Deb Marlowe grew up in Penn book. Luckily, she's read enoug[...] true modern hero she met at a col[...] though he wore a tuxedo T-shirt [...] boots. They married, settled in North Carolina, and produced two handsome, intelligent and genuinely amusing boys.

Though she spends much of her time now with her nose in her laptop, for the sake of her family she does occasionally abandon her inner world for the domestic adventure of laundry, dinner and car-pool. Despite her sacrifice, not one of the men in her family is yet willing to don breeches or tall boots. She's working on it. Deb would love to hear from readers! You can contact her at debmarlowe@debmarlowe.com

Don't miss these other Regency delights from Mills & Boon® Historical romance's bestselling authors!

REGENCY PLEASURES
Louise Allen

REGENCY SECRETS
Julia Justiss

REGENCY RUMOURS
Juliet Landon

REGENCY REDEMPTION
Christine Merrill

REGENCY DEBUTANTES
Margaret McPhee

REGENCY IMPROPRIETIES
Diane Gaston

REGENCY MISTRESSES
Mary Brendan

REGENCY REBELS
Deb Marlowe

REGENCY SCANDALS
Sophia James

REGENCY MARRIAGES
Elizabeth Rolls

REGENCY INNOCENTS
Annie Burrows

REGENCY SINS
Bronwyn Scott

REGENCY
Rebels

Deb Marlowe

All the characters in this book have no existence outside the imagination
of the author, and have no relation whatsoever to anyone bearing the same
name or names. They are not even distantly inspired by any individual
known or unknown to the author, and all the incidents are pure invention.

Mills & Boon, an imprint of Harlequin (UK) Limited,
Eton House, 18-24 Paradise Road, Richmond, Surrey TW9 1SR

REGENCY REBELS © Harlequin Books S.A. 2011

The publisher acknowledges the copyright holder of the individual works
as follows:

Scandalous Lord, Rebellious Miss © Deb Marlowe 2007
An Improper Aristocrat © Deb Marlowe 2008

ISBN: 978 0 263 88738 9

052-0911

Harlequin (UK) policy is to use papers that are natural, renewable
and recyclable products and made from wood grown in sustainable
forests. The logging and manufacturing processes conform to the legal
environmental regulations of the country of origin.

Printed in the UK
by CPI Mackays, Chatham, ME5 8TD

Scandalous Lord, Rebellious Miss

To my husband—supporter of dreams
and builder of sheds extraordinaire

And to Susan—for cracking her whip
and wielding her red whip with flair

Chapter One

Charles Alden, Viscount Dayle, sank into his favourite over-stuffed chair in the morning room at White's. It was early; the porters had not yet let down the awnings and bright light flooded through the floor-to-ceiling window. At his elbow sat a pot of coffee, a plate of muffins, and a pile of papers. He snapped open *The Times,* sank his teeth into his first, hot, buttery bite and let out a heartfelt sigh.

He revelled in the peace of the morning all the way through the first paper. Unfortunately, peace was a commodity hard to come by anywhere in England in the spring of 1817, even for a viscount. Charles first noticed something amiss as he set aside *The Times* and reached for the *Edinburgh Review.*

A space had cleared all about him. The morning room, usually full of gentlemen either beginning one day or ending another, was empty but for a few souls gathered in whispering knots along the walls. One man caught his gaze, blasted him with a look of utter scorn, and stalked out, calling for his hat. A wrench of foreboding seizing his gut, Charles looked up into the sympathetic eye of one of the porters, come to refresh his coffee.

'Well, Bartlett,' he said quietly, 'I can see you are not half so ignorant as I. Tell me.'

Bartlett cleared his throat. 'I have taken the liberty of adding a copy of today's *Oracle* to the stack of your usual papers, my lord. Perhaps you would care to peruse the editorial section?'

'The *Oracle?*' It was little more than a scandal sheet. 'Thank you, Bartlett.'

Charles picked up the paper with trepidation and turned a few pages until he found the item he sought, directly under a scathing response to Lord Sidmouth's call against 'seditious publications'.

Tory Darling or Wolf In Sheep's Clothing?

They do say that a Reformed Rake makes the Best Husband—but what kind of Politician does he make?

Just such a man is Lord D—, a Rakehell of the First Order, now converted into a Responsible English Peer. Or is he? Based on certain, recent Rumours, We wonder if he has changed pastures only in search of fresh prey.

Lord D— has been seen often lately with the notorious Lady A— on his arm. Perhaps this is not so surprising when one considers his past taste for women of immodest character and her known taste for the rising young members of her husband's political party. What is surprising is that a man previously known for living on wit and instinct could have fumbled this situation so badly. No other explanation presents itself for yesterday's dramatic events, when Lord A— returned home unexpectedly only to find a dark-haired gentleman departing the house by route of Lady A—'s bedchamber window.

The lady has reportedly been duly chastised and banished to the country. But as for the gentleman?

It cannot be denied that Lord D— is a man of many talents. Indeed, it is rumoured he is to be groomed for High Office. We at the Oracle cannot help but wonder if the Tories should reconsider the notion. Surely a candidate exists who can demonstrate a higher standard of character. For if the Tories cannot trust Lord D— with their women, then why should they trust him with the Nation?

For a long minute Charles sat rigid with anger. Bloody, damnable hell. Months of hard work. Weeks of toadying. Countless gruelling hours spent constructing a careful façade. All destroyed in a moment with the vicious swipe of an acid pen.

Normal, everyday sounds drifted in from the adjoining rooms: the rustle of freshly ironed papers, the soft clink of china, the low murmur of men whose lives had not just been turned inside out. Charles sat frozen, trying to wrap his mind about the disaster that had befallen him with the turn of a page.

He nearly jumped out of his skin when grizzled Lord Rackham paused behind his chair and thumped him soundly on the shoulder.

'Just so, my boy!' the old relic bellowed. 'Brazen it out. Don't let them see you with your head down, that's the wisest course! Tomorrow some bloke will get caught hammering his rocks in someone else's quarry and they'll all be talking about that. It will blow over soon enough.' After another encouraging cuff he stalked off to rejoin his friends, the whole pack of them muttering darkly as they crossed into the coffee room.

With quiet, deliberate movements Charles finished his coffee. Old Lord Rackham had the right of it; he would not let anyone think he was ashamed. Once he had finished he stood, tucked the copy of the *Oracle* under his arm, and with a flash of a gold coin in Bartlett's direction, Charles walked out of White's.

He stood a moment on St James's Street, dazzled by the bright sun and annoyed at the bustle of traffic. Then he let loose a great laugh. Who in the world did he think he was— the heroine in a gothic novel? Should lightning crack the sky and mere mortals scurry for cover because Viscount Dayle's political career lay in ruins?

As if in answer, a brisk breeze riffled his hair, and Charles set off towards Mayfair. *Who did he think he was?* That was the question of the hour—no, of the entire past year—was it not?

There was only one answer. He was Viscount Dayle, a carefully constructed facsimile of the man who should hold the title. And Viscount Dayle was nothing without his political career.

His mind darted from one scenario to the next as he approached Piccadilly, scrambling to come up with some way to salvage the situation. Lost in his own whirlwind of thoughts, he failed to notice both the rising wind and the increasingly strident sound of his own name. It wasn't until someone grasped his arm that he came awake to his surroundings.

'Dayle, did you not hear us calling you, man?' It was Henley and Matthews, two of the more degenerate hangers-on of his old crowd. They were still in their evening clothes and looking the worse for wear. Charles winced. These two would tear him apart after reading that piece.

'Sorry, chaps. Lost in the fog of my own thoughts this morning,' he said, striving for a light-hearted tone.

'A bit dense in there, eh?' laughed Matthews. 'I trust it's not as thick as the fog at Hyde Park this morning.' He leaned in and spoke confidingly. 'Blackmoor met Ventry at dawn. Ventry was shaking so hard his gun went off before he'd got his hand half-raised. Hit the ground not ten feet in front of him, the poor sod.'

Charles felt like shaking himself, in relief. Obviously they didn't yet know. 'Blackmoor didn't kill him, did he?' he asked with nonchalance.

'I should say not,' Henley drawled. 'Pinked him in the arm, which is far less than the upstart deserved, should you ask me.' He shot Charles a conspirator's grin. 'It's good to see you, Dayle. It's been an age since you've been out and about with us. Leave the debates to them what can't get a rise out of St Peter, if you catch my meaning, and come on with us. You're too young to bury yourself in the House.'

Matthews chimed in. 'We're off to breakfast, old man, before heading home,' he said. 'Been to the new bawdy house on Bentinck Street? Opens in the morning and lays out a breakfast buffet. Mrs Pritchett guarantees a bellyful and an armful to send you sweetly to your dreams. Care to join us?'

The desire to yield and go along with them was almost visceral. How easy it would be to forget, to lose the pain of the last year and the humiliation of the morning in the burn of good liquor and the hot sweet flesh of a woman. He could just let it all go. End the charade.

He shook his head to rid himself of the notion. No. Charles Alden was dead. Slain by the same wild round that had stolen his brother, buried by the despair that had seduced his father. There was no going back.

He went forward instead, resolutely and one footfall at a time. Good-naturedly refusing the offer, he saw Matthews and Henley into a passing hack before crossing over Piccadilly. By the time he passed Devonshire House and headed into Berkeley Square, temptation had been safely locked away. Viscount Dayle was once again in full possession of all his faculties and putting together a plan of action.

The wind had become quite forceful by the time Charles reached his Bruton Street townhouse, and the sunlight dimmed by fast-moving clouds. Perhaps fate had indeed meant to give him the backdrop for his drama, and had only missed her cue.

'My lord,' his butler gasped as the door swung in. 'Forgive me, we were not expecting you back…'

'No need for apologies, Fisher.' Charles headed for the library. 'But could you please send round a man to fetch my brother? Drag him from his books, if need be, but tell him I need him now. And send some coffee in, too.'

'Wait, my lord!' the butler called as Charles stalked away. 'You have a visitor awaiting you.'

'At this hour?'

The butler had no chance to reply before the library door slammed open. 'Dayle!' The shout rang in the cold marbled entry. 'This time you will pay for your perfidy. Name your seconds!'

'Lord Avery, how kind of you to call,' Charles said, running a hand across his brow. 'Better make that something stronger, Fisher. Brandy will do.

'Now, my lord,' Charles spoke soothingly as he ushered the man back in the room and away from the staring eyes of the servants, 'we are a bit precipitous with this talk of seconds. But I would be happy to discuss the upcoming Poor Relief Bill, even at this early hour.'

'There's no distracting me, you philandering dog! I know what you've done with my wife, all of London knows!' The older man was nearly grey with fatigue and emotion. Charles guided him to a chair. The last thing he needed was for the fool to collapse in his study.

'You know no such thing. It's nonsense. I dined at the Clarendon, and stayed there talking most of the night. You will easily find a roomful of gentlemen to corroborate the fact. We can send for one or more of them right now.'

'I know what I saw, you young rakehell.'

'I don't know what you saw, my lord, but I know it was not me.' Charles's tone grew more firm.

'Do you think me a fool? I've seen you together with my own eyes! And all of London knows of your rackety ways.'

'I've never had more than a casual public conversation with your wife, sir. I own that she is charming, and exceedingly handsome, but whatever trouble lies between you has nothing to do with me.'

Charles saw the first sign of uncertainty in the man's face. He felt for him, but he could not let this go any further. He hardened his expression and said with finality, 'If you choose not to believe me, then I will indeed give thought to finding a second.'

Jack arrived just then, excited and fully ready to defend his brother's honour, but the fight had gone out of Lord Avery. He hung his head in his hands while Charles greeted his brother and while the brandy was brought in. He accepted a drink, threw it back, and held out his glass for another. Then he stood.

'I will accept your explanation for now, Dayle, but I shall check out your claim, and if I find it's a lie, I'll be back. Why would your name be mixed up in this if you weren't involved? Makes no sense.'

'You echo my own thought exactly,' said Charles.

Lord Avery bristled. 'This is no laughing matter! My honour, and my wife's, has been destroyed.' He looked thoughtfully at Charles. 'I know that there are those in the Party who believe in your transformation. The rake reformed.' He snorted. 'I know your history, and today's work smacks of it. Blatant. Insulting. Just like your soft-hearted politics. It's bad enough to side with the unwashed masses against your own kind in the Lords, but this! Unforgivable is what I call it, and so will many a Tory, after I am through with you.' He marched to the door and paused on the threshold. 'If your whereabouts last night are uncertain, then tomorrow morning's will be assured.'

The echo of the slamming door was much quieter on this side. Charles looked away and began to pace, from the sidebar to the crackling fire, then away to the full wall of books. He couldn't bear to look upon his father's portrait above the mantel.

'I'm sorry, Charles.' Jack's tone was quiet, careful. 'God knows I don't understand it, but I do know how important your political interests have become to you.'

Charles nodded again and drank. He crossed to the window and watched as the rain began to come down in sheets.

'Throw me a bone, would you? I'm trying to play the supportive brother here.' Jack rose and came to stand behind him.

'He'll check your story and find that it's true. After that it's only a piece in a scandal rag. Is it really so bad?'

Charles stared at his brother's reflection in the window. 'It's bad, and it couldn't have come at a worse time. The Board of Trade is looking for someone to head an investigative committee on distressed farming areas. My name has been mentioned. It could set me on a path to much higher places.' He scrubbed a hand through his hair. 'I've worked hard, and come so far. Take a good look around, little brother, this country is in an horrendous mess. I have finally got myself into a position where I can do something about it...I could *help*.'

He slammed his fist into his hand. 'And now someone wants to use my past against me? No one will consider me seriously. I'll be just another *ton* wastrel who cannot keep his bodkin buttoned up. This could ruin me. My political career could be over before it has truly begun.'

'Would that be such a terrible thing?' His brother's hand was suddenly heavy on Charles's shoulder. 'Phillip is dead. You are not. Perhaps it is time to let all of this go. You could get back to your own pursuits, spend some time at Fordham with Mother.'

'No,' Charles barked. 'I could not.' He stared down into his drink, but there were no answers there. And no solace either, as he had good reason to know. How could he explain his desperation to his little brother? There were some things that Jack could never understand. 'I need this, Jack. I can't explain it, but I need to do this, and I need you to help me out of this mess.'

There was a moment's silence, and then Jack took his hand away and went to pour himself a drink. 'Is the situation salvageable? What do you mean to do?'

'I suppose I must demonstrate a higher standard of character,' Charles said with a wry twist of a grin.

'Higher than what?' Jack laughed suddenly and the tension in the room became a little more bearable. 'That wasn't really you climbing out of the old jade's window?'

'Good Lord, no! I'm willing to sacrifice a good deal in the name of politics, but that's taking the matter too far. In any case, I believe she only flirts with us young bucks to stir her husband up, to get his attention off the quarter of a million military men set adrift with no pensions and back on her. But she's evidently gone too far this time.'

Charles scrubbed a hand across his brow while he thought. 'Still, I have to admit this was a master stroke. Whoever is behind this is clever. They've negated months of work, and done it by painting me with my own brush. All with no hint of his own identity or agenda.'

'Someone doesn't like the influence you've begun to gain. How do we track the whoreson down?'

'First I'm going to find the baseborn idiot who wrote that piece for the *Oracle*. Whether he wants to or not, he's going to tell me who his sources are. But it's not going to be enough to find out which coward is behind this. The damage is done.' He moved back to the window and gazed out at the gathering intensity of the storm. 'I'm going to have to give them all something better to talk about.'

Jack nearly choked on his drink. 'Better than sex and scandal? There isn't anything the *ton* loves better.'

'Oh, yes, there is, little brother.'

'What?' Jack demanded as an enormous branch of lightning split the sky.

Into the brief moment of calm, Charles spoke. 'Marriage.'

His brother's jaw dropped. Thunder broke open in the heavens. The house shuddered.

'Marriage? To whom?' Jack managed to ask.

'To the most priggish lady you can drag up from the muck of the *ton,* I should imagine.' Charles shrugged. 'It seems clear that the only way I will ever live down the excesses of my past is to secure the dullness of my future. I don't know, draw up a list. Only the primmest and most proper to be considered. I'll marry the one at the top.'

Thunder throbbed through the house once more. The windows shook in their frames. Behind them their father's portrait rattled off its moorings, crashed into the mantel, and flipped face down in front of the fire.

Chapter Two

Her step light, her portfolio swinging and her maid scurrying to keep up, Sophie Westby strode through Cheapside. A gusting wind swept past in brisk imitation of the traffic in the streets, whipping her skirts and challenging the knot holding her bonnet. Sophie raised her chin, breathed deep of the pungent air and grinned in delight. London might be dirty, occasionally rank, and surprisingly lacking in colour, but it was also a huge, bubbling cauldron of *life*.

After years of quiet country living and near isolation, Sophie's own life was suddenly beginning to simmer. Furniture design had long been her passion, and in an effort to ease her dearest friend Emily Lowder's unusually long and difficult confinement, she had indulged them both with an extensive nursery project. It had been a smashing success. They'd had such fun and Emily had been so enchanted with the result, she had quickly swept Sophie up into a redesign of her dark and cluttered drawing rooms. The new suite had been unveiled at little Edward Lowder's birthday celebration and, to Sophie's chagrin, the room had nearly eclipsed the cherubic infant.

The grandest lady of the neighborhood, Viscountess Dayle, had been most impressed. Lady Dayle had run an assessing eye over both the new room and its designer, and in a bewilderingly sudden turn of events, she had them all established in town for the Season and for a large, mysterious design project.

Almost before Sophie could catch her breath, she found herself out of Blackford Chase, ensconced in the Lowders' London home, and finally encouraged to pursue her design work. The result was one ecstatic young lady.

A young lady who perhaps should not have left her coach behind, stuck in the snarl of vehicles blocked by an overturned coal cart. Against her maid's protests Sophie had climbed down, left instructions with the driver and set off on foot. And she could not bring herself to regret the decision. Walking was so much more intimate. She felt a part of the city rather than a bystander.

'Paper! The *Augur!*' The newsboy hefting his heavy sack of papers looked perhaps ten years old. He had inked-smeared hands, a scrupulously clean face, and eyes that made Sophie's fingers positively itch for a pencil. An old soul smiled hopefully out of that young face.

'Paper, miss? Only sixpence and full of society's latest doin's.' He spotted a pair of well-dressed young ladies emerging from a shop across the street and waved his paper high to get their attention. 'Paper! The *Augur!* More exciting tales of the Wicked Lord Dayle!'

He could not have used a more enticing lure. Sophie promptly bought a copy, then turned to Nell, the maid assigned to her from the Lowders' town staff. 'Will you tuck this away in your bag, Nell, just until we get home?'

The maid looked startled. Sophie smiled at her. 'I promise to share as soon as I've finished.'

Gossip was like gold below stairs, and Sophie knew she had an ally when Nell, her face alight with mischief, took the paper and shoved it under the mending in her bag. The newsboy flashed them both a gap-toothed smile, then a cheeky wink. Nell giggled, but Sophie caught herself unthinkingly reaching for her sketchbook.

No. Not this time. She took a tighter grip on her portfolio and firmly set herself back to the task at hand: reaching the shop of a particularly well-recommended linen draper.

It was a scene that she had replayed with herself countless times in the past week. With so much history, so much energy and so many human dramas unfolding about her, the temptation to put it all down on paper was nearly overwhelming. From the towering glory of the churches, to the saucy curve of the newsboy's cheek, to the flutter of the fine ladies' dresses, London was full of sights, textures, and subtle images that she longed to capture in her sketchbook.

But she did not intend to succumb to the temptation. Sketching meant taking a step back, imposing a distance, becoming an observer, and Sophie Westby was done with being an observer.

Fate had finally smiled upon her and she meant to make the most of it. That was one reason why today's errand was so important. Though she as yet had no idea what project Lady Dayle had in mind, Sophie intended to dazzle her. Themes, colour schemes, and any number of preparatory steps could be readied ahead of time and individualised later. When the time came Sophie would be ready with an array of ideas and choices that would quickly highlight the viscountess's tastes. And when the project was complete, she vowed, Lady Dayle would have reason to be proud.

Sophie could do no less for the woman who had been so kind and generous. And indeed, Lady Dayle had no true idea just how much her kindness had meant, for she could not know that in the very act of bringing her to London, she had brought Sophie that much closer to two of her most heartfelt desires.

First, of course, were the incredible opportunities that could arise from a London project. She smiled when she remembered thinking that Emily's drawing room had been such a coup. As wonderful as that had turned out, it was as nothing compared to what exposure to the *ton*'s finest might do. So much might be accomplished if her designs were well received.

Second, and somehow more importantly, Lady Dayle had placed Sophie squarely in a position where she might see Charles again. Her pulse leaped at the thought.

She wondered what Lady Dayle knew of their relationship—but perhaps relationship was the wrong word. Friendship, then, because he had indeed been her friend. Her friend, her companion, her confidante, the knight of her youth.

Anticipation brought a secret smile to her face when she thought of the paper hidden in Nell's bag. How she loved to read of his exploits. Through the years she had followed his nefarious career with the same glee that she had felt hearing of his schoolboy stunts. She could scarcely wait to tease every scandalous detail from him. It was her favourite fantasy; the pair of them, reunited, sharing laughter and dreams just as they had used to do.

Sophie had always known that some day they would meet again. But now that the distant promise had become a near certainty, she found that it had gained new significance.

How had he changed? What would he have to say to her? Sophie knew she stood at a crossroads in her life, a rare point filled with promise and possibilities ahead. Yet she also knew that she would not be able to settle to any one of them until she had the answers to those questions.

'Miss!' came a gasp from behind her. 'Is it very much farther, miss?' Nell sounded breathless. Apparently Sophie's pace had quickened along with her thoughts.

'Not much farther, I don't believe.'

For Nell's sake she slowed her steps and resolved to keep her mind off of the distant past and the uncertain future, and firmly on the task in the present.

It proved easier than she might have imagined, for Cheapside was a treat for the senses, populated as it was with all manner of shops and craftsmen. Sophie wrinkled her nose at the hot smell at the silversmiths, and again at the raw scent of fresh dye at the cloth weavers. She marvelled at the crowded windows of the engravers, but it wasn't until she reached the tea merchant's shop that she came to a delighted stop.

The merchant had at one time been blessed with a bowed shop window, but the area had been converted, or inverted, and now held a charming little protected alcove. Like a miniature Parisian café, it held a small table, meant, she supposed, for customers to sit and experience some exotic new flavour before they parted with their coin. It was the seating, in fact, which had so caught Sophie's attention.

'Nell, just look at those chairs. If I'm not mistaken, those are true Restoration pieces, sitting right out in the street! Yes,' she said, rushing forward to stroke one lovingly. 'The Portuguese arch. Oh, and look, Nell, you must hold my portfolio while I examine the *pé de pincel.*'

She could never truly say, afterward, just what went wrong. Perhaps the clasp had already been loose, or perhaps she herself accidentally triggered it. In any case, one second she was absentmindedly passing her portfolio back to Nell, and the next it was dropping wide open. Another gust of wind hit just then and all of her sketches and designs were sent skyward in a veritable cyclone of papers.

For a moment Sophie stood frozen in panic and watched as her life's work scattered about the busy street. Then she sprang into action. First she sent Nell after those that had skipped back down the way they had just come. Then an enterprising street sweeper approached and offered to help retrieve the papers that had fluttered into the street. Sophie gave him a coin, entreated him not to place himself in any danger and sent him off.

She herself set after the bulk of the lot, which had gone swirling ahead of them. She was not heedless of the sight she must present, chasing, stooping, even jumping up to snatch at one desk design that had impaled itself on the pike of an iron railing, but she was beyond caring. These designs were her hopes for the future; she could no more abandon them than she could go quietly back to Blackford Chase.

At last, after much effort, there was only one paper left in sight. It led her a merry chase as it danced mere inches from her fingertips more than once. But each time she drew near another mischievous breeze would send it bounding ahead. Sophie's back ached and her gown grew more filthy by the minute, but she refused to give up.

And she finally had a stroke of fortune. Just ahead a gentleman stalked out of a printer's shop, right into the path of the wicked thing. It fetched up against a pair of well-formed legs, then flattened itself around one shining Hessian.

With a triumphant whoop Sophie swept down and snatched the paper up. *Oh my,* she thought as she caught sight of her own distorted grin, *you truly can see your reflection in a gentleman's boots.*

'Of course. It only wanted this.' The voice above her was heavy with sarcasm. 'I can now officially brand this day one of the worst I have ever endured. Now my valet shall berate me as soundly as the rest of London.'

Sophie fought the urge to grin as she slowly straightened up, her gaze travelling the unusual—and unusually pleasurable—path up the form of a well-formed gentleman. A well-heeled gentleman too, judging by the quality of the small clothes, which were buff, and the morning coat, which was, of course, blue, and the scowling face, which was…

Charles's.

The shock was so great that her stomach fell all the way to the pavement and the rest of her nearly followed.

He saw the danger and grasped her arm to steady her. She looked again into his face and saw that it was true. His face was not quite the same, the handsome promise of youth having hardened into a more angular and masculine beauty.

His eyes were different as well, so cold and hard as he scowled down at her, but it was undeniably, without a doubt, her Charles Alden.

Sophie was so happy to see him, despite the awkwardness of the moment, that she just beamed up at him. All the joyful anticipation she'd felt for this moment simply flooded out of her and she knew that her delight shone all over her face.

It was not a shared emotion. In fact, he dropped her arm as if he'd suddenly found her diseased.

Sophie's smile only deepened. He didn't know her! Oh, heavens, she was going to have some fun with him now.

'I don't know what you are smiling at. That was the worst example of unfeminine effrontery I have ever witnessed, and in the street, no less.' He raked the length of her with a hard gaze. 'You look the part of a lady, but it appears to end there. Where is your escort?'

'My maid will be along in a minute,' she replied almost absentmindedly. She couldn't take her eyes off of him. It was no wonder he'd had such a reputation as a rake; he had grown almost sinfully handsome. She would bet that women threw themselves in his path on a regular basis.

'Please, stop that infernal smiling,' he ordered. 'If you need a good reason, impudent miss, just look at my boots!'

She obediently arranged her face into a more sombre mien. 'Please, do forgive me, sir.' She smoothed the chalked design that had indeed smudged the high polish off one of his Hessians. 'Let me assure you that I do not usually behave in so reckless a fashion. But I had to have my papers back, you see.'

'No, I do not see.' He stopped suddenly, an arrested look

upon his face. He glanced back at the building he had just exited; with a closer look it appeared to be a publisher's office. 'Are you a writer, a reporter, by chance?' he asked.

'No, sir. I—' She was not allowed to finish.

'Damn. I could do with someone from the press in my court.' With a sudden motion, before she could protest, he had reached out and smoothly snatched the paper from her grasp. 'But please, enlighten me as to just what is worth making a spectacle of yourself.'

Sophie looked as well and saw that it was a design of a *chaise-lounge* she had specifically drawn for his mother, complete with a complementary colour palette and notes on specific fabrics and trims.

'Furniture,' Charles said with a deprecating snort.

'Décor,' she corrected as she just as smoothly retrieved the design and tucked it with her others.

'Pray, do excuse me,' he drawled in exaggerated tones. For a moment he reminded her forcefully of his younger self, and her reaction was instantaneous and purely physical. And yet, something distracted her and slowed the melting of her insides. She'd heard that mocking tone before, but never with so hard an edge. He wasn't taking her seriously, true, but he wasn't being nice about it either.

She narrowed her eyes. 'No, I don't believe I will,' she replied.

His eyes widened in mock dismay. 'Was that meant as a mortal blow to my pride? Unforgiven and despondent, the gentleman prostrates himself and begs for mercy. You have read one too many novels, my dear,' he said.

'Just look about you,' he continued with an encompassing wave of his hand. 'There are a good many things in this world in need of attention, even some worth making oneself a fool over. But let me assure you—' his voice was getting louder now '—that furniture is not one of them.'

Sophie raised her brow in the very arrogant manner that he himself had taught her. 'Perhaps not to you, sir, but our circumstances are quite different. You haven't a notion of my concerns. To me, this is very important.'

'Important, of course,' he said, the sarcasm growing heavy again. 'You will forgive me if I don't raise décor to the same level as perhaps, the plight of the English farmer, or the suspension of Habeas Corpus.'

'And you will forgive me if I place it a little higher than the shine on your boots.'

Charles stopped in the act of replacing his hat, clearly taken aback. He opened his mouth, then closed it. He jammed the beaver on to his head. 'I concede you the point.'

Suddenly his shoulders slumped. He tore the hat off again and bowed his head. 'What on earth am I doing?' He heaved a sigh and the tense lines of his neck and shoulders relaxed.

When he looked up at Sophie again, it was as if a layer of cold stone had fallen from him. 'Listen, I do apologise.' He scrubbed a rough hand through his hair and flashed her a half-grin that was awkward and thoroughly familiar.

'It's not my usual habit to go about berating young women in the street, but then nothing has been usual in my life for— well, it feels like for ever. It has been so long since I had a normal conversation,' he continued, 'I scarcely recall how to go about it.'

The indefinable pull that emanated from him had doubled in its intensity. Sophie could not make herself respond, could not tear her gaze from his. There they were at last, warm in their regard, Charles's eyes. Her Charles.

He didn't seem to notice her lapse. 'Allow me to help you.'

With brisk efficiency he soon had her designs in order and her portfolio securely fastened. Another awkward silence followed her thanks. Sophie desperately tried to gather her wits. She knew she should either take her leave of him or reveal her identity.

He spoke before she could choose either option. 'You seem to have a great many ideas. It must be a very large project you have undertaken.'

Sophie flushed. How to answer that without making a fool of herself? She should have told him who she was at the start. 'Yes, at least I believe so. The truth is, I do not really know yet.'

He shifted and she could almost feel his restlessness, his need to escape. But she was not ready to see him go yet, nor was she quite sure she had forgiven him his harsh manner. She curved her lips into a smile and cocked a brow at him. 'If not normal, then what sort do you usually have?'

He was puzzled. 'Pardon?'

'Conversations. You say you are unused to the normal variety. I am perishing to know what kind of conversations you usually have.'

'Oh.' He paused and she thought that he might not answer, that he would put an end to this improper tête à tête and go about his business, but instead he glanced carefully about, then flashed her a wicked smile. 'Do you wish for the truth or for a properly polite answer?'

Sophie tossed her head, her chin up. 'Always the truth, please, sir.'

'Very well, then. The truth is that for most of my days my conversations tended on the coarse and bawdy side. More like the seasonal bawling of young bucks and the bleating of...available females than true human exchange—'

Sophie interrupted him with a sigh. 'You did warn me. I am sure I should be slapping your face, or stalking off in high dudgeon. Fortunately I am not so faint-hearted.' She smiled. 'Do go on.'

He shrugged. 'Now I have political conversations. Long, relentless, occasionally monotonous, but in the end productive and worthwhile. Both sorts, I find, have their own drawbacks and pleasures.'

The playful gleam returned to his eye and he leaned in a little closer and lowered his voice. 'But I will let you in on a little secret. Sometimes, especially when the stakes are high, political debates are remarkably similar to primitive mating rituals. There is a little polite cooing, leading to an extravagant display of superiority, then a mad scramble as everyone pairs off. Occasionally there is a show of temper and brute strength. In the end someone wins, the victor takes the spoils and the next day we all ever so politely begin all over again.'

Sophie laughed. 'Fascinating. It gives one a whole new perspective on Parliament, does it not?

'It helps me get through some very long days in the Lords.'

'It makes me wish I was indeed a reporter. Imagine the story I could write: "Wild Westminster, The Secret Life of Parliament." Every paper in London would be at my feet. Alas, my talents lie in another direction altogether.'

Charles eyed her portfolio, then slid his gaze down her

form. A swift, fierce heat swept through her, following its path. 'I beg you won't be insulted if I say that you decorate the city with your mere presence.'

Before she could gather herself enough to respond, his face suddenly contorted into a grimace of dismay that had her following his gaze. An elegant carriage pulled by an exquisite team passed them by. Very obviously staring was a pair of wide-eyed feminine faces. One even craned her neck to look back as the equipage moved on.

'Oh, hell,' he breathed before turning back to her. 'As stimulating as this has been, I cannot afford any more gossip just now. Neither would I wish to harm your reputation with my tarnished presence.' He sketched her the curtest of bows. 'I wish you the best of luck with your endeavours.'

She returned with a curtsy just as brief. 'Indeed, I understand, sir.' She watched as he turned to go and called after him, 'Off you go to save the world. I will content myself with dressing it up.'

He tossed a scornful glance over his shoulder at her. 'Unworthy, my dear, and just when I had begun to judge you a promising opponent.'

Sophie watched, amused, as he stalked away. Let him have the last word for now, she thought. Oh, she was going to enjoy their next meeting even more than this one.

She became aware, suddenly, of a faint panting just behind her. She turned and found Nell, who handed over a sheaf of papers and wiped her brow. 'Who was the gentleman you was talking with, miss? He looked a mite put out.'

'That, dear Nell, was none other than the Wicked Lord Dayle.'

'No!' The maid's gasp was more titillation than shock.

'Indeed, although I recall him more fondly as my very own knight in shining armour.'

Nell had been pushed too far this morning to be discreet. 'Happen that armour's tarnished some.'

'It does appear so,' Sophie mused. 'Though the polishing of it could be quite a bit of fun, indeed.'

Nell only shook her head. 'If you say so, miss.'

Chapter Three

Miss Corinne Ashford's hand was limp and cool as Charles bent over it. As was the expression on her face while he took his leave of her. Even so, Charles's step was light when he stepped into Portman Street and set out for home.

He felt as if he could breathe again, as he hadn't been free to since that cursed piece in the *Oracle.* He had been exonerated, of course, once it had leaked out that the dark-haired man sneaking out of Lady Avery's window had been none other than Lord Avery's valet. And society had quickly sunk their teeth into new and even more delicious gossip when the old girl had run off with the young fellow, the petty cash, and the family jewels.

Yet the damage had been done. The thinly veiled references were in every scandal sheet. Suddenly his old peccadilloes were fodder for gossip again.

Wild, reckless, restless—these were the epithets he had become accustomed to in his seven and twenty years, the labels a scandalised society had readily laid at his door. They were well and truly earned, too. He had misspent his youth in a frenzy of hard living, soft women, and outrageous pranks. He had, in short, enjoyed the hell out of himself.

But such carelessness belonged to another lifetime. Charles Alden might have spent his time in carefree pursuit of pleasure, but Viscount Dayle was not so lighthearted. Two years ago his brother had died, his father had shortly followed, and Charles's life had been transformed.

It had begun as a penance he had embraced in a fury of remorse and determination, and, though it was true that grief and guilt still lay heavy on his shoulders, Charles could not deny that it was the work that had saved his sanity.

With fierce devotion he had immersed himself in the estates, the accounts and the politics. Somehow he had survived, had even reached a point where he could draw breath, enjoy the success he had wrought and begin to envision a future.

Until that ridiculous article. Now his name had once again been associated with scandal and vice, and his reception had significantly cooled, both in the corridors of Westminster and the parlors of Mayfair. He found the setback infuriating, and despite his best efforts, he still hadn't a clue as to who was behind it.

So, he had temporarily abandoned his search for the villain, dragged out his original plan, and after careful deliberation decided that Miss Ashford might be just the thing to cure his ailing reputation. She was the daughter of a baron and a member of a notoriously staunch conservative family. Elegant and tall and proud to a fault, she wore respectability like an enveloping mantel. Charles just hoped that it was large enough to cover his own sins.

In truth, he had half-expected to be left standing in the street when he began to pay his addresses to the lady, but the past year's good works—or his title and fortune—had proved credit enough to get him in the door. Whether he progressed any further remained to be seen.

He crossed his own portal now, satisfied for the moment, and more in charity with the world than he'd felt in weeks. He found his mother descending the stairs, straightening her gloves. 'Going out, Mother?' he asked.

'Indeed, as are you. Please have the carriage sent around, dear. We won't wish to be late.'

Charles nodded to a footman to deliver the message. 'Late for what?'

Only a mother could fit so much meaning into a sigh of exasperation. 'I knew you would forget. We are promised to call at Mrs Lowder's, *both* of us. And do not even think of trying to wiggle out of it. You know that Edward Lowder is influential in some very important political circles. And in any case, Emily Lowder has something in particular at her house that I wish to show you.'

She had reached the bottom of the stairs. Charles smiled and offered her his arm. 'Wiggle out? I wouldn't dare. Not since the Aunt Eugenie incident.'

She laughed. 'I would never have banished you to your room if I thought Phillip would do such a thing. I thought we were going to have to break the door down. Do you know, to this day we have never found that key?'

He couldn't hide the twinge he felt at Phillip's name. She saw and stopped to put her hand on his cheek. 'They were good times, Charles. It is fine to remember them.' She smiled and straightened his cravat. 'And we will have good times again, I feel it.'

Charles could almost believe her. His mother was smiling again. She had come up from Fordham Park with a spring in her step, a list of some kind in hand, and he had barely seen her in the weeks since. He had warned her of the Avery scandal, but she had only laughed and dared anyone in society to vilify her son to her face.

'How went the hunt?' she asked now. 'You have certainly given the rumour mill enough grist. Word is out that the Wicked Lord Dayle is looking for a wife to tame his ways. Surely the worst must indeed be past if such a high stickler as Lavinia Ashford gave you entrance to her drawing room.'

The arrival of the carriage saved him from a response, but his mother would not let the subject drop. She teased a list of names from him and then cheerfully dissected each one, as callous in her regard for the young ladies as if they were no more than choice offerings at the butcher's stall. 'If what you truly wish is to wed a pattern card of propriety, Charles, then there are in truth only three or four girls who will do. Nearly everyone of consequence is in town now. There should be plenty of time for you to meet them all and select the best.'

Charles suffered a little qualm hearing his mother discuss his marriage in such cold-blooded terms. He suffered a bigger qualm picturing the many long years ahead leg-shackled to a cold-blooded shrew. Then, like a sudden summer breeze, the image arose in his mind—dark, windswept tresses, laughing eyes, a radiant smile. The chit from Cheapside.

The exotic little beauty had invaded his thoughts more than once since their encounter. That smile—it kept coming to mind. Perhaps she reminded him of someone? And perhaps it was only a knee-jerk reaction to the course he had chosen. Intelligent and witty as well as pretty, she would be a far more pleasing prospect to face every morning over breakfast.

Except that such a prospect did not exist. Nor should it. He could not forget the near panic he'd felt during the lowest moments of the last weeks. The thought of failure was insupportable. He had hit upon the best path out of this mess and he was going to follow it right into a cold and sterile marriage.

He gave a cynical shrug; it would be a fair trade, surely. A cold marriage bed for a lifetime of credibility. And he should be down on his knees thanking the powers that be for even such dim prospects, for he was lucky to have a future at all.

These reflections left him in a mood of grim determination. He would prevail, would sacrifice anything to ensure his success. His resolution lasted across Mayfair, through all of his mother's chatter, and right up until he entered the Lowders' family drawing room. It might have lasted through the entire Season and seen him through the tedious weeks ahead, had it not encountered the pair of ankles.

A very fetching pair of ankles, framed by a scalloped flounce and situated right at eye level. Grim determination stood not a chance; it melted under a combined onslaught of shock and pure male appreciation.

'Have the guests arrived, Thomas?' asked a voice situated somewhat above the ankles and the stepladder they were perched upon. Charles couldn't see how far above because his gaze remained locked where it did not belong. 'Hold a moment and let me hand down my things. I wouldn't wish to be caught at work.'

'Too late, my dear,' his mother chirped. 'Come down, please, you frighten me out of my wits on that thing.'

But the unexpected reply had disturbed the girl's balance, both mental and physical. A surprised 'Oh!' came from above and then the ankles and the stepladder began to sway.

The footman who had admitted them—the recalcitrant Thomas, no doubt—lunged for the ladder, but it was Charles who, without conscious thought, reached out and plucked the girl from the air.

'Charles, dear, I did particularly wish for you to meet Miss Westby today,' his mother said, her voice wry.

But Charles was staring at the woman he held in his arms. She was a beauty indeed, and she'd had quite a fright. Large dark eyes stared apprehensively into his, her arms were locked tight about his neck and her soft, full bosom was pressed quite delightfully into his chest. But pleasure faded as realisation dawned, and then it turned to growing outrage. 'You!' he gasped.

Sophie's heart was beating so fast—partly from fear, partly from exasperation at the absurdity of the situation, and partly from sheer feminine appreciation—that she was sure Charles could feel it. To view Charles from a few feet's perspective was a delight; the prospect from a few inches was awe-inspiring.

It was as if he had been designed to be pleasing to every eye. His hair was the colour of chestnuts, thick and luxuriant, his eyes a deep brown that clearly signalled his shock—and his interest. Strong cheekbones, stubborn chin, every inch of him solid, authoritative, and somehow *English*. It was enough to tempt one to sing in praise of a nation that could produce such a specimen.

She'd forgotten that smug English superiority. Ever so slowly the astonishment faded from his face, only to be replaced once more by haughty disdain. *What was it?* she wondered. What had happened in the intervening years to turn her laughing boy into this proud, imposing man?

This proud man who still held her tight in the incongruous safety of his arms. Sophie took encouragement where she could find it, and forged ahead.

'Well, my lord, you have caught me—literally—at a disadvantage once again.' She peeked over his shoulder, 'Really, Thomas, it was too bad of you to neglect to warn me. I'm sure we have embarrassed Lord Dayle past all bearing.' She handed the footman her wet paintbrush and cut off his apologies. 'No, it's fine, really, just remove my equipment, please, and we shall muddle through, shan't we, my lord?'

Charles did not reply, although the stark lines of his face tightened, and so did his grip.

'Do put her down, Charles, for heaven's sake,' Lady Dayle commanded.

He flushed and immediately set her down, with a bit more force than was necessary, Sophie thought. She flashed him an unrepentant smile, and wiped her paint-stained fingers. She would break through his stone-sober demeanour, she thought, if she had to take up a chisel and hammer to do it.

'I'm fine, truly,' she said as Lady Dayle fussed over her. 'I should have known not to ask Thomas to warn me, he's started up a flirtation with the parlor maid and was bound to forget.'

'Mother,' Charles said tightly, 'you seem to have some idea just what the dev—deuce is going on here. Perhaps you will enlighten me?'

'It is what I have been trying to do, my dear, indeed, it is why you were invited today.' Beaming, she took Sophie's hand. 'Allow me to reacquaint the two of you. I do not say introduce, for, if I recall, the two of you did bump into each other in Dorsetshire in years past.'

'We have indeed bumped into one another,' Charles began in an acid tone, 'and only too recently—' He stopped. 'In Dorsetshire?'

'Yes, dear. May I present Miss Westby? Sophie, surely you remember my son?'

Sophie could only nod. Her heart was, unexpectedly, in her throat and she could not tear her eyes from him as she waited for the truth to strike. She could almost see his mind spinning behind the dark and masculine beauty of his eyes. 'Westby,' he repeated. And there it was, at last, shining in his gaze, knowledge, and a flash of pure, unfettered joy. 'Sophie?'

A weight of uncertainty dropped from Sophie's soul. He knew her. He was glad. She felt as if she could have floated off with the slightest breeze.

He stepped forward and took her hands. His grip was warm and calloused, and so longed for, it almost felt familiar. 'Sophie! I can scarce believe it! It's been so long.'

'Indeed.' She smiled. 'So long that you did not know me— twice over! If I weren't so pleased to see you again, I should feel slighted.'

'It was you in the street that day, and you did not reveal yourself—minx. I do not know how I failed to realise. I should have known that only you would back-talk me so outrageously!'

'Back-talk? I only gave back what you deserved. You were so high in the instep I barely knew it was you at all.'

The door swung open and in swept Emily. 'Oh, do forgive me,' she said, her voice shaky. 'I should have been home an age ago, but you'll never believe it.'

'Emily, are you well?' Sophie turned as Charles dropped her hands. 'What is it?'

'We have been caught up in a riot!' Her hand shook a little as she returned Sophie's embrace.

'A riot?' gasped Lady Dayle. 'My goodness, are you unharmed?'

'Perfectly well, do not fear.' Emily removed her bonnet and moved to a chair. 'Perhaps riot is too strong a word, though it was unsettling!' She tried to rally a reassuring smile. 'It was only a group of mourners who had come from that poor Mr Cashman's funeral. They were quite well behaved, but there were ever so many of them! It was a little frightening to find ourselves in their midst.'

'No weapons, no looting?' asked Charles. His voice had gone cold and harsh, so different from just a moment ago that Sophie could scarcely credit it. His smile was gone. All traces of warmth had vanished and he stood, shoulders squared, solid and unmoving. Sophie instinctively took a step towards him. He looked as if the weight of the world had descended upon him.

'No, thank the heavens.' Emily sighed. 'I own that the man was used rather badly, but I have no wish to be drawn into the situation.'

'Used indeed!' said Sophie, still eyeing Charles uneasily. 'And then cheated, robbed, and made a terrible example of by the very government he risked his life to protect.' She allowed Lady Dayle to pull her to a chair. 'I wish I might have paid my respects.'

The man's story was tragic, and all too common. A navy man, the 'gallant tar' had faithfully served his country for years. The war at last over, he'd been discharged, but unable to collect his arrears in pay and prize money. He'd pursued his claim, but had been insulted and ignored. The same day as his last curt dismissal by the Admiralty Board, spurred by drink and anger, he'd become caught up in an angry crowd bent on riot, and he'd been caught and arrested for stealing arms from a gunsmith's shop. Tried, convicted, and publicly hanged, he'd become a symbol for thousands of the discontented across the nation.

'In any case, it is too upsetting to contemplate,' shuddered Emily. 'Let us order tea and talk of pleasanter things.' She rang for a servant, and then settled on the sofa next to Lady Dayle. 'Well, Lord Dayle, tell us how you are getting on after that absurd Avery situation.'

Charles paled even further and shot a wary glance in Sophie's direction. Clearly he did not account this a more pleasant subject.

'I am faring little better,' Charles responded, 'though the truth is out.' He spoke tightly, his face a mask of control. 'I prefer not to discuss the subject, ma'am.'

'I don't know who could have believed such nonsense in any case,' the viscountess complained. 'As if you would have been interested in such a nasty old piece of baggage.'

'Mother,' chided Charles.

'I'm sorry, my dear, but it is the truth. Lord Avery and his wife have antagonised each other for years, each trying to outdo the other in their outrageous bids for attention. I wish they would finally admit their feelings for each other and leave the rest of us out of it.'

'Charles is not the first young Tory she has used to stir her husband's jealousy,' Emily agreed.

'Nor am I the first whose career has been jeopardised,' he added, 'but I am the first to be so publicly reviled for it.'

'It is your past exploits that make you so irresistible to the papers, my lord,' Sophie teased, hoping to restore his good humor. 'They think to line their pockets with so long a list.'

'I would that that were the only motivation behind this constant attention. But someone seems determined to unearth every scrape I've landed in since I was breeched.'

Sophie deflated a little with this answer. It would appear that Charles could not be coaxed back to his good humour. If anything, he looked more morose as the tea things were brought in and he took a seat. Emily poured, and, after she had offered around the biscuits, she exchanged a pointed look with Lady Dayle.

'I know it has been an age since you were last in this room, Charles,' his mother said, setting her tea down, 'but have you noticed the changes that have been wrought?'

The question appeared to startle him. As it would any man, Sophie supposed. Yet she could not suppress the nervous chill she felt when she recalled his scorn at their last meeting.

He glanced about, and Sophie followed suit. She could not help but be well pleased with what she saw. Emily had held a definite vision for this room, and between them they had created something special. Much of the woodwork had been painted a dark green, softer shades of the same hue graced the walls and were incorporated into the upholstery and curtains. Rich cherry furniture, including a stately grandfather clock, contrasted nicely. It looked well, and, most importantly, it satisfied a secret longing in her friend's soul.

'It is very peaceful,' Charles replied, sounding surprised.

'Exactly how I hoped it would feel,' Emily agreed. 'I wanted to step in here and feel as if I were hidden away in a forest glen. It is only just finished, and I could not be happier with the effect. I am extremely pleased with the artist who helped me with the design. In fact, although it is supposed to be a secret, I believe I will share one aspect that was done just for me. You will not spread the tale, and I am convinced no one else would have done the thing so well.'

Sophie held her breath. The viscountess looked intrigued. Charles appeared to be looking for a back way out. But Emily was not to be deterred.

'When I was a girl,' she began in a dreamy voice, 'I was fascinated with fairy rings. I searched our home woods diligently, and when I found one I would spend days there, making wishes and dreaming dreams of the fairy realm.'

'Your mother and I did the very same thing, dear, when we were young.' Lady Dayle's voice was gentle.

'I know,' Emily said fondly. 'She discovered me one day. She joined me, plopped herself right down amongst the toadstools in her best day dress. We spent many a happy day so occupied.' She sat quietly a moment and Sophie's heart ached for her friend.

'So when we began this room,' Emily continued, 'I tried to convince…ah…my designer, to use a fairy wallpaper pattern I had seen in a design guide. It really was quite loud and colourful, though, and not nearly so tasteful as what we have here now. It was my designer who convinced me and still found a way to incorporate the youthful fantasies of a silly, nostalgic woman.'

'Don't keep us in suspense, dear,' said Lady Dayle. 'Where is it?'

'All around us,' said Emily, 'and neither of you had any idea! But if you look closely, you'll see a pixie here and there peeking out at us.'

The viscountess immediately rose and began to search, but Charles looked straight at Sophie's green-stained fingers then right at the high spot where she had been when he entered the room. And there she was, a tiny green and gold-haired sprite, peering at them from the top of the curio cabinet.

He looked back at her and Sophie smiled and gave a little shrug.

'Well, Charles,' his mother said with a touch of sarcasm as she returned to her seat, 'that's a sour look you are wearing. Have you too much lemon in your tea, or are you in some kind of pain?'

'No, no.' He let loose a little bark of laughter. 'No more than any other gentleman forced to listen to a pack of ladies fussing over *décor.*'

It was Sophie who was in pain. He was being deliberately cruel. But why?

'Well, pull yourself together, dear,' his mother was saying, 'for you are in for more than a little fussing.'

'Yes, for we have saved the best surprises for last,' Emily said.

'I think he has already discerned one of them,' said the viscountess shrewdly. 'And you are correct, my son, it was indeed Sophie who envisioned the design of this room. She has done a magnificent job, both here and at Mrs Lowder's home in Dorsetshire.'

'I congratulate you on your fine work, Miss Westby,' he

said, his voice coldly formal. 'I wish you equal success in your début.'

Sophie was growing tired of Charles's swaying moods. What on earth was wrong with the man? None of this was going as she had planned. 'I am a designer, my lord, not a débutante,' she said firmly.

He cocked his head as if he had heard her incorrectly. 'Nonsense. You are an earl's niece. You are of good birth and good connections.' He nodded at the others in the room. 'Why else come to London at the start of the Season?'

'She has come at my invitation, Charles,' his mother intervened. 'Both to be introduced to society and to aid me with your birthday present.'

His look was so frigid that Sophie wouldn't have been surprised if the viscountess had sprouted icicles. 'I beg your pardon?'

Lady Dayle was a warm-hearted and giving woman. She was also still Charles's mother. 'Do not practise your high-handed ways with me, sir.' She softened her voice a bit and continued. 'The Sevenoaks house, dear. A politician needs a place to get away, to invite his cronies and plan strategies, to entertain. The place is run-down and shabby. For your birthday, I would like to ask Miss Westby to help me with the redecorating of it.'

Sophie could have cheerfully kissed Lady Dayle's hem. A house. A nobleman's house. It was exactly what she hoped for.

'I appreciate your thoughtfulness, Mother, but such a large undertaking is unnecessary. I would not wish you to tax yourself. Nor would I wish to be responsible for taking so much of Miss Westby's time away from her first Season.'

Sophie could have cheerfully punched Lord Dayle's nose. Was he insane or merely trying to make her so? Who was he? Haughty aristocrat or charming gentleman? She was beginning not to care.

'Nonsense,' returned his mother. 'I shall see to it that we both divide our time favourably. And with Emily's help as well, we shall have a grand time with it all. You will,' she added her *pièce de résistance,* 'be in no way discommoded.'

'But, Mother,' he returned gently, 'perhaps this sort of project should be undertaken by my bride?'

'I should place a great deal more weight with that argument if such a person existed.' The viscountess sniffed. 'You haven't won the hand of a dyed-in-the-wool puritan yet, my boy.'

Emily spoke up. 'I dare say that your mama should derive more enjoyment from such a project, in any case, my lord,' she said with a significant look.

This argument did indeed appear to sway him. 'Oh, very well,' he capitulated with bad grace. He turned, his eyes narrowed, to Sophie, 'But I beg you both, here and now, to leave me out of it. It is entirely in your hands. I do not wish to be conferred with, consulted with, or called on. In fact, I would be mightily pleased if I hear not another word on the matter until it is finished.'

Even before he had finished his sentence Sophie was swallowing her disappointment, pushing away a deep sense of betrayal. She had been so humiliatingly wrong. The Charles Alden she had longed for was nothing more than a foolish girl's fantasy. A ghost of a man who might have grown from a good-hearted boy.

The real Charles Alden, she was forced to conclude, was

this hard-eyed monument, more marble than flesh. He had no inclination to renew their friendship, and she—well, she was long past the time she should be indulging in daydreams.

She met his stony gaze and nodded her agreement as Lady Dayle and Emily chattered, full of excitement and plans. Sophie would easily—gladly—meet his terms. She would do her very best for the viscountess and she would make the viscount's home a place of beauty and harmony. But another ten years would be too soon for her to ever see Lord Dayle again.

He stood. 'I shall leave you ladies to your fairies, furniture, and furbelows.' He bowed and took his leave, never quite looking Sophie's way. She watched him go, felt her dreams dragging out behind him, and took some small satisfaction in the cheerful green handprint showing clearly on his left shoulder.

Charles clutched his hat with shaking fingers as the door closed firmly behind him. For several long moments he stood, shoulders hunched to ward off the pain. Sophie.

When he had first realised who she was—for the briefest moment—he had forgotten. Elation and an odd possessiveness had surged through his veins. At last fate had smiled upon him and sent the one person who in some elemental, deeply satisfying way, understood him completely.

The flash of joy and relief had been overwhelming. His ally, his friend, his very own Sophie.

Then Mrs Lowder had come in talking of riots, and he had remembered. Realised. She didn't know, could never understand. They couldn't ever go back. The thought hurt on a nearly physical level.

She had grown up, his childhood friend. She was all vibrant

energy and exotic beauty, as passionate and unconventional as ever. Still, he had longed for her company. He wanted to tell her everything and hear everything she had done over the years.

He could not. Judging from their two unconventional encounters, she had not changed. She was impetuous, opinionated, and always in trouble. A friendship with her would be dangerous. Poison to Viscount Dayle, the only part of him still living. He had realised it at once; he could not have her. Ever.

So he had acted like the juvenile she had known and he had flailed at her in anger. Now she would despise him, and it was better that way. Easier.

Charles straightened and dragged himself off. He would go home and examine this situation in the way that it deserved—through the bottom of a bottle of blue ruin. Then he would live the rest of his life the way he deserved. Alone.

Chapter Four

'Sophie, you are not attending me.' Lady Daylc's words barely penetrated the mist in Sophie's head.

'What?' She blinked her eyes and focused on the jumble of fabric swatches and wallpaper patterns spread before her. 'Oh, yes, that combination is lovely, but I don't know how much more we can accomplish until I have seen the house.'

It was a true statement, but what she left unsaid was that though this was the chance of a lifetime, she could scarcely concentrate on plans for the house without succumbing to a barrage of conflicting thoughts about its owner. One minute she was wishing him to perdition where she would never have to lay eyes on him again. The next she wanted to knock him to the floor, sit on him, and flick his ear until he confessed just what it was that forced him to act like an ass, just as she had done when she was twelve and he had hidden her favourite box of coloured chalks.

'I know, dear, but it will not be long before we see it. I've already sent word to the staff to remove all the covers and shine the place up, so you'll see exactly what you have to work with. In a day or two we can visit and— Oh, I've had the most fabulous idea! Let us make a party of it!'

'Party? But we will have much work to be done if we are to be there for only a day.'

'True, but we can at least make a picnic of it. Emily, and her dear little one, will enjoy it. Jack can come, he needs to get away from his books occasionally. And Charles can escort us. How refreshing it will be to get away together!'

A little *frisson* of panic travelled up Sophie's spine at the mention of his name. 'I do not think we should bother Lord Dayle. I promised he should not be troubled by this project, if you will remember.'

'Don't be such a widget! We are his family. It is his house, for heaven's sake. In any case, we'll invite that dreadfully prosy Miss Ashford along and he can feel as if he is putting his time to good use.'

A different kind of twinge struck Sophie. 'Miss Ashford?'

'The leading candidate for dullest débutante in London, and therefore the main focus of Charles's attention. He has a notion that marriage to a strait-laced girl of impeccable family and no two thoughts to rub together will settle all his troubles in one fell swoop.' Lady Dayle paused. 'Although he could not have picked a more unlikely miracle worker, should you ask me.'

'Miracle worker?'

'Indeed. An alliance with such as her, he expects, will reassure the party, restore his standing in the *ton,* and stop the papers' infernal fascination with his old exploits.'

Surely it was a sudden onset of the putrid fever that had Sophie's throat closing and her eyes watering, not the tight fist of jealousy or the realisation that if *that* was the sort of girl Charles was looking for, it was no wonder he wanted nothing to do with *her*.

'In any case, we'll ask him tonight at Lady Edgeware's ball,' continued the viscountess, unaware of her protégée's distress.

'I know you went to a deal of trouble to have me invited, my lady, but I am of a mind to stay quietly at home tonight. You know that going about in society is not my true reason for being here, and, indeed, I am not feeling all that well.'

'Nonsense. All work and no play, and all those other adages, my dear. In any case, I think we are avoiding the real issue.' She stroked the back of Sophie's hand. 'You must face him some time, you know. Emily and I will be with you, there will be nothing to fear.'

Indignant, Sophie sat up straighter. 'I am not afraid of Lord Dayle.' She might not have the pedigree or propriety of a Miss Ashford, but she was no coward.

'Good Lord, why should you be? I was not speaking of my addlepated son. I meant Lord Cranbourne, your uncle.'

Her uncle. A man for whom she had given up all feeling, confused or otherwise. Would that she could do the same for Lord Dayle. 'I'm not afraid of him, either, but neither do I wish to rush a confrontation.'

'There will be no confrontation, of that I can assure you. Just a polite, long-overdue meeting.' Dismissing the subject, she forged ahead. 'We've been so busy lately with plans for the house that we have quite neglected our social obligations, and this will be just the thing to liven you up a bit. And in any case you must come tonight and see Lady E's Egyptian room. It is quite famous, and you will not want to miss it.'

'Oh, very well…' Sophie paused. 'Did you wish me to bring my notebook? Are you thinking of something similar for the Sevenoaks house?'

'Heavens, no! She has taken Mr Hope's ideas and run wild. It is a dreadfully vulgar display.'

Sophie thought longingly of her own bed and her previous plans for the night: a quiet meal in her room, a nice long soak, the pages of portraits she would like to draw of Lord Dayle before she shredded each one and consigned it to the fire. Then she thought of him dancing with the faultlessly lineaged Miss Ashford, or perhaps taking her for a stroll in the garden, where he would kiss her eminently respectable lips.

'In that case, how can I resist?'

Miss Ashford, Charles thought as he led the lady out for their set, was everything he was looking for in a bride. She did everything proper and said everything prudent. She even danced in an upright manner, perfectly erect and composed, with no expression, of enjoyment or otherwise, on her face.

Why, then, was he trying so hard to discover some chink in her flawless façade? He had spent the evening trying to uncover something—addiction to fashion, a sweet tooth, a secret obsession for nude statuary, anything.

He had failed. The lady seemed to be everything reputable and nothing else. No flaw, no interests or passions or pursuits. And no warmth for him, either. She accepted his attentions with calm dignity and with no sign of reciprocal regard or even disfavour. He felt as if he was courting a pillar. Lord, it was a depressing thought.

Their set finished, he led her back across the ballroom, exchanged all the correct pleasantries with her equally bland mama, and took his leave, trying not to yawn.

A slap on the back from his brother brought him awake.

'Evening, Charles,' Jack said, 'you look like a man who could do with a drink.' He signalled the footman and when they both had a glass of champagne, said, 'Just thought you might want to celebrate a bit—your name hasn't been in the papers for a week, but it has shown up in the betting book at White's.' He swept his glass across, indicating the crowded ballroom. 'They're betting which of these dull-as-ditchwater debs will have the chance to tame you.' He drank deep again.

Charles grinned, feeling more than a little satisfaction. Things were finally progressing according to his own plans. He still had much political ground to make up, and, ridiculous though it might be, his social success would help him cover it quickly.

'I am happy to report that Miss Ashford is the filly out in front,' said Jack. 'Wouldn't be surprised if your attention to her tonight makes it into the *respectable* social columns tomorrow.'

Charles's good humor deflated a little. He glanced over at Miss Ashford, who stood in unsmiling, serious conversation with some matron or other. This marriage-of-convenience business was a bitter brew to swallow. But swallow it he would, and be thankful for it, he thought. The bitterness he undoubtedly deserved, and some stubborn, wilful part of him welcomed the challenge.

'Good.' That same stubborn part of him yearned to find the person responsible for stirring up this hornet's nest of scandalbroth. 'Unfortunately I haven't had the same luck finding the editor of the *Augur.*'

'Someone's tipped him off,' said Jack.

'It is a convenient time for the man to have developed a far-flung sick relative. I doubt I'll get anywhere with him if he's anything like the one at the *Oracle*. He makes Lord Avery's talk of a peasant revolution look quite sane. Hates the nobility, took a satanic glee in rubbing my nose in my own misdeeds.'

'He certainly did his research.' Jack grinned. 'Honestly, Charles, even I did not know that you were the one who painted old King Alfred's statue such a heavenly shade of blue. There's a certain justice in it that you must pass the old boy every day on the way in to the Lords.'

Charles firmly suppressed his answering smile. 'Somebody's feeding them information, and being bloody clever about it. My man hasn't found a scrap of a clue.'

'So what shall we do now?'

'I meant to ask you to take over the search for the missing editor.' He clapped his brother on the shoulder. 'Sorry, old man, I know it means time away from your research.'

'It's no matter, I find I quite enjoy this sleuthing. It's not so different from scholarly research, except for the venue. And I never had to buy so many rounds in the university library.'

'I appreciate it, Jack. In the meantime I have taken a lesson from this tricky cove and decided to fight him with his own weapons.'

'Do tell!'

'One of my footmen has been "bribed" by the press.'

Jack laughed. 'Damn me if you aren't brighter than you look, big brother. Brilliant idea. Now you can leak the information you wish to hit the streets.'

Charles smiled. 'Before long there will be an entirely different view of the "Wicked Lord Dayle" circulating.'

'I'd drink to it, but my glass is empty. Ah, well. Perhaps I will dance, since I am all rigged out and actually made it to one of these intellect-forsaken functions.' He surveyed the room, then nodded his head and raised a brow. 'And there is just the creature to make me willing to dredge up the memories of those nightmarish dancing lessons— Mother's protégée. Take a look, Charles, she cleans up excellently well.'

Charles did not turn. He had spent the evening purposefully trying not to notice Sophie. And yet he knew how incredible she looked in her exquisitely embroidered ivory gown. He knew how the scarlet of her overdress contrasted so richly and set off the lustrous sheen of her ebony tresses, and he could probably calculate to the smallest measurement just how much of her smoothly glowing skin was displayed.

He did not look, for every time he did he found himself mocked by his own thoughts. *He would prevail, would sacrifice anything to ensure his success.*

He'd had no idea just how much he would be asked to sacrifice.

Jack was leaning in closer. 'Tell me, what do you think of that whole situation? There's been a bit of gossip there as well. None of it malicious, so far, just curious, what with the estranged uncle and the unflagging interest in design.' He nodded again towards the corner where their mother stood with Sophie and a group of friends. 'Although I did hear a few catty whispers from the younger set, something about the girl having trouble with society at home.'

Charles unclenched his teeth. 'I think that her presence makes Mother happy, and for that we owe her much.'

'Without a doubt. I haven't seen Mother so animated since… well, in a long time. But I confess, at first I thought that Mother was matchmaking.'

This time Charles could not stop the grin that came at his brother's words. 'It occurred to me as well. In fact, I scrubbed up the courage to confront her, thinking to forestall any hopes in that direction, only to be unequivocally warned off.'

'I was read the same lecture.' Jack rolled his eyes and imitated his mother's stern tone. '"The dear girl has suffered enough at society's hands. I mean to ease her way, not subject her to the wayward attentions of a man too busy with his nose in a book to treat her properly."'

Charles laughed. 'It was my boorish moods and general crankiness.'

'Well, she's right, old boy. You are a cranky boor and I am in no way ready to acquire a leg shackle, but that doesn't mean I can't dance with the little beauty.'

Charles watched him go. Watched him receive a smile from Sophie and a warning look from their mother. Watched the other men watching her as she gracefully took the dance floor, smiling her evident enjoyment. Then he turned, heading for the card room, where one of the members of the Board of Trade was reportedly diminishing his own cash flow.

Sophie watched him leave the ballroom as the dance began. She had been surreptitiously watching him all evening, all the while painfully aware that he was nearly the only person present not watching her.

The *beau monde* did not know what to make of her. Her birth was good, her fortune respectable, though it had a slightly mercantile taint. But she was undeniably not one of them. At three and twenty she was a bit long in the tooth to be entering society. Worse, her manner was too direct, her looks too exotic, her passions too strongly expressed. She was *too much* of everything, she felt, for them to be comfortable with her.

They studied her like a rare insect, some with fascination, some with revulsion, and Sophie wouldn't have cared a whit, yet she knew Lady Dayle would be distressed should she be found wanting.

Not to mention that she was absolutely determined, even more so as she pretended to ignore Charles ignoring her, that he would not find her alone and friendless today as he had so many years ago. Especially not when his own social standing appeared to be so fully restored. The 'Wicked Lord Dayle' might not play well in Whitehall, but since the rumours began of his search for a viscountess, he was a hit in Mayfair.

So she had smiled. She had sparkled. She had danced and talked with a great many boring gentlemen, and she had secretly studied Charles the way the rest of the room studied her, trying to fathom his mysteries.

He was incredibly handsome tonight, in deep blue and creamy white. Someone had tamed his wayward hair; like him, it was shining and gorgeous and contained.

When, she wondered, had he donned this mask of control? She knew he must be relieved at his restoration, but there was no sign of it. No sign of any emotion, except for a few moments of obvious camaraderie with his brother. He remained calm and cool, receiving attention from every woman in the room as if it were his due. He spent a good deal of time in corners with other gentlemen of a political bent, danced only a few dances, and twice only with Miss Ashford.

She could not like the man he had become. But though she wavered between hurt and disdain, she had to admit also her fascination. How and when had he changed so completely? She was not ready to give up on her questions, to give up on him.

Let him bask in the admiration of the silly women of this world. Sophie knew her man, and with the old Charles a little disdain went a long way. Perhaps, with this stranger, it would as well.

So she thanked his brother prettily for the dance and bided her time. When she grew tired of feeling like a new species of insect at a naturalists' gathering, she retreated to the ladies' retiring room. She dawdled for a bit in front of the mirror, gathering her determination. She was no stranger to disapproval. At the tender age of seven she had been orphaned, uprooted from her home in Philadelphia, and unceremoniously shipped to England. She'd dreamed of a warm welcome and a loving uncle. Instead she'd been shuffled off to a lesser estate, hidden away along with her eccentric aunt, who sometimes thought that she was seven years old as well.

The people of Blackford Chase had taken their cue from the earl and done their best to forget her existence. She'd been so lonely until she found Charles, and again after he left. Still, she had managed well enough for herself and eventually found a way to be useful. She could do the same here. And here she still had a chance at unravelling the mystery that was Charles Alden.

Still lost in thought, she headed back, but was surprised when she heard a step close behind her and felt a hand on her shoulder.

'Good evening,' a strangely familiar voice greeted her.

Sophie froze. It wasn't her chance. It was her uncle.

She forced herself to breathe deeply and turned. She'd known she must face him some time, but still she found herself unprepared for the pain. 'Hello, Uncle.'

He had grown older. The broad shoulders she remembered were a little stooped, the dark hair shot with grey.

'It has been a long time,' he said.

She inclined her head. There was no polite reply to that.

'You are doing well for yourself. You've shown initiative getting yourself to London.' He smiled for the first time and looked her over like a horse at Tattersalls. The smile did not reach his eyes; they glittered, reminding her of a hungry spider. 'Quite a change from the snivelling chit that landed on my doorstep.'

He would find her no easy prey. 'Indeed,' she politely agreed. 'Many changes take place over the course of so many years. The most important one is that I no longer need, or desire, your approval.'

Her rudeness didn't faze him. 'You've got your mother's spirit as well as her looks.'

'Enough of it to tell you that you may go to the devil, which is exactly what she said to you, is it not?'

'Clever, too. Young lady, you have far more potential than I have given you credit for.'

'Lord Cranbourne,' a clear voice rang out, and Lady Dayle materialised behind Sophie. 'We so hoped to see you tonight. How nice to see that Sophie has at last tracked you down.'

'She has indeed, and I see how wrong I have been not to search her out sooner. But I shall make amends and call on you soon, my dear.' He made his bow and departed.

Lady Dayle turned and stroked Sophie's face, her own dark with concern. 'Are you all right?'

'Perfectly.'

'I am sorry I was not here sooner.'

'Do not worry.' Sophie made herself smile for her friend. 'The worst is over. It will only get easier from here.'

'I hope you are right.' She sighed. 'But he did not seem upset in the least, did he? I had worried that he would resent my interference. Well! Everyone is still at supper. If you have finished, then perhaps we should take a look at the Egyptian Room?'

'Lead on, my lady.' But Sophie drew her shawl closer to her for warmth, and tried to ignore the fact that her hands were shaking.

She forgot her discomfort once they entered the Egyptian Room. Sophie's shawl fell along with her jaw as the door closed quietly behind them. It was unlike anything she had ever seen. She had expected something cold and sterile. Instead her senses were under attack. The vibrant warmth of the vivid blues and oranges contrasted strongly with the antique red and black. It was astonishingly busy, yet the lines were straight and clean. It was alien, spectacular, and oddly compelling.

'Dreadful, isn't it?' asked Lady Dayle. 'I don't think this was what Mr Hope meant at all.'

'In fact, I believe this is quite close to the spirit of some his work,' came a voice from deep within a lionskin chair. 'Except for all the odd animal parts. I believe that little touch is all Lady Edgeware's.'

Charles stood and Sophie's heart dropped. She was shaken still, and edgy from her encounter with her uncle. Not at all up to dealing with him, or the way he made her feel.

'Charles! What are you doing in here?' Lady Dayle's tone was sharp.

'I've come to see Lady E.'s latest acquisition.' He gestured and Sophie swept around a sofa with legs fashioned after an elephant's.

'Oh!' she gasped. It was a monstrosity of a stuffed crocodile, frozen for ever in a snarling pose of attack.

'Good heavens,' complained Lady Dayle, 'the woman has gone too far. Charles, you shouldn't be hiding away in here. Some baron from the north has stolen a march on you and taken Miss Ashford in to supper.'

'I make it a point to come in here every year. It helps to distract myself from my own folly when I contemplate someone else's.'

'Yes, well, perhaps you should not encourage Lady Edgeware. I don't find this place at all comfortable, but there is an appealing piece here and there. This, for instance,' and she swept toward the heavily adorned marble mantel.

'Hold, Mother,' Charles warned, but it was too late. The short, pearl-encrusted train of her gown had caught in the jaws of the stuffed crocodile. The tear of fabric sounded loud in the room, along with the pinging dance of scattered pearls.

'Oh, the horrid thing,' huffed the viscountess. 'Do untangle me, Sophie, and tell me how bad it is.'

Sophie knelt to examine the hem. 'I'm afraid it is quite a long tear, my lady. Let me help you to the retiring room and we'll find a maid to stitch you back up.'

'No, no, dear. You stay and finish your look around. If you find any of my seed pearls, do be so good as to tuck them into your reticule. No, Charles, you go on to the dining room. I shall be back in a trice to fetch Sophie.'

She was gone from the room before either of them could protest. Neither of the pair left behind would have been comfortable had they seen the crafty smile she wore as she went.

Sophie, who felt that her current mood could rival any of Charles's most cranky moments, bent again and began to gather the pearls. 'You should go, my lord. I doubt Miss Ashford would be happy to know you were alone in here with another woman.'

He stood, silent and cold, for a moment. 'Perhaps you are right.' He turned to go.

Perverse disappointment bit into Sophie. 'Incomprehensible.' She said it just loud enough for him to hear.

'I beg your pardon?'

Defiant, Sophie lifted her chin. 'I was remarking to myself that I find you incomprehensible.' She pursed her lips and shook her head. 'But upon reflection I find that I don't even want to try to understand it.'

'Understand what?' he demanded.

'How the boy who faced down Otto, the village bully twice his size, the same boy who climbed the maypole just to win a bet, the man who swam naked in the Serpentine with two of the city's most famous high flyers—how that person somehow metamorphosed into the pluck-less specimen before me.'

Charles just blinked for several seconds. 'Did you say pluck-less?'

'Yes, but I could have substituted faint-hearted, mean-spirited, dandified, or, let us not forget, hen-pecked.'

For a moment he looked as if he might explode. Then he laughed. And laughed. Then he sat down in the lion chair and laughed some more.

'Damn you, Sophie,' he said when he had recovered, 'you always did bully me out of a bad mood. I should have remembered.'

He met her gaze as he smiled in remembrance and Sophie's breath caught. Here it was, the look, the feeling of friendship and something indefinable, but *more*. This was what she had been looking for when she found him again. It was sweet to discover it at last, but also painful, because she knew it was fleeting.

'I? Bully?' she asked. 'You are the one who has yelled at, insulted, and ignored me. A little name calling is the least you deserve.'

He grinned. 'How did you hear about the Serpentine?'

'The same way the rest of England did—in the papers. I dare say I've heard of every scrape you've been in since you were fifteen.'

'Good Lord, I hope not. Some of them were never meant for ladies' ears.'

'No one has ever had cause to call me faint-hearted,' she said with pride. 'You know I've never cared for what people say of me. You never did either.'

The challenge hung in the air between them, and Sophie held her breath. For a moment she thought she had done it, that he would tell her what haunted him, but then he grimaced and the light in his eyes died. The mask was back.

'Now I do,' he said, his voice harsh, 'and it is past time you did too.'

'I never thought to see the day I could say this with honesty.

I don't like you, Charles. I can't abide the person you have become. You are closed, cold, and cruel.'

'Good. It's better that way.' His voice was as remote as his expression.

'Why are you trying to drive me away?' she whispered.

His eyes closed. He was fighting some inner battle while she waited alone. He knelt and took her hands. His were warm. He smelled of masculine things, smoke and expensive cologne and raw male sensuality. 'Things have changed,' he said gently. 'You are right, I've changed. We cannot be to each other what we once were.'

'Why not?' She had to fight to keep the anguish from her voice.

'Don't, Sophie,' he said, dropping her hands and rising. 'If you only knew how hard it has been.' He was pacing now and she was shaking. 'And you come along and make it so much more difficult.' He turned to her. 'You're not…I cannot…' It was panic in his voice and on his face. Something out of proportion for the situation as she knew it. He began to pace again.

He stopped. 'Listen, Sophie, let's agree to be friends, then. I cannot offer any more. Please.'

He was hurting and, in some way she didn't understand, it was her fault. She wanted to ease his pain, wanted to know what it was that frightened him. 'We have always been friends, Charles. We always will be.'

'Thank you.' His relief was palpable.

Confused, she bent back to her forgotten task. The tiny pearls blurred as she fought the tears that threatened.

'Here, let me help you, then I shall escort you to Mother.'

She blinked furiously. He didn't truly wish for her friendship either, he just wanted to be rid of her.

They worked quietly for a moment before he said, 'I believe there are some still trapped in the creature's jaws.'

Sophie struggled to regain some semblance of herself. Never would she allow him to see the depth of her humiliation. She summoned a smile from some buried vein of strength she didn't know she possessed. 'Shall I leave them to you, then?'

He made a face and knelt down, picking a jewel from the crocodile's teeth. 'You always did leave the nasty work to me.'

'How can you say so?' she protested, leaning back on her heels. 'I believe it was I who pulled the leeches off you when you would go into the South Bog after those berries.'

'Very true,' he returned, 'but who had to muck out the gardener's shed when you decided to raise a goat in there?'

Her smile was a true one this time. At least they had not lost this, the ease they felt together. It had been present since their first meeting and was the part of their relationship that she would have mourned most. Perhaps she could be content with this. 'Poor William,' she sighed. 'He's still a terror, you know.'

He made a strange, strangled noise. 'William!' He began to chuckle. 'I'd forgotten the goat's name.' He began to laugh in earnest again. 'Because Billy was undignified!' he whooped, and set himself off again into gales of laughter.

This time she joined in, because it was easier to laugh than to cry.

'Ah, Sophie,' he said a minute later as he wiped his eye, 'we always laughed, didn't we?' He leaned in close to pass her his handful of pearls, his gaze suddenly serious and locked with hers. 'I'd forgotten how much I missed it.'

Now it was her turn to experience a twinge of panic. He was close, so close. He looked relaxed, almost happy now that he had settled her firmly in a distant sphere.

Biting her lip, she asked herself just what it was she wanted. She scarcely knew. She'd come to London telling herself she only wanted to renew their friendship. Now he offered just that and she felt—what? Disappointment. Dissatisfaction. She yearned for that connection that lit her insides, ignited her passion, made her feel whole.

Very well, she breathed deep. She would take what was offered. For now.

She schooled her expression and lifted her gaze to meet his. But didn't.

Because his was locked on her mouth, and the atmosphere had suddenly, subtly changed. She could almost feel the hot touch of his gaze as it travelled down the column of her neck and across the expanse of her shoulder. The air between them danced with the hard beat of her pulse.

Slowly, his hand rose. Sophie's eyes closed as, whisper-soft, his fingers brushed along her collarbone. Her head tilted as he caressed the one heavy lock that lay against her nape.

It was the tinkling of the scattering seed pearls slipping through her fingers that allowed sanity to intrude. Just in time, too, for once she was released from the sensual spell of Charles's touch, her brain began to process what her ears had been trying to relay.

'I'm sure he must be in here, dear, I left him here gathering up the jewels from my dress.'

Lady Dayle. Right outside the door. Sophie only hoped it was the proximity of the viscountess that caused the horrified expression on her son's face as they both clambered to their feet.

'There you are, my darlings.' Lady Dayle had a distinctly sour-looking Miss Ashford in tow. 'Haven't you found all those pearls yet? I was just telling Miss Ashford about our plans for a picnic, Charles, and felt sure you wouldn't mind if I invited her along.'

'What plans are those, Mother?'

Charles walked away without a second glance, and Sophie had the distinct impression that that look of horror would have been there even had his mother not appeared.

Chapter Five

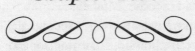

Perfect morning light, a soft haze of chalk dust, the quiet scratch of a pen—it was a recipe for contentment. Alone in her room, enveloped in her beloved things, Sophie should have been content. Ecstatic, even.

She wasn't, because the air also hung with the heady fragrance of lilacs. He had remembered her favourite flower. A glorious full vase of lilacs rested on her dressing table, their scent teasing her, their beauty distracting her, the card that had accompanied them tempting her to read it just one more time.

Friends, then.

That was all it said, all he offered.

Sophie flung down her pen and gave up her work as a lost cause. It was time she was honest with herself, she thought as she began to pace the room. Her real problem, the true source of her agitation, was the certain realisation that what he offered was not enough.

She wanted the old Charles back, him and their rich, easy friendship. She wanted the laughing, carefree Charles, the one who, when left alone with a pretty girl, would have gone far beyond one burning caress.

She pressed one hand to the spot he had touched and dug her other palm into her brow. She was mourning the passing of a rake! She must be the only person in all England who wasn't completely enamoured of the new Lord Dayle. It was the new Charles they admired, the one who was productive, and prudent, and moody, and so incredibly handsome.

The horrid truth was that she wanted that Charles too.

She groaned and started to pace again. She was as inconsistent as he! He who asked for friendship with words and pen, and something else entirely with stormy eyes and fervent touch.

Sophie sighed and came to a stop. There was only one thing she could be certain of: her need for some answers. She had to know where that mask had come from, what had caused that haunted look in his eyes, where the old Charles had gone. Perhaps a better understanding of Charles's feelings would clarify her own.

Very well, they would be friends. She would chip away at the stone, remove what obstacles she could from between them, and then? Then she would see what happened next.

She dipped her nose in the bouquet one last time, then turned and rang for Nell. If she was going to begin to look for answers, there was no time like the present.

'Nell,' she began when the maid appeared, 'will you let me know right away when Emily returns from the park with the baby?'

'Yes, miss.' Nell stopped and looked surprised at the stacks of papers and designs covering the bed, the table, and nearly every flat surface in the room. 'Lordy, miss, I hope you don't mind my saying it, but you have been busy. I thought you'd done all you could until you saw the big house?'

'I have. All this—' she gestured '—is for another project. Something very special indeed.' In fact, this work represented a dream very close to Sophie's heart. It was nearly complete, but she was not quite ready to confide in anyone just yet.

'Mrs Lowder did send word that you should be ready for callers this afternoon. Shall I just run a brush through your hair?'

Sophie laughed. 'Nell, you are wonderfully circumspect. Yes, thank you, I always do muss it dreadfully when I am working.'

She sat quietly while Nell plucked the pins from her hair. Once the maid had begun brushing with long, rhythmic strokes, she asked, 'How long have you been with the Lowders, Nell?'

'Oh, going on seven years now, miss. Usually I'm just the upstairs maid, so I was ever so glad when you came.' For the first time Nell sounded shy. Sophie guessed she was not used to talking of herself.

'You've done a wonderful job,' Sophie said warmly, 'and I shall be sure to tell Mrs Lowder so.'

'Oh, thank you, miss. I did get to help with Mr Lowder's sister when she made her come out, and I watched her dresser do her hair ever so many a time, so I had an idea what was needed.'

'Seven years. And you've been in the London house all this time?'

'Yes, miss.' The maid sounded a little wistful. 'Though I've thought a time or two that I might like the country.'

Sophie chuckled. 'I always felt the same about the city. I suppose it's natural to wonder about what you've never really experienced.' She was quiet a moment and then she cast a glance at Nell in the mirror. 'I suppose you've heard a good deal about Lord Dayle's adventures, then? He did keep the London papers busy for a good number of years, did he not?'

Nell ducked her head and kept her brush busy. 'They say he's reformed now, Miss. Though I admit I was surprised when such a good girl as you are had an acquaintance with him.'

'Oh, yes...' Sophie did her best to sound nonchalant '...I've known Lord Dayle since we were both practically in leading strings.' She cocked her head. 'I never truly knew his older brother, though. But you would have been working here when the previous Lord Dayle died?'

'Oh, yes. Such a shame. I even saw him a time or two, he was as wrapped up in politics as Mr Lowder is. That sorry I felt for his poor mother. Bad enough the son, but then her husband gone so soon after.' Nell shivered as she twisted Sophie's hair up and reached for the pins.

'Phillip died at Waterloo, but I was home in Dorset when Lord Dayle took sick. We all thought it just a minor illness. No one expected he would die as well.'

Nell pursed her lips and concentrated intently on her work.

Sophie watched her in the mirror. 'There were vague rumours of trouble in the family at home. Did they reach town?'

'Almost done, now. Such hair you have, miss! You must remember to wear your new bonnet for the picnic tomorrow, it brings out the light in your hair so well.'

'Nell?'

The girl sighed. 'It's just servants' gossip, miss.'

Sophie sat silent, questioning.

'They whispered below stairs that Lord Dayle died because he wanted to.'

Shocked, Sophie said, 'Surely no one believes…?'

Nell shook her head. 'No, they just said he gave up. Got ill and didn't fight it, then he just slipped away.'

Sophie turned around in her chair and gave Nell a measuring look. 'The next time we are at Lady Dayle's house, do you think you could…?'

Nell's bright eyes shone. 'Ask some questions?'

'Discreetly.' Sophie paused. 'You've already shown yourself to be loyal and trustworthy, Nell. I know I can depend upon you in this matter.'

The maid straightened, her face proud. 'Of course, miss.'

A knock at the door startled them both. Sophie called entrance, and a footman opened the door deferentially to announce a visitor waiting below.

With a flustered glance towards the lilacs, Sophie rose. Was it Charles? She gathered her shawl and steadied herself. Good, she could begin finding some answers straight away.

She entered the drawing room a moment later at a sedate pace, chin up, only to draw up short.

'Lord Cranbourne, miss,' the butler intoned.

Once again she found her uncle where she had been expecting someone else entirely.

'Uncle,' she said in the frostiest tone she could summon.

'Niece.' He was equally formal as they seated themselves and the butler offered to go for the tea. He watched her the entire time, his gaze sharply calculating.

As the servant's footsteps faded in the marbled hall, her uncle spoke. 'I was annoyed when I first heard you had come to town, I admit.'

'I am amazed you thought to care one way or another.'

He crossed his legs negligently. 'It doesn't look well, you coming here without my sponsorship, but, after meeting you, I'm willing to overlook the matter.'

Sophie inclined her head regally. 'That does seem to be what you do best.'

He leaned forward, suddenly intent. 'Look here, niece. We can sit here all afternoon while you flail me with the sharp edge of your tongue, or we can get straight to the point. Which would you prefer?'

'Whichever gets us finished quickest.'

He chuckled. 'I'm impressed, my dear, and that is not something I say with any frequency.' He shook his head. 'I just never guessed you had any fire in you.'

The tight control she held on her rage snapped. 'It is impossible that you would know anything about my character!' She struggled to regain herself as the servants returned with tea.

Heavy silence hung in the room as she poured for them both and wished mightily for Emily's return.

Her uncle was still entirely at ease. 'I know more about you than you would think, young miss, never doubt it. I know you resent me, but what's done is done. We find ourselves now in a situation where we can help each other.'

Determined not to let him see her out of countenance again, Sophie sipped her tea. 'Your offer comes fifteen years too late, sir. I'm not interested.'

'Don't go missish on me now, girl. It took brains and courage to get here without my help. Now I can make sure you go much, much further.' He leaned back. 'I have connections. What is it that you want? To be a leading lady of the *ton?* A political hostess holding her own salons?' He gestured to her colour-stained fingers. 'A patroness of the arts?'

She merely shook her head in reply.

'There is power to be had behind the scenes. True power. Empires are won and lost by chance meetings at a ball, by a loose word let slip over drinks. You could be a great help to me, and I can make sure you meet all the right people.'

Sophie closed her eyes in pain. She'd spent too much of her life hoping for some kind of attention from her uncle. Now here he sat and she only felt ill. He wasn't interested in her, only in what she could do for him. Perhaps, she thought for the first time, she had been better off without his attention.

'You are more like your mother than I thought possible,' her uncle continued. 'She had beauty and intelligence and spirit as well. But she chose poorly, and look what it got her. A few years of love in a colonial backwater and a watery grave.' He sat straighter and stared intently at Sophie. 'Don't repeat her mistakes.'

'I thank you for the confidence you have finally shown in me, sir, but I am not feeling at all well just now.' She could stay no longer. What he did not know was that Sophie had her mother's temper as well, rarely raised, but devastating in scale. One minute more of this and she would be throwing his offer, along with her cup of tea, in his face. Only the thought of Lady Dayle's and Emily's disappointment stayed her hand. She took comfort instead in imagining his reaction when all of her plans were revealed. 'Pray, do excuse me.'

He rose and gave a short bow before declaring in a hard voice, 'I'll give you some time to consider. Don't dawdle, Sophie. Together we can accomplish much.'

Shaking, Sophie rose. It was the first time he had ever called her by her name. Her anger fled, leaving her aching and empty inside. With a barely audible farewell she hurried out and up the stairs. The lilacs mocked her as she entered her room and flung herself upon the bed. First Charles and now her uncle— who would ever have guessed that getting all the things she thought she wanted would be so horribly disappointing?

She cried then, hard, racking sobs for the little girl who had only wanted someone to love her, and for the grown woman still searching.

Lord Cranbourne watched her leave. He turned and stalked out to his waiting carriage, fiercely ignoring the pain once again radiating down his left arm.

The chit was going to be a problem. He had enough trouble this spring chasing after a political appointment that should have come easily, and, far more worrying, dealing with his own body's betrayal. Throw a headstrong brat into the brew and he might not be able to vouch for the outcome.

Inconstancy. Unpredictability. He was unused to such, yet they seemed suddenly pervasive, hanging thick in the air, obscuring his vision, fouling his plans. He was a man used to being in a position of strength, of knowing all the variables in myriad situations and understanding ahead of time where the players were connected and how the final act would play out.

In a world where knowledge was power, he was a very powerful man indeed, albeit, as he had hinted to his niece, behind the scenes. For most of his life it had been enough, but lately, when faced with these reminders of his mortality, he found he wanted more. He wanted just a bit of the glory and recognition due him, and he wanted it with a fierceness that surprised even himself.

Now he stood on the verge of gaining his objective and his carefully laid plans were fragmenting. He clenched his fist to his chest against another pain and cursed out loud. He was not going to go down without a fight.

When the carriage rocked to a stop, Cranbourne stepped down on to Green Street and walked gingerly up the stairs. He'd feel better after a good stiff drink. He left his coat with a footman, and calling for his secretary, headed for his study.

'You're sure that message went off to Philadelphia as planned?' he asked the compact, extremely efficient man.

'Indeed, yes, sir.'

'And we can expect a reply, when?'

'Two weeks…maybe three at this time of year.'

Cranbourne grunted. Three weeks. He was glad he'd had the foresight to send his inquiries earlier. Judging by the obstinate look on his niece's face, he might need some help from that direction.

'If I may, sir? You have a visitor in your study.'

'Wren, is it?

'No, sir. It is Mr Huxley.'

'What? Old Huxley, here?' he paused outside the study door.

'No, sir, the young gentleman with the maps, if you will remember?'

Cranbourne wrinkled his brow and longed for that drink and a few minutes of peace. Serious matters were afoot. He needed to think. 'Maps? Oh, yes.' He sighed. He'd done a favour for a very useful friend, and hired one of his sons to do some detailed survey work. Heaving a sigh, he went in.

'Lord Cranbourne, sir.' The young man rose, blinking like an owl from behind a thick set of spectacles. 'I have good news. The project is completed.'

But inspiration had hit Lord Cranbourne just as the mid-afternoon sun glinted off Mr Huxley's dishevelled blond hair. The boy was the right age, tall, shaped well, and easy enough to look at if he would lose the barnacles. 'Good, good,' the old man said as he took the papers the puppy handed him. He barely glanced at them. 'Yes, you'll do. Sit down, my boy.' Cranbourne sank gratefully into his own chair.

'You will find the map completely updated, sir. I walked practically every inch of Lancashire myself. Every lane, farmer's track and footpath is noted.' He handed over another folder. 'The only thing missing, I dare say—' he smiled '—is who is on the roads at present.'

'Yes, very thorough,' agreed Cranbourne, but his mind was racing. Perfect. At the least, young Huxley would serve as a very creditable distraction, but if matters came to a head between his niece and himself, then the man might be more useful yet.

'Here's the additional information you requested as well: innkeepers and way-station holders in the district, and what I could find on meeting places, debating societies and reform-ist connections.'

'Excellent. Tell me, do you go out into society much, Mr Huxley?'

The boy blinked again, startled. 'No, sir.'

'It's time you started, then. How many years have you, three score?'

'Just eight and twenty, sir, but I fail to see how this relates to the project you hired me for.'

'I've got a new project in mind. Got a niece coming out this Season. I could use a good man like you to squire her about a bit, ask her to dance, take her for a drive now and then.'

'I hadn't really thought to…'

'Nonsense. The girl's a beauty, educated; she's just new to town and doesn't know many people in society. You can't stay a bachelor for ever, sir. I thought to give you first crack at her.'

'You do me an honour, sir, but I have given no thought to taking a wife at present.'

'Oh, well.' Cranbourne shrugged. 'The chit's got no money, unfortunately, but I'd be disposed to look kindly upon her husband. To be his patron, perhaps.' He gazed shrewdly at the young man. 'I belong to a committee of importance or two, you see, and I had thought to propose a few more mapping expeditions. Who knows what might come of it? A project encompassing the entire island, perhaps.'

Mr Huxley blinked once more. 'Perhaps if I just met her, sir.'

Chapter Six

The day of the proposed expedition to Sevenoaks dawned bright, with a slight crispness in the air that boded well for comfortable temperatures later. The company gathered early in Bruton Street and quickly separated into travelling groups. Lady Dayle elected to ride with Emily, her husband and their little boy in the closed carriage. Jack enticed Sophie into his showy cabriolet. Two more carriages, carrying servants, the baby's nurse, and the picnic, stood waiting. And Charles? He stood on the steps, suppressing a sigh as his own smart curricle rounded the corner, heading back to the mews.

'I don't mean to be a bother, Lord Dayle,' Miss Ashford assured him again, 'but a journey of several hours in that contraption? And all the way back, too? I'm not sure Mama would approve.' She gave him an arch look. Charles had the impression that it was meant to be flirtatious.

Charles smiled at her. 'I would gladly give up the chance to drive my bays in exchange for the pleasure of your company, Miss Ashford. We are very glad you could join us today.'

She thanked him with pretty words, but her eyes did not meet his. In fact, Miss Ashford was directing a look of displeasure somewhere else entirely.

It was a man who drew her attention, a battered-looking man in a ragged regimental coat. He walked slowly towards the group, until he was a few feet from Jack's rig. There he stopped, snatched his hat from his head and spoke in urgent tones too low for Charles to hear.

'I'm sure I feel all the pity that is due someone like that, and the compassion for which my own gender is known,' Miss Ashford said in an equally low voice, 'but I cannot think Mayfair a suitable place for him to wander. Should you do something, my lord?'

'I am confident that Jack will handle the matter appropriately,' Charles answered. And, indeed, he saw his brother reach for his purse. He was stalled by Sophie, who leaned down to speak with the grizzled veteran. Clearly startled to be so addressed, the soldier answered her. Sophie continued to speak—indeed, it looked as if she were questioning the man closely. Soon she reached into her reticule, pulled out a scrap of paper and scribbled something on it.

The open barouche arrived just then, and Charles, busy handing Miss Ashford in, missed the end of the strange encounter. He gave the order for the party to set off, and noticed as they drove past the unfortunate man that he clutched the paper tight in his hand and stared after the departing Sophie with a look of dazed surprise.

Charles could not know what she had said to the man, but he recognised that vacant look. It was an expression commonly seen in Sophie's vicinity. He'd worn it himself more times than he could count.

She was a force of nature, his Sophie, and he suspected that her power, like her beauty, had only grown with her. Just look what had happened at Lady Edgeware's ball. A few minutes alone with her and he had forgotten his role. Forgotten his debt. Let down his guard and laughed like he hadn't since Phillip had died.

She fascinated him, yet he was terrified of her. She knew him too well. So easily she had discovered the chinks in his armour. He could never let her look inside. She might discover that there was nothing left underneath.

They would be friends, he had told her, though they both felt that spark, that potential for more. It was that instantaneous jolt he felt in her presence, perhaps, that sizzling reminder that a man did indeed exist under the viscount's shell, that frightened him most of all.

Because she was still Sophie. Still outrageous, outspoken and slightly out of step with the rest of the world. They were qualities he had always enjoyed in her—now they were the very reason he must avoid her.

He had already lived life his own way, for his own pleasure, ignoring the strictures of society, and what had it got him? Only a hellish reputation at first, but too quickly followed by a dead brother, a dead father, a lifetime of remorse and a title that he hadn't ever wanted.

He'd never coveted the viscountcy, but he was saddled with it now, and it came with an enormous debt to repay. It was clear that, if he ever meant to pay that debt, sacrifices were required, the first and greatest of which was his freedom.

He knew now that his theory was sound. Society was quick to judge, but easier to manipulate. They had fussed and worried over his past like a dog with a bone, but all he had needed to distract them was a bigger prize: his bachelorhood.

A few dances with the right debs, a compliment here, a witty rejoinder there; all he'd had to do was show a proper interest in making one of their darlings his viscountess, and suddenly his wickedness became youthful high spirits, his transgressions were forgiven, and invitations began piling up again.

His political prospects had improved as well. He'd been approached at Lady Edgeware's ball by Sir Harold Luskison, an influential member of the Board of Trade. The gentleman had stuck to polite conversation at first, but eventually he had given Charles a friendly slap on the back and approved his attention to Miss Ashford.

'I know you've been down a rough road recently,' Sir Harold had said. 'Avery's nonsense is easy to ignore, but together with the character assassination in the papers? It becomes more difficult.'

Charles had started to speak, but the man had stopped him. 'I know I'm not the only one who has noticed that all of those published escapades are shades of a murky past.' He had flashed Charles a conspiratorial grin, 'Do you know I myself was caught up in one of your pranks, once?'

Charles groaned, but Sir Harold appeared lost in fond remembrance. 'It was that contretemps you got up to at the Lady's Slipper. Do you recall it?'

Recall it? How could he forget? The tavern in the Strand was the scene of the most notorious brawl he and his cronies had ever got mixed up in. The owner had been in a fury and had had Charles and his friends thrown into the street. He'd even threatened to send the bill for repairs to Charles's father.

Sir Harold was still grinning. 'You make a fine rum punch, lad. Not too proud to say I sampled a cup myself.'

Charles rubbed his brow and hid his eyes. The very next night, he had set up camp outside the pub, with a small cauldron fitted out like a woman's shoe, in the likeness of the tavern's famous sign. He had mixed up his best rum punch and ladled it out for free to every comer, ruining the pub's business and infuriating the owner all the more. The man had called the watch and Charles had been lucky to escape.

'It took me all day to put together that cursed shoe.' He dropped his hand and returned Sir Harold's smile. 'Do you know I still have it?

The man laughed. 'I dare say there's not one among us who couldn't rake up a hairy tale or two from our youth. I just wanted you to know you have your defenders. The energy and dedication you've shown since you inherited has done you good.'

Sir Harold had gestured toward the dance floor then. 'Good gracious, not since that dreadful Fitzherbert woman has anyone's courtship been so closely examined. But you are doing well. A steady girl of good family and reputation will prove your sound judgment and lay your past to rest.'

Charles had been thrilled at the reassurance. His instincts had been correct, his gambit had worked. He had, in fact, felt completely vindicated in his course of action.

Until he had almost kissed Sophie.

'What do you think, my lord?'

Even her interruptions were timed perfectly, Charles thought, mentally noting the addition of another 'Reason to

Marry Miss Ashford'. More than happy to be distracted, he fixed his attention on the young lady. 'I beg your pardon, my attention was drawn elsewhere for a moment.'

'I asked,' she said again, allowing the smallest hint of exasperation to colour her question, 'how you think I might best approach Miss Westby. You seem to know her well, so I thought you could advise me.'

'Approach Miss Westby?'

'I think she might benefit from my influence. I shall take her under my wing, as they say. With my help I dare say she shall go on very well here in town.'

Charles shrugged. 'It's very kind of you, but I think she's doing well enough on her own. I can see no need for you to so trouble yourself.'

Miss Ashford threw Charles a significant glance and favoured him with a very small, tight smile. 'Naturally a busy gentleman such as yourself would not encounter the same sort of small talk that a lady would. Normally I would not deign to pass on such, well—let us call it what it is—petty gossip. But a few things have been brought to my attention, since I am known to also be an acquaintance of your family's.' She paused and this time her speaking look was even more pointed. Charles would have been amused if he hadn't had a sudden chilling vision of the thousands of such arch glances the lady's husband would be subjected to, day in and day out. Chalk one up for the 'Reasons to Consider Someone Else'.

'Fortunately there is nothing that cannot be overcome with my help. The incidents are mostly small and insignificant, in the manner of what we saw this morning, when Miss Westby engaged that beggar man in conversation.'

Charles knew, without a doubt, that he should be grateful to Miss Ashford. She only sought to please him. She only echoed his own doubts about Sophie's behaviour. She only offered to help Sophie in exactly the manner that he wished for himself, if on a larger scale. There was no earthly reason for him to feel such indignation on Sophie's behalf. Yet feel it he did. Indignation and irritation flashed through him at the thought of Miss Ashford's forcing Sophie into a mould fashioned after herself.

'That military man, and all his like, deserves our condescension and compassion, Miss Ashford. God knows they have obtained precious little from the government they risked all to defend.'

'I agree. Yet for a lady to be seen in conversation with them in the street is not at all the thing. If Miss Westby has a charitable bent, I have a far better notion of how she may proceed.'

Charles's interest was piqued. Perhaps Miss Ashford had more bottom than he had suspected. He hadn't had an inkling that she participated in charity work. He couldn't help but approve. 'How so?' he asked.

'I, and a few of my peers, have organised our own charitable society. I mean to ask Miss Westby if she would like to join us.'

'I dare say she would,' Charles said warmly. 'I'm very interested myself. Tell me about your works, perhaps I could help in some way.'

'Oh, it is nothing you would be interested in. We are a small group, and new.'

'Nonsense. I would be glad to help in any way I can. What have you accomplished so far? Have you a board? A charter? Perhaps I could serve as financial advisor and take that burden from you?'

Miss Ashford was looking more and more discomfited. 'I am afraid you have surpassed me already, my lord. As I said, it is a group of *ladies.* We meet every week or so over tea to discuss society's ills. We have not progressed so far as you imagine.'

Charles did his best to hide his disappointment. For a moment he had thought…but no, it was clear that Miss Ashford's society would never progress as far as he imagined. Oh, she might throw a charity ball, but she would never truly interest herself in the plight of the less fortunate. The 'Not Miss Ashford' column was coming on rather stronger than he was comfortable with.

'I fear I must warn you,' he said, 'Miss Westby was never a fan of discussion. If she sees a wrong being committed, she is far more likely to intervene herself than to sit and talk about it.'

'Yes,' agreed Miss Ashford, 'and that is precisely the character flaw I hope to eradicate. Do you know what she said to the Duchess of Charmouth?'

Charles did not know, but he could well imagine. 'No, but I would wager that she criticised that cold and draughty ballroom that her Grace is for ever entertaining in.' The *ton* had suffered, silently shivering, through year after year of the popular event. He almost laughed at the picture of Sophie haranguing the old termagant.

'Worse,' Miss Ashford declared, 'she pointed out everything architecturally wrong with the room, then she came right out and told her Grace that she knew of a builder who could repair it…' and she lowered her voice to a dreadful whisper *'at a good price!'*

Unexpected laughter burst out at the mental image, but

Charles tried hard to contain himself when he noticed Miss Ashford's shocked countenance.

'It is no laughing matter, my lord. Such pretension on Miss Westby's part must not be encouraged.'

'And was the duchess insulted?' he asked.

'No, she was not.' Clearly Miss Ashford was puzzled by this. 'But she very easily could have been.'

'What, exactly, was her reply to Miss Westby's advice?'

'She said she was glad indeed to meet someone who would talk sense to her despite her title, and would be gladder still to hear of a man who would not cheat her because of it.'

Charles chuckled, but he could see Miss Ashford's point. Yet even though his head conjured images of Sophie suffering a scathing set-down and social disgrace, urging him again to distance himself from the girl, he knew in his gut that he would not.

She very likely would get herself in some sort of trouble this Season. With Sophie, it just seemed inevitable. But she was the closest friend of his childhood. He would stand by her, come what may.

It is a shameful thing, some deeply buried part of himself whispered, *that you won't trust her enough to allow her to return the favour.*

The party made good time on the roads and arrived in Sevenoaks just past mid-morning. Everyone welcomed a stop in the village centre to stretch weary limbs and to admire the stand of trees that bestowed on the little town its name.

After a brief respite they climbed back aboard and travelled the short distance to Lord Dayle's dilapidated house. For a few moments chaos reigned as the house servants came out to greet them, the stable hands swarmed to take charge of horses and vehicles, and those servants who had accompanied them from town set about unloading and locating the best spot to set up the picnic.

For Sophie, their arrival came not a moment too soon. She had fidgeted her way through the entire journey, apologising to Mr Alden and explaining it away as anxiousness to begin her project. What she could not admit to him was how unnerving she found the sight of Charles and Miss Ashford together.

The ride had been bad—the thought of watching them strolling together in the gardens, rowing on the lake, or doing any of a thousand things that courting couples do, was insupportable. She made haste to befriend the housekeeper, therefore, and swept away with her and Lady Dayle, happy to bury her anxiety in her work.

Confused feelings were easy to ignore when one had an entire house to bury them under. Sophie had poured over plans of the estate; she had imagined the rooms as she concocted colour schemes and design themes, but nothing compared to this: walking into the house and knowing that the transformation of it belonged to her. Touching the walls, studying the light, draping fabrics across furniture, and mentally turning a musty, neglected old house into a place of warmth and life.

Sophie had measured, climbed, scraped, pulled, and scribbled page after page of notes and sketches for several blissful, uninterrupted hours. This, this was heaven, and she resisted when Lady Dayle and Emily finally came to insist that she come join the party and eat.

'Do come now, dear,' wheedled Lady Dayle, who had kept

up with her for most of the morning. 'You must feed your body as well as your soul. And as much as I enjoy seeing you so happily engaged, it's past time we go and save Charles from Miss Ashford.'

'Save him?' Sophie asked. 'I rather thought he was happy for the chance to continue his courtship.'

'Yes, well, a few hours of the lady's unrelenting company should have cured him of that notion,' Lady Dayle answered with a wry twist of a grin. 'Let's go down.'

The viscountess marched out. Sophie shot a questioning glance at Emily, who only shrugged. Feeling intrigued and more than a little hopeful, Sophie took her friend's arm and followed.

She was quickly happy that she had given in. Charles, she found, had directed the picnic to be spread out in a sun-dappled grove overlooking the lake. The air was soft and full of birdsong, the company was in high good humour and a bountiful feast of cold meats, cheeses and fruit lay spread before them.

'Which is the tree in which you hid Cabot's teeth, Charles?' Jack Alden called.

Charles's only response was to roll his eyes at his brother.

'We had a litter of new puppies in the stables,' Jack confided to the company. 'The butler refused to allow them in the house. Charles had to exact his revenge somehow.'

'It isn't nice to tell tales on your brother, Mr Alden,' Emily said with a meaningful glance in Miss Ashford's direction.

Jack only laughed and they all went forth to the feast. True to her word, Lady Dayle enticed Miss Ashford into conversation and into a seat next to her. Sophie noted that Charles did look grateful as he took his plate and joined his brother. She carried her own and settled beside Emily and her family.

Emily was slicing fruit for her young son. 'You must see my little Edward, Sophie,' her friend said joyfully. 'He's walking so well!'

'The springy turf and even ground have inspired him,' chimed in Mr Lowder. 'He'll be running soon, though I think now he likes the falling down as much as the walking.'

'Sophie, there is dust on your skirt, a cobweb in your hair, and a smudge on your cheek,' Lady Dayle spoke up. 'All sure signs that you are enjoying yourself rather well.'

'I am enjoying myself immensely,' Sophie said complacently. 'Later today the builder arrives, and I predict that my appearance will suffer further, but my enjoyment will increase in proportion.'

'Speaking of which, Lord Dayle,' Sophie called. 'Forgive me for interrupting, but I must ask if you've any objection to my tearing down the wall between the two parlours at the back of the first floor?'

She hesitated to ask, after his harshly declared intention to have nothing to do with the project, but did not feel comfortable undertaking such a large change without his approval. Fortunately he appeared amused instead of annoyed. 'I give you full *carte blanche,* Miss Westby. The house is entirely in your hands.' He looked directly at her, and she caught her breath. Breathtaking was how he looked, sitting relaxed, with the wind ruffling his hair and a smile tugging at the corner of his mouth. 'I only ask that you don't attempt to bring the wall down yourself.'

Sophie gathered her composure and wrinkled her nose at him. 'I appreciate your confidence, and promise to leave the demolition to the men.'

She smiled as little Edward, appetite assuaged, toddled over to her and patted her face with sticky hands. 'I don't know why you berate me for my untidiness, Lady Dayle. Just look at this little gentleman—covered in peaches and grass stains! You'll never win the ladies' hearts that way, my boy,' she admonished him.

The boy laughed and plopped himself into her lap. 'Well, perhaps you shall,' Sophie said, gathering him close for a squeeze.

Emily smiled at her son's antics. 'Better grass stains than bruises, Sophie.' She raised her face to the sun filtering through the new leaves and leaned back against her husband. 'Oh, this was a marvellous idea.'

'Yes, a lovely day,' Miss Ashford agreed. 'It is a shame that you may not relax and appreciate it as the rest of us have, Miss Westby.'

Sophie did not wish to think about how Miss Ashford had been spending her day. 'I thank you, but beg you not to worry for me. I am more than content.'

'It seems an odd sort of thing to gain such pleasure from,' Miss Ashford remarked.

'It is unusual, but there can be no doubt of your talent,' Mr Alden intervened. 'I wandered in earlier and caught a glimpse of some of your colour and fabric combinations. Won't you please tell us how this project came about?'

Lady Dayle answered him. 'Sophie is too modest to tell the story correctly, so we shall have to enlighten you. It started with the baby,' she said, gesturing to the boy growing heavy-eyed in Sophie's arms. 'Tell them, Emily, dear.'

Emily rose to fetch her son. 'It did indeed start with

Edward,' she said as she settled back with him. 'Shortly before *his* arrival came the arrival of a very large packing crate at our home. I couldn't imagine what was in it.' She paused to adjust the baby's weight in her arms.

'Shall we guess, Mrs Lowder, or will you tell us?' Mr Alden laughed.

'I shall tell you, Mr Alden, if you will be patient.' She smiled over at him. 'It was a cradle. A marvellous cradle, with a mighty castle, and knights and horses, and even a princess in her tower carved right into the wood, like they had grown there. I confess, it took my breath away.'

'Beautiful piece,' Mr Lowder agreed. 'Never seen anything like it.'

'It was from Sophie, of course, and we asked her right away where she had found such a treasure, for we hoped to get some matching pieces.'

'Was it Spanish?' asked Miss Ashford. 'I've seen some lovely pieces from Spain and they are a fanciful people.'

'No indeed,' replied Emily. 'Sophie had designed it herself, and had a gifted friend of hers do the woodwork. We were amazed, of course.'

Everyone proclaimed their admiration. Sophie, blushing, tore her eyes from Charles, who had appeared very far away while Emily talked.

'Due to some previous difficulties, the doctors had insisted I stay off of my feet,' she continued. 'I thought I would go out of my mind! So I struck upon the idea of redoing the entire nursery, to keep my thoughts occupied.'

'She was the brains of the project,' Sophie laughed. 'I was only the hands and feet.'

'That is not at all the truth,' Emily protested. 'But it turned out so well and we had such fun that, after little Edward was born, I decided to ask Sophie's help in redoing some other rooms.' She turned to Miss Ashford. 'I assure you, they turned out beautifully. You've never seen anything so comfortable and elegant at the same time.'

'How nice,' murmured Miss Ashford.

'And upon seeing their handiwork, I decided that a big redecorating project would be just the thing for me as well,' interjected Lady Dayle. 'I came up with the idea of doing this house for Charles's birthday and enjoying the Season at the same time. And here we all are.'

'Yes, here we are all, and here I am going to stay, at least for a bit,' said Sophie, more than ready to change the focus of the conversation. She looked to Charles. 'Your mother and I have packed a few things. We mean to stay for a day or two, to get the work started off in good fashion.'

'Won't you be missed in town, Mother?' he asked.

'No. We intend to stay only tonight and tomorrow night. We shall be back in time for Almack's on Wednesday.'

'Good. I would hate for Miss Westby to miss any of the excitement of her first Season.'

Irritation straightened Sophie's spine. 'I do not know why you must insist on thinking of me as an empty-headed débutante, intent on flirting my way through the Season and into some peer's pocket.'

Charles cast a lazy eye over her. 'That was not my meaning, but since you brought it up, I shall remind you that decorating as a hobby might make you an eccentric, but as a career it will place you out of consideration for nearly any gentleman of birth.'

'That is just as well, then,' she returned. 'I have as much talent, vision, and will as any man, not to mention enough money of my own to gain me something that few other women possess: choice, free will, and independence.' She raised her chin, more than ready to continue, but was forestalled by Miss Ashford.

'I'm sorry to hear that you will not be returning with us, Miss Westby,' the lady said smoothly. 'I am hosting a gathering of young ladies tomorrow to discuss some charitable works, and I had intended you to join us.'

Sophie blinked. The woman sounded as if she fully expected a reversal of their plans. 'I am most obliged, Miss Ashford, but I must stay. The plasterer cannot come until tomorrow. I must be sure everyone comprehends what I have in mind. The first stages of a project such as this are critical.'

'Of course, I understand.' Her tone said otherwise. She accepted a glass of lemonade from a servant and turned back to Sophie. 'What I would like to hear is how you developed such a passionate interest in design, Miss Westby. It is a most unusual accomplishment for a young lady.'

Sophie fought back a grin. Clearly in Miss Ashford's eyes, *unusual* was not a compliment. 'Oh, it was born of necessity, I'm sure. My singing voice is not fit for public hearing, my needlework skills are mostly of the practical variety, and my musical ability, though competent, is nothing special.'

'Her artistic talents, however, are unsurpassed,' Charles broke in unexpectedly. 'I don't believe I have a single memory of Miss Westby without a sketchbook close at hand.' He smiled at the company in general. 'Unless, of course, I had squirrelled it away and hidden it. It was the greatest torture I could devise.'

Despite the tension that still crackled between them, Sophie was warmed by Charles's defence of her. And by the brightness of that smile. It sparked a longing to see it more often.

She forced herself to laugh and keep her tone light. 'I, on the other hand, devised any number of ways to torture you.'

'Yes, and I still bear the scars of a few of them,' he said with mock-severity.

'I know Miss Ashford would love a hint on how to beat Charles into submission, Sophie dear…' Lady Dayle spoke with the indulgence of a fond mother hen with a brood of wayward chicks '…but it will have to wait for later, for isn't that the builder's cart travelling up the drive?'

'Oh, it must be,' Sophie said, rising to her feet. 'He is due to arrive some time this afternoon.' Pausing, she flashed Charles her biggest smile, then stopped and bent down to Miss Ashford. Still holding Charles's gaze, she said in a deliberately loud stage whisper, 'Ear flicking, he hates that', before striding off to the house.

Chapter Seven

The afternoon sun was still high when Charles entered the house in search of Sophie. Though there was plenty of daylight left, most of the party wished to return to London before dark. He'd avoided the bedlam of repacking, calling to his mother that he would find Miss Westby so that she might bid everyone farewell. Now he wandered the empty rooms of a house that had never been meant for him, searching for a woman who was undoubtedly wrong for him.

There were signs of her everywhere. Long shrouded furniture lay newly uncovered, the discarded linen lying in heaps in the corners. Sunlight and fresh breezes poured through the place, as every window had been thrown open to let the day in. Splashes of colour, in swatches and sketches, sat prominently in each room.

She was up a ladder again when he found her, measuring a window for curtain lengths, he surmised. He stood, unnoticed in the doorway, watching the graceful bend of her body, the sunlight fighting against the glorious night of her hair, the gentle sway of her dress in the breeze.

He was a fool for being here. He was playing with fire and likely to get burned. But there was a part of him that could not resist her call, the young man in him who missed her chaotic friendship, and perhaps also the dark part of him that had always relished such danger.

'Don't fall,' he said softly, remembering the last time he'd discovered her on a ladder.

She turned her head and gifted him again with that dazzling smile—all white teeth against soft, exotically toned skin. 'Don't worry, Charles, I'm not going to fall.'

Her mocking tone made him wonder if she referred to something other than the ladder.

'The rest of the party is preparing to leave, I thought you might wish to come and see them off.'

'Yes, of course, just let me finish these measurements.' She bent again to her task. It grew quiet, with only bird sound from the open window to break the silence. Charles leaned on the doorframe and stayed where he was. He almost started when she spoke.

'Tell me, Charles, do you see much of Lord Avery lately?'

She surprised him with the question. 'Only in Westminster.'

'How does he go on?'

'I have not the faintest idea, except for the fact that he does go on about my reformist leanings every time we meet. He and his cronies keep up a continuous dark mutter when I am present.' He shivered. 'It is deuced unsettling. Why do you ask?'

'An odd notion. I know you feel you were sorely abused in that whole strange situation, but I can't help feeling sorry for him and his wife, as well. It seems to me that they were quite as ill used as you.'

'I agree, in large part, but I assure you my sympathy is the last thing Avery wishes. He persists in blaming me, at least in part, for the whole débâcle.'

'I suppose there is no one else for him to concentrate on, is there? It's human nature to look to others instead of yourself when something goes wrong. But I still feel for him. Has he heard from his wife?'

'After she ran off with the valet? I've no clue, but I don't wish to know anything else about the tawdry affair. What has brought all this on?'

'It's nothing. I just hate to see a relationship—and they do seem to have loved each other, in an odd way—come to such an end.'

Rolling up her tape, she climbed down and tried to put herself to rights. The familiar sight caused an unexpected ache, but still made him smile. It was so easy and comfortable, being with Sophie.

'What is it?' she asked, rubbing a grubby hand against her cheek and only making it worse.

'Nothing.' He chuckled. 'It's just with dirt smudges all over you and your hair coming down like that, you look about eleven years old again.' He let his gaze roam over curves and valleys that had never graced her younger figure. 'Well, perhaps not,' he said, unable to keep the husky appreciation from his voice.

She stilled and did not reply; a wild thing scenting something dangerous.

He advanced into the room, trying not to feel like a

predator. 'I didn't wish to discuss it in front of everyone, earlier today, but I remember the first time we really discussed your designs. Do you remember?'

She still had not moved. 'Yes.'

Her caution, her attitude of expectancy, of uncertainty, was affecting him. His heart was pounding. God, she was beautiful.

It was warm in the room, and the space was somehow growing smaller as he drew closer. 'It was summer, and we were trying to keep cool in the gazebo by the lake. You were drawing another of your infernal rooms, another place that existed only in your mind. I remember the breeze teasing the edges of your paper.' His own voice filled the small distance between them, wrapping, winding about them both and carrying them somewhere else entirely.

'I had never asked you before why you created those imaginary parlours and kitchens, ballrooms and stillrooms, instead of sketching flowers or houses or landscapes like every other girl. But that day I watched you, the intensity in your eyes, the heat of the day in your cheeks, and the wind whispering in your hair. And I asked. Do you remember what you answered?'

Her eyes were closed, but he knew she wasn't here any more. She was lost in the sweet summer's warmth of long ago. 'Yes.'

'You spoke of your father's warehouse, how he would take you there with him. You described the dust in the air, the sunlight spilling into the shadowy places, illuminating boxes, and crates, and barrels, of furniture, and paintings, and pottery. You told me how, just a small girl, you would close your eyes and dream of the homes those beautiful things would go to, of the rooms they would adorn.'

Sophie's eyes snapped open, and the spell was broken by the spark of fear shining there. Charles knew she did not want him to go any further. She lifted her chin. 'Pray don't mention this to Miss Ashford,' she said. 'I've only just been warned not to discuss my mercantile background.'

He accepted her retreat, knowing they both recognised it for what it was. 'I'm sorry if she offended you.'

Sophie shrugged. 'I am sure she meant it well.'

He sighed. 'I am sure that is what she tells herself, at any rate.'

'What's this?' The old Sophie was back, grinning her mischievous insight. 'The courtship's path travels over rocky ground?'

'No, maybe I would prefer that it did. Anything would be better than the bland, unexceptional terrain we've already traversed.'

'I'm glad to hear you say that. I was afraid you hadn't seen it.'

The relief in her voice puzzled him. 'Seen what?'

'Seen how ill the two of you would suit.' She smiled again. 'I thought I was going to have to exert myself to disentangle you from her clutches.'

Charles flinched. 'You misunderstand. I shouldn't have spoken so, it was a mistake.'

She stared. 'The only mistake would be to continue to pursue her.'

'Don't be ridiculous. It's an advantageous match for both sides.' This was not a conversation Charles wanted to have with Sophie.

'Charles, I've seen you with her. Watched you.' She spoke carefully, patiently, like he was a child, too young to see things clearly. 'In her company you disappear. There is only some sober, solemn stranger standing there in your skin.'

'That is exactly the intended effect.' His voice sounded as tight as the constriction in his chest.

'I don't understand. You mean to say you wish to be rigid, humourless, and unapproachable?'

'No, I mean I wish to be seen for what I am—an adult, a responsible, respectable peer of the realm.'

'Oho! Convenient, but unoriginal, Charles. I never thought to hear you playing Lord of the Manor. Does it all come back to the title, then?'

The scorn in her tone infuriated him. 'Of course it comes back to the title!' he said harshly. 'The bloody thing hunted me, laying waste to my family. Now it's got me. The duties and responsibilities are mine now; some of them so heavy, you cannot comprehend.'

'Balderdash! Do your duty, accept the responsibility, but don't let it change who you are.' Her hands were moving, sharp and fast, emphasising the force of her words. If he hadn't been so angry, Charles would have laughed. You knew Sophie was in a passion if she started talking with her hands. Then he heard what she was saying and any urge to laugh died instantly.

'You may not believe it, Charles, but I remember many things as well. I remember a girl making herself miserable, turning herself inside out trying to please the adults who tried to forget her existence. I remember the boy who taught her to find her own happiness. I remember the small confessions, the shared stories. My uncle, your father. My sad aunt, your over-burdened brother. I remember the words too. Do you want to hear them?'

'No,' he said harshly.

'"We'll think of the others, but live for ourselves." That's a wondrous piece of wisdom for a mere boy. Too bad the man's forgotten it.'

Her voice was heavy with disdain, and Charles shocked himself by welcoming it. Yes, he deserved nothing but her contempt, however misdirected its focus might be.

Sophie turned away from him and gripped the faded curtain. 'That's what you're doing now, isn't it? Living the life that others expect of you?'

She would never understand. He felt a sudden, insane urge to blurt out the truth, all of it. But he couldn't bear to see her reaction.

She'd grown tired of waiting for one. 'It's just a title, Charles. It may define your station in life, but naught else. You've hidden from yourself for so long, I think you've forgotten who you are. You're more like Phillip now than I ever thought you could be.' She paused a moment, as if digesting her own words, then realisation dawned on her face. 'It's Phillip,' she breathed.

This time, Charles knew, his flinch was noticeable. He'd known she was dangerous. Now he struggled to gain control, to throw the mask back up before it was too late.

It already was too late.

'My God, Charles! Is that what this is all about? Phillip was a serious man, a good and studious man. But it was his nature; the title didn't make him that way. Do you think to turn yourself into your brother?'

Charles's heart was pounding, his breath coming fast. 'We're not children anymore, Sophie. You don't know me as well as you think you do.'

'I know you well enough. Don't throw yourself away in such a marriage. Phillip would not approve. He would want you to be happy.'

Charles almost choked on the conflicting emotions within, all trying to fight their way out. She was beautiful in her passion, terrifying in her perception. He wanted to run, back to London, if necessary, where he could bury himself in work and never hear his brother's name again. He wanted to drop the mask and let the warmth of her affection and acceptance flow over him, absolving him of his sins. He wanted to shout the terrible truth at her: *I can't be happy. I don't deserve to ever be happy again.*

He couldn't do any of those things. So he buried his hands in her already dishevelled hair and kissed her instead.

For a moment, a shocked Sophie could only stand frozen, stunned. It was a short moment. Then she came alive under his hot and insistent mouth.

She couldn't push her mind past the miracle of it: Charles kissing her. She was overwhelmed by the taste and scent of him, the wonder of the dark need curling through her.

Through the long, lonely years, when Charles had been a companion only in her mind, he had represented safety, acceptance, and warmth. Then she had found him again, and he wasn't her best friend anymore, just a stranger who had shown her mostly arrogance and disapproval. Now, with his mouth slanting hotly over hers, he radiated something else entirely: risk, danger, molten excitement that welled deep in her belly.

She welcomed it, thrilled to it, reached for him so she could demand more. He groaned as her arms went around him, and the sound made the throbbing deep within her that much stronger.

He was barely in control of himself. She didn't care. He drove her head back with his hard, brazen kiss. She yielded to the assault and met him kiss for kiss. He backed her against the wall as his hands crept up to crush the curves he'd admired so boldly. She clung to him as if her life depended on it.

She had cracked his armour, touched the man underneath. His passion served in part as a stalling technique, a way to avoid dealing with the emotions that frightened him. But it was true, and it was hers. She accepted it and while the wind gusted through the open window, draping the faded curtains over them and enclosing them in a cocoon of desire, she gave him back all the fervent warmth in her heart.

He wasn't ready to accept it.

With a despairing moan he tore his mouth from hers and slid his hands up to grasp her shoulders. His chest heaved as his eyes closed and he rested his forehead on hers.

'I remember it all, Sophie,' he gasped, 'even the part you didn't wish to hear. I asked you that day why the rooms you drew were always empty. You said they were waiting for the happy people who would come to live in them.'

Sophie closed her own eyes in pain. She'd pushed him too far. She deserved this, she knew.

'Don't do it here,' he whispered. 'Don't create rooms for *my* happy family. They don't exist. They never will.'

He loosed her abruptly and strode out of the room. He didn't look back.

Chapter Eight

This was the last in a high stack of forms. Resolutely, Sophie dipped her pen again and signed. She paused, staring at the bold scrawl of her signature, contemplating everything that this step meant, then she pushed the papers over to her guest. 'Here you are, Mr Fowler.'

'Thank you, Miss Westby.' The man ran a practised eye over the contracts before putting them away in his case. Only then, Sophie noticed, did he visibly relax, take a sip of tea, and smile. 'I admit this is far more pleasant than my usual business meetings, but then, everything about this venture is unusual.'

Sophie sighed. There was that word again. *Unusual.* In the fortnight since that fateful day at Sevenoaks, it had echoed repeatedly in her head. Always in Miss Ashford's ever-so-slightly condescending tone. She took a deep breath. Perhaps it was time to make *unusual* work for her, rather than against her.

She raised her cup and an ironic brow. 'Then let us drink to the unusual success of our enterprise, sir,' she said.

'Hear, hear.' Mr Fowler drained his glass and began to

gather his things. 'I have no doubts on that score, however. Your work is delightful. It is sure to make us both a success.'

'I sincerely hope so,' Sophie said, standing to bid him farewell.

He took her hand, but paused. 'I feel I have to ask again. Are you certain you wish your portion of the proceeds to be paid to this…gentleman?'

'Mr Darvey, yes.' Sophie fixed her guest with a penetrating look. 'He may not be a gentleman, as you have obviously discovered, but he is a good and worthy man, and he will see that the money goes where it is needed most.'

'He's a lucky man, to have attracted a patroness like you, miss.'

'As I am a lucky woman to have found a friend like him.' She smiled. 'Nor am I unaware of my good fortune in securing a publisher of your calibre, Mr Fowler.'

He grinned and picked up his case. 'I'll send you round a copy of the book as soon as it is ready. It has indeed been a pleasure.'

Sophie watched from the window as Mr Fowler descended to the hired coach that had brought him. His cheerful whistle and jaunty step only served to frustrate her further. Her temple rested against the cool and soothing glass long after he had gone.

It was disheartening, really. She had accomplished so much. She'd found friends who felt more like family as each day passed. She was in London, with a major design project coming along relatively smoothly, and now this. A design guide of her own. It was a victory, a culmination of a dream that she had worked towards for years. More importantly, it was a means of helping those who might otherwise have no chance of a future.

Fate had surely had a hand in her meeting with Mr Darvey, all those months ago, for it had come at a time when they had both been in desperate need of some hope. The combination of her vision and his talent had resulted in some lovely pieces, such as little Edward Lowder's cradle. But that had only been the beginning. With a bit of Sophie's money, Mr Darvey's good sense, and a few members of his former regiment, they had created more than beautiful furniture, they had manufactured opportunity. They had given hope to others as well as themselves. This book could lead to more of the same.

She should be flush with success, awash in triumph, but she had found that she couldn't truly enjoy any of it. Instead she was only filled with a ceaseless, restless anxiety.

It was all Charles's fault, damn his eyes. She had neither seen, nor heard from, him in the fortnight since that unexpected, heart-pounding, earth-shattering kiss. And unsettling though his continued absence may be, worse was her inability to reconcile her unruly feelings.

Once she had recovered from the pure, physical shock of their embrace, she had been furious. How dare he resurrect a moment of their past, seduce her with the beauty and intimacy of it, then use it to push her away!

A little more thought, however, had reinforced the notion that his kiss had been an act of self-defence. She had touched him. Her patient chiselling had succeeded at last, and she had found a tiny breach in the stone rampart around him. She had reached the man inside and it had frightened him. Typically, like a scared little boy, he had pushed back, trying to scare her off in the same manner.

Perversely, his tactic had had the opposite effect on Sophie.

And perhaps that was characteristic of their relationship as well, she thought with a smile. But she could not help the feeling of intense relief that had swept over her with the realisation that there was indeed a mystery to be solved here. It wasn't a natural tendency for prudery and sanctimony that had changed Charles. Something had happened to induce this drastic alteration in personality and demeanor, to cause him to retreat behind that bulwark of prickly pride. Something to do with his dead elder brother.

What could it have possibly been? As far as she knew, Charles and Phillip had had the normally contentious relationship of brothers a few years apart in age. They had been especially close as young boys, tumbling through the home woods, racing their ponies, and perpetrating endless pranks. Even later, when separated by school and their father's increasing demands on Phillip's time, they had maintained the rough-and-tumble, slightly competitive regard of adolescents.

Had something happened to change that? Sophie did not know, but she was going to find out. It was a relief to have the task before her. It gave her hope, at least, that if Charles faced whatever it was he was hiding from, he might have a chance to be happy.

That, at the last, must be her goal. With everything in her, she longed to see her tousle-haired, smiling Charles again, even if it meant he found his happiness without her.

Such a thought, of course, led right back to that burning kiss. Good heavens, but every girl dreamed of such a kiss, when not only lips and bodies mingled, but souls brushed each other as well. Heat, desperation, spiralling desire—it all came rushing back. A small, triumphant smile escaped her as she touched her lips. Let him kiss Miss Ashford and see if he felt like that.

She drew away from the window. He could not escape her tonight. Lady Dayle was throwing a dinner party and expected him. It was time she prepared herself for the confrontation ahead. A silk gown would be her armour tonight, her weapons nothing more than determination and a smile. But perhaps she would carry along her chisel as well.

'That's all I know, I swear on my mother's grave!'

Charles tightened his grip, choking off the remainder of the man's lies, along with most of his breath. 'Your mother is alive and well and living in Kensington,' he said in disgust. 'How do you think I tracked you down?'

Like her son, the mother of the editor of the *Augur* liked money. Charles wasn't complaining, however. Greed was far easier to get past than radical fervour—which still blocked any progress with the *Oracle*'s editor.

'That's all you can give me?' Charles released the man, allowing him to slump back against the wall. 'A small, dark, wiry man. No name? No idea for whom he worked?'

'No, no,' Mr Mills said, rubbing his throat. 'He came around at night, left me a fat file of papers—all dealing with you.'

'And a fat purse, I'll wager.' Charles snorted. 'Do you still have the file?'

'Aye.' The man turned sullen now. 'I left it at my mother's place.'

No wonder the old woman had looked at him so strangely. 'What, exactly, was in this file?' Charles asked.

Now the little editor was eyeing him up and down. 'A right

long reckoning of your career as a hellraiser, my lord.' He chuckled. 'And may I salute your creative thinking too! We never got to print half the juiciest stuff.'

'You're sure this small, dark man never mentioned where he got this file?'

'No, it was always "my employer" wants this, "my employer" wants that. But whoever it is—it seems they have been watching you a long time.'

Charles had come here expecting to solve this mystery; instead it was only growing deeper. Frustrated, he sat abruptly down upon a nearby chair. His opponent watched him warily as he drew a purse from his pocket. He tossed it on to the scarred desk the man was obviously using as a temporary office. 'That's a sign of good faith. I believe you have told me everything you can, and I believe that if you remember anything else, you will contact me right away.'

The scoundrel snatched it up. 'I swear, that's all of it.'

Charles drew out another, fatter purse. 'This I will give you if you agree to print another story about me. A remorseful story. A favourable story.'

The man weighed the first purse in one hand while eyeing the other. 'No insult intended, but your randy youth is the most interesting thing you've got. What else is there to draw the readers in?'

'The truth. An apology for the damage you've done me. I don't know, something about the good I've accomplished in Parliament, the charities I support, something. Do your own research this time, man. Write a real story.'

He nodded agreement and reached for the second purse.

Charles tucked it back into his coat. 'You will receive it

on the day the story is printed.' He stood. 'I want that file delivered to me tomorrow.'

Without waiting for a response he turned and strode out.
Once outside the man's dingy little hideaway, Charles vaulted
back into his curricle, took the reins from his groom and set
his bays off sharply. He had several hours before he had to be
back home in time for his mother's blasted dinner party. The
idea had him groaning out loud. A house full of people. It was
the last thing he wanted when this whole mess had him feeling
so desperate.

Despite his best efforts with the *ton,* despite his obvious
perusal of the available debs, despite his intensifying courtship of Miss Ashford, the tide of public opinion was turning
against him again.

He wasn't a madman. Someone, for some unknown reason,
was orchestrating this siege against him, but this time the tactics
had changed. Nothing new was in the papers. Instead, the attacks
came in the form of vague rumour and untraceable innuendo.
He was living a masquerade, people whispered. He hadn't
reformed, he'd just taken his illicit activities underground. He
was lulling Parliament, pulling the wool over society's eyes. He
was a secret radical, a closet Catholic, a Whig sympathiser, a bac-
chanal, or an opium addict, depending on whom you spoke
with, and whose friend of a friend they knew.

Charles would have laughed if he hadn't known that the
truth about himself was far worse than anything society could
come up with. And he would have realised the serious nature
of the situation, nipped it in the bud earlier, if he hadn't been
obsessed with Sophie.

A discreet cough from his groom recalled his attention to

the road. Just in time too. He pulled his pair up as traffic slowed at the crossing of the Westminster Bridge. He was doing it again. Obsessing. And on the road, no less.

He sighed. It was still early, but he could not go home, it would be under siege, buried in a flurry of activity as his mother prepared for her party. As his wheels met *terra firma* once more, he turned the curricle smartly and set off for his club.

It appeared that even this small pleasure was to be denied him. There was a crowd of gentlemen at White's. Charles pushed his way through the crowd, looking for an empty seat. He finally found one, at a corner table. The vacancy was probably owing to the cloud of gloom that hung over the pair of occupants, nearly as tangible as the heavy haze of smoke in the air.

Charles paused as he grew closer. It was that infamous pair of his erstwhile friends, Matthews and Henley. What the hell.

'Gentlemen,' he bit out. 'Do you mind if I join the ranks of your dismal consortium?'

Matthews did not even look up. Henley rolled one bleary eye at him and waved for him to take the remaining seat.

Charles dropped into the chair and waved at a passing porter. Glancing at the empty brandy bottles still on the table, he sent the man off for another.

A brooding silence reigned in the corner, which suited Charles perfectly. A swirl of troubles floated through his head. He had to focus, had to find a way to salvage what was left of his life. But only one thought consistently rose to the top of the maelstrom: Sophie.

Good Lord, he'd kissed Sophie. Devoured her, more like, as he thought back to that shockingly intense embrace.

He'd had no business kissing her. It had been an idiotic thing to do. Cruel, even, when he thought of the harsh words he'd uttered afterwards. But how could he not have kissed her? When she had stood there, so beautifully tousled, so danger-ously perceptive, so close to the unspeakable truth? And why, then, had he spent the fortnight since reliving it?

Because it was nigh on impossible not to, that's why. Bad enough that he was obsessed with thoughts of the dratted female, but suddenly so was everyone else in London, and as much as he bemoaned his own notoriety, he almost cringed more at Sophie's.

The porter returned with the brandy and with a clatter began to clear away the empty bottles. Matthews looked up in surprise, and then started even further at the sight of Charles. 'Good Lord, when did you get here, Dayle?'

'A good ten minutes ago, you drunken lout,' snapped Henley. He gave Charles a good once over. 'Though I must say, Dayle, you look as bad as I feel.'

'Just looking at the pair of you makes me feel worse,' Charles retorted. He sighed, then. 'Sorry. What is the trouble with you two?'

'Female trouble, what other sort is there?' asked Henley.

Matthews was pouring them all a glass of the brandy. He flourished his own high. 'Women, bah!'

Charles lifted his own glass in a show of solidarity and they all drank deep.

'Got to get leg-shackled, Dayle,' Matthews said in a voice of deepest mourning. 'Don't want to. Family insists.' His head lolled a bit, but he got himself under control and fixed a reddened eye on Charles. 'M'father put his foot down. Cut my quarterly allowance. Refuses to cover my expenses. Not even my debts of honour, not until I fix my attention on some deb.' He shot a hateful look over at Henley. 'And my so-called friends have deserted me in my hour of need.'

'I'll tell you one final time—you keep away from my sister!' Henley shouted. 'When she marries it will be with far better than the likes of you.' He turned to Charles. 'Tell him, Charles—you wouldn't want a sot like him marrying your sister, would you?'

'Dayle ain't got a sister, toff head,' snorted Matthews. He stopped and Charles suffered an instant dislike for the light dawning in his unfocused eyes. 'But you do got that pretty little filly your mother has been squiring about town,' he said with sudden enthusiasm. 'She'll do. Will you do it, Dayle? Fix me up with an introduction to the girl? Slide in a good word for me?'

'No,' Charles spat.

Matthews gasped, then looked like he was going to cry into his brandy.

'See?' Henley crowed his triumph. 'Dayle don't want you pawing any of the females in his family, either.'

'She's not family,' Charles said, trying to keep his temper. He tried to look apologetic. 'Listen, Matthews, Miss Westby is not your conventional débutante. She's not the sort of girl your father would probably even wish for you be courting.'

'Don't try to turn me up sweet, now. It must be me you object to. Nothing wrong with the girl. She's got breeding, and money. Your own mother dotes on her, and so do the Lowders.'

'Seen the Duchess of Charmouth take her up in her carriage at the park, myself,' Henley put in. 'Heard her Grace asked for the girl's advice on her new ballroom. If the duchess embraces her, the rest of the *ton* will have no choice in the matter, even if the chit has spots and six fingers on each hand.'

That was the problem, Charles thought. Embrace her the *ton* already had, with a vengeance. Her name was on everyone's lips, as much as his own. Suddenly everyone had an amusing little tale to tell of Miss Westby. The events she attended were an instant success. The vivid colours of her gowns were touted as a natural expression of her artistic temperament and were aped by matrons, widows and any woman old enough to escape pastels. The Prince Regent himself demanded an introduction, examined her portfolio, and spent an hour discussing designs with her. Now her passion for décor was an asset, not an oddity, and the fickle *haut monde* clamoured for her advice.

It was galling. He behaved like a monk and was cursed for a fiend. She broke half of polite society's rules and they worshipped her for it.

Not that he could blame them. She'd hit their insular little world like a mortar shell, scattering insipid young misses like shrapnel, but she'd done worse to him. She'd bewitched him with her beauty, seduced him with her laughter. She'd made him forget.

He had forgotten his companions. They were both staring at him with knowing expressions on their faces.

'Perhaps you aren't the problem after all, Matthews,' Henley mused. 'Perhaps Dayle wants the chit for himself.'

'You got the Ashford girl all wrapped up,' complained Matthews. 'You don't need both of 'em.'

Charles had had enough. He stood. 'I must go. I wish you good hunting, Matthews.' He threw a handful of coins down on the table, enough to pay for the entire evening's tally of drink, and he strode out, calling for his vehicle.

He had wasted enough time, mooning like a schoolboy. He didn't have time for it. He had to concentrate. He must work out this mess that passed for his life—for the sakes of those who no longer had one.

He forced his thoughts back the encounter he had had with Mills this morning. A small, dark man. A file tracing his activities. It was devilish little to go on. Though he racked his brains, he could not think who might hate him so. The only people he'd ever truly wronged were dead. And now to find his enemy had been watching him so closely for years? It made no sense, but it sent a shiver of unease up his spine.

Perhaps Jack had made some progress. With luck, his brother would be in his rooms and they could have a private word before the party. He took the ribbons from his groom and set out.

He was passing Humphreys, the renowned print shop, where the usual crowd gathered to see the new prints in the windows, when the cry went up.

'It's him!'

'Hey, Dayle! Can I have an invitation to your next party?'

A chill descended over Charles and he pulled the horses up short. On the street, an older woman pulled a young lady away. 'Don't look at him, dear,' she said, with a sniff. 'Let us go.'

Tossing the reins to his groom, he approached the window, already certain what he was about to see.

It was worse than he imagined. Burning rage twisted in his gut, bubbled up and spewed out of him in a particularly inventive string of blasphemies. Stalking inside, he snatched one of the offending things off the glass. The catcalls and ribbing continued as he accosted the first apprentice he found. 'Where's your mistress?' he barked.

'U-upstairs,' the boy stammered.

'Lead on,' Charles said.

'Oho!' The involuntary chuckle escaped Jack when Charles handed the paper to his brother. 'Oh, my.'

'Is that all you can say?' growled Charles. They were in Jack's cluttered bachelor's quarters and Charles was trying to pace without toppling one of the many towers of books and papers.

'No, as a matter of fact. I have to say I'm insulted that you never invited me to any of your orgies.'

Despite himself, Charles laughed. 'Damned caricaturists. Yes, they're clever, but it doesn't sit so well when it's you they ridicule.'

'Yes, but Cruikshank, no less! No one is truly notorious today until Cruikshank mocks them!' Jack bent to examine the piece more closely. 'Well, old chap, sorry to say it, but he is very clever. Portraying you entertaining the *ton* in one room while the wild orgy is going on behind partially closed doors! And the detail is brilliant.'

'Brilliant and devastating.'

'Look—half the patronesses of Almack's are on one side, while on the other…' Jack looked up. 'Did you truly have an affair with *the* Annie Ewing?' he asked, his voice filled with awe.

'Of course not,' Charles snapped.

'Oh, well, I've always enjoyed her singing. It's clear from this how she came by her nickname.'

'You are missing the important part, Jack.'

'More important than Amply Endowed Annie's bared breast?' his brother asked, grinning.

'Take a look at what the half-clothed revellers are reading.'

'Hmm, yes, that lucky fellow is holding a paper, isn't he? *The Radical Review?* And look over here, on the floor next to these energetic ladies, a book, *The Real Rights of Man.* Bad form, my boy, to mix pleasure and politics.'

'But that's just it, it's the same thing as last time. An attack on my morals and my politics in one fell swoop.'

'So you think that the same person is behind both?'

'I feel that it must be. But who?'

'I feel sure that it is not Avery,' Jack said with a sudden serious turn. 'I've kept an eye on him, as you asked. He truly is miserable, Charles. I don't believe it is an act, and I don't believe it is only his honour that is damaged. I think he misses the old girl.'

'But why should he continue to stir up trouble for me? He certainly does it openly at Whitehall, if not clandestinely with these attacks.'

'You're an easy target, and a natural one for him. You're mixed up in the business that has humiliated him, and there is a true political divide between you. Frankly, I admire the old man for staying in town. Many a lesser man would have fled home in the face of such embarrassment, and never been heard from again.'

Charles stopped pacing and turned to face his brother. 'Perhaps that is the whole idea. Perhaps either one or both of us were supposed to withdraw, to tuck our heads and hide, but from what?' He sat in the chair across from Jack and scrubbed his hair to help him think. 'It must be me, since the latest round was aimed at me as well.'

'But perhaps the caricature is only the natural result of all the rest, and not a new attack.'

'Ah, but I haven't told you all of it.' Charles told his brother of what he had learned from the *Augur*'s editor. 'And, when I found that—' he gestured toward the cartoon '—I had a little talk with Hannah Humphreys.'

'She gave up Cruikshank?'

'Told me where I might find him, rather. He was not a bit apologetic, but he did tell me something interesting.'

Jack only raised a questioning brow.

'He said he would never have had the idea for that thing if he hadn't met someone new at his regular coffeehouse.'

'A small, dark, wiry man?'

'Who got into a political discussion with him one afternoon, and bought him dinner one night, so they could continue their interesting debate.'

'And you were served up along with the chops, I gather.'

'Not outright, but very subtly.' Charles stopped. Something was nagging at the back of his mind. 'There is something familiar about all of this, but I can't quite place it.'

'Familiar?' Jack laughed. 'Good Lord, if this sort of thing is familiar, then I don't envy you.' He rubbed his eyes and shook his head as if to clear it. 'It's still not a lot to go on. Even if we could find the right man, what would we do, charge him with scandalmongering?'

'I'd find out who he works for, by God, and I'd make his life as miserable as he has made mine.'

'It wouldn't fix the damage already done,' Jack said philosophically, 'and it might send you fleeing for the continent. No,' he mused, 'I know I scoffed at your idea at first, but I'm beginning to think you have had the right idea all along. Ignore the rumours. If you aren't visibly affected, maybe he'll grow tired and move on to play games with someone else.'

'It's too late for that,' said Charles.

'No, it isn't. Focus on your work, and your search for a wife. If everyone is discussing which lady you are courting now, they will not be talking about who you poked last year. Even if it was Amply Endowed Annie Ewing,' he finished with a grin.

'I'm not sure even that will save me now. The highest sticklers were already avoiding me. That—' he gestured to the caricature '—may well be a killing blow.'

Jack stood, an odd gleam in his eye. 'It has been a hard couple of years, Charles, for all of us. I would not wish to be saddled with some of the burdens you have carried. But you've done well.' He approached, and clasped Charles's shoulder. 'It's the perfect time for you to take a step back. Look around. Decide, once and for all, what it is that you want. What *you* want. And I'll do whatever I can to help you get it.'

Jack grinned, lightening the mood. 'But for now, you had better get home and get ready for Mother's dinner party. She'll shoot us both if we're late.'

'I forgot.' Charles dashed back his drink and rose to shake his brother's hand. He clasped it longer than necessary, trying to convey his gratitude and so much more. 'Thank you, Jack.'

It started to rain as he set his tired horses for home. Charles shrugged out of his greatcoat and gave it to his ever-patient groom. He hunched his shoulders as his brother's words echoed in his head. *Decide what it is that you want.*

Chapter Nine

Sophie entered Charles's house poised for battle. If nothing else, at least she would see him, and this interminable wait would be over. She was not good at waiting, and hadn't been since she was eight years old, and had decided that a year was long enough to wait for an uncle who was never coming. That fateful day she had shed her good-little-girl persona along with her pinafore, climbed the tallest oak in the forest, and found a tousled-haired, kindred soul at the top.

It was poetic justice, she thought as she smoothed her long gloves and twitched her gown into a more graceful fall, that Charles should reap some of the forceful nature he had helped to sow.

Sophie had brought Nell along, and, after a few whispered words of instruction, she sent her off on her covert mission. Before long she was entering the parlour on Lady Dayle's arm, confident that she looked well, and confident that, whatever the outcome, Charles would no longer be able to ignore her.

Her poise faltered a bit when the first person she saw was her uncle. She arched a brow at the viscountess, who only grinned and urged her forward to greet him. A hostess's duties soon called her away, and Sophie was left alone with her uncle once more. She had seen him only once since their first, distressing private interview, and that had been at Mrs Dawson's musical evening. She had been relieved that it had been a public scene with no chance for private conversation. He asked her now if she would join him on the corner settee.

'I've been hoping for a moment with you, niece.'

Sophie agreed. He looked tired, his once-handsome face pinched, as if he were in pain. Fleetingly, she wondered if her father would have resembled him as he grew older.

He didn't waste any time. 'I wondered if you had given thought to our last discussion?'

'I've thought much on it, Uncle.'

'And?'

Sophie breathed deep. Daringly she took his hand—it was cold and thin. 'There was a time, sir, when I would have given anything to have received such a show of interest from you. But I've had to make my own way, forge my own happiness, for too long now to submit myself to anyone else's ideas for my future.'

'Stubborn girl! You could choose—'

'No, sir,' she interrupted. 'I'm afraid we are both too wilful to get along together in the manner I think you are suggesting.'

He withdrew his hand from her grasp. 'I'd expected as much.' He gave her a look she thought might be regretful. 'But I'd hoped I was wrong.'

'I would like it if we could find our way toward some kind of relationship.'

He was silent a long time. So long she thought he might not answer at all. When he finally spoke, he avoided her eye. 'I wondered if perhaps you remember… Did your father ever speak to you, of me, when you were a child?'

'Yes, of course. He had your likeness in a miniature, which he often showed me. He told me tales of your childhood. He loved Cranbourne House.' It was the earl's principal estate, situated five and twenty miles from the small estate where Sophie had grown up. She had never seen it.

'And, your mother?'

Still, he looked away, where Sophie could not read his face. She understood what it was he was asking. 'She spoke fondly of you.' Now Sophie was the one looking down at her hands in her lap. 'It was one of the reasons I was so looking forward to living with you.'

A trill of nearby laughter distracted them both from their sombre thoughts. It was a party, after all, and life did go on, despite old hurts.

'Well, then…' Her uncle had recovered and was motioning someone toward them. 'You'll recall Mr Huxley, won't you?'

The gentleman reached them and made his bow. Sophie and her uncle stood to greet him. She did indeed remember him—her uncle had gone out of his way to present him at Mrs Dawson's. Sophie had wondered at it, as the two seemed as unlikely a pair as she had ever seen.

An odd, but likeable gentleman, Mr Huxley had talked at length of his map collection.

'A pleasure to meet you again, sir.'

'The pleasure is mine, Miss Westby. Will you take a stroll about the room with me?'

'Yes, you young people run along,' her uncle agreed. 'There's a discussion on the Corn Laws going on over there that needs my insightful input.'

The realisation struck Sophie suddenly that her uncle might be matchmaking. Nevertheless, she laid her hand on Mr Huxley's arm and allowed him to lead her off.

'Your uncle tells me, Miss Westby, that you have been travelling a great deal into Kent.'

'Why, yes, I am involved in a project that takes me there every few days of late.'

'Which roads do you travel? I'll wager a monkey that I know a route that will shorten your travel time by at least a quarter of an hour.'

Finally dry and presentable, Charles made his entrance after most of the guests had arrived and dinner was nearly ready to be announced. He went first to his mother, to apologise for his lateness, and found her chatting with Miss Ashford.

His mother simultaneously scolded and embraced him. Miss Ashford greeted him with her customary cool courtesy. He supposed he should be grateful that she acknowledged him at all, considering the escalating scandal surrounding his name. Indeed, he was grateful, he told himself sternly. He noticed that a few of the other young ladies his mother had invited for his benefit were not to be seen. Her very presence tonight was a testimony to Miss Ashford's loyalty and character. He resolved to devote himself to her this evening, and to firmly suppress the small part of him that wished to feel more than gratitude for his future bride.

Miss Ashford's father, however, requested a moment of his time, and Charles could not but agree. The baron drew him aside, and gestured to the long, crowded room full of glittering guests.

'A nice evening,' he said. 'Perfect mix of business and pleasure.'

'Thank you, sir. I hope you and your family will enjoy yourselves.'

'No doubt. Womenfolk are in alt planning that charity ball.'

Charles nodded his sympathy. Miss Ashford had indeed struck upon the idea of a charity ball, and showed more enthusiasm for it than anything he had yet seen in her. 'It is very good of your daughter to devote herself to such works.'

Lord Ashford gave an indulgent smile. 'She's a very good sort of girl, Dayle. Just what a lady ought to be.'

'I hope you are aware of my agreement on that score,' Charles said easily.

'Well, that's the subject I wished to discuss with you. I thought we had an understanding regarding your intentions, but now I find myself unsure.'

Startled into stupidity, Charles just gaped. 'Sir?'

'Rumours are one thing, Dayle. A man can't help what the tabbies will say about him, most especially if he possesses as chequered a past as your own.' He nodded his head in approval. 'You've had a rough spot recently, and I thought you were handling it well. Some kind of ruckus seemed inevitable, and I thought you might as well put your past to rest early in your career rather than later. Good for you too. Tempered steel is stronger, as they say.'

'I can honestly say, I never thought about it in that light.'

'But this broadsheet's another thing entirely. Takes it to another level, so to speak. Can't have my girl mixed up in such.'

'Surely you don't believe such rubbish, Lord Ashford?' said Charles, his temper starting to get the best of him.

'Don't matter what I believe, when it gets to this point. Matters what the rest of the world believes. I have a good bit of political weight. Meant to throw it behind you, if you and my girl found you suited. But I don't mean to hitch my girl to a runaway wagon, if you understand. Want what's best for her.'

'I comprehend your meaning, sir,' said Charles. And he did indeed understand the most salient point: his unseen opponent was gaining ground.

'Now, don't fret. You just keep your feet on the straight path and the situation will right itself.' He squeezed Charles's shoulder in a fatherly gesture. 'My girl rather fancies you, I believe. At least she likes you as well as she's ever liked anyone. If you need my help, you need only to ask.'

'You are most generous,' said Charles. It was a struggle to keep the bitterness from his voice.

The baron departed in search of his spouse, and Charles returned to Miss Ashford and his mother. Once there, however, he found it difficult to concentrate on the conversation. The events of this long and trying day were beginning to take their toll. He could swear the universe was conspiring against him. The harder he tried, it appeared, the heavier his burdens grew.

Suddenly the crowd in the parlour shifted. His gaze fell on Sophie, and the weight of his troubles was instantly forgotten. She was stunning. Her shining dark tresses were arranged in an elaborate coiffure that accented the length and slenderness of her neck. Her shimmering gown, dark blue over a white satin slip, had the same effect on her frame, without hiding her luscious curves. She was standing with Mrs Lowder and a blonde gentleman he had never seen before. A gentleman who had taken the opportunity of her turned head to run an appreciative gaze over her décolletage.

'Is that Mrs Lowder over there with Sophie?'

'Indeed it is,' his mother answered. 'Does she not look divine this evening? I believe motherhood agrees with her.'

'I had a mind to speak to her husband. If you will excuse me, I believe I'll go and ask if he is here.'

Oh, Lord, but he was seven kinds of an idiot. He'd just spent a fortnight avoiding Sophie, trying to forget how she'd felt in his arms. He'd thought long on what to say to her tonight, and promised himself that he'd make sure he never found himself in that situation again. He'd just determined to spend the evening securing another woman's favour, and been warned by her father to keep his nose clean. Yet one glance had him abandoning all those good intentions, stifling the warning ringing in his head. He cursed himself for a fool all the way across the long, crowded parlour, but he didn't stop.

'Good evening,' he said when he reached them.

'Charles! You have finally come!' Sophie said, reaching out to him. Was that relief he heard in her voice? And was she relieved to see him or to be distracted from her companion? 'Please, allow me to present Mr Huxley? Mr Huxley, this is our host, Viscount Dayle.' They greeted each other and Sophie continued, 'And of course you are already acquainted with Mrs Lowder.'

'Of course. May I present my compliments? You look lovely this evening.'

Mrs Lowder thanked him with an amused look and a brow raised in Sophie's direction. Sophie, predictably, was not impressed.

'There, Emily, now you have experienced first hand a bit of Lord Dayle's famous charm! Come now, Charles, enough flattery, what we really wish to see is your hand.'

'My hand?'

'Oh, yes, my lord!' Mrs Lowder was smiling quite genuinely now. 'You see, Miss Westby and I were walking in the park today.'

'Which park?' asked Mr Huxley.

'Hyde Park, of course,' said Sophie, 'and we walked there via Brook Street to Park Lane.'

'I've always found Mount Street to be superior,' Huxley answered. 'Less traffic, you see.'

'In any case, we were introduced to a most impertinent young lady there. She knew we were acquainted with you, Charles.'

'But what does any of it have to do with my hand?' asked Charles.

'She wished to know if it were true that you were part-Selkie, Lord Dayle!' interjected Mrs Lowder. 'Can you imagine?'

Despite himself, Charles laughed. 'Unfortunately, I can imagine.' He shot Sophie a look of mock-severity. 'I can also imagine you telling the poor child it was true.'

'Well, I did assure her we would check for webbed fingers when next we saw you, but considering the light such a thing would cast upon Lady Dayle, I felt compelled to deny the charge. In any case, I told her, you most assuredly have your father's nose.'

Charles just shook his head. He didn't know which was

more outrageous, the rumours or her method of dealing with them. 'I must thank you for defending my family's honour.' His mother, he could see, stood in whispered consultation with the butler, and was turning to leave the room. He turned to Mrs Lowder. 'I remember your skill on the pianoforte very well. I hope you will play for us all after dinner, but right now I must whisk Miss Westby away, as my mother has requested her assistance.'

'Of course, I would be honoured,' Emily answered with a smile.

'Mr Huxley, grand to have met you,' said Charles as he firmly grasped Sophie's elbow, ushering her away before she had a chance to protest. He led her out the door his mother had just exited, and stood a moment in the hall, debating. Likely, his mother had been called to the kitchens. The dining room, he knew, would be swarming with servants. As he hesitated, Sophie pulled her arm from his grasp.

'Where is your mother, Lord Dayle?'

'Soothing the cook, I imagine.'

'She doesn't need my assistance.'

'No, I do. We have to talk.'

Ah, the bookroom. He herded Sophie in and carefully left the door partially open. She looked around curiously, and then turned to him with a frown. 'How disappointing. Nary a radical nor a ladybird in sight.'

'Very amusing.' Charles grimaced.

'Well, I do have first-hand knowledge of what you get up to in empty rooms.'

'Stop it, Sophie, can we not talk seriously for a moment?'

She took a calming breath and threw back her shoulders.

He wished she wouldn't—it strained both her neckline and his control. 'You've ignored my existence for a full fortnight, but you are compelled to talk now, in the middle of your dinner party?'

'My mother's dinner party, but yes.'

She waited; he stared, trying to gather his thoughts. What was there to say? There were at least a thousand thoughts crowding his brain, he had to tread carefully and choose just the right one.

'You'd been kissed before,' he said.

Her jaw dropped. He groaned and pushed a hand through his hair. That had not been the right one.

Her décolletage was heaving now, in perfect time with his gut. 'I beg your pardon?' she gasped. 'That's what you dragged me in here to discuss? That's what you took away from our—encounter?'

Lord help him, but it was true. Though he hadn't articulated the thought to himself, it had been nagging at him, poking and prodding, making him squirm perhaps even more than his other troubles. 'You knew how to kiss. Someone had to teach you.'

True to form, Sophie laughed, but it was a desolate sound. Despairing. She turned and walked away.

Well, what did he expect? She would be well within her rights to leave the room and never speak to him again, but he couldn't stop himself, he had to know.

'Was it Sean Hill?'

'The blacksmith's boy?' Anger brought her back, and Sophie was angry indeed. Her dark eyes flashed, her cheeks flushed, and she advanced on him like Ney and d'Erlon into Wellington's centre line.

'You were gone, Charles. You left for school and never looked back. I didn't blame you. I knew how things were with your father.' She stopped before him, magnificent in her fury. 'But I was still there. I might be there still if not for Emily and your mother.'

She turned away again, and retreated to the far side of the room. 'Did you think because their mamas disapproved of me, the boys would steer clear of me? Foolish—don't you know that that made me even more interesting?' Her voice fell away to a whisper. 'I was alone, Charles.'

She rallied and shot him a look of defiance. 'Thank God for Emily. If we hadn't struck up a friendship, I might have done far worse than allow a boy to kiss me.' She gave an ironic snort. 'I might have run off to Gretna with the first man old enough to ask me, just for the conversation on the way. Had any of them paid me any serious attention, I think I might have done almost anything.'

Charles found himself barely able to respond. The picture she painted was devastating. 'I didn't know—I never thought…'

Undaunted by her own admission, she faced him squarely. 'You judge me if you wish, Charles Alden. But you remember that I never judged you. I cheered when the rest of the world reviled your exploits, and wished I could be kicking up rows right along with you. Nor did I judge you when you stayed away all those years, with never a word or a letter. You returned home for what—a mere two days—for Phillip's funeral? Less than that for your father's, but you never came to see me.'

Her anger seemed to have fled. It was disappointment he read in her eyes now. 'I didn't judge you, Charles. Even when you forgot me.'

Her skirt flared as she turned her back on him. This time she was the one to sweep out of the room without looking back.

Had he forgotten her? Charles sat through dinner ignoring his food, nodding as Miss Ashford talked—she had decided her ball must be a masquerade—and trying to answer that question.

He remembered the brash youth he had been, daring anything, risking everything, determined to force his father's displeasure, since nothing had ever earned his respect. He had indeed left for school, but he had always looked back—back to be sure his father was watching.

No, he hadn't forgotten Sophie. Unconsciously, he had held her memory close, sure as he raised every kind of hell he could imagine, that there was one person in the world who would forgive him. But he had held her static in his mind, never considering her growing older, becoming a young woman. She had always been his pig-tailed, adventurous partner in crime.

He hadn't forgotten her, but he had failed her.

That truth gnawed at him throughout the evening as he watched her. Another sin to shoulder responsibility for, another person who had suffered while he exercised his fertile imagination and frittered away his life. He wasn't sure his soul could bear another such burden.

Oddly enough, though, he found a measure of peace while he watched her. She had been hurt—perhaps only he knew how much—yet she had risen above it. Sophie had grown up, and Lord knew she had turned out to be unconventional, but she was also good natured, amusing, and intelligent. She was a beacon of light in the room, smiling and animated, and the people around her responded. She charmed her partners through dinner and was kept happily occupied in the drawing room afterwards. He noticed Mr Huxley was often at her side.

Watching her gave him hope. And that was only the top reason on a long list of them to stop.

Nevertheless, he was achingly aware of her as he circulated through the guests after dinner. There was excited talk of costumes for Miss Ashford's masquerade, and much animated gossip over the state of Prinny's health. The knot of young people about Sophie all seemed to be embroiled in a discussion on fashion, and of course, there was a good deal of political debate going on in pockets about the room.

At his request, his mother had invited a few members of the Board of Trade. Charles knew he should be courting them, but he was more worried about the young men courting Sophie. Was this the sort of attention she had craved? The thought had him contemplating mayhem, not party platforms.

But he knew his duty. Resolutely he turned his back and joined the men plotting the course of the nation.

He found his own situation to be nearly as dire as England's. Though the men here tonight supported him, there were others, they reported, who felt that his character was not steady. Charles sighed. Before all this he'd been at the top of the list to chair their new committee; now he'd be fortunate to be invited as a committee member.

Sir Harold commiserated with him, but advised him to be patient. 'Now is perhaps not your time, Dayle,' he said. 'Wait until this gossip dies down. There will be other committees, other paths to the ministry.' He sympathised with him on the simmering scandal broth as well. 'Still no idea who your enemy might be?'

'No.' Charles did not go into detail. 'Jack seems convinced that it is not Avery, however.'

'Hmm. His antipathy doesn't help your situation, for certain, but I tend to agree. Avery's style is to confront you directly, just as he has been doing. He's not the sort to sneak behind a man's back.'

Sir Harold was quiet a moment. 'I have the feeling that whoever is behind this is more powerful than we suspect. It won't be easy rooting him out.'

'I begin to wonder if the struggle is worth it,' Charles said. This setback disheartened him. He was tired, tired of fighting, tired of trying to prove himself to a world determined to see only the worst in him.

'Don't give up, Dayle. You've a great future ahead of you. Find the man behind all this and give him back a taste of his own misery. Once you've done that, take a little time for yourself. Concentrate on choosing one of these fine young ladies. Set up your nursery. Show the doubters that your judgment is sound, that you've finishing sowing oats and are ready to reap a more steady crop.' He gestured to the others, still energetically debating the latest Poor Relief Bill. 'We'll still be here for you.'

His mood low, Charles shook the man's hand and thanked him for his kindness. He stood alone a moment, wishing all his guests back to their own homes, himself to his favourite brooding chair, and his unseen enemy to the devil. He sighed. If wishes were horses, beggars would ride. The way Charles's luck was running, he'd likely be trampled instead. He would do better to seek out his brother.

He'd just spotted Jack in animated conversation with a crowd of young bucks when the sound of Sophie's name, spoken with derision, drew him up short. He glanced quickly around and saw a cluster of dandified gentlemen just off to his right.

'Impudent chit. I don't care if she is an earl's niece; she has spent her life buried in the country. What does she presume to know of fashion?'

Charles stared. Was that his cousin Theo rigged out in that hideous get-up of turquoise and buttercup yellow? Yes, he rather believed it was.

'Didn't like your waistcoat, old boy?' sniggered one of Theo's companions while gesturing to the elaborately embroidered disaster.

'Don't you dare laugh—this is the height of fashion, and cost me ten guineas! No, the chit betrayed her own ignorance when she said that not only should *I* not wear this colour combination, but no one in all England could pull it off.'

'Except for a jockey on the back of a deep chestnut bay!'

Peals of laughter rang out from the group, heightening Theo's colour, along with his temper, Charles surmised.

'Theo's right,' interjected a gentleman arrayed in silver and puce, 'the girl has no business giving fashion advice.'

'Well, you cannot deny her success, and certainly I've never seen her look anything less than smashingly gorgeous,' someone argued.

'True enough!' came a chorus of agreement.

'I wonder what her dowry is like?' someone wondered out loud. 'I think I shall ask her to partner me in whist.'

'You shan't get a jump on the rest of us,' someone cried and as a group they moved off to seek out the lady's attention, leaving only Theo and the other malcontent still grumbling.

Moving forward, Charles decided to nip that little bud before it could bloom into a larger flower of disgruntlement.

'Good evening, Theo. It has been a while, has it not?'

'Dayle,' returned Theo, still in a pout over the attack on his sartorial splendour.

'My mother must be pleased to have you tonight, I know she wants all the family to meet her particular friend, Miss Westby.' As a warning it was not much, but it was all that was required. Mumbling his agreement, Theo and his friend took themselves off.

Charles watched them go. He was annoyed with Theo, but, oddly enough, the bulk of his irritation lay on Sophie's shoulders. Just once he wished she would hold her tongue and not say the first thing that leapt to mind. Yes, Theo was ridiculous, but must she point it out in such a public forum?

Who was he to conjure criticisms? His life was unravelling faster by the minute. He left in search of a drink.

He found one, but his mother also found him.

'Charles, dear,' she fussed, drawing him aside. 'Do you think you could influence Sophie and persuade her to allow me to make an announcement about her book?'

He lifted a questioning brow. 'Her book?'

'Yes, her book.' His mother sounded exasperated, but when she saw his puzzlement she relented. 'Do you mean she hasn't even told you? Oh, she must indeed be serious about keeping it quiet.'

'Explain, please, Mother.'

'Well, I suppose it's too late now, and I'm sure she doesn't mean to keep it from you. And at least I can break the news to you, if to no one else.'

'Mother…'

'Oh, yes. Well, isn't it the most wonderful thing?' She leaned in and lowered her voice. 'Sophie has written her very own design guide! And a very reputable publisher has agreed to take it on. The proceeds, of course, will be donated, but I know you can appreciate what such validation means to her.'

Indeed he could. Charles was sure that the accomplishment left Sophie feeling deeply satisfied. Unfortunately it left him feeling frustrated and strangely upset. He shook his head. Why should Sophie's good news make him furious? He murmured something to his mother about finding a drink and wandered off, quite forgetting the one he held in his hand.

The party broke up soon after, but far too late for Charles's peace of mind. He caught Sophie alone as her party was preparing to leave. In the dark corner of the hall he caught up her hand and held it, searching for something, anything, he could say to express the myriad of emotions that swamped him. It was all too much. He'd schooled himself to feel nothing save ambition for so many long months, and now Sophie had him twisted in ten different knots in one evening.

He couldn't just stand here, dumb as a doorknob. He opened his mouth to speak, but she stopped him with a shake of her head. Her hand lingered in his, however, and they stood together, silent, connected in a way that went beyond touch. The moment stretched on, but Sophie never looked up. Instead she kept her gaze locked on their clasped hands, until Emily Lowder cleared her throat, then Sophie recalled herself and her hand and swept away.

* * *

Somehow Charles got through the next hour. He bid goodbye to all the guests, kissed his mother goodnight, bade the servants to go on to bed and leave the mess for the morning. He took himself to the book room and shut the door. He poured a brandy, but didn't drink it. He stared long at the fire, without seeing it. He sat down in his favourite chair and slowly descended the slippery slope into insanity.

It must be what this was, insanity—or as close as he'd ever come to it. His mind was whirling, events and voices from the past weeks were haunting him. *Sacrifice anything…decide what you want…you forgot me.*

They were all slipping away, all the reasons that had given him purpose, allowed him to go on. If Viscount Dayle faltered, would there be enough left of Charles Alden to survive?

All of his hard work had been for naught. The progress he'd made in redefining his character, his potential—wiped clean. His committee position—gone. Even his social standing stood in jeopardy. He was a joke again, Wicked Lord Dayle who had played the greatest prank of his career on his peers.

He stood and leaned into the mantelpiece. It had been so hard, and now he must start again. But damn it, he would. He would. Just as soon as he could focus his thoughts, just as soon as he could deal with Sophie.

His heart began to pound, his hand, still holding a drink, to shake. He regarded the trembling amber liquid in a vague, detached way for a moment, wishing it contained the solace he needed. His goals were ripped out of his reach, his life was falling apart, and all he could think about was Sophie.

He stood abruptly and flung the glass into the fireplace,

where it erupted into a flash of blue flame. He left the book room, grabbed a walking stick from the urn in the entry hall and strode past his startled footman into the night.

Damn her. Damn her for coming back into his life at the worst possible time and wreaking her own special brand of havoc. Damn her for being beautiful, and funny, and irresistible. Damn her for waking him up, making him laugh, making him *want.*

He walked far and long, but he could not escape his thoughts. The past had often haunted him, but now the future loomed troublesome as well. He didn't know which terrified him more—possibilities he feared might be closing to him, or the ones that he sensed might open.

Decide what you want. Perhaps Jack was right, perhaps it was time he faced the truth. It was simple and frightening at once. He wanted Sophie, passionate, beautiful, impossible Sophie.

She was intoxicating in a way that spoke directly to his soul. She comforted his battered spirit, captivated his wary mind, and tempted him with her exotic beauty.

For a dangerous moment he allowed himself to imagine what life might have been like if Phillip had never come to him on that fateful day. He might have reunited with Sophie a free man, unencumbered by grief and guilt. They could have met by chance in Dorsetshire or here in London— No, down that path lay madness. The nightmares were real. He would never be free.

Not even for her could he abandon the vows he'd made. There it was, plain and simple, the festering truth that had tormented him. He'd wanted her since she'd nearly knocked him down in the street. He'd known, almost since then, that to choose her would be to forsake everything he owed to his dead brother and father.

He'd told himself many times that Charles Alden had died right along with his brother. Viscount Dayle had sprung from the ashes of his former life, a shell of a man whose only purpose was payment of dark and deep debts.

Sophie had changed all that when she fell back into his life. Suddenly Charles Alden was alive again, resurrected by the laughter in her eyes, and torn between heart and mind, want and need.

He'd become a living cliché. A stone bench sat up ahead—he sank on to it and buried his head in his hands. It was an age-old dilemma. He supposed he was no worse off than a thousand poor devils before him. But who would have thought it would hurt so much?

A book. Charles could hardly believe she'd done it. He had given her her first design guide himself, to help her fill the imaginary rooms she created. His mother was right; he did know how much this meant to her, not just the book, but everything.

He felt a twinge of guilt. After a lifetime of censure, Sophie was finally enjoying what she longed for: welcome, acceptance. He should be happy for her, not begrudge her this first real triumph. But begrudge it he did, because her unconventional, meteoric success pushed her beyond his reach.

He was afraid for her too. Fickle society loved to force people on to pedestals, if only to watch them fall. Look at what had happened to Byron. Look at what had happened to *him*.

A cool breeze swept by, ruffling his hair and just possibly, bringing the idea with it. *Look at what had happened to him.* He lifted his head. It seemed so simple. Was it possible? Could both Charles Alden and Viscount Dayle have what they wished?

He looked about and found himself near the gates of the

garden in Hanover Square. How long, he wondered, had he been here, across from the house where Sophie slept? A light came on in one of the upper windows, and Charles laughed softly. Perhaps Fate had finally taken pity on him and come to intervene on his behalf. There could be no other explanation. It must be Sophie up there, stirring long before anyone else would dream of doing so.

One way to find out. He searched out a few small stones, and, stifling a strong sense of *déjà vu,* launched them at the window.

Sophie had spent a restless night, but to no avail. Finally, just before first light, she gave it up as a bad business. She hadn't slept a wink, and still her thoughts were in a worse tangle than her sheets.

She had spent half the night fuming over Charles's perfidy. 'You'd been kissed' indeed! How dare he? When he'd spent years wenching his way through the female half of the population? He was no better than a child; he didn't want her, but he didn't want her playing with anyone else either.

Never would Sophie have imagined Charles indulging in such hypocrisy. She shook her head. But then, neither had she predicted the change in his temperament. And now his vacillation between hot and cold had taken on new and frightening dimensions.

She'd been so naïve! She had longed for the connection she'd felt with him so long ago, and had allowed her fantasies to run away with her. The understanding and intimacy that they had enjoyed had been so strong, so vital to her, that she'd assumed they would survive the years apart.

She sighed. There had been too many changes. He'd been

correct, she didn't know the new Charles, but she was beginning to suspect that he didn't know himself either.

The thought led her back to Nell's attempt with the family's
servants last night. Though Nell had enjoyed the idea of
intrigue, she hadn't been very successful. The only thing of
interest she'd heard was that old Lord Dayle had been furious
when Phillip had accepted Lord Castlereagh's mission, and
travelled with important papers to Wellington in Brussels.
Sophie still wasn't sure just how he'd ended up at the battle at
Waterloo, but she supposed it made no difference. Phillip had
died, just as many thousands of other good and gallant men had.

Could she be making too much of the situation? Perhaps
there was no mystery, only her own desires and the wish to
fuel her own fantasies. There could be a simple explanation
that she didn't wish to see. People changed. Or perhaps
Charles's wish to mould himself into his brother's likeness had
simply been the desire to impress his hard-to-please father?

Something kept her from embracing such an idea. She
hoped it wasn't her own self-indulgence, but she couldn't
shake the feeling that Charles was hiding something. There
was a desperation about him that she could not explain. He
seemed *driven* to succeed in politics, to impress the men in
government with his solidity and responsibility. It must go
deeper. Also, she thought, why wouldn't he have eased off
after his father's death? And why the strange talk about old
Lord Dayle's death? No, there was something more here she
couldn't yet see.

Sophie shook her head and rang for Nell. She might suf-
focate if she stayed in this room any longer. She needed to get
out, to breathe fresh air, to walk and clear her mind.

A small clattering sound, quite nearby, had her suddenly jumping back into her bed. Heart pounding, feet tucked safe away under her night rail, she inspected the floor. The noise came again, there by the window, but she could see no sign of a rodent invader. Once more, louder this time, and Sophie recognised the sound for what it was. Laughing despite herself, she climbed down, threw back the curtains and looked below.

Charles. He stood there on the pavement, wearing a grin and last night's clothes.

'Are you insane?' she called in a loud whisper. 'What are you doing?'

'Come down!'

'Now? Can't you pay a morning call like all the other gentlemen?'

'Where would be the excitement in that?' He gestured to the burgeoning light in the east. 'It's morning. Come! We have to talk.'

Behind her a drowsy Nell scratched on the door and let herself in. She came wide-awake, however, when she took in the situation. 'Miss!' she gasped.

'I'll be down presently,' Sophie called to Charles. She turned to the maid. 'I know, Nell. Pray, don't look at me like that! Just fetch my wrapper, quickly.'

Oh, Lord, but she was a fool. She couldn't help it. This smacked of older, better times, and was nigh irresistible. She hurried into a heavy robe, allowed Nell to put her hair up loosely, and crept quickly down the stairs.

The night footman dozed in his chair. Nell put her mouth to Sophie's ear. 'It is Richard. He sleeps like a stone.'

Sophie held a silencing finger to her lips and slowly turned the lock on the front doors. With a sigh of relief she stepped out into the cool, early morning air. The street was deserted except for Charles, beckoning her from the gate to the square. Leaving Nell to quietly close the door again, Sophie ran lightly across the street.

'You imbecile! I thought it was your wish to stay out of the papers!' she scolded.

'I had to chance it. In any case, I knew it must be you waking. Anyone else would have been too cruel.'

Sophie drew back. 'Are you drunk, Charles?'

He grasped her hands tight in his. 'No, I'm just… Oh, I don't know. I feel as if I am waking from a long and terrible dream.'

She looked him over carefully and tried to calm the pounding of her heart. Her mind was racing almost as fast. What could it mean? She didn't know whether to dread what he had to say, or to long for it. The only thing she knew was that a rumpled and unshaven Charles was devilishly more handsome than the usually immaculate Charles. The image of her tangled sheets came to mind before Sophie could curb her wayward imagination. Blushing, she reined it in. 'Where is your coat, your hat? Heavens, but you are a mess!' She laughed. 'I've spent too much time with your mother. Never mind! What is it that you must say, that couldn't wait until a decent hour?'

'I had to apologise. The things you said tonight—they are burnt into my mind like a brand. I'm so sorry. I can't bear the thought that I added even a jot to your unhappiness.'

'No.' She bowed her head. 'I do beg your pardon for attacking you so unjustly. You owe me nothing, I shouldn't have implied that you do. You were, in fact, the one who

taught me to be responsible for my own happiness. I'm sorry
I failed to heed your perfectly correct advice.'

'You haven't failed.' He lifted her chin. 'Look at what
you've done, Sophie. I saw you talking—cordially—with
your uncle tonight. We thought such a thing would never
come to pass! You've learned so much, and used your talents
to make people happy. You should be proud of all that you've
accomplished. I am. And I do owe you, for being such a good
friend to my mother. But none of that is why I wished so desperately to speak with you.'

Sophie's eyes closed and she allowed a sigh of pleasure to
escape her. She knew it was wrong, even dangerous, to allow
his praise to warm her. But there was no fighting it. His understanding meant so much because only he knew how hard it
had been for her to get to this place in her life, how much it
had cost her. When she opened her eyes again, she knew her
pleasure shone transparently, and probably more as well.
'Why then?' she asked.

'Miss!' Nell hissed from her position across the street.
'The baker's girl is coming up the street. We must go back in!'

Charles reached out and clutched both of her hands in his.
'Not yet,' he pleaded. He glanced about wildly. 'The servants'
stairwell,' he exclaimed. 'Come, we can talk there.'

He pulled her across, to the stairwell at the front of the
house. Sophie looked doubtfully down at the landing at the
bottom, but she could not resist the imploring look on
Charles's face.

'Please, Nell?' she asked. 'Just keep watch for us a bit longer.'

The maid did not look happy, but she nodded. Sophie
turned and followed Charles down the stairs.

The temperature dropped several degrees as they descended. She shivered and pulled her wrapper more tightly about her. The light was murky down here; Sophie could only dimly see Charles's expression. He was gazing at her in a way that made her heart begin to trip.

'You are so incredibly beautiful,' he whispered.

'You brought me down here for a reason,' she reminded him tartly in a vain attempt to cover her reaction to him. She hoped it was too dark for him to see her flushed cheeks. 'You were going to tell me why you were so desperate to speak to me.'

'Because I couldn't let you go on thinking I had forgotten you,' he said, his voice rough with emotion.

'I don't, truly—'

He moved so quickly she did not see it; she only felt his closeness, and his warmth. He stopped her words with his hand on her lips, and desire burst past all her restraints. Swelled with new hope and old dreams, it coiled through her, igniting every dark recess of her body.

'You couldn't have known,' he whispered. 'I don't think I even knew, but you've always been with me. No matter what infamous prank I pulled, no matter how deep the grief, no matter how hard the task I faced, you were there. Tucked away in a safe corner of my heart, you were there, smiling at me, comforting me, forgiving me.'

His hand dragged slowly away, only to be replaced by his mouth, soft and sweet. From the moment his lips touched hers, she was lost. She'd known it the first time he'd kissed her, but she'd ignored it, hidden from the knowledge that might destroy her. This was home, where she belonged, in his arms. The lonely orphan inside her knew it and rejoiced, but there was still a coldly sane and logical bit of her that rang out a warning. *Be careful.*

She ignored it, let the heat of the moment wash over her, and allowed the kiss to deepen. His mouth was hot and demanding and she surrendered to it. Charles groaned and his own restraint fell before the onslaught of desire. She could feel his desperation as he pulled her tight against him, the rasp of his beard rough against her jaw, and down the length of her neck.

She held him tight, drew him closer, wordlessly asking for more. He gave it, burying his face in the smooth juncture of her shoulder and bringing his hand up to mould the weight of her breast.

Oh, yes, she thought. Or perhaps she said it out loud. She could not be sure; all she knew was that suddenly her back was pressed against the wall. She was trapped between the cold, hard brick and the throbbing heat of Charles's body, and she never wanted to be anywhere else. Ever.

Somehow her wrapper had come open and his clever fingers were making quick work of the tiny buttons of her night rail. His mouth, hot and wet, traced a fiery trail across the skin of her shoulder. The heat of it chased away the chill of the morning, rendered inconsequential the impropriety of what they were doing and where they were doing it.

His hand faltered a little, hung for a long moment over her breast. Her nipple was taut, thrusting against the thin linen of her gown, aching for his caress. She held her breath, waiting.

At last he gave her what she wanted. Suddenly impatient, he pushed the gown away, baring her body to the dim morning light. His fingers touched her, ever so softly circling, and then, finally, brushing over the hard, yearning peak.

Her breath slid out of her in a soft, satisfied sigh. It turned rapidly to a moan when he bent over and took her in his mouth.

His tongue worked magic. He licked and sucked and nipped and sent rivers of pleasure, of pure unadulterated *want* down to the spot where she pulsed with need for him, and down into the depths of her soul. Her passion only grew when his fingers found their way to her other breast. She moaned and clutched him to her, letting her head fall back against the wall.

Yet still that small voice inside of her tried to be heard, tried to clamour a warning. She ignored it, had no desire to listen. At long last Charles was in her arms and giving her her first true glimpse of passion. It was a victory of sorts. He had not wanted to want her; she knew it. But there was no mistaking the heat and tension and longing in him now.

She forgot to feel triumphant a moment later. She forgot everything as he raised the hem of her night rail. His bold touch on the naked flesh of her thighs sent a tingling sensation up to her very core.

He touched her, then, where no one else ever had before. He tangled his fingers in her curls and trailed them over her feminine folds. He made her ache, he made her gasp when his finger slipped inside of her.

The shock of it was sweet, but the sound of a loudly and repeated clearing throat was not.

'Nell,' Sophie gasped. 'Charles, we have to stop.'

He slid his hand away, and grasped both of her shoulders, breathing heavily and resting his forehead on hers.

'Miss!' Nell's voice was strident. 'We must go back in now! The sun is high and the maids are out to clear the steps.'

'We can be together, Sophie. I know we can manage it.'

Charles's voice was as urgent as Nell's. He drew back a little and stared into her eyes, his face serious. 'Where do you go tonight? We must meet, I have to tell you.'

Sophie slumped a little. 'We cannot. I leave today with your mother, to Sevenoaks. There are things there that require our attention. We don't return until Saturday, for Miss Ashford's ball.'

His hands slid down her arms, finally grasping both of hers once again. 'Saturday, then. I have an idea. A plan, perhaps.' He smiled. 'I know it's a stretch, but just keep out of trouble until then. I'll find you at the ball.' He raised her hand and kissed it.

'Miss!' hissed Nell.

'Saturday!' Sophie smiled, and watched as Charles backed away, then turned and vaulted up the stairs, disappearing into the bright morning light.

Chapter Ten

The grinding of the carriage wheels, the creak of the harness, the *clop, clop* of the horses' hooves—the regular everyday racket of a slowing carriage was as nothing compared to the sound of her own pounding heart. Sophie bounced in her seat, impatient with waiting for the footman, and leaned forward to open the door herself. She found her hand stayed by Emily Lowder's.

As part of the evening's entertainment, Sophie and Emily had come early to the Argyll Rooms, the site of Miss Ashford's charity ball. 'I'm having second thoughts,' Emily said.

'About what?' Sophie asked. Finally the door opened and, without waiting for an answer, she eagerly alighted. The rooms were ablaze, but the spectacle couldn't compete with the glow of excitement in Sophie's breast. This was it. Tonight Charles would declare himself. She knew it.

Emily slowed once more as they crossed the threshold into the empty foyer. 'Perhaps we should reconsider this scheme. I'm afraid there might be some backlash. For you, Sophie.'

Sophie was flabbergasted. 'Emily Lowder, you've helped

with every step of Miss Ashford's plans! What is it that is bothering you?'

'It's…well, it's your costume.'

She raised a brow in question. 'What objection could you possess? Nearly every square inch of me is covered. Far less of me shows in this than in the average ball gown.'

'I know!' Emily cried. 'That's why I thought it nothing more than a lark—but the overall effect—I couldn't have imagined.'

'Rubbish,' she said, tugging at the cords of her cloak. 'Come, let's find Miss Ashford. She herself condoned the idea, and you don't think she would countenance anything remotely scandalous tonight?'

'I don't think you should put your faith in Miss Ashford's judgement in this case.'

'Emily, I swear I don't know what has got into you. You could look the world over and not find anyone more closely acquainted with propriety than Miss Ashford.'

'Yes, but I see something in her eyes, occasionally, when she's watching you.'

'Shh. Here she is.' Sophie gestured as Miss Ashford, dressed in the flowing robes of the goddess Diana, entered the entrance hall with a gaggle of servants on her heels.

'Mrs Lowder, Sophie, dear!' she exclaimed upon sighting them. 'You are here at last. Do take their cloaks,' she said to one of the footmen. 'I'm so glad, I have been waiting to show you…' She faltered as Sophie's cloak came off.

'Not you, too,' Sophie groaned. She thought she looked rather well, especially for the role Miss Ashford had asked her to play. She wore *churidar,* or baggy silk trousers of deepest blue, an upper garment whose close-fitting bodice was of the same hue, with long, tight sleeves of white. Over this she had a tunic of pale blue, richly embroidered with silver and white, and reaching to her knees. Her hair hung loose in dark waves, adorned only by a plain corded band, with a single jewel—a sparkling tear-shaped sapphire—centered on her forehead. On her feet were velvet slippers of the same dark blue. A necklace of gold coins and bangles at her wrist and ankle completed the ensemble.

'Is this not what you described?' she asked. 'Don't I look like I could be Scheherazade's sister?'

'Indeed, it is what we discussed,' said Miss Ashford, 'and you do look very…erm…authentic.'

'You look like you walked straight out of a harem!' Emily said. 'Even when we assembled the pieces I could not object, and on me or Miss Ashford there would probably be no concern. I don't know how to say it, but somehow, on you, this outfit is very—' she lowered her voice to a whisper '—sensual.'

Sophie laughed. 'All well and good then, I should draw my share of donations.'

Instead of soliciting donations in a large bowl at the entrance of the ballroom as the guests entered, Miss Ashford had hit upon the charming scheme of offering entertainments in exchange for her guests' generosity. All of the young ladies on her committee were cooperating and she had struck upon the idea of Scheherazade's sister as a way of utilising Sophie's artistic talents.

Sophie's remark seemed to recall Miss Ashford to her senses. 'Yes, we must keep our goal in mind, after all. But come, you must see what we have prepared for you.'

They entered the ballroom and Sophie was transfixed. 'Oh,

how delightful.' The galleries were draped with rich fabrics and musicians tuned their instruments on a dais in the back. Hundreds of candles and a forest of fresh blooms had transformed the room into a sparkling fantasy.

'It has turned out well, hasn't it?' Miss Ashford asked with a satisfied smile.

'The vignettes are darling,' Emily said.

Miss Ashford had set up separate areas around the room for each of her planned entertainments. The ladies who had agreed to perform were all present; they quickly gathered to exclaim over the new arrivals' costumes and to show off their own.

One young lady in an ephemeral white gown had a small stage with a grand floor harp. Another had a banner-draped corner with a small table and was dressed as a fetching gypsy girl. A painted backdrop set the stage for a charming girl in scarlet who meant to sing.

But none held a candle to Sophie's vignette. A shimmering ivory tent took up one corner of the ballroom. The flowing fabric was pulled wide, exposing an opulent scene straight out of *Arabian Nights*. Swathes of silk were everywhere, large pillows and rose petals covered the floor, and in the middle of this decadent Eastern scene sat a large easel and a pair of chairs.

'Miss Ashford,' Sophie said, trying to take it all in, 'you have been hiding a decided flair for the dramatic.'

'Indeed,' agreed Emily as they approached the tent. 'It is nothing less than awe inspiring. Sophie will fit right in. I am still worried, however, about the stir it might cause.' Her voice grew firm. 'I will not have her thought of as *fast.*'

'Nor would I,' agreed Miss Ashford. 'We must take care to see that all the proprieties are met. Would it suffice if we agreed that she shall have one of us as a chaperon at all times?'

'Well. Yes,' Emily said slowly. 'That should do. I shall take the first shift.' She turned to Sophie. 'You must promise to be on your best behaviour tonight, my dear. The costume alone is risky; we dare not give the gabble-grinders any further ammunition.'

'I do promise,' she agreed, stroking the rich fabric of the tent.

'Good, then I shall return when I find a chair to position at the entrance, for I will not recline on those pillows, even for a charitable cause.'

Sophie waved her off and turned around inside the tent. 'How wonderful! I feel positively transported.' She beckoned Miss Ashford in. 'Come along, as this was all your idea, you must be first to sample Dunyazade's talents.' Lowering her voice and attempting an Eastern accent she cajoled, 'Come, my dear, sit, make yourself comfortable. I shall draw you a picture of your fondest dreams.'

'No, no,' Miss Ashford protested. 'I still have much to do.'

'Nonsense. You have worked long.' She gestured to the glittering ballroom. 'All is set for a magical evening.' Sophie pulled her to the comfortable chair across from the easel. 'Sit back. Take a minute for yourself.' She took up Miss Ashford's hands and began to rub them, waiting for the tension to ease from her arms and shoulders.

'This is silly,' Miss Ashford protested weakly.

'Indeed, it is not. Close your eyes,' she directed softly.

Sophie took her seat. Paper was already tacked up, a box of coloured chalks sat at the ready. 'Now, bring your mind to your favourite place. Where would you most like to be? It needn't be a spot in the true world—perhaps it is where you have always dreamed yourself to be.'

She saw the moment when Miss Ashford gave in. She began to sketch quickly while her subject sat silent, still a moment. When she could see that Miss Ashford was absorbed in her own private world, she said quietly, 'Tell me what you see.'

'A garden. Full of blooms. The sky is very blue. It is lovely.' She sighed.

'Are you alone?' Sophie pitched her voice lower still as her fingers moved swiftly on the page.

'No. There are many people here. They are watching me.'

'Look down,' Sophie directed. 'What is in your hand?'

'More flowers. Lilies. I can almost smell them.'

'How do you feel in your beautiful garden?'

Miss Ashford was quiet a long moment. 'I feel…at peace. Appreciated.'

Sophie heaved a sigh. If this could work so well on practical, prudent Miss Ashford, then she could put away her last worry for the evening. She sketched in a few last details. 'You may open your eyes now, Miss Ashford, though I would not blame you should you wish to stay in your garden.'

Her eyes popped open and she blinked to focus. 'Oh. Yes. Well, I should run and check the kitchens.'

'Wait a moment,' Sophie called. She pulled the thick vellum from the easel and handed it over. 'Don't forget, a memento of your visit to Dunyazade.'

'Oh, my,' Miss Ashford whispered in awe. 'It is just as I imagined.'

'How lovely,' Emily said as she entered. She directed a servant to place the chair and peered over Miss Ashford's shoulder.

Sophie had drawn Miss Ashford in her garden, surrounded by a bower of fresh greens and pretty blooms. She wore a flowing white dress with tiny, capped sleeves, a wreath of flowers in her hair, and carried a group of vibrant lilies.

'I hope you have many happy moments there,' Sophie said, watching Miss Ashford's reaction. She looked on the verge of tears.

'Thank you,' she whispered again.

'Now then,' Sophie said, turning to Emily and giving Miss Ashford a chance to gather her wits, 'you must be my assistant as well as my duenna. Where are those ribbons we spoke of when we were planning this scheme? Ah, there in the basket. Let's tie up Miss Ashford's picture so that she may put it away until after her evening is done.'

'Yes, thank you,' said Miss Ashford, recovered now. 'I must be off. I see they still do not have the bookcase in place for Miss Harraday's poetry reading.' She strode away, the golden ribbons in her hair catching the light as she left the darker environs of the tent.

'Perhaps this will turn out well, after all,' Emily said.

'I do believe it will, at that,' Sophie agreed.

In fact, it turned out to be a very near thing. Before long the rooms began to fill. Milkmaids mixed with kings, pirates led medieval princesses onto the dance floor. Miss Ashford's young ladies began their performances and the silver bowls at each vignette began to fill.

Except at Sophie's tent. Lady Dayle sat for Dunyazade.

The Duchess of Charmouth told Sophie to draw her in her new ballroom. No one else ventured close. People gawked, whispered, and walked repeatedly past, but no one entered.

'What is it, Lady Dayle?' Emily asked from her post at the entrance to the tent. 'Why aren't they coming in?'

'There's talk of Sophie's trousers, but even the highest sticklers cannot refute that she's more than decently covered,' the viscountess answered, her voice troubled. 'But there is another problem. Someone is spreading rumours, accusing Sophie of being difficult and temperamental, of trying to outshine the other young ladies.'

'I feared something would happen,' moaned Emily. 'What are we to do?'

In the end, they did not have to do anything. Charles's cousin, Theo Alden, of all people, saved the day.

He didn't mean to. He entered the lavish tent with malice, intending to take advantage of the wave of malicious gossip and take the impudent Westby chit down a notch or two. He settled in the chair with bad grace and pictured Sophie's downfall instead of his own piece of heaven.

Sophie gave it to him anyway. His jaw dropped and his heart swelled when she handed him his picture, effectively expelling all of his ugly intentions.

She'd drawn him strutting in the park, dressed to perfection in an elegant, only slightly showy ensemble, while jealous dandies and worshipful females looked on.

'The green of the coat exactly matches my eyes,' he exclaimed. 'The pleat in these pantaloons showcases the length of my limbs.'

He tore his gaze from the drawing. 'I have wronged you,

Miss Westby. You have the eye, the soul, of an artist. I will take this to my tailor tomorrow and have it exactly replicated.'

Sophie smiled. 'I'm glad you approve.'

'What shade of gold would you call this waistcoat?'

There were no more problems after that. Theo's set crowded in and soon there was a line waiting to sit in Dunyazade's chair. Sophie drew until she thought her fingers would fall off. The bowl outside her tent filled and had to be replaced. She hadn't had a rest or a dance all evening, but she barely noticed. Always she kept one eye on her latest subject and the other trained for any sign of Charles.

Charles swore as his valet struggled with the high boots of his costume. He was going to be late again.

Truly, though, it couldn't have been helped. He'd been closeted with the committee on farmland distress all day, and they had made significant progress. 'Sorry, must go and gather my costume for tonight's masquerade' wasn't an excuse that balanced against the fate of desperate English farmers.

His valet, Crocker, had done wonders without him, however. Now Charles stood and allowed him to drape the billowing black cape over his shoulders. There, he was the image of an eighteenth-century highwayman, lace collar, cuffs, and all. He had balked at donning the old-fashioned shirt, but Crocker had insisted. 'No,' his man had said in his usual raspy voice and blunt manner, 'my lord must be the romantic, noble thief of the last century, not the ill-bred, dirty, illiterate road agent one encounters these days.'

Charles had looked askance at the man and wondered briefly just what it was he did with his off days. He decided it was wiser not to know. He threw back his cape, strapped the light rapier to his side and bade Crocker not to wait up.

It was a sorry highwayman who rode through town in a carriage. Outside his groom waited with two restive mounts. They set off, and Charles chuckled, wondering whom he might startle in the streets of Mayfair tonight. It was a fitting disguise, for tonight he meant to defy both fate and his enemy and steal back his future.

His future with Sophie. Just the thought fired his soul, filled him with a longing so intense it was almost frightening. His plan would work. It must. Sophie could do it—she could become the steady, respectable lady he needed. All this time he had fretted and worried that she might be a threat to his plans. It was the height of irony that she was now in the position where she might be the one to save them.

He needn't have worried about frightening anyone in the streets, for everyone in London was obviously at the charity ball. Impatience winning out over manners, Charles made his way through the multitude of revellers just waiting to get in. He stood in the entryway and marvelled at the crowd. Good heavens, but the modistes must have been burning the midnight oil for weeks. He saw mermaids, chevaliers, and Roman senators. If he was not mistaken, that was a member of the Royal Family dressed as old Boney himself. But nowhere did he see the smile he was looking for.

He did catch site of Miss Ashford as he entered the ballroom, dressed as one of the goddesses. Diana, judging by the purely decorative bow she had slung over one shoulder. She must be in alt at the success of her ball, and as heartily as Charles commended her, he most definitely did not wish to see her now. He ducked to one side of a bookcase as her gaze wandered his way.

Hold a moment. A bookcase? In the ballroom of the Argyll Rooms? He peeked out and noted a pretty young lady taking a stand on a carpet just in front of his hiding spot. A group was gathering politely before her. The young lady breathed deep.

> When Man, expell'd from Eden's bowers,
> A moment linger'd near the gate,
> Each scene recall'd the vanish'd hours,
> And bade him curse his future fate.

Not Byron, Charles moaned.

'I say,' a nearby satyr said to his companion, a robed wizard, 'had you heard the story of when Dayle dressed as Byron and visited the Mayfair Ladies Byron Appreciation Society to sign copies of the latest edition of his poetry?'

Charles dropped his head in his hands. At least this was a short selection. Soon the masked audience was applauding and depositing coins and tokens in the silver bowl on a nearby stand. Then, vaguely, Charles remembered Miss Ashford prattling about the performances at her ball.

A sudden, uneasy prickle tripped its way down his spine. He'd better find Sophie, fast.

His anxiety increased as he paced the length of the ballroom and noted each of the performers as he passed. Singer. Harpist. He shook his head. Sword dancer?

When he caught site of the tent, he knew. He knew, and his blood began to boil.

It nearly erupted out the top of his head when he grew close enough to see inside. Long, curling hair pulled back from her face, hanging loose to her waist. Smouldering, painted eyes. Long slim legs in *trousers,* though they were baggy, and a tight-fitting bodice exposed under the covering tunic as her arm lifted to the easel.

She was sex personified, igniting fantasies of long desert nights and secret Eastern skills. His heart contracted, his body tightened at the sight of her and he wanted to scream his rage—because he knew every other man here was having the same reaction.

Desperately trying to clamp a hold on his anger, he stalked to the tent.

Sophie was tiring a little of her role and wishing she could get up to see some of the ball. She brightened, however, when her uncle stepped into the tent, bringing someone with him.

'Uncle! How good of you to come. I'm sure Miss Ashford will be grateful.' She smiled. 'Shall Dunyazade draw your portrait? At least you have no mask to remove. Just have a seat and throw back the hood of your domino.'

'Your uncle is always ready to support a worthy cause, my dear. But see, here is the reason I've come tonight.' He motioned to the man accompanying him to step forward. 'I've brought you a surprise.'

Sophie smiled and studied the man as he drew closer. Tall and slender, he was dressed soberly, with a broad-brimmed black hat over dark curls. He seemed familiar, but she did not recall that they had met. 'Sir? Are you a Quaker, come to remind me of my old home?'

'Dressed as a Quaker, for expediency's sake, and definitely here to remind you of home,' he returned with a spark-ling smile showcasing white teeth against dark skin. 'I do not expect you to recognise me, Miss Westby, but I would know you anywhere. You are the very image of your mother.'

'My mother?' Sophie stilled and cast a questioning glance to her uncle.

'It's been a long time,' her uncle said, 'but I'm sure you'll remember your cousin, Mr Cardea.'

A sudden vision flashed in her mind. A curly-haired boy, eyes alight with mischief, tugging her braids, chasing her through her home while she shrieked in glee. 'Mateo?' she whispered.

'Indeed, it is I!' He swept her up in an impulsive embrace and twirled her around. Emily gasped from the entrance where she had once again taken up her post, and Mateo threw her a wink before he set Sophie down.

'But what brings you to London?' Sophie asked, smiling.

'Lord Cranbourne and I have business dealings. I was already contemplating coming to London, but when one of his letters mentioned you, my fate was sealed. I hopped aboard the first one of our ships leaving port, and here I am.'

'Here you are,' echoed Sophie. His blithe statement raised several questions in her mind. What sort of business dealings? And surely the timing was off, was it not? But before she could find a polite way to ask, some small, inarticulate sound made her turn to the wide opening of the tent. It was filled with a large figure in tight black clothes, long dark boots and a small black mask. Her heart began to pound.

'Charles!'

'Sophie,' he said abruptly. He advanced into the tent,

changing the atmosphere with the dark menace of his assumed identity. Sophie swallowed and hoped it was only the costume. 'Lord Cranbourne. And?'

'Oh, Charles, please, allow me to introduce my cousin. Mateo, this is Lord Dayle. Charles, this is my cousin, Mr Cardea.'

Mateo flashed his charming smile and made a very credible bow. 'Delighted, Lord Dayle.'

'As am I, Mr Cardea.' He turned to her uncle. 'Congratulations, Cranbourne. I heard you had won the chairmanship for the Board of Trade's committee. I missed you at the preliminary meeting today, but I look forward to working with you.'

Cranbourne grinned. 'Thank you, Dayle. I'm sure we'll accomplish much.'

Charles nodded. 'I hope you will all forgive my rudeness, but Sophie is promised to me for this set.'

Sophie blushed with pleasure and laid a hand on his arm. 'Oh, that sounds lovely. I haven't had a dance all evening. Pray, do excuse us, Uncle, Mateo.'

His eyes warm with regard, her cousin pressed her free hand. 'We shall see each other again soon, I hope.'

Sophie could only nod as Charles stalked out, his hand tight on hers. She struggled to keep up with his long stride.

'The sets are forming this way, Charles.'

'We are not dancing,' he growled.

She swallowed her disappointment and surprise and looked at him in question. His eyes were cold and hard again, a study in opposites from the warm openness of her cousin's. 'What is it?' she asked.

He didn't answer. It appeared that he was looking for something. He stopped when his gaze fell on the galleries overhead and then he headed for the nearest stairway at the front of the room.

They had to manoeuvre through quite a crowd and by the time they reached the stairs, Sophie was tired of feeling like a toy on the end of a string. All of her happy anticipation was draining away. 'I'm not going a step further until you tell me what has upset you now.'

He paused part way up and threw a heated glance over his shoulder. 'We have to talk, and the things we must say to each other are not for other ears.'

She hesitated a moment. His walls were back and up and she was tired of trying to breach them. On the other hand, she'd heard of the cosy alcoves located above, and some of the things that were rumoured to go on in them. The thought of that early morning encounter and the way it had made her feel floated through her mind and sent a shiver of excitement through her. Before she could formulate another thought, her feet were mounting the steps right after Charles.

Oh, my. She'd come to the top and could see why the galleries were so well known, and masquerades so popular. Charles had passed by several alcoves, some with curtains drawn, some not. He drew her now towards a small room with a door, but Sophie's attention was caught by something else. 'Charles,' she whispered, 'is that shepherdess kissing the knight who I think she is?'

'Yes, but you are not to repeat a word of it,' he said in a harsh whisper.

'I wouldn't. I don't think her husband would approve, though.'

He pulled her into the room and shut the door. It was a subscription room, or something like. The walls were covered with shelves of books and periodicals, but Sophie barely noticed. 'Well,' she said, her mind still on what she had just witnessed, 'they shouldn't be able to get up to too much mischief. Just think of the noise, with all that armour.'

Charles laughed, the sound soft and bitter. Sophie looked at him in concern. She didn't wish to deal with one of his moods. In fact, she wanted him in another mood altogether. Like he'd been last time. Perhaps now she had a better idea on how to achieve that. 'Are you going to tell me what has upset you so?'

'I'm amazed that you must ask.'

'How could I know? You barely speak, you won't dance, you drag me up here like a toy you've found someone else playing with.' She was staring at his mouth while she spoke, unable to tear her gaze away. She bit her own lip in nervous agitation. 'You're certainly in a different temper from the last time we met.'

She sounded wistful even to her own ears. Edging closer, she saw the anger that had been haunting his eyes turn to wariness. And something else—desire. Slowly she raised her hand, placed it on his chest. Hard, like marble, but so warm. 'Perhaps we should just forget whatever's bothering you and pick up where we left off.'

He groaned, either in agony or amusement. Perhaps both. 'Sophie—you're driving me mad.' He reached out and wrapped her in his arms and she thought she'd gladly join him on the trip.

He smelled of sandalwood and leather and virile male. His vexation was apparent in the hard crush of his mouth on hers, but she didn't care. She opened her mouth, drank it in, and gave it back as hot, slick passion.

He shuddered and pulled her tighter, running his warm hands under her tunic. She gasped when he cupped the swell of her breasts. Then those large hands were moving, flowing around the curve of her waist and tracing the thinly disguised line of her buttocks. She pressed tighter to him and he kissed her deeper yet, while she savoured the heat and the strength and the taste of him.

Sophie was briefly bereft when his mouth abandoned hers, only to trail over the line of her jaw and down her throat. The rough cloth of his mask brushed her soft skin, arousing her almost as much as his searing kiss.

His hands came back up to her breasts, kneading her through the tight bodice. She felt her nipples swell, and her body arched, answering the rough caress with a pulsing throb that travelled from the point of his possessive caress to the coiling heat in her belly.

With a moan, Charles pushed a leg between her thighs. With no enveloping skirts in the way the contact was close and powerful. She could feel his full arousal against her most intimate spot, and she suddenly understood why a woman in trousers was so scandalous. She also understood for the first time what true passion was. Not restless longing and vague, unrelenting craving, but a powerful, lust-filled whirlwind that stole away all reason, crushed resistance and blew her inevitably toward her final destination.

Sophie couldn't summon the will to resist; she just clung to Charles and hung on, ready to follow the destructive vortex to the end. Charles, however, was made of sterner stuff. Eventually he wrenched his mouth from hers and pulled away.

Sophie breathed deep, desperate for air, for something to replace her abrupt loss. Charles was panting as well and glaring at her as if she had been the one to call a halt to the proceedings.

'Do you see?' he demanded. 'What you drive me to? What every man down there wishes to get a chance at?'

Sophie was shocked. 'Don't be ridiculous.'

'It's a far cry from being ridiculous, it's the truth. What was it I asked of you when we last parted? Just don't get into any trouble. But you take the first opportunity to make a grand spectacle of yourself.'

'A spectacle? It's a benefit. Other young ladies are performing as well.'

'None of the other ladies look like they sprang from a bordello's re-enactment of the *Arabian Nights!* You're wearing trousers! They'll have to destroy half the forests of England to print all that will be said of you in tomorrow's broadsides and papers.'

'You are overreacting. And in any case, what if they do?' she asked, tossing her hair. 'I told you once before—you cannot control what others think. I don't care what people say of me.' If she did, she'd have broken long ago.

'And I told you then—you should care.' He groaned and ripped off his mask. 'If you hold any hope of becoming my bride—you must.'

Sophie froze. All the elation she'd been feeling these past days began to wither. 'Pardon me?'

'You know my situation, what I've been doing this Season. I must find a bride of sterling character and reputation. People are watching me, judging me by the choices I make. I have to live down my past; I must show good judgement and an eye for the future when I wed.'

Sophie tried to breathe, but it seemed each word fed the pain that was building in her chest, cutting off her air, her blood, her belief in Charles and his in her. 'Choosing me would be a show of bad judgment?'

'I don't think so, but others will.'

'All this because of a masquerade costume?'

He took her hand, led her over to a little chair, then pulled up another close to her. 'It's not just the costume, Sophie. It's—it's more. I don't know. It's not always the things you do, it's the way you do them.'

She couldn't speak, couldn't force any words past the fist of agony inside her. All the taunts, all the rejections of her childhood—none of them had hurt so badly as this. It was *Charles* throwing these barbs at her now, and hitting her most vulnerable spot with devastating accuracy. She could only look at him with accusing eyes.

He misunderstood. 'No—it's more than your designs— because it's not *just* your designs. You don't just have an interest in décor—you publish a book. You trade fabric swatches with the Prince Regent, for God's sake!'

He took her hand, clasped it in his warm grasp. 'Please, just listen to me for a moment. We can make it work,' he said. 'I'm sure we can. But it will take some effort from you, Sophie.' He smiled, tried to rally her. 'It won't be so bad. Mother will help. I know you disapprove of Miss Ashford, but her reputation is spotless. We can use her as a model of sorts.' He smiled again. 'If I can go from England's worst profligate to a politician on the path to the ministry, then you'll have a much easier time.'

The air was cold in this little room, or perhaps it was just her frozen heart. She shook her head. He didn't even know that he was betraying her, killing the one belief that had given her hope, kept her sane. 'What you are saying—' her voice was dangerous '—is that we can be married, once I learn to behave?'

He heaved an exasperated sigh. 'Don't phrase it in such a way. You know the situation. We just have to change society's image of you.'

The cold was disappearing fast, fleeing before the heat of her rising fury. 'Oh, but why stop there?' she asked. 'For you surely did not. No—you changed their perception of you and then you continued on, changing your personality, your heart, and your soul. You've changed more than I suspected, to be able to say such things to me.' She turned, not wanting him to see the tears that she couldn't hold back.

He moved closer, until she could feel his breath close to her ear. Before he could insult her any further, voices echoed in the hall, just outside the subscription room door.

'Do not look at them, Corinne,' someone commanded in a sharp, nasal tone. 'Oh, I shall shake the wretched girl. I do hope you are wrong, but we must look into it, I suppose.'

'I'm sure it is not what you might be thinking, Mama.' Miss Ashford's usually calm voice sounded almost smug.

The door opened and the two ladies peered in.

'Miss Westby!' Lady Ashford gasped. 'I am sure I did not believe the vile rumours that have been circulating about you tonight, but I see I have been proven wrong. And you, of all people, Lord Dayle!'

'It is perfectly all right, Mama, as I have tried to tell you,' Miss Ashford said. 'Lord Dayle and Miss Westby are old friends. They grew up together and regard each other more as brother and sister than anything else.' She ran an assessing eye down Sophie. 'No one who is familiar with them would suspect anything untoward. I am sure the situation is perfectly innocent.'

'Is my daughter correct, Lord Dayle?' Lady Ashford demanded.

He did not answer, did not even look her way. His gaze remained locked with Sophie's. She turned from him, avoided the questioning eyes of the Ashford ladies, and moved to brush past them.

'Please,' he said to her. 'I wish it were otherwise. Is it really too much to ask, when you consider what might be gained?'

She closed her eyes as the rage drained away. It left behind an empty husk in its wake, all too vulnerable to the pain that was quick to rush back. She turned to him, looked him in the eye. 'Yes,' she said simply. 'It is too much. If you knew me at all in the way that I thought you did, you wouldn't have to ask.'

She fled, fighting tears, running from the ache of despair. Her feet flew down the stairs as she struggled to rein in her emotions. She must get away. She absolutely could not break down in front of so many witnesses.

Her every resource was focused inward. She did not see the two men whispering together at the bottom of the stairs until she had run into them.

'I do beg your pardon,' she said thickly, without stopping.

'Sophie!' It was her uncle, and her cousin. 'Are you well? You look upset.'

'I am not feeling at all the thing, Uncle. Do excuse me.'

'Then of course you must go home at once.'

Sophie had to fight off a bitter comment about the extreme lateness of his solicitude.

'Mr Cardea will escort you, will you not, sir?'

Mateo bowed low. 'I shall be delighted.'

Sophie hadn't the energy to decline. She left a message for Lady Dayle and departed with her cousin.

She never felt the weight of two separate, but very satisfied, gazes as she went.

Chapter Eleven

The worst part was knowing that Charles was right. That he could breathe a sigh of relief with each new broadsheet posted across London, that he could thank his lucky stars that he was not involved, as each vile rumour grew worse with repeated whisperings.

Sophie had lived most of her life at the mercy of talebearers and scandalmongers. She had long ago learned to rise above such nonsense. But not this time. This time the whisperers had sharper tongues, wicked wit, and a broader audience. The tales circulating about her were outrageous. She'd worn trousers, she'd worn *transparent* trousers, she'd worn next to nothing at all. She'd danced a harem dance, she'd danced with the Prince Regent, she'd danced down the centre of the supper table. There was no end to the inventiveness.

Still, strange things had been said of her before, and she had held her head high and taken the high road. She had even used her reputation as an eccentric to her advantage a time or two. It might have been the same with this, after enough time had passed, if this time, the scandal hadn't become the embodiment of her deepest insecurities. This time each fabricated account of her wickedness hit her like a blow, drumming the ugly truth deeper. *Not good enough. Not good enough.*

Oh, he hadn't said it in so many words, but the meaning was clear. She should know. She was an expert at being not good enough.

She'd been a disappointment to her uncle, a failure in reaching her aunt, a pariah to the people of Blackford Chase. Only Charles had ever made her feel truly appreciated just for being herself. The rest of London could go hang; it was the loss of that certainty, the sure knowledge of Charles's regard, that caused this pain, this blinding agony that only seemed to grow worse with each drawn breath.

She wandered the house, emotionally adrift. Only now was she coming to realise how deep her dependence had gone. She'd spent half her life on the wrong side of public opinion, but always she had clung to the rock of Charles's faith in her. Now she floundered. She hadn't felt this lost since the death of her parents.

She had to fight, to keep afloat, to flail blindly if need be, until she found something stronger to hold on to. But it was so hard. She couldn't think. It was all she could do to breathe, to ignore the hurt and make it to the next moment.

Emily's family was suffering as well. That first day her drawing room was a scene of frantic activity, as society came to sympathise, to gloat, or just to be in the centre of the scandal broth. Sophie stayed in her room and waited with a mixture of dread and anticipation for Charles to come. He didn't. And then neither did anyone else.

The number of visitors trickled, and then stopped. An air of dread inhabited the house. Deep silences, long faces, hushed voices. Sophie grew tired of mourning her reputation and heartily sick of waiting for Charles. Finally she could take no more. She packed her bags and went alone to Sevenoaks.

It was exactly what she needed. She threw herself into the dirtiest projects she could find. No job was too small to command her attention. Stripping paper, hanging fabric, and restoring plasterwork occupied her thoroughly. She concentrated on soothing the Italian *stuccatore*'s wounded vanity instead of nursing her own wounded heart. She spent her time curbing the hanger's passion for red-flock paper instead of dwelling on the passion that had flared so easily between her and Charles.

She worked almost unceasingly each day, falling into bed exhausted late each evening. As a plan for avoiding painful memories, it had merit. Unfortunately, it did not meet with success. In the quiet darkness her mind was too busy to allow her body to rest.

A thousand times during those lonely nights she changed her mind. Charles was right, he wasn't asking too much. Not if they could be together. Tired, heartsore, and more alone than she had ever felt in her life, she thought of marrying Charles, spending their lives together, and she knew she would do it. She would change. She would change into an elephant if he wished it.

Yet each morning found her back at work rather than on her way back to London. As much as she yearned for Charles in the night, in the clear, dawn light harsher memories returned. Cold eyes, hard words, high, strong walls keeping her out. She'd been exasperated by that side of Charles, but she could not deny that she had found him intriguing and ir-resistible in his own way.

Was that the sort of person he wished her to become? Even here, alone and covered in grime and plaster dust, she shook her head. Through years of loneliness and neglect she'd battled bitterness and despair. She'd refused to become closed and angry. She couldn't give in now, even for the sake of love.

That was the crux of it: love. Charles desired her, he wanted her, but he didn't love her. Love supports, love nurtures, it doesn't require you to change.

So, with stiffened resolve, Sophie laboured right along with the workmen, and slowly over the next few days the project drew close to the end. It was a bittersweet realisation.

The house had turned out to be even more beautiful than she had hoped, and now that it was nearly complete, she could picture Charles here all too easily. His image sprang to mind everywhere: in the library, in the hall, in the bedroom. He would spend many happy hours here. Without her.

Finally she had accepted the truth. She'd had time for a lot of relentless soul searching over the last days, and she wasn't sure she liked what she'd found.

No matter what she had told herself upon coming to London—regarding both her designs and her relationship with Charles—she had to admit now that some part of her had been hoping to have both. Well, she couldn't. He had changed, and so had she. And it was past time she changed again.

These days of grief and regret had been disturbingly similar to the days after her parents' deaths. As a scared little girl, suddenly alone in the world, she'd put all her hopes and dreams into the image of a loving uncle, a man who would love and care for her the way her parents had. When that fantasy had died, she had focused all the love in her lonely little heart on the one person who had cared. Even after he'd left, she'd carried that dream in her heart.

No longer. She was a woman now, and it was time to finally recognise the difference between dreams and reality. Charles was a dream. But what was her reality?

This, she thought, gazing around her. No matter what society thought, no matter what Charles believed, she knew the kind of person she was. Not perfect by any means, but she did have talent, the ability to bring beauty to people's lives. More importantly, she could use that talent to accomplish something useful, to help those who had so much less than herself.

Society was closed to her now and she wouldn't give tuppence to have it back. But she had her designs. Her book. Mr Darvey and the workmen back at Blackford Chase. She could use her skills and accomplish some good at the same time. She would be content with that.

It was not long after reaching that conclusion that she stood in the drawing room, staring with a frown at the continued chimneypiece. She'd had the wood painted white to match all the moulding in the room and to complement the elegant plasterwork. But she could not decide on a painting to mount there. She had two candidates, but neither was quite right.

With the rest of the room she was more than satisfied. Here her ardent hanger had had his way, and the room was resplendent with red-flock paper. It contrasted beautifully with all the white. Here was a room a statesman could be proud of. Fit for entertaining royalty, visiting dignitaries, or just close friends and loved ones. It was grand, impressive, yet somehow it also maintained the warmth of a home.

She could even think of it that way without regret. Almost.

As luck would have it, some sort of disturbance began at the front of the house and she was given no time to dwell on it. She had only just turned towards the door when it opened.

'Now that I see what occupies you so far from London, I must say it is worth the trip.'

'Mateo!' Sophie gasped.

'Indeed, it is I. You fled the city just after I arrived and I have chased you down, just as when we were children.' He smiled and entered the room to take her hands. 'The sight of you alone was worth the chase. This—' he waved his hand at the room '—is—what do the English call it—the cream.'

She laughed. 'How did you find me?'

'I have pestered the good viscountess day and night until she finally relented and allowed me to travel here with her. She will be in directly, she was delayed by the housekeeper, and I had the bad manners to come straight in here.'

'Well, I am glad you are here.' She surprised herself by meaning it.

'As am I.' He dropped her hands and began to circle the room. 'Lovely. Exquisite, in fact. If this is an indication of your work, then I can see why the Prince Regent adores you so.'

Sophie grimaced. 'I think you exaggerate.'

'Oho! So you have not been reading the papers here in your retreat?'

'No.' She could not keep the hard edge from her voice. 'And if you have, then you'll know why.'

Mateo tossed his head, setting his shining dark curls to

bouncing, and laughed long. Sophie stared, filing the image away in her mind, knowing she would sketch it later. Young, handsome, confident, carefree, he was the very image of…something. Life, perhaps.

'Trust you, Sophie,' he crowed, 'to turn London upside down and not even realise it.'

'He's right, my dear.' Lady Dayle came in, and Sophie went straight into her embrace. She clung a little longer than she meant to, and when the viscountess finally set her back, she began, 'I'm so sorry, my lady—'

'No,' interjected Mateo. 'You do not apologise. It is these English. Such a fuss over such a small thing. They do not know how to enjoy life, Sophie. You have no wish to be like them.'

Despite herself, she smiled. 'You sound just like Nona Celeste. Nevertheless, I am sorry for any distress you have suffered, Lady Dayle.'

'Not at all, dear. You must listen to your cousin. The circumstances have changed since you left.' She looked around with pleasure at the room. 'How lovely it has turned out, Sophie. Let us sit while we speak.'

They all took seats, but Sophie could wait no longer. 'Circumstances have changed?' she prompted.

'Yes, they have realised that they have put their temper in a teacup,' Mateo said.

'Tempest in a teacup, Mr Cardea. In any case, Sophie, it is over.' The viscountess took her hands in hers and smiled.

'Over?' Sophie was perplexed.

'Over.' Lady Dayle said in a firm voice. 'After you left, the furore died down a bit. Only to be stirred up again every day or so with some new story or published account. Soon people began to notice that many of the articles printed about that night and your supposedly shocking behaviour were very similarly worded. As if it were one person behind all the stories, stirring the scandal broth, as they say.'

'But your defenders, they were legion!' her cousin said. 'The viscountess has stood your truest friend, and Mrs Lowder and many more.'

Sophie couldn't help the tears that rose. No one had ever defended her before. Except Charles. The stab of pain was acute, but she had to know. 'And Lord Dayle?'

'I haven't seen him since the masquerade,' Lady Dayle said, sounding troubled. 'Jack said he was locked up with his committee, but Sir Harold said they had adjourned several days ago to await a report from the north. No one seems to know where to find him. I thought perhaps he might have told you his plans?'

Mute, Sophie shook her head.

'You have no need of his aid, Sophie,' said Mateo. 'Your friend the Duchess declared she would cut dead anyone who spoke a wrong word of you. The cold one, Miss Ashford?' She nodded and he continued. 'Even she finally declared that the costume had been her idea and was unobjectionable. But the final blow to your detractors came when the Prince Regent spoke on your behalf.'

Sophie could only cover her mouth with her hand. 'He didn't,' she whispered.

'Indeed.' Lady Dayle smiled.

'He said that your talent is great and that the artistic temperament must be allowed more latitude than the average person's. He would be very displeased to hear anyone disparaging you. He may not be much of a ruler,' Mateo said with condescension, 'but he is a man who knows how to get the most out of life.'

They all laughed and Sophie began to feel a little better.

'The truly funny thing is that once Prinny made his pronouncement, everyone pulled out their drawings to prove him right and show their support. Now a Dunyazade original is quickly becoming the most fashionable object one can own.'

'Indeed, it is most unfair that I, your cousin, do not possess one.'

Sophie smiled. 'I'm afraid that Dunyazade is permanently retired, but I would dearly love to draw your portrait.'

Mateo's eyes lit up. 'Now?'

Sophie laughed. 'I'm sorry, but no. I have too much to do today. But perhaps tomorrow morning, when the light is best, we could begin some sketches. That is,' she said, turning to the viscountess, 'if you both mean to stay the night?'

'We do,' said Lady Dayle, 'and I really must get upstairs to help with the unpacking. Winston will not know which dress to leave out for dinner. By the way,' she said casually, 'I stopped at Emily's and brought Nell along, and the rest of your wardrobe.'

'Thank you. I have missed Nell. I hope you won't be disillusioned by my sad wardrobe while you're here, Mateo, but the work is hard on my gowns.'

'You would be divine in rags,' he professed. 'Business calls me back to London in a few days, but I intend to enjoy my time here with you, cousin.'

'I will see you both at dinner, then,' Lady Dayle said, rising to leave. She paused by the chimneypiece. 'The white is such an improvement! But do you mean to hang one of these here, dear?' She gestured to the two paintings propped against the marble hearth.

'I suppose so. Neither suits me exactly, but I haven't found anything else in the attics.'

'Then don't hang anything just yet. I have just the thing. I will send to Fordham—it should only take a few days to arrive.'

'Thank you, my lady. Now, Mateo, I hope you will excuse me.'

'Indeed I will not. I shall be one of your drudges, if you permit.' He chuckled. 'I suspect it is the only way to spend some time with you, cousin.'

Sophie accomplished much that day, even with Mateo's help. Actually he possessed a keen eye and a willingness to lend a hand to even the meanest task. He kept her laughing with his chatter and unflagging good spirits. She enjoyed the day, and later they all enjoyed a fine dinner, cosy in the breakfast room, as the dining room was not yet complete.

Afterwards, the three of them took tea in the less formal parlour at the back of the house. Sophie avoided the window where Charles had first kissed her.

Mateo did not. He stood right in the spot where Charles had and assessed the room. 'Sophie,' he said, 'this house will make your name.'

'If it does not, I shall set out a shingle as Madam Dunyazade,' she teased.

'Mateo is right,' Lady Dayle said, 'I cannot wait for everyone to see it.'

'You shall have to write and tell me how Lord Dayle's first entertainment is received.'

The viscountess set down her teacup and exchanged a glance with Mateo. 'I won't have to, dear,' she said.

'Why not?' Sophie looked from one guilty face to the other. 'What is it?'

'Charles's birthday, you know, is at the end of the week.'

'Yes.'

'I've invited some people here to celebrate. It is to be a house party.'

Sophie's jaw dropped. 'But, my lady! There is still so much to be done!'

'Nonsense. It is magnificent. What is left can easily be accomplished in time.'

Sophie was doing rapid calculations in her head. 'Perhaps.' She was quiet a moment. 'Yes, I believe we can manage it, but we must not delay. If we work very hard for the next few days, I should be able to be finished and out of the way in time.'

'Indeed, you will not. You will not be in the way and you will not be skulking off. You must be here.'

'I would rather not.'

'But you must, for they are your guests as well. I issued the invitation in both our names. It is to be a birthday celebration and an unveiling at once.'

Sophie sat very still. 'You…' She felt the urge to laugh, but was afraid it would turn into a sob. Charles. A house party. 'You do not play fair, Lady Dayle.'

The viscountess chuckled. 'True. All's fair in love and war…and decorating.'

'Ah, but the lady is right, Sophie. This is perfect.' Mateo's voice was intense. 'It shall be a triumph for you. After this you will be able to go anywhere, do anything you wish with your designs.'

'I agree. I have no doubt you will receive another commission when this is seen. In fact, I predict you will receive many offers.'

'Ah, but you are wasted on these rigid English.' Mateo was leaning forward in his chair, regarding her intently. 'I agree, you must receive due credit for this beautiful work, but then you must come home to Philadelphia with me. There you will be appreciated, revered. A lady designer with the ear of the English prince! They will be fighting over you like dogs in the street.'

'Such a charming picture.' Lady Dayle rolled her eyes. 'Sophie is well loved and appreciated right here. Surely the last few days have shown you that.'

'Yes, but here she will not be allowed the sort of success she could find elsewhere. In America, it is different.' He looked into Sophie's eyes, earnestness shining in his own. 'You think on it, eh?'

She would. After she found a way out of this house party.

Chapter Twelve

Charles was fifteen again, and finally going off to school. At last his father had relented, though he grumbled about throwing good blunt after bad and predicted his wayward second son would be sent back down before the quarter was out.

Charles didn't listen. He'd heard it all before. His father's grumblings couldn't touch him now, he was finally getting away and the world lay open before him. The only dark spot in his bright future was the interview immediately ahead. He had to say goodbye to Sophie.

He found her sitting on the lowest branch of the tree where they had first met. Her ebony hair curled down her back and silent tears streamed down her face. He sat down close beside her on the gnarled branch and her head fell to rest on his shoulder. They stayed—silent, beyond words—for a while. Then he gave her a parting gift: a book. Thomas Hope's *Household Furniture and Interior Decoration*. She smiled her thanks and he said something to make her laugh.

Her laughter rang out in the quiet glade, fluid, almost

tangible, then suddenly it *was* tangible, moving in sensuous tendrils, surrounding him. No, those were her arms sliding up his hard body, encircling him. They weren't children any longer. Sophie was a woman in his arms, hot and wanton, eager as she pressed herself against him, pressed her lips to his with a breathless sigh.

Charles moaned and buried his hands in her thick hair, clamped his hard and desperate mouth over hers and tightened his grip on her soft, writhing body.

In an abrupt change of mood that made him want to howl, she pushed him away. The forest had faded, she wiggled from his grasp and marched to his bedchamber door. Turning, she regarded him with a sneer, dark eyes flashing indignation and anger.

'No, Charles,' was all she said, then she slammed the door with a crash.

Bang! She slammed it again and the noise made his brainbox rattle.

Bang! Why was she still slamming the door? Somehow the racket had gotten inside his head and was set to explode out through his pounding temples.

'Don't you have a key?' Sophie said, still irritated. Wait, no. That was Jack's voice.

'He's got it in there with him,' someone answered.

Bang!

'Damnation!' Charles shouted, then clutched his head. 'Stop that bloody racket or I'll strangle you with my bare hands!' He lay back, bending over in agony. He wasn't going to kill anybody; he was going to cast up his accounts right in his own bed. Then he was going to die.

'At least he's alive,' his brother said, laughter and relief in his voice.

Bang!

The last great crash did kill him, or at least sent him spiralling past the pain and into a blessedly quiet, dark void.

He awoke to find his brother and his valet standing over him. Staring in horrified fascination.

'Any idea where he's been all this time?' Jack asked.

Crocker grunted a negative. 'Two gentlemen brought him in. Found him at Bellamy's. I don't know what he's been drinking, but he didn't get it there.' The valet's cragged face twisted in disgust. 'I left to brew some coffee and when I come back, the door was locked. Figured I needed to get in here, so I sent a man for you, sir, before I started taking the door down.'

'You did the right thing.'

Crocker wrinkled his nose. 'I'll fetch up a hot bath.'

Charles just moaned and rolled over.

'When I told you to decide what you wanted, I wasn't thinking of suicide as an option.' When he received no response, Jack continued. 'Well, come along, lay-a-bed! While you've been on a three-day binge, I've been a busy boy. I've brought a visitor for you.'

'Go away and let me die.'

'Not today, big brother. Come on, here's your man with some coffee.'

'Go. To. Hell,' Charles said succinctly.

Jack laughed. 'It looks as if Old Scratch has already ejected one Alden from his domain today, so I dare say I won't take you up on that.'

'Coffee, my lord,' Crocker said, holding a steaming cup and saucer under his nose. Charles tried manfully not to gag and waved him away. A regiment of footmen entered and the racket they made pouring his bath sent him diving back under the covers. But between them, Jack and Crocker got him into the steaming tub and the conviction that he was going to die out of his aching head. After half a pot of coffee he felt almost human again. Almost.

'I'm not even going to ask what precipitated this,' Jack said once Charles was propped in a chair, wearing a robe.

'A woman,' Crocker said darkly as he cleaned away the shaving implements. He had the grace to flush when Charles eyed him with distaste, but stood firm. 'Nothing else brings a man so low.'

'Lord knows you're entitled to a binge, but we need to get back to business now,' said Jack. 'I meant it when I said I had brought you a visitor, and trust me, you'll want to hear what he has to say.'

Charles heaved a great sigh and allowed Crocker to brush back his wet hair. Lord, every strand on his head was a needle of fire piercing his scalp. 'Bad enough you expect me to be coherent, you shan't get me to dress. Unless I see him here, he'll have to wait.'

'I'll bring him up.'

When Jack came back he had a stripling lad with him. Charles grimaced at his brother and hoped the sight of such dissipation wouldn't ruin the boy.

'Charles, this is Mr Lionel Humbert, apprentice typesetter. Mr Humbert, Lord Dayle.'

The boy bobbed his head and wrung his hat in his hands. 'Good morning, my lord.'

'A debatable opinion, but I'm not up to arguing it, Mr Humbert.' He indicated a chair close by. 'Won't you sit down?'

The boy paled. 'No, thank you, my lord. I mean, I'll stand, my lord.'

'Do you care for coffee?' Charles tried to put the poor boy at ease.

'No. I mean, I do sir, but I better not drink it now. I'm too nervous, sir.'

At least they had gone from 'my lord' to 'sir'.

'Don't be nervous. I may look a fright, but I don't eat young men for breakfast. Tell me, what can I do for you this morning, Mr Humbert?'

The boy glanced at Jack, who nodded encouragingly. 'I think I'm to do something for you, sir. You see, I'm apprenticed to Mr Prescott, a printer.'

'One of Mr Prescott's accounts is with the *Oracle*, Charles,' said Jack.

'My sympathy is with you, for having to deal with the editor of that scandal rag.'

'Thank you, sir. Mr Griggs is a mite dicked in the nob, if you catch my meaning.'

'More than a mite, I would say,' Charles agreed gravely.

'Tell him about the man we discussed,' urged Jack.

'Well, a while back, I delivered the proofs to Mr Griggs, like always. It was about when they started hounding you in their paper, sir, if you'll forgive me. That's when I first saw the man that Mr Alden says you are looking for.'

'A short, dark, wiry man?' Charles asked, sitting up with interest.

'Aye, sir. An odd one, that. Moves quick and sharp, like a bird. That's what made me remember his name.'

'His name? What was his name, son?' Charles asked gently.

'Wren, sir. Wren, like a bird, see?'

'I do indeed. Smart boy,' Charles said with approval. 'Do you know what Wren was doing with Mr Griggs?'

The boy pursed his mouth and thought. 'Well, it looked summat like he was checking the paper and putting his stamp on it—like Mr Griggs usually does.'

'Hmm.'

'They looked at the articles about you, sir. They had a good laugh about 'em before giving me the go ahead to print.'

'You've indeed been a big help to me, Mr Humbert. Now I want you to think very carefully. Did Wren ever mention who *he* works for?'

The boy was silent a long moment. 'Nooo,' he said, and Charles slumped. 'But he did say once, "His lordship will be pleased."'

'Lordship?' Charles looked at Jack.

'Aye, but he said it funny—mean funny, you ken? Like he was mayhap making fun?'

Charles had a sudden thought. 'Does Wren still come around to look at the proofs?'

'No, sir. Since Griggs quit riggin' you in the paper, I haven't seen him back.'

'Thank you, Mr Humbert, you have been very helpful indeed.' He gestured to Crocker. 'Why don't you show our young friend down to the kitchens? I'm sure Cook has something for a growing lad. And give him something for being so co-operative.' Charles rose and shook the boy's hand. 'I hope we may do business together again someday.'

The boy, looking relieved, went off with Crocker. Charles sat down and looked at Jack.

'Thank you. It's more than we had before.' He sat silent a moment, before pounding his hand on his chair in frustration. 'It's still so little! Why can't we pin him down?'

'We have a few days. Perhaps we can find something else.'

'A few days?'

'Before your birthday.'

Charles rubbed his temples. Oh, Lord, this could not be good. He wondered what else he'd missed in the past week. 'My birthday?'

Jack looked at him in surprise and then laughed out loud. 'If you had been reading your mail instead of bending your elbow, dear brother, you would know that our dearest mother is planning a birthday bash for you.'

'How bad is it?'

'You really don't know? She's invited a slew of people to a house party this weekend.'

'A house party? All the way at Fordham?'

'No, Charles. At Sevenoaks. She means to unveil the new house at the same time.'

Charles slumped in his chair. His gut started roiling again, in time with the percussion in his head. Jack and Crocker had been wrong; he was going to die. He only hoped he could manage it before his birthday.

Chapter Thirteen

Of course, he didn't die. He didn't even get out of the house party. In the end, it wasn't worth it. It would have insulted his guests, hurt his mother, and given the score keepers one more black mark next to his name. He'd given them enough ammunition with this last trip below the mahogany, and they had revelled in it. He had a flock of reporters following him now, all poised with pencils and pads, waiting for him to speak in tongues or start fornicating in the streets, he assumed. He ignored them. He had other things to worry over.

When Sophie had walked out on him at that charity ball, he'd been shocked. As angry as he'd been, he'd thought they could come to an understanding. He'd still thought it an inspired solution to all their problems. He'd quickly moved from shocked to furious, and had spent the next couple of days cursing the inconstancy of women in general and Sophie's misplaced pride in particular.

And then, in the middle of a committee meeting, right in the midst of a report documenting bread riots in Birmingham, the realisation had struck him. How his brilliant idea might have sounded to Sophie. How it must have made her feel.

Gone were the disturbing details of protesting farm labourers refusing to work and harvests rotting in the field. Instead, images of Sophie began to flash in his mind. The hurt on her young face when her vague aunt forgot her name again. The defiant squaring of her shoulders when her birthday came with no acknowledgement except his own. Her reluctance to be drawn into the social whirl. Her grim pronouncement that she was a designer, not a débutante.

She put up such a brave front that even he—who knew what hurts lurked behind her bright vitality—had forgotten. He knew the frightened little girl who hid behind the beautiful woman. Yet he had been so wrapped up in maintaining his own façade, that he'd forgotten hers.

It was then that he'd realised the magnitude of what he'd done, how his callous words would have hurt her. It was then that he'd gone on his carouse. Lord Cranbourne—her uncle, no less—had shaken him back to reality when the meeting ended. Charles had thanked the man and left. Unable to bear the thought of the damage he'd inadvertently caused, he'd left Westminster, gone straight to the nearest grogshop, and washed away the agony brought on by his latest bout of selfishness with a river of cheap gin.

Unfortunately, one could only hide in an alcoholic haze for so long. Jack and Crocker had fished him out, and he'd tried to get on with his life. Only to find he could not. Politics, Miss Ashford's expectations, even the thought of the elusive Mr Wren—none of it could hold his interest. He'd wandered through the next few days numb, lost. He didn't know who he was any more. Not rakish, carefree Charles Alden, and no longer Viscount Dayle, young politician on the path to the ministry. Who was he then? He didn't know or care.

His only thought was that he must see Sophie. He burned to see her, with an aching desperation that obliterated all else. He had to know what they might salvage out of the mess he'd made. He had to tell her he finally understood how profoundly stupid he had been. He had to make amends.

He'd latched on to that thought like it was a lifeline. With his brother and his father there had been no opportunity for apologies, but with Sophie he had a chance to make everything right again. He didn't mean to waste it.

Thus he stood now, on the threshold of his newly redecorated house, and at a crossroads in his life. He breathed deeply and entered.

The entrance hall was bright with sun and welcoming with the gleam of polished wood and crisp, whitewashed stucco. Charles advanced, breathing in the homey, welcoming smells; beeswax and biscuits and the faint tang of new paint.

The dining room to the right stood empty, of both people and furniture. The paint smell was stronger here. He turned to the left and approached the entrance to the drawing room.

Sophie was there, with his mother. They were both bent headfirst into a packing crate. Bits of straw floated in the air above, and when his mother straightened, he could see it stuck in her hair as well. But it wasn't that that brought him up short. It was her face, alive with mischief and laughter. His mother, he realised, was happy.

Sophie stood then, laughing as well. She had a smudge on her cheek and a huge stain down one arm. Her dress was old and faded. Her dark tresses, once gathered simply at her nape, were a dishevelled mess. She was beautiful. Charles stood, absorbing the brightness of her smile, drinking the music of her laughter, and knew, with sudden clarity, what a colossal fool he was.

Sophie was a shining light in a world of dark indifference. She'd borne so much, and never broken. She might have become bitter and withdrawn; instead she gave of herself with every word, every smile. She didn't hide behind superficialities, or stifle her talent because it wasn't fashionable. No, she laid her true self before every person she encountered and she risked censure and disdain to make others happy.

Like his mother, who must endure one of life's worst hardships. Like Emily Lowder, who had faced the same sort of disappointment and heartache, yet emerged victorious. Like she might have done for him, had he been clever enough to recognise her for the treasure she was.

She might have shone her light into his darkness. He closed his eyes and imagined it. Gentle smiles, healing hands, forgiveness. He could have cherished her, pleasured her, buried his hurt in her lithe body and emerged clean, and nearly whole.

It was more than he deserved. He had disparaged her, lectured her, hurt her. She was open and generous, while he had secrets he could never share. But his yearning for her purity, her warmth, her love, was visceral and undeniable. He didn't deserve her, yet he wanted her with a desperation that was nearly palpable.

'Charles!' His eyes opened. His mother had noticed him in the archway. 'You're here!'

'Yes,' he said, trying to hide his need, his confusion. 'I thought I should be here when the guests begin to arrive tomorrow.'

Sophie stood silent. His mother was fluttering, placing the top back on the crate and signalling the footman who had appeared behind Charles to take charge of it. 'I'm so glad you've come, dear. We are nearly ready. I do need to see Mrs Hepple about the dinner tomorrow, though, so I'll let Sophie give you the tour of the house.' She gave him an affectionate peck on her way out. 'I shall see you a little later, hmm?' and then she was gone.

He advanced cautiously into the room, his mind awhirl with so many regrets. She dropped her eyes when he grew close. He stopped. 'Sophie.'

'I didn't expect you until tomorrow,' was all she said.

'I wanted to see you. I thought it might be awkward were we to meet again in company.'

She risked a fleeting glance. 'Yes, it might have been awkward.' A flash of a quick smile gave him hope. 'But so is this.'

He grinned back, with relief. 'Yes, but at least there are no witnesses.'

Her face fell and he cursed himself for a fool. 'I didn't mean it like that.' He took a step closer, fighting to keep from just taking her in his arms. He wanted to kiss her, softly, until the wounded look in her eyes was gone. 'Every time I try to hold a conversation with you, I'm suddenly a gawky boy again.' He waited but she gave no response. 'I have to tell you how sorry I am. It finally penetrated my feeble brain just how my idiotic ramblings might have hurt you. I never meant to, though. It nearly killed me when I realised it.'

She drew a ragged breath and he stopped. 'Please. I accept your apology.'

Charles sighed his relief. 'Thank you.' He couldn't help

himself then; he reached out and took one of her hands. Stained and callused, with ragged nails, it was a physical representation of all that she'd endured, of the generosity of mind, spirit and talent that set her apart. Ridiculous as it might seem, the touch of that worn little hand was more beautiful, more dear, more arousing to him than the boldest caress from any other woman in the world.

'I know I've been selfish, blind, and testier than William the Goat—' there, almost a smile '—but I also know that my feelings for you are real and abiding. Can't we salvage something from the wreck I've made of our friendship?'

The smile disappeared and she pulled her hand from his. 'No, Charles. You were right all along. We can't go back. I was foolish to think we might.'

Charles's breath caught. 'But, Sophie, there's so much I want to tell you—'

There was panic in her face now. She stopped him with a sharp motion of her hand. 'I'm sorry. No. I cannot have this discussion with you now. This house party is going to be very difficult for me. If I am going to get through it with any semblance of dignity, then I have to ask you to wait.'

'Wait?'

'Yes. All the…things we need to discuss will still be there later. Perhaps they will come easier then, too.'

'I understand.' Charles thought a moment. 'I don't want to make this more difficult for you. Shall I go then, make an excuse for abandoning the party?'

'No.' Her reply was instantaneous. 'It means so much to your mother.'

He should have expected her reaction. He was truly a fool.

'Perhaps, then, we can try something new. Grant each other a clean slate. Spend these days as new acquaintances.'

Her look was speculative. 'Yes, I think perhaps I should like that.'

'Good. Well, then, Miss Westby, as a new acquaintance who also happens to be my designer, will you escort me on a tour of the house?'

They were both able to relax a little as he inspected the reno- vated rooms. It was easy to show his approval of her work. She'd turned a musty old house into a vibrant, welcoming home.

He was especially pleased with the library. The old pair of windows, tall and narrow with a padded seat at each base, had been ripped out, along with the entire wall between them. In their place stood an entire bank of windows, turning a gloomy room into a warm and sunny retreat. Outside the lawns stretched in a gorgeous, gradual slope down to the lake. Dappled sunlight danced on the water's surface and reflected back from something shiny on the far side.

'What is that, across the lake?'

'A folly, a very beautiful one in the classical style. Your mother specifically requested it and has overseen its installa- tion. She walks out there most mornings.'

'Shall we go out and inspect that as well?'

'Perhaps later.' She smiled. 'The reflection is from the copper cupola. The effect won't last, though. Once it weathers a bit it won't bother you.'

'It doesn't bother me now.' Charles strode about the library, admiring the new bookcases, the tasteful refurbishings, the elegant carpet. 'Is this new?'

Sophie's smile was genuine now. 'No, we only cleaned the old one. I don't think it had been done in years.'

'It's beautiful.' He trailed a finger over the immaculately shining, nearly empty desk. 'I see my correspondence hasn't caught up with me.'

Sophie winced and Charles chuckled. 'Yes, I can well imagine the tone of your own correspondence of late.' He grew more serious and looked her in the eye. 'I'll only mention it this once, until you are ready to talk, but I want you to know that I am glad you emerged from that situation unscathed. For your sake,' he emphasised.

Her face was pale, and she only said, 'Thank you.'

He lightened his tone a bit. 'There's something you might have missed, if you've been neglecting your post.'

She raised a brow in question.

'Lady Avery has returned.'

That did capture her interest. 'Has she?'

'Indeed. She ran out of money and the valet ran off with the jewels. She's returned to London.'

'And what of Lord Avery?'

'By all accounts, he's taken her back.'

'Oh, but I am so proud of him! How he must have missed her. I hope they can find happiness in each other, now.'

'I do as well, for he's little chance of finding it elsewhere.'

Her brow furrowed. 'What do you mean?'

'I mean the poor man's a laughing stock—even more so than before.'

'Because he loves his wife?' She looked indignant.

'Because he looks a besotted fool, and men are...well, men. Society will shun them. They may establish their own circle, as Lord and Lady Holland eventually managed, but Lord Avery's political influence will falter as his supporters scurry away.' Much like his own, Charles thought with some irony. 'Like rats before a fire.'

The dismay on her face both touched him and ignited a twinge of exasperation. 'Have you learned nothing from my situation over the last months? From your own dip in the scandal broth?'

'Yes,' she shot back. 'I've learned that London is full of hypocrites, people who won't hesitate to criticise others even while perpetrating worse behind closed doors.'

'Exactly!' Charles said. 'Then you've learned the most valuable lesson regarding the *ton*. You can get away with almost any evil if you are discreet. The only unforgivable sin is to get caught.'

She was ablaze with anger now. 'Token sanctimony. It is ridiculous! How can you so calmly accept such a gross injustice?'

Lord, but she was beautiful when she was in a passion. Charles shook his head as the import of her question sunk in. 'Because I've already tried to fight it, and lost. Can you have forgotten my misspent youth? I broke every one of society's rules and flaunted each misdeed. I flung their hypocrisy into their faces—and what did I reap? Ruination and destruction.'

'Destruction?'

He'd said too much. The warning was in the arrested look on her face. 'Yes,' he hedged, 'even now, after so much time, it is destroying my political career. I fashioned my detractor's most lethal weapon myself.'

She didn't look entirely convinced that's what he had meant. 'Lord and Lady Avery know this, Sophie,' he said, trying to get her back on to the thread of the conversation. 'I'm sure they've accepted it. They'll be happy in their private life, even if they must give up their public one.'

'They should have both. They've harmed no one but themselves. If they can forgive and embrace each other still, what can anyone else say of it?'

Her anger faded, and the look in her eye became thoughtful, crafty. Charles sucked in a breath. He'd seen that look enough to know that trouble followed.

'All that is required is a little help.'

'Help?' he asked.

'Yes, someone to show their acceptance and support.'

Charles considered. 'You may be right. Some of Avery's cronies are very well placed. He might muddle through with their assistance.'

'I hope so.' She sighed. 'Have you seen them?'

'Me?' Charles snorted. 'I have no doubt that mine is the last face either of them wish to see.'

'On that score I would guess you are wrong. Lord Avery strikes me as a very honourable man.' She lifted her chin, looking him direct in the eye. 'They would both be easier if given the opportunity to apologise to you, I imagine. At the very least you might let them know you hold no grudge. Your good wishes would probably hold more weight than anyone else's.'

Charles closed his eyes and rubbed his brow. He had always hated it when she was right. 'No doubt you are correct. I shall call on them.'

'Good.' Now that she had won her point, she grew brisk, businesslike. 'I hope you enjoyed the tour and approve of the house,' she said, turning to the window as if unsure of his answer.

'You know I do. It is lovely.' *Like you,* he wanted to say.

'I'm so glad you like it.' She turned back. 'It's time I changed for dinner, and I must speak with your mother first. We have been dining early. I hope it will be acceptable? It's a bit late to ask Cook to put it back.'

He nodded and she continued. 'Shall I see you in the drawing room around six, then?'

'Six,' he affirmed. He watched her go, and then sank into the chair behind the desk. His head was spinning. He stared out of the window, the glinting light catching his eye again, and decided what he needed was a walk. Time to think, to sort all the conflicting loyalties that beset him, to decide what it was he wanted. Of Sophie, of his life. Perhaps he would have it all solved by dinner.

He would not care to wager on it.

Chapter Fourteen

Sophie sat before her mirror as Nell brushed the plaster dust from her hair and wrestled it into a semblance of decorum. She'd waited too long for a bath, but she'd had to speak with Lady Dayle. Lord Avery and his wife were in need of aid. She knew she was right about their situation. It could be brought about, with just a little nudge. It was fortunate indeed that Lady Dayle agreed; it would be so much easier with her help.

She had a plan, but it was risky. It would also provide the definitive answer to her lingering questions about Charles's character. Would he prove himself to be her Charles or Miss Ashford's? It was time he made a decision, so they could all get on with their lives.

Her Charles. How beautiful it sounded. She'd thought she'd been ready for his arrival, armed against him with logic, determination, and a healthy dose of fear for how easy it had been for him to hurt her. She'd meant to take this opportunity to begin the process of withdrawal, to begin to unravel the ties that bound them. It hadn't been easy when, instead of resentful and angry, he'd been apologetic and sincere. Yet she had held firm.

Until she heard Lord and Lady Avery's story. Now she wavered. Sophie had felt for the couple since she'd first heard of their strange relationship. She had wanted to help them, would have helped them in any case. To see love triumph over anger, hurt and betrayal was a worthy cause on its own. But now she had an ulterior motive.

The situations were not exact, but similar enough. Surely if Charles saw Lord Avery survive such a scandal with social acceptance and political influence intact…

'Would you hand me the comb, miss? The one with the pearl inlay?' Nell broke into Sophie's scheming.

'Thank you, almost done.' When the maid spoke again, she sounded hesitant. 'I know we haven't spoken of it for some time, but I thought you might like to know that the servants here are a good bit freer with their gossip than the viscount's London help.'

Sophie started to turn, but stopped at Nell's cry of dismay. 'Sorry, Nell. Have you heard something of interest?'

'Something small, but I thought you would want to know.'

Sophie nodded encouragingly.

'There's talk of old Lord Dayle's death, like we'd heard before.' Their eyes met in the mirror. 'There's also a footman here who says that old Lord Dayle was furious with his lordship at the time.'

Sophie snorted. 'That's nothing, Nell. They didn't get on at all. The old gentleman was angry at Charles for half of his life, at the very least.'

'Not just angry, John says, but furious.' Nell insisted.

'Wouldn't talk to his lordship after the bad news of his brother came, wouldn't be in the same room with him. Not even for the funeral.'

'That does sound excessive. And hurtful.' Sophie sighed. 'Poor Charles, I wonder what was going on between them?' It would explain a few things too. If Charles's father died before they made up the quarrel, then it was no wonder he was sensitive about the subject.

'It's led to some pert talk about his lordship below stairs, miss.'

Sophie sent her a sharp glance. 'I hope you set that right?'

'You can be sure of it, miss,' Nell said with firm satisfaction. 'It won't be happening again.'

'Thank you, Nell. I'm sure his lordship would thank you for your loyalty as well.'

'I do my duty.'

Sophie turned and clasped the girl's hand. 'You do so much more than that, and I hope you know I appreciate it.'

She was still coming to grips with this latest piece of the puzzle as she made her way to the drawing room a little later. Charles and his father had a turbulent history, it was true, but surely such a breach was extreme, even in a time of grief. She wondered if she dared to ask Charles about it. She would gauge his mood before she considered it.

It didn't look promising. Charles was already in the drawing room when she entered, frowning up at a painting hung in the formerly blank spot on the chimneypiece.

'Oh,' Sophie exclaimed. 'Lady Dayle has had the portrait hung!' She stepped up next to Charles to examine the effect.

It was all that she could have asked for. The colours blended well with the room and the subject matter was both appropriate and heart-warming. It was a lovely painting of Lady Dayle, clad in a crimson gown of the old, panniered style, her arm around two of her young sons, and the youngest seated on the floor at her feet. Phillip, the eldest, stood at her side, staring forward with a serious mien. Charles stood next to his brother, with an armful of squirming puppy and an eager look on his face as he looked up at his elder sibling. Jack, still a toddler, sat on the floor surrounded by blocks and more puppies.

'I like it there very much,' Sophie said. 'What do you think, Charles?'

She could see what he thought on his face. His expression was pained, haunted. 'Are you all right?' she asked with concern.

'Yes.'

His voice sounded strained. Sophie could see that his colour was pale as well.

'Do you think that it is formal enough for this room?' he answered at last. 'The family has more than its share of masterpieces, I'm sure we could find something more appropriate.'

'It's a Reynolds,' she said simply. 'I find it charming.'

He stood, silent. Sophie pursed her lips and decided to say what was in her heart. 'I think that it is a matter of significance that your mother chose it. After all the pain she's endured in the last two years, don't you think it is a sign of healing that she can look on this with pleasure?'

Charles flinched as if her words had actually hurt him. Still he did not respond. His eyes were closed now, as if he couldn't bear to look at it any more.

'Charles?'

He started and opened his eyes. Sophie began to be concerned.

'Shall I remove it?' she asked.

'No.' He sighed. 'I can endure it, for my mother's sake.' He turned then and went to pour himself a drink.

She watched him down his drink and pour another. She thought of what Nell had told her earlier, remembered the accusation she had flung at Charles in anger, in this very house. *Do you think to turn yourself into your brother?*

'What happened to Phillip, Charles?' she asked softly.

'What?' His head snapped toward her and he nearly dropped his glass.

'What happened to Phillip? Everyone in Blackford Chase knows he died at Waterloo, but no one is sure just why he was there. It's something of a mystery.'

Charles's gaze burned into hers. He didn't want to answer, she could tell. Though his face was rigidly set, emotion churned in his eyes. For a moment she feared he would walk out, rather than answer.

Eventually, though, resignation replaced the stiff wariness. He set down his drink and moved away from her, away from the painting. His eyes, when he finally began to talk, were focused on the fancy scrollwork before him, but Sophie guessed that what he saw in his mind's eye was very far away indeed.

'Phillip was very interested—obsessed, almost—with the war.' His voice was distant, unconnected, as if he was merely repeating a story. 'From the beginning, when we were younger, he would read every article, every dispatch printed. He longed to purchase a commission, to serve as an officer. I think he would have if it hadn't been for...'

'His duty?' prompted Sophie.

'Yes, duty.' He made it sound like a dirty word. 'And Father. You can imagine his feelings on the subject.'

Sophie grimaced. 'Yes. I think I can.'

'Though he couldn't follow his inclination, Phillip became involved in the war effort here at home. He worked with the Foreign Office. He was very busy, and happy, I thought.' Charles fell silent a moment. When he continued, he spoke low, and Sophie had to strain to hear him. 'Until Napoleon escaped and returned to France.'

'What changed then?'

'Phillip did. He was in a frenzy. So was everybody, if you remember, so I didn't place too much importance on it. Until it was too late.'

Silent, Sophie waited.

'You would have thought that Boney's sole purpose was to give Phillip a second chance at him. He was wild to go to Brussels, along with much of society. Father, of course, would not hear of it. But when Castlereagh himself asked Phillip to carry important messages to Wellington, Phillip agreed.'

She was in complete sympathy with Charles's brother. She knew how difficult it was to yearn, with no hope. She could well imagine what had happened next. 'He got there, and he stayed, didn't he?'

Charles glanced askance at her. 'Yes, he did.'

She understood about Phillip, then, but not about the level of pain in Charles's voice. It was not just the pain of loss. There was something more here.

'Yes. I'm sure he was useful, and wildly happy,' Charles continued. 'Wellington's staff was swelled with all manner of people who didn't belong there by the time they engaged the French, but Phillip made himself valuable.'

'And he fell at Waterloo, along with so many other good men,' Sophie mused.

'No.' The single word was harsh, as if ripped from Charles's soul.

'No? But the lists, I'm sure—' Sophie stopped, horrified by the look on Charles's face as he turned around.

'Yes, that's what everyone believes.' Charles spoke in a rush now, as if in a hurry to spit the story out and be done with it. 'The truth is that Phillip died before the battle even began. Wellington went out riding that morning, inspecting the area and the troops. Phillip numbered among the men with him. There was a battalion positioned on the edge of the Hougou-mont fields, close to the French. They lost nerve and broke position, turned to flee long before even a shot was fired. The Duke saw them, rode them down and rallied them.' Charles stopped and drew a deep breath. 'But as he rode back, a few of the disaffected men fired shots after him. None hit him, as you would know,' his voice was but a whisper when he finished, 'but one killed my brother.'

'My God,' Sophie said, sinking into a sofa.

'It was remarked how history might have changed, had those men been better shots.' His voice was bitter. 'I can't help thinking I might be tempted to exchange history for my brother's life.'

'Oh, Charles, I am so sorry. Such a waste of a fine man.' It was tragic, even more so for the reckless stupidity asso-ciated with it. 'No wonder your father was inconsolable.'

Charles winced and paled even further. Sophie stared as he

visibly gathered himself back under control. 'Wellington himself came to give my parents the story and to express his sorrow.'

'A fine consolation that was to your grieving mother, I'm sure,' Sophie said, just as bitterly.

'It did help my father. A bit.'

'Thank you for telling me.' She could see what it had cost him.

'It's time you knew. But I would ask you not to mention it to my mother. She's so improved.' His look was intense. 'I know I have you to thank for that.'

'She's a lovely woman, I love her very much.'

He didn't reply, but he took a step towards her, eyes fastened on her face. Sophie drew a deep breath.

'Such serious expressions!' Lady Dayle had arrived. 'Charles, you are not forcing Sophie to talk of dismal economics, are you?'

'No, nothing so bad as that, Mother.'

Sophie watched as he summoned a smile from somewhere and returned his mother's embrace.

'Good, you'll have plenty of time for that later. I want to know what you think of the house!'

Chapter Fifteen

The tragedy of Phillip's death was still echoing in Sophie's head the next day, as she rearranged yet another group of fresh flowers and tried to calm her nerves. The guests would be arriving soon, but that was only one of her worries. Her thoughts were in a whirl, and she couldn't choose one to focus on for very long. So many fragmentary troubles, and they seemed to be converging on her now.

Phillip's story, though horrifying enough, still didn't seem to explain the depth of Charles's pain. No, depth seemed the wrong word. Was there a *timbre* of something like pain? It also failed to explain the strain between Charles and his father. Sophie remained convinced that there was still a piece of the puzzle missing.

On top of that mystery, she was going to have to deal with Mateo, whose hints had been growing broader and more insistent, and, she was very much afraid, were leading to a proposal of marriage.

Lord and Lady Avery's situation still troubled her, as did her uncertainty about her own future. And then there was her biggest problem of all…poking his head around the dining-room door.

'Ah, Sophie,' Charles said, entering with a paper in hand. Obviously ready to greet his guests, he was immaculately handsome in high boots, buckskin breeches, and a form-fitting coat of soft brown. 'Here's a note from your uncle, saying he cannot join us until tomorrow. Mr Cardea, however, will be coming in today as planned.'

'Thank you.' She took a deep breath. Charles was not the problem so much as her undisciplined reactions to him. 'I'll be sure to tell your mother. It will throw off her seating at dinner.'

Sophie wondered if Charles knew why her uncle was delayed. If he didn't, she didn't wish to be the one to tell him. Mateo had written to her with the news.

'It appears we must congratulate him when he arrives.' Charles spoke with studied casualness. 'He's to be appointed Treasurer of the Board of Trade.'

She spoke carefully. 'I know it must be difficult for you to see him succeed further. After he won the position you had hoped for, I mean.'

'I'm not so shallow as that. I'm pleased for the man. I'm sure he'll perform splendidly.'

'Of course. Thank you for sharing the news.' She turned back to her arrangement, but he didn't leave. She could feel his presence hovering in the doorway.

'Didn't I see you arranging those flowers earlier this morning?' he asked.

She laughed and tucked the last bit of foliage back in among the blooms. 'Yes, I suppose I'm trying to entice the butterflies in my stomach to abandon me for greener pastures.'

'You're mixing your metaphors,' Charles said with a quick smile. 'You are nervous.' He came into the room, all solicitous concern. 'You cannot be worried about the house—it's superb. Everyone who sees it will fall in love.'

Sophie took a step back. She exercised her woman's prerogative and changed her mind—Charles was indeed the problem. There was something seductively different about him since he'd come back to Sevenoaks. His eyes were less guarded; he spoke to her more easily and openly. He'd shared the story of his brother's death.

Her reaction was confusing and convoluted. Part of her rejoiced. *At last.* At last he was accessible, approachable, sharing himself with her. The other part of her didn't trust it. She kept waiting for the walls to slam back up, for his eyes to turn cold and for him to shut her out. It was nerve-racking, especially when she thought of the invitation that had gone to London this morning. 'No, I'm satisfied with the house. It has turned out to be more beautiful than even I had hoped.'

'What is it, then?'

She shook her head.

He rounded the corner of the dining-room table and paused. 'Never tell me you are worried over your own reception?' He raised a brow and his voice grew slightly mocking. 'What happened to the Sophie who didn't care what others thought of her, who didn't need anyone?'

She met his eye with an unwavering gaze. 'I've learned the danger of needing people in a hard school, haven't I?' She didn't add that the blow he had dealt her had been the hardest lesson of all.

He blanched. She might not have accused him outright, but he understood.

'Perhaps you have taught me something after all,' she continued. 'I've grown up a little. I may not enjoy depending on the goodwill of others, but I can see that it is sometimes a necessity.'

He acknowledged her barb with a nod. 'Truly, though, you have no need to fear. You, at least, have champions and they have defended you well. When you are ready, you will be speedily accepted back into society.'

'I have no wish to go back into society,' she said firmly. 'I only wish to be free to continue my work.' She folded her arms in front of her and shot him a defiant look. 'It's quite ironic, isn't it? In Blackford Chase they abhorred me because I was different. But it is those very differences that titillate the *ton,* my eccentricities that distract them from their deadly *ennui,* and win their acclaim.'

'But don't you see,' he pleaded harshly, 'that is the very type of notoriety that will have them turning on you in the end. The acclaim won't last. That's why I—'

'I don't care,' she interrupted. She couldn't bear to hear it all again. 'I don't wish to be a darling of the *beau monde.* As long as I can use my momentary popularity as a springboard for my design work, I shall be happy.'

'And if you cannot?'

'Then there are plenty of wealthy cits who need furniture too. Or perhaps I will heed Mateo's advice and pursue my career in America.'

'What?' His shock was genuine. He moved away from the table and towards her. 'That is the most ridiculous thing I have ever heard. Absolutely not.'

Her anger was genuine too. Was it the same old reaction? Indignation at the thought of someone else using his plaything? Or perhaps worse. Perhaps he didn't believe she could succeed there either. 'I beg your pardon?' He was nearly upon her now. He was coming too close. 'You have no right—'

He silenced her with his kiss, deep and dark with instant desire. His arms encircled her, crushed her to him.

No, this is wrong, she thought, even as she melted into his arms. She needed to be free of him, of her frightening dependence on him, because she didn't know yet if she could trust him. But the orphan inside of her refused to listen. *Home,* that voice said, revelling in the taste and scent of him, relishing the warmth and security of his embrace.

It's an illusion, her logical self insisted, *not real.* But logic was soon silenced by sensation, drowned in desire. Instead of pushing him away, her hands were wrapping about him, pulling him close, curling through his hair.

No, she wasn't fighting him. She was opening wider, inviting him in. He tasted of coffee, and rich, bittersweet sin. She was meeting him stroke for stroke, entwining her tongue with his in a thrilling, languorous dance.

Charles groaned in response, further drowning any voice of protest. His hand was low on her back, urging her against him. She went willingly and allowed her own hands to roam, to trace a restless path over the muscles of his back and then lower. He returned the favour, cupping her bottom and pressing her closer still.

It was lovely, it was intoxicating, it was dangerous. Slowly, fear began to succeed where logic had not. He had hurt her, badly. How much worse would it be if she let this go too far?

She was a woman grown, a lonely little girl no longer. She dug deep, summoned her strength and her hard-won wisdom, and broke away.

He protested and reached for her again, but she stepped back. 'No, Charles.' Her anxiety threatened to spill out of her in a heartrending sob, but she forced herself to stand firm.

'Nothing has changed,' she said. 'Yes, we still have this between us—' she made a vague, encompassing gesture '—but so do we still have all the problems.'

'Then let us face them together,' he said.

'I—' She couldn't say the words out loud. *I'm afraid.* So she took the coward's way out. 'I'm sorry.' She kissed him softly, and then she turned, fighting tears, and slowly climbed the stairs.

It was only a little later, after Sophie had had a chance to gather her wits and her resolve, when Nell came to her room.

'Mrs Hepple's having a tussle with the drapery in the blue guest room,' the maid said with a grin. 'She asks if you would lend a hand?'

'Of course,' but it was with a heavy heart and a slow stride that she entered the hall and headed for the blue room. Lady Dayle, climbing the staircase, list in hand, hailed her as she passed.

'Nearly time, now. Are you dressed and ready, my dear?'

'Yes, my lady.'

'Oh, my darling, what is it? You look positively blue-devilled!' The viscountess bustled over and, a hand on each shoulder, looked searchingly into her face. Clucking to herself, she took Sophie's hand. She glanced about the empty hall then shrugged, and perched herself on the first shining oak step, patting the spot beside her invitingly. 'Come now, sit, and I'll soothe your nerves.'

She was so warm and motherly, Sophie couldn't resist. She chuckled and sat down. 'I can't stay, Mrs Hepple needs me, and what would she say if she came out and found you like this?'

'Pish! If she caught a look at your face, she'd hustle off to bring you a dish of tea, then she'd likely perch on your other side.'

Sophie laughed.

'That's better. Now, what is it that has brought you so low?'

She sighed. The truth wasn't an option. But her troubles with Charles were only a part of it, in any case. 'I'm not certain, exactly. Did you ever have the notion that you've arrived at a short time in your life that will affect all the rest of your years? It's ridiculous, really, since I suppose one could say that about nearly any moment.'

Lady Dayle smiled. 'Not ridiculous. I understand that feeling. It's wonderful and terrifying at once, isn't it?'

Sophie could only nod. To her horror, she felt tears gathering again.

The viscountess took her hand and sandwiched it between her own. 'Let me tell you what it is that I admire most about you.' She brushed a wayward curl off Sophie's face and continued, 'You've faced a great many challenges in your young life.'

Sophie tried to protest, but Lady Dayle shook her head and went on. 'I know, we all encounter our own obstacles in life's path. Sometimes they appear so large they blot out the sun, the other side, and it seems, any possibility of happiness, ever again.'

She took Sophie's chin in her hand and smiled into her

eyes. 'But you never let those obstacles stop you. Oh, I've heard you rail in shockingly unladylike language, when things don't go your way.' She let Sophie go and grinned. 'And sometimes it feels as if you're doing nothing but pounding your head against it in frustration, but you are strong. Always, you pick yourself up and find a way to scramble over.'

'Or chisel through,' Sophie said softly.

'Or chisel through,' the viscountess agreed. 'I've never seen you give up, Sophie Westby, and that is a rare thing in this world.'

Lady Dayle dropped her chin and put her arm around her. Sophie leaned gratefully into her comforting embrace. 'The bright side, I've found,' the viscountess continued, 'is that once you make it past the hard spots, there always seems to be something good on the other side.'

'Like you,' said Sophie, a single tear sliding down her cheek.

'No, it's you who has been a blessing to me, dear child. And I promise, even if we hit some obstacles in the next few days, there will be better things to come.'

They sat then, arms around each other, drawing strength, until the jingle of harness outside announced the first guests.

'I'll wager you a bolt of fine sarcenet that it's Emily who's here first.' Lady Dayle grinned.

'I'm not fool enough to take that bet.' Sophie laughed.

Arm in arm, they went down to greet their guests.

Chapter Sixteen

The afternoon had been taken up with the greeting of guests and with showing off the splendours of the newly refurbished house. It had been hectic and chaotic, leaving Charles no time to consider what he'd done with Sophie in this very room this morning. Now, however, he found himself seated at the head of a happy, boisterous group, the recipient of enough birthday toasts to float a fleet on, and in possession of plenty of time for reflection.

Ignoring his guests was a bad idea, though, and useless besides. Only one thought continually emerged from his self-absorption. He wanted Sophie, needed to have her in his life. Whether he should, or could, have her were two very separate issues that he still had no answer for, but on that one point, he was firm.

It was with some trepidation, therefore, that he had welcomed the Ashfords to his home. They must suspect that their inclusion in this gathering meant more than it did. In truth, what it meant was that his mother's vaunted perception must be a little slow in this instance. Now he must find a way to communicate the change in his intentions without insulting them.

It seemed an easy feat compared to the Herculean task of keeping his temper around Mr Cardea. The man's charming manner, his easy smile, and, above all, his constant, adoring attendance on his cousin infuriated Charles, as did the suspicion that Sophie's uncle might be promoting a match between them. He resolved to watch the man carefully once he arrived.

Another toast was proposed, this time by Sir Harold, and echoed by Mr Chambers, the young nephew who had accompanied him. Charles smiled, drank, and tried not to gauge just how far down Sophie's décolletage Mr Cardea, seated next to her, could see.

At last the final cover was removed. Charles relaxed a little as his mother led the ladies away.

Too soon.

'Another ridiculous English custom,' Mr Cardea announced in ringing tones. 'In Italy we know that it is the ladies who make such gatherings interesting.' He stood and Charles gaped as he saluted the astonished men and followed in the ladies' footsteps.

Silence reigned a long moment as the port was brought out. Yet soon a strange, creaking sound echoed in the room. It was the protest of Lord Ashford's corset, as he wheezed with laughter. Soon all the men were howling along with him. Even Charles chuckled a bit and raised a glass in salute to a brilliant manoeuvre.

He found he was not alone in his disgruntlement, however, when the gentlemen did rise to join the females in the drawing room, only to find them clustered around the pianoforte, listening, enraptured, to Mr Cardea's pleasing baritone.

'I can see what the man's about,' complained Mr Huxley. 'There's no doubt the ladies adore him, but his attention to Miss Westby is too marked. I shall mention it to the lady's uncle myself, for I can't approve of such close cousins as a match.'

'Why ever not?' asked Mr Chambers. 'It's done all the time.'

'Useful means of keeping property in the family,' added Mr Lowder.

'I believe the ancient Egyptians actually married their siblings for just that reason,' Jack said helpfully.

'I still think the relationship too close. I just cannot like it,' said Mr Huxley, and he went to extricate Sophie from her cousin by means of an argument over the superiority of English versus American roads.

For once Charles found himself in sympathy with the man, but not for the professed reasons. Watching the others squabble over Sophie made him insane. It roused some hidden primitive instinct that made him want to snatch her away, warn them off, and shout 'Mine!' to every male in the vicinity.

But he had no right to do so. Worse, he didn't know if he should.

He eased his way through the room, stopping to laugh at a ribald joke told by the lively Mr Chambers, exchanging a few comments with Sir Harold, but gnawing on that thought all the while.

He must own up to the truth. Much as he might wish it, perhaps he wasn't the man for Sophie. All the harsh words he'd spoken to her haunted him. The stark memories of her sweet offers of friendship and his own emotional retreats mocked him. He'd been horribly unfair to her. No doubt she would be better off with someone else.

He distinguished her throaty chuckle of delight from across the room. It triggered the image of her radiant smile and shining eyes. She'd brought laughter back into his life, and companionship and passion.

He watched her, studying the lovely angles of her face, and recalled how her eyes looked when heavy with desire, how ripe and full her mouth appeared when she'd been kissed. He remembered how she felt in his arms, all curves and tangible need. And he knew. Without further doubt. No, she wasn't better off with any of these milksops. She was his. He would find a way to make it so.

He would begin this very moment, he pledged, as he saw a pained expression cross her face, by rescuing her from Miss Ashford and her mama.

His mother, he found, was there before him. 'I think that Hannah More is a very fine person,' Lady Dayle was saying.

'Yes,' agreed Miss Ashford, 'Mama is a great admirer of hers.'

'But in this time of post-war distress, I think there are very many other charitable institutions you might consider,' Emily Lowder said with conviction.

'Mama and I have agreed to donate the money to the Society for the Suppression of Vice. Mama has had the fortune to meet both Mr Wilberforce and Mrs More, and has high hopes of being mentioned in that great lady's next edifying book.'

Charles was standing behind Mrs Lowder and heard her mutter something under her breath about not seeing Lady Ashford's performance at the ball.

'Indeed,' said Lady Ashford, 'Hannah More is a saint. She does so much for the unfortunate, all the while encouraging them to become honest, industrious and accepting of their lowly path, which was, of course, assigned to them by the hand of God.'

Charles decided it was time to interrupt. 'May I join you, ladies?' he asked.

'Please, sit down, dear,' his mother replied, moving over and indicating the bench she was sitting on. 'This is sturdy enough to hold two.'

Charles sat, admiring the bench as he did. It was a clever piece; the scrollwork was a mirror image of the moulding on the wall behind it. 'This is one of my favourite changes in the room,' he said with a nod to Sophie.

'Indeed, I am very proud of you, Sophie,' said Mrs Lowder. 'The whole house is quite transformed. It's hard to believe how much you've accomplished since we picnicked here.'

'It was clever of you to design the features in the room to match the furniture,' conceded Lady Ashford.

'Actually, it was the other way around. I designed the furniture to match the lovely plasterwork done in the last century,' Sophie replied in a pleasant tone.

'Ah, I'd forgotten that you dabble in furniture design as well.' Charles thought Miss Ashford sounded sour.

'Now here is an example of a worthy charity for you, my dear,' his mother said.

Sophie made a sound of protest, but his mother did not heed her. 'Please, Sophie, this is exactly the sort of effort that Miss Ashford might not be familiar with.' She turned back to the ladies. 'Sophie founded the workshop that makes her furniture with her own funds. Her foreman, Mr Darvey, was in the Corps of Royal Engineers. He lost a leg in the march on

Toulouse, unfortunately, and was sent home with no pension, a broken man.'

Charles did not miss the look of distaste that passed over Lady Ashford's face, but his mother seemed oblivious. 'Sophie found him selling exquisite little carvings in the street, just trying to survive. Now he has a respectable position and recognition as a talented artisan.' She beamed proudly at Sophie. 'They have provided work for local men as well as taking on quite a number of veterans with no place to go.' She gestured to the room at large. 'You can see the quality of the work they have done.'

Charles did not hear the Ashford ladies' responses. He had been seized by a flash of memory. Sophie, leaning down from Jack's cabriolet, talking earnestly with a man in a ragged regimental jacket. He remembered the slip of paper and the look of bemused hope on the man's face.

He remembered the thick portfolio she'd had the first day they had met again in London. He remembered his mother mentioning to someone that the proceeds from Sophie's book were to be donated to a veterans' charity.

He'd just spent over a year toadying, courting the goodwill of influential, but inflexible, men. All for the greater good, he'd told himself. Once he had achieved his goals, he could be of use; help his fellow man, help his country through the time of transition that lay ahead,

And all the while he had been making grand plans, telling himself and others how many issues they faced, how many people stood in need of their support and assistance, Sophie, this little slip of a girl, had been out there providing it.

His thoughts flew back over the months. He'd dragged

himself out from his dark and dank hiding hole of grief, talked fustian with narrow-minded fools, listened to self-serving rationalisation, smiled when his heart was breaking, danced when he wished nothing more than to lie down and die. And what did he have to show for it?

Nothing. An anonymous enemy, a shattered reputation, a stalled political career. He lifted his gaze, stared at Sophie's embarrassed countenance. Thwarted love.

He knew then, with an excruciating pang, that she'd been right all along. They had never really known each other.

Sophie was no flighty, capricious girl. She was an incredible woman, more beautiful on the inside than the out. And he, he was a hopeless fool.

He could stand it no longer. He had to get away. He rose, took his leave of the ladies, excused himself to the gentlemen, then left the drawing room, went out the back and set out for the lake.

Sophie watched Charles leave the room. The look he had given her before he stood to go had been disturbing, unfathomable.

She couldn't blame him if he was disgusted with her. She was ashamed of herself. Today, for the first time in her life, she had acted the coward and let fear rule her.

The question was, was she going to continue to allow it?

'Wherever has Lord Dayle gone to?' Lady Ashford asked after a little while had passed. 'I can't approve of a host who deserts his party without a word.' She looked at her daughter with displeasure, as if it were her fault.

'I notice that Sir Harold has also absented himself,' Lady

Dayle answered. 'No doubt some vastly important political matter is detaining them in the library.'

'Oh, I'm sure you are right,' the baroness said, somewhat mollified. 'Do you believe they will return soon?'

'Hard to predict. Sometimes these political conversations can take hours,' Lady Dayle said with a shrug of her shoulders. 'Would you care for more tea? Miss Ashford, if you feel up to it, I shall bring out the backgammon board.'

'Thank you, but no,' Lady Ashford said, getting to her feet. 'Travelling always tires me. I believe we shall retire. Come, darling, a little extra beauty rest shall not harm us.'

It shan't harm any of us either, Sophie thought uncharitably as the ever-obedient Miss Ashford rose and followed her mother out. She was glad to escape the tiresome pair. Neither seemed inclined to forgive her for bringing the taint of scandal to their ball.

Their exit appeared to be a signal to the rest of the party. Most of the ladies followed suit and retired upstairs. Some of the gentlemen did as well, while others settled down to a game of cards. Sophie rose and made to bid Lady Dayle goodnight.

The viscountess had seated herself at the escritoire, and was scribbling out a note. 'Sophie, dear, before you go up, would you mind leaving this note in the kitchen for cook? I wish for her to see it first thing.' She lowered her voice and leaned in close. 'Grant me a favour, dear, and make sure the kitchen door is unlocked?' she said. 'Cabot said that Charles has gone out walking. I wouldn't wish for him to be locked out.' She stood. 'I always sleep so well in the country, do not you?' She blew Sophie a kiss and started up the stairs.

* * *

The kitchen was quiet and dark, the servants gone to their rest. Sophie placed the note square in the middle of the scrubbed oak table and then checked the door that led outside. Locked. She drew back the bolt and stood with her hand on the knob.

Lady Dayle's words today had greatly affected her. This time the obstacle she must overcome lurked within her own heart. Would she continue to allow fear to rule her? There was only one way to find out. She turned the latch and slipped outside.

It was a gorgeous night. The air was fresh and clear, free of the tension that had lingered in the drawing room. A heavy, nearly full moon hung low over the lake, making magic of the ordinary park.

She stepped away from the door, made her way past the kitchen garden, and set out across the lawn. She knew what she was doing. There was only one reason, after everything that had passed between her and Charles, to seek him out like this.

The risk was huge and potentially disastrous. The heartache would be far worse, if he left her, than the pain that had already scared her so. Yet still she walked, her feet heading unerringly to where the moonlight beckoned her, winking off the waters of the lake, calling to her from the copper cupola of Lady Dayle's folly.

She knew that's where he would be, and she was right. The effect of the moonlight on the Doric columns turned the place into a study of light and shadow. Charles sat in the dark, in one of the comfortable chairs Lady Dayle had had placed here, his head hung in his hands.

She spoke softly into the gloom. 'Charles.'

He raised his head, no hint of a surprise in his face. 'I should have guessed,' he said, no discernible emotion in his voice.

Sophie entered and took a seat near to him. They sat in silence a bit. 'What's wrong?' she finally asked.

'Me. You. The whole damned world. Take your pick.'

She sighed. 'I'm sure it's a tangled combination of the three.' But no problem, however convoluted, stood a chance against his strength of character, his determination to do the right thing. 'I'm also sure that, however problematic, you'll be able to fix it.'

He snorted. 'Now that's where you're wrong. Oh, I might have been arrogant enough to think so, just a few months ago. But you've changed all that.'

She was horrified. 'I have?'

With a muffled oath he stood, banging the chair back against the stone floor. 'Sophie, you don't even know what you've done to me! Before you came back, I was firm in my goals, sure that my redemption was possible, if only I worked hard enough, long enough.'

He strode away from her, striding between the columns with the sinewy grace of a cat. 'Then you slammed into my life like cannon shot, and tempted me.' He glanced back at her, his face twisted. 'So beautiful, so full of life and laughter. I resisted, though, for, as much as I might regret losing you, I knew that there were other things that would haunt me even more.'

She sensed a hint of the answers she had been looking for. She sat up straighter, started to ask, but he continued on, unaware of her reaction. 'Now I see what you have done—with just your stubborn will and your generous heart—and I am ashamed. All my great and lofty goals, all my hard work, and nothing to show for it.'

He turned to face her then, and she thought her heart would break at the grief and chagrin and tenderness she saw in his face. 'You put your talent and your determination to good use. You're the one who has made a difference, in a concrete, human way that I never gave a thought to.'

'I did what I could, based on my circumstances, but you are different. You have a chance to help thousands, to change the course of so many lives.'

'Perhaps once, but my chance seems to be slipping through my fingers. Worse, I don't even know if I want to hold on. Oh, God—' he groaned '—what if I've been wrong all along? I don't know what to think, what to feel. All I know is that I'm tired of pretending.' He turned, propped a hand on the nearest column and stared out again at the lake. 'I don't suppose you know what I mean, do you? You don't pretend, you throw yourself out to the world with no thought of what you might suffer. You put others before yourself and they love you for it.'

'Stop it, Charles. I'm not a saint. Look at all the times you've railed at me for my behaviour, and don't make me out to be something I'm not.'

He laughed, a harsh, ironic sound, and spun abruptly around. Slowly he began to stalk toward her, the moonlight alternately lighting his face and casting it into shadow. 'Sophie,' he said, his voice low, seductive, 'I'd be the last one to call you a saint.' The deep timbre of his voice somehow echoed in the pit of her belly.

'Do you know what you are?' He lifted his hand and tenderly cupped her jaw. 'You're a terror.' His thumb caressed her chin, then brushed her bottom lip, gently, sweetly. 'A beautiful, exasperating, unselfish, great-hearted monster.'

Her every nerve ending was focused on his touch, on the promise of more implicit in his voice. She allowed him to pull her closer, into the shadows as well. 'Thank you,' she said, her voice husky.

He laughed, and this time it was genuine and a little rueful. 'Ah, Sophie, you've turned my world upside down.' He dipped his head to brush her lips with his. Sophie's head swam. A stab of fear tried to surface, but she closed it away, opened instead the door to her longing and let it flood over her.

'You've been the only thing keeping my world right side up,' she whispered.

Her words seemed to snap his restraint. He kissed her again, deeply, surging inside her mouth with quick, possessive strokes, claiming her, marking her as his.

She surrendered to it. Passion flared, hot and low in her belly. A sense of recklessness made her bold and she answered him in kind, entwining her tongue with his with hot, silky strokes.

So long had she dreamed of this. So many nights imagining the tenderness of his touch, the sweetness of his kiss. How often in life are we granted what we want most? And this might be all she ever got. She had no idea how he would react when he discovered her latest scheme. She felt like a thief, stealing these few minutes of happiness when their future was so uncertain, but she didn't care. If the worst happened, she would accept the pain, in exchange for the rare wonder of a dream come true.

Her hunger grew as she gave herself up to the moment, and she slid urgent hands up and over the expanse of his chest, to the barrier of his neckcloth. She tugged experimentally. It loosened a bit, but Charles gave a sudden growl, then quickly unwound the thing and flung it away.

She smiled and he buried his face in the crook of her neck, nipping and kissing. Her chuckle turned to a gasp and then a low moan as his fingers sought the hidden fastenings of her gown.

Suddenly he stopped. 'Wait,' he said. Her breath caught, as effortlessly he took her in his arms and carried her the few steps to the *chaise* that Lady Dayle had placed facing the lake. Crouching down beside her, he smiled up into her eyes and slowly raised her skirts, stopping when they had just topped her knees.

'Ahh,' he said, tracing reverent fingers up one leg and turning it to explore the dark birthmark on the inside of her knee. 'There it is.' He leaned down and pressed a warm kiss on it. Heat flared and travelled the short distance straight up, to where she pulsed with need for him.

He flashed his devil's grin at her. 'Do you know how many times you flaunted that at me when we were children? Every time you ran fast or climbed a tree or hiked your skirts to wade. I never thought a thing of it, then. But I watched you dancing, that first night at Lady Edgeware's ball, and I suddenly remembered. The thought of it has driven me mad ever since.'

She smiled down at him. 'Now it's yours.'

His eyes darkened and he surged up against her. She clutched his shirt, pulled him down to her, kissing him deeply. Quickly then, they tugged, and pulled and tossed clothing aside, neither heeding anything except the next exposed spot to touch, caress and kiss.

When at last Sophie lay in naked splendour before him, Charles could only gaze in awe. He'd been right, she was a terror, but she was also a miracle. She'd forced him to rediscover his heart, an organ he'd done his best to forget. She'd forced him to realise that pain was not the only thing he could feel. He was alive again and free to experience pleasure, and passion.

Neither of which adequately described how he felt looking at her now. He stared, wanting to imprint this image, never to forget. She lay reclined on the *chaise,* a glorious vision of ebony tresses and creamy curves. The moonlight caressed her, flowing over her high and heavy breasts, kissing their taut peaks.

He bent to do the same. His breath flowed hot over her skin, making her gasp in anticipation. He smiled up at her, detoured to place a soft kiss on her mouth, then leaned down and drew her breast into his mouth. Her shoulders slammed back, lifting her breasts higher in a wordless plea. He answered it with hot and languid kisses until she began to squirm in pleasure.

He lifted his head. She cried out, and reached for him. 'You are the most beautiful thing I have ever seen,' he said, his voice rough with emotion.

He turned his attention to her other breast, loving her that way for long moments, while his hand travelled the length of her, exploring and teasing. She tensed a little when his hand strayed lower, but he kissed her worries away. He cupped her, teasing her with strokes as light as a feather, until she relaxed. Then he bent to her breast again, sucking hard and nipping as his fingers spread her, delved deep and drew forth the hot, slick evidence of her desire.

'Oh, my,' she said, sounding breathless with surprise. He found the tender nub at the heart of her, and began a slow, enticing stroke that had her twisting and turning, clutching him like he was her anchor in a storm of passion.

'Charles,' she gasped, 'I want to touch you.'

Already hard as a pike, his shaft stood ramrod straight at the mere thought. With a wordless moan of assent he rolled over, taking up her former position as he reclined back against the scrolled arm of the *chaise.*

Sophie leaned on one elbow, her dark hair spilling down and caressing his chest. Her fingers followed, touching him with the endearing curiosity of innocence, and raining soft little kisses on his neck. He reached for her breast, tracing a slow path around her nipple, but she gave a little shake of her head and pushed his hand away. Deliberately she looked down the length of his body. His manhood stood at attention, pleased with her look of awe.

At her questioning glance he nodded and her hand skimmed downward, grazing him with soft fingertips.

Slowly she slid up and over him, testing the weight of his shaft, eventually wrapping her fingers around the throbbing length. Without thought he placed his hand over hers, showed her how to stroke him and drive him mad. She was a quick learner. Within seconds he was ready to explode.

'Stop,' he rasped, stilling her hand.

She released him as if his heat had scalded her. 'Did I do it wrong?' she asked, frowning.

'No—just right, too right. Any more right and I won't be able to stop.'

Her brow cleared and she leaned down, her breath hot against his mouth. 'Don't stop,' she said, before pressing her mouth to his in a devouring kiss.

He let loose a helpless sound, somewhere between a choke and a sob, and pushed her over and down. Her thighs fell apart and he wedged a knee in between them.

Eyes shining, she gazed up at him, reflecting moonlight and trust. 'Show me what to do,' she whispered.

'Are you sure? We don't have to—' He stopped, praying she said yes.

'Yes.'

He parted her with his fingers once more, feeling a surge of power at her wet, inviting warmth. Her nub was swollen, and he teased it again, softly, then harder, until she was wild again beneath him. He replaced his finger with the head of his rod, rubbing and groaning out loud at the feel of her, wet and slick.

Need hit him like lightning, but he had to go slow. He must. Gently he probed her swollen flesh. Her innocent, uncontrolled movements pulled him in deeper and he groaned. Ever so slowly he tilted his pelvis, stretching her, giving her time to accommodate him. And then he reached her barrier.

He bent and kissed her. 'Hold on,' he whispered, and surged into her, burying himself deep in her sweet flesh.

She gasped and froze. He stilled, sweating and fighting to wait while she grew accustomed to his invasion.

'All right?' he asked quietly.

She nodded and with a heartfelt moan he began to move.

Oh, Lord, but she was tight. She began to move with him and he surrendered to her warm, wet welcome. He lost himself in her, set free from his burdens by the sweetness of her flesh, and the warmth of her spirit.

He thrust hard, settling into a sweet, rocking rhythm. This was going too fast, he was already on the edge, and she couldn't keep up. He eased a hand between them, gently rubbed.

She clutched him, her eyes opening in surprise as sensation overcame her. Her breath came in quick, panting gasps now. Charles kept his rhythm steady and suddenly she moaned into the night. Deep within her, he felt her passage tremble, convulse, pull him even deeper.

It was too much. The pleasure was unbearable. Harder he thrust, deeper, every fibre of his being focused on the hot, sweet feel of her, until, with a shout, he shattered. Pieces of his soul scattered, leaving his heart free to soar in the healing darkness of peace.

They came back to earth together, leaving a trail of tender sighs, soft whispers and gentle laughter. Sophie regretted nothing, was happier, in fact, than she had ever been in her life. This, this was what she had been longing for: this utter contentment, complete acceptance, pure happiness that only grew with each touch.

Anxieties tried to crowd in, but she forced all doubts, all fears from her mind. She breathed deeply, determined to absorb everything while she could. The alien planes of his body, hard and flat where hers was soft and curved, the weight of his limbs entangled with hers, his easy laughter and smooth brow, the pleasure in his eyes when he looked at her; they were a gift to her. These were the things she would remember.

Eventually, of course, reality intruded. But it was with soft laughter and unhurried movements that they dressed and prepared to go back to the house. They took their time, enjoying each other and absorbing the peace of the night. When they reached the low wall that surrounded the kitchen garden, Charles sat down upon it, pulled her on to his lap and wrapped her in his embrace. They stayed and watched as the moon began to sink behind the temple, reminiscing, and talking of inconsequential things, each avoiding any mention of the future.

'Jack mentioned that you have made some progress towards finding your secret enemy,' she said, just to put off their leave-taking a little longer.

'Very little.' Charles sighed. 'It's naught but a wild goose chase. Almost literally.' He made a face and asked, 'You haven't seen any small, wiry men skulking about here, have you? Especially one who moves like a bird?'

Sophie laughed. 'No, none that I've noticed. If he wasn't a plasterer or a carpenter, then I probably wouldn't take notice of him, in any case.' They sat quietly a moment. After a moment's reflection she said, 'I did know a man like that once, though. He even had the name of a bird.'

She felt Charles stiffen behind her. 'You did? What was his name?'

'Mr Wren. He worked for my uncle. It's strange that I remember him, I haven't seen him in years.' She reconsidered her words. 'Well, perhaps not so strange.'

'Why do you say that?' Still wrapped in Charles's arms, she could still feel the tension growing in his frame.

'Oh, I don't know, it's silly, I suppose. I didn't like him. He was the one that always came in my uncle's stead when there was business to be done with our steward. He carried messages and bank drafts and such, and communicated my uncle's wishes.' She paused. 'I used to dread his visits.'

'Why?' The question was low, dangerous.

She considered her words. 'I was young. He was a visual reminder of my uncle's neglect. And not only to me, I think. Whenever he stayed with us, the talk in the village always seemed to start up again. You know what I mean—talk of my uncle's estrangement from my aunt and me, of my father's disgrace, of my unsuitability. All the usual gossip.'

His grip on her tightened. He held her close for a long minute, and then kissed her softly. 'I am so very sorry,' he said.

She twisted in his embrace and smiled into his eyes. 'It's long over. We've come a long way since then, haven't we?'

He kissed her forehead and pulled her close again. 'And this is only the beginning. We'll go on together.'

Sophie wanted it to be true. A little *frisson* of panic seized her at the thought that it might not be so. She sank into the warmth of him, seeking again that feeling of content abandonment. It escaped her, perhaps because Charles's focus suddenly seemed to be far away.

'Charles, what did you mean tonight when you spoke of your redemption?' She regretted the words almost as soon as they were out of her mouth. But perhaps it was for the best, she thought a little desperately, to know where they stood right now.

He said nothing for a long moment, yet his stillness held a different quality now. Wariness? Regret? She wasn't to know.

'It didn't mean anything. It's not important.' He dropped his head, breathed deep in the crook of her neck. 'Let's just enjoy each other tonight.'

The spark of hope born inside her tonight flickered and died away. Her eyes closed. So much lay between them, but not enough. Charles had shared much with her, but he still couldn't open his heart, gift her with his trust.

This was it, then. This time, stolen away from the real world, was to be all they had. She clutched him tightly, determined to wring every drop of happiness she could, to help her survive the cold and lonely years ahead.

'The sky is starting to lighten,' he said, his breath hot against her skin.

She glanced over at the house. 'We should go in separately, don't you think?'

'Yes.' He turned her and kissed her once more, his eyes intense. 'Everything is going to be fine, do you understand?'

She nodded, even though she didn't believe him.

'You go on,' he said. 'I'll stay out here for a bit, then follow you in.'

She went, wrapping tonight about her like a blanket, refusing to think of tomorrow.

Chapter Seventeen

Charles was inside waking his brother before the eastern sky had fully lightened. He was on the road to London before the sun had fully crested the horizon. He still couldn't quite grasp the truth. But he had had it from Sophie's own lips.

Lord Cranbourne was his unknown enemy? It seemed absurd. All this time he'd assumed it would turn out to be someone he had wronged in the past. A cuckolded husband, a woman scorned, a victim of some mindless prank. He could think of nothing he'd ever done to Sophie's uncle.

But perhaps it was the future that concerned Lord Cranbourne? He'd always been involved in politics, always been known to be influential, but in a quiet way, in the background, so to speak. Until recently. He'd won the chairmanship that Charles had wanted, hadn't he? And it had led to even higher placement in the Board of Trade. The ministry was the next logical step. It was working out for Cranbourne just as Charles had hoped for himself. Perhaps that was it? Perhaps it was the talk of Charles's potential that had represented a threat?

His horse was fresh and almost as eager as Charles. The miles sped by quickly, but could not match the fast pace of his churning thoughts. He might not know precisely what Cranbourne's motivation might be, but he meant to find out. And then what? He might expose the man and clear his name. He could have his political future back.

But what would that do to Sophie? One thing Charles knew beyond the shadow of a doubt. He would do nothing that might harm Sophie, not ever again. He had caused her enough pain—it was time he put her happiness first.

What of his own happiness? For so long he had been convinced that such a thing did not exist, that his only path led inexorably toward a future in the government.

Except that path was truly Phillip's. It was Phillip who had paved the way for him, Phillip who had lived for it, who had been talked of as a potential Prime Minister. Charles knew now that his own reach would likely never be as lofty. His past would always block the way to such a future.

For so long he'd been certain, sure that to follow Phillip's dream was the only way to redeem his mistakes. He would take the place of the brother who should have lived. But, just perhaps, there might be other ways to help, other ways he could give back. Sophie had shown him that.

Sophie. Just the thought of her calmed him, gave him hope. They'd exchanged no promises, but last night had changed everything. He knew now that she cared for him as he did for her. Somehow he would sort out this mess, and then they would plan the future, together.

It was mid-morning when he reached London. The streets were bustling and Charles was tired and hungry. He considered stopping at his own house first, but there was no time to waste. He went straight to Green Street.

'Yes?' Lord Cranbourne's butler was cordial, but clearly not impressed with the grubby viscount on his steps.

Charles was in no mood to deal with the snobbery of an upper servant. 'Has Cranbourne set out yet?'

The man looked him up and down a moment, as if deciding whether to answer or not. 'Yes, sir. Not half an hour past.'

A sudden notion hit him. 'Let me see Mr Wren, then.'

The servant looked startled, but recovered quickly. 'I'm sorry, but I don't know who you mean, sir.'

'Do you know who I am?' Charles barked.

'Yes, sir.' There was a wealth of contempt in the simple words.

'Then you know that I have personal as well as political dealings with your master. He's on his way to my house as we speak. Now tell me where I can find Mr Wren.'

The autocratic tone had the desired effect. The butler let down his guard enough for Charles to see his genuine bewilderment. 'But I can't tell you, sir. Wren comes and goes as he pleases, at every hour, but he does not bide here.'

'And you don't know where he lodges?'

'No.' The impudent blighter actually cocked a brow at him. 'I'm sure Lord Cranbourne has that information.'

'Fine, now listen closely. If you see Mr Wren, you be very sure to tell him that his lordship has need of him in Sevenoaks. He is to get himself there, straight away.'

'Yes, sir.' The man watched as Charles began to search his coat pockets. 'I'm to see Cranbourne's solicitor next, but I've lost the direction on the trip.' When he withdrew his hand there was a glint of gold in his palm. 'What was the name, again?'

After a long moment of consideration, the butler answered at last. 'Bridewell, sir, of Bridewell and Locke.'

'Thank you.' Charles tossed the coin and didn't wait to see if the man caught it. He mounted, and then paused to think. After a moment's reflection he turned the horse's head towards St James's Street.

His instincts had been good. Just a quick question to a porter at White's and he had the solicitor's address. A scant few minutes later he was being ushered into the comfortable offices of Bridewell and Locke.

'Good morning, my lord.' The young man rising from behind the formidable desk was definitely not either of the portly gentlemen whose portraits hung in the reception area.

'Good morning. I am Dayle. I'm here to see Mr Bridewell.'

'Alas, Mr Bridewell passed on last year. I am Mr Locke.' At Charles's sceptical glance he added, 'Mr Locke, the younger. My father's health is unfortunately tenuous as well. He has been forced—and I mean that almost literally—to hand the reins over to me.'

'Including the affairs of Lord Cranbourne?'

'Most of them,' Mr Locke said with a cheerful grin.

'Then you may congratulate me, for I am to wed Cranbourne's niece.'

'Indeed, I do offer my felicitations. Are you here, then, to discuss the settlements?'

'Only briefly. We must save the meat of it for a time when Cranbourne and my own man are available. I only wished to inform you so that you may begin to draw up the papers.'

'I don't blame your impatience, when such a sum is involved. You understand, though, that there is little I may do for you until I have word from Lord Cranbourne himself?'

'I see.' Charles spent a fleeting moment wondering if a flash of gold would work as well on Cranbourne's solicitor as it had on his butler. His instincts said not.

'But may I ask you to pass along my best wishes to Lord Cranbourne,' Mr Locke continued, 'and, of course, to your intended?'

'I shall be sure to do so.' Charles began to rise. It seemed useless to question this young man. He doubted he could tell him anything, in any case.

'Thank you,' Mr Locke continued. 'Though it may be a blow to his purse, I'm sure Lord Cranbourne is thrilled to see his niece happily settled at last.'

Charles sat back down and fixed an eye on the man. 'A blow to his purse?'

'Yes. The lady's fortune has been held in trust for her, but it is meant to be a marriage settlement.' Mr Locke returned the same sort of measuring stare Charles had just given him. 'May I ask how long you have been acquainted with the lady?'

'For ever.' Charles smiled, but he could see that the man was serious. 'Since she came to England as a child.' He hesitated, then said, 'I care for her very much.'

Mr Locke smiled. 'I am glad to hear it. Every young lady needs someone who is looking out for her best interests.' His smile faded and he was quiet a moment. 'I shall tell you something that I likely should not. Someone else should know, I think.' He met Charles's eye. 'There is a stipulation in her father's will. If Miss Westby does not marry by the age of five and twenty, her annual stipend will increase a bit, but the bulk of her fortune will pass to the trustee.'

'And the trustee is—?' Charles knew the answer already; he would stake his life on it. But he wanted to hear the words.

'Lord Cranbourne, of course.'

'I see.' And he did. Indeed, suddenly so many things were becoming clear.

'May you put it to good use, sir. Many things can be accomplished with eighty thousand pounds.' He leaned forward, catching Charles's eye again and said in a level voice, 'Many things might be done to gain such a vast sum.'

The man was trying to warn him. It wasn't necessary. His eyes were wide open, now. Charles stood and gripped his hand. 'Thank you for your help, Mr Locke.'

'Congratulations again, my lord.'

Charles vaulted to his horse, his mind awhirl. It was growing late and he still had a long ride ahead of him. Cranbourne might even be at Sevenoaks by now. So much deceit, and over so many years. By God, the coming confrontation was going to be ugly, but the old fraud had much to answer for. Charles's only regret was the thought of what this would do to Sophie.

He turned south, then paused, seized by a sudden thought. Coming to an abrupt decision, he changed direction, heading for Mayfair. He had one more call to make before he returned.

Sophie came late to the breakfast parlour that morning, and had to endure some good-natured teasing from Jack Alden about being the last to rise.

'But she is not the last,' Lady Ashford said, pointedly looking at the empty chair at the head of the table.

'Ah, but she is,' said Mr Alden. 'Charles was actually the first to rise this morning. An urgent matter in town had him gone at first light.'

Lady Ashford had much to say at that news, but Sophie heard none of it. Charles was gone? And at first light. He must have set out just after she left him. Her eggs grew cold as she was beset by a surge of conflicting emotions. She didn't know what to think, to feel. Her insecurities told her that this development could not bode well. Yet she could not help but feel a reluctant relief at the thought of not having to dissemble in front of everyone. How could she pretend not to be affected by his presence after all that they had done to each other last night?

But neither of those reactions was the one that cut most deeply. Without a doubt her overwhelming response was an abiding sense of loss. One night only? It hardly seemed fair. Her appetite fled along with her hope of extending their idyll a little longer. So few moments together—she'd hoped for just a few days more, a few more memories to carry with her once he was gone.

The sound of Charles's name broke into her reverie. 'I'm going to agree with Lady Ashford this time,' Mr Huxley was saying. 'It's raggedy manners indeed to leave us all in the lurch. Wouldn't you agree, Miss Westby?'

'No, I would not,' Sophie said firmly. 'Lord Dayle's work is important. I'm sure he had a good reason for leaving.'

'Indeed,' Mr Alden agreed, casting an approving glance her way. 'Nor are you left in the lurch, or even to your own devices. Charles has asked me to act as host for him today, and he fully expects to be back with us by this evening.'

'Given the state of the country,' said Emily with a quelling glance at Lady Ashford, 'I would say we can forgive Lord Dayle one day.'

'We shan't miss him a bit,' Lady Dayle put in. 'I have a full day planned, and for this evening, a truly splendid surprise.'

Mr Alden set his cup down and stood. 'Miss Westby, if you have finished, will you join me on a walk along the lake path?' He looked over the crowded table. 'Anyone who wishes may join us, of course.'

Nearly the whole party decided to go along, and in the end, Sophie was kept so busy she did not have time for reflection. It was a very good thing too, for last night had provided plenty of fodder for her unruly mind to dwell on. The rest of the group might exclaim over thrilling vistas and picturesque views, but Sophie was preoccupied with the memory of Charles's hands on her body, the musky scent of his skin and the feel of him under her own roving touch.

Such thoughts had to be banished, however, as the party had gathered at the small dock. Sophie fanned her hot cheeks and hoped the sun was bright enough to account for her flush. She watched as the guests separated into groups of two and four and set out in the boats for a leisurely row. Mateo tried to coax her into his boat, but she smilingly declined and urged Miss Ashford to take her place. As the awkward pair attempted to paddle together, she retired to a bench in the shade with Emily.

'You are singularly quiet today, Sophie,' Emily said. 'Are you feeling well?'

'I am fine, thank you.' Sophie summoned a smile for her friend. 'Actually, I was going to make the very same remark to you.'

Emily sighed. 'It's little Edward. He's teething and not sleeping well. I relieved the nurse for a bit last night, and did not get much rest at all.' She glanced about at the few people left on shore. 'In fact, perhaps I shall take this opportunity to go in and check on him.' She grinned. 'If my husband notices I am gone, tell him I may also take the opportunity to take a nap.'

'I shall do so,' Sophie agreed. She sighed as Emily set out for the house and she was left alone on the bench. She was tired as well, albeit for a much more wicked—and more pleasurable—reason. Her thoughts wandered back to the first day they had picnicked here; it seemed so long ago. That day Charles had rowed Miss Ashford on the lake. But then he had come to her, and shocked her with that heady, passionate kiss. Her eyes drifted closed at the memory. Then he had kissed her in self-defence, trying to distract her from probing into his wounded past. Had last night been the same?

She didn't believe so. He'd been open with his feelings last night. They had, at last, come together with all barriers down, and it had been as exquisite as she had dared to dream. Charles had, in fact, already shared the secret he'd been trying to protect that long ago day, or at least a part of it. He'd trusted her with the truth about his brother's death.

And yet, Sophie was not fool enough to believe that Phillip's secret was all that Charles was hiding. She knew instinctively that he hadn't shared everything, and she suspected that whatever the problem was, it was all mixed up with his feelings about his father, his brother, and his political career.

She sighed again, mourning the brevity of the time she'd had in Charles's arms, missing the sense of peace and security that came with his embrace. Already she was back to the familiar realm of doubt, anxiety, and uncertainty.

'Would you, Miss Westby?'

She opened her eyes with a start. 'Excuse me?'

The boats had come back to shore. The little beach was a milling mass of bodies as the gentlemen helped the ladies to dry land and others to their places in the boats. Mr Huxley was standing before her looking earnest. 'I asked,' he said with exaggerated patience, 'if you would pardon me for speaking out of turn this morning. I didn't mean to disparage our host, but I am moved by his neglect of Miss Ashford.'

'Miss Ashford is a guest in Lord Dayle's home, as are we all,' she replied, rather more sharply than she had intended. 'I know of no reason she should feel more slighted than any one of the rest of us.'

He looked a little hurt at the sharpness of her tone. 'I know nothing has been officially announced, but I feel sure there is some understanding, or at least some sort of expectation, between the two of them.'

'Between the two of who?' Mateo asked as he dropped into the seat beside Sophie.

Mr Huxley looked definitely disgruntled by her cousin's lack of formality. 'Between Lord Dayle and Miss Ashford, if you must know,' he answered.

'Mateo, show some manners,' chided Sophie.

'I am sorry. It has been too long since I have actually rowed a boat and it has tired me. I am too much accustomed to standing at the wheel and shouting orders.' He turned to Mr Huxley. 'I do beg your pardon for interrupting. To make amends I shall give you a piece of advice. If nothing has been

announced, my friend, then I would not be so quick to allow
Lord Dayle to cut you out. Miss Ashford's dowry, I hear, is
formidable indeed.'

'I am surprised you do not pursue the lady yourself, then,'
Mr Huxley said stiffly.

'Not I! These English girls are not for me.' Mateo grinned
and raised a brow in Sophie's direction. 'I prefer a woman
with some fire in her blood.'

'But Miss Ashford is no wilting flower,' Sophie protested.
'She tells me she has travelled extensively. I understand she
has been to Bath, and even, I believe, has journeyed to visit
family in Wales.'

'Indeed?' Mr Huxley did seem impressed. 'Perhaps I will
just take this opportunity to ask her about the state of the
Welsh toll roads.' He bowed to Sophie, cast a distasteful look
in Mateo's direction and went to Miss Ashford's side.

Sophie exchanged a grin with Mateo. 'Yesterday I asked you
to cease baiting the man,' she said, 'and what do you do today
but dangle Miss Ashford in front of him like a worm on a hook.'

'Yes, but it was you who gave it that enticing little wiggle.'
They both laughed.

'I suppose we should be ashamed of ourselves,' Sophie said
eventually.

'I refuse. In any case, they will hopefully keep each other
occupied for a bit.'

'Oh, look, an added benefit.' Sophie gestured to Lady
Ashford, who was heading in a determined fashion to the
spot where her daughter stood in conversation with Mr
Huxley. 'Perhaps Lady Ashford will find a new target for her
sniping.' She smiled at her cousin. 'For that I bless you.'

Mateo took her hand. All the laughter had died out of his face. 'I am happy to hear it.' He spoke in the most serious tone she had yet heard from him. 'You give me hope where I begin to fear there is none.' He met her gaze with wistful eyes. 'Perhaps you will bless me in other ways as well?'

Sophie could not mistake his meaning. Indeed, somehow she had known this moment was approaching. Gently she withdrew her hand from his. 'Mateo. I'm sorry, but I cannot. I care for you a great deal though, my cousin, and am so happy to finally have a family again. I hope we can remain so?'

Something dark swam in his eyes, just for a moment. Sophie caught her breath. Then he was Mateo again, shrugging in nonchalance. 'Ah, well.' He reclaimed her hand and pressed an ardent kiss upon it. 'I had to try, did I not? And yes, rest assured, we shall for ever be family.' He smiled. 'Now that I have found you again, you will find it difficult to shake off your cousin Mateo.'

'Miss Westby!' A shout hailed them from the water's edge. Mr Alden waved from one of the boats. 'We've room for one or two more!'

Sophie returned Mateo's smile, pressed his hand, then turned and waved back at the pair in the boat. 'Yes, I'm ready!'

Chapter Eighteen

Charles had still not returned as the dinner hour approached and Sophie's nerves had worked themselves into a frazzled snarl. Bad enough that she had no idea what his absence meant for the two of them, but she was certain that it spelled disaster for the scheme that she and Lady Dayle had already set into motion.

She tried to distract herself by spending a bit of time with her uncle, who had arrived this afternoon. He was in good spirits and eager to talk about his new position. She listened, happy that things were moving smoothly for someone, but after a few minutes Sophie noticed that he was repeatedly rubbing his left arm.

'Are you well, Uncle?' she asked, with a nod towards his arm.

'What? Oh, yes, fine, fine. An old complaint, no need to worry.' He pulled his watch from his waistcoat pocket. 'You'll have to be dressing for dinner soon, girl, so send your cousin in to me on your way out, will you? We've business to discuss.'

Thus dismissed, Sophie did go up to prepare for the

evening's festivities. She dressed carefully, but for once Nell's chatter did not help to ease her nervousness. Heart fluttering in anticipation, she met the rest of the party in the drawing room, only to find that she had not been included in all of Lady Dayle's scheming. She gaped in wonder along with the rest when the viscountess led them, not to the dining room, but outside, to a magical twilight picnic.

Surely the old gods must have conspired with the viscountess, for the evening was idyllic, full of soft light with just a touch of a fresh breeze blowing off the lake. On the other side the folly gleamed in the late sun, rivalling the nearer display of sparkling silver and crystal. The tables stood in readiness, as did an array of servants, ready to serve a lavish feast fit for the Regent himself. A trio of musicians played soft dinner music, adding a final touch of elegance.

The guests were enchanted. Moods were light and conversation flowed as easily as the wine throughout dinner. But all talk ceased as the evening faded and darkness set in. To a man they watched, entranced, as the full moon rose over the lake. Only Sophie closed her eyes against the beautiful sight. In the face of all her uncertainties, she could not bear to look. It was too painful to be reminded of what had transpired under that moon last night.

The sound of wheels in the drive had her snapping to attention, though. She looked to Lady Dayle, but the viscountess had heard it as well. She directed a nod towards Sophie and set out for the house. Sophie saw her whisper something to the staff on the way, and a few moments later the guests' attention was diverted. Everyone gasped as tiny lights began to wink on in the trees. Even Sophie was awed.

The effect was magical, a bit of the vast heavens come to earth for their delight.

The last lantern had only just been lit when the shadowy figure of Lady Dayle could be seen, returning on the arm of a gentleman.

'Oh, good,' Lady Ashford said. 'Lord Dayle must have come back at last.'

Sophie knew better. She clutched the table as the viscountess stepped into the island of light with an older gentleman on her arm. They stood a moment and Lady Dayle cleared her throat and loudly asked for everyone's attention.

'My very dear friends, I ask you to welcome some distinguished new guests to our party. Of course, most of you are already acquainted with Lord Avery.' The gentleman bowed, and a woman stepped from behind them into the light. 'And of course you will remember Lady Avery as well.'

A moment of silence met her pronouncement, broken only by a gasp of outrage from Lady Ashford. Sophie's knuckles grew white as she waited, then she could stand it no longer. Into the breach she stepped. She stood, and dipped a curtsy. 'Welcome to Sevenoaks, my lord, my lady. I'm afraid you've missed dinner, but there is still a sweet course to be served.'

She breathed a sigh of relief as Emily rose then, as well. 'Indeed, come and be welcome. There is a pair of empty seats here next to my husband and I.'

Lady Avery went to her with a grateful look, while Lord Avery stopped to shake hands with Sir Harold. 'Beg pardon, didn't mean to be so dreadfully late,' he was saying, 'one of the horses threw a shoe and we were forced to wait with the carriage while another nag was found.'

Sophie was ready to collapse under the weight of her relief. She and Lady Dayle had taken a definite risk tonight. It had taken courage for Lord and Lady Avery to agree to come, as well. For a moment, she'd thought that, without Charles's influence, their scheme was doomed. But the first step had been taken. Perhaps it was going to come about all right on its own.

But suddenly Lady Ashford was on her feet. 'I will not,' she flung at her husband, before turning to glare at Lady Dayle. 'The effrontery of this is beyond belief! First we are abandoned by our host, then we are subjected to—this!' She waved a hand in Lady Avery's direction. The poor woman kept hold of her dignity and kept her chin in the air.

Lady Ashford grabbed her daughter's hand and hauled her to her feet. Her husband merely hung his head. 'My daughter is an innocent. She is not to be exposed to such—persons. Come, Corinne.' She stalked past the tables, nose held high, and paused to sniff at Lady Dayle. 'We will be packed and gone by morning.'

'That is well—' it was Charles's voice, ringing out of the darkness. Sophie was not the only one startled. She could see several of the ladies in the company clutching their dinner partners '—because I will not tolerate such rudeness to a guest in my home,' he finished.

Everyone watched, spellbound, as Charles stepped forth into the light. Sophie sighed. He was rigged out in full evening garb, all in black and gleaming white. He looked as starkly beautiful as the night sky, but his expression was as formidable as the darkest thundercloud.

Lady Ashford merely continued past him, dragging her daughter behind her. Sophie noticed that Miss Ashford kept her gaze down and did not look in Charles's direction. Lord Ashford rose slowly from his chair, murmured a soft apology to the company at large and stopped to shake hands with Charles. 'Not the outcome we hoped for, eh?' he said with resignation. 'Ah, well.' He trailed after his family.

Another moment of silence hung in the air, but not for long. The sound of a clearing throat brought all attention to Mr Huxley, who had, in his turn, risen to his feet. 'I am sorry to say it, but Lady Ashford's right in this case,' he said, shaking his head. 'Unmarried girl and all, it ain't proper.' He cast a look at Sophie and followed the others towards the house.

'If anyone else is of the same opinion, I suggest we hear of it now.' Charles's tone said clearly that he would not welcome an answer. He cast a stern glance over the group.

After a moment, when he received no response, Charles continued. 'Well, then, let us make our new guests welcome, shall we?' He chuckled and went to shake Lord Avery's hand. 'I would suppose this explains why you were not at home when I stopped today to call on you, on my way out of London.'

Lord Avery shook Charles's hand heartily.

'Come, Avery,' Sir Harold said, 'Tell me what the blasted Whigs have been up to in Parliament since we left.'

'Come and sit with me, Annalise,' Lady Dayle cajoled the still-silent Lady Avery, 'Charles's cook has prepared these marvelous *petite souffléts au chocolat*. I give you my word, it is like tasting a cloud.'

At last Sophie could relax. A bit. The remaining guests erupted into enthusiastic chatter. Lord and Lady Avery were accepted into the group with a graciousness that was clearly meant to outshine the bad grace of those who had gone. Sophie saw them exchange an emotionally charged look across the crowd. Lady Dayle trailed past and paused to share a glance of warm accomplishment with her.

It was a start. Lady Avery might never be welcomed by society's highest sticklers, but she had a foot in the door now. They could claim acquaintance with Viscount Dayle and his family, at least. And it might lead to more, thanks to Lady Dayle, and Emily and the other kind souls here, wise enough to embrace forgiveness and eschew judgments. But first and foremost it was thanks to Charles.

Sophie looked for him, praying he could forgive her meddling and find hope for their own tangled situation in the older couple's success. He was mixing with his guests, making sure that Lord and Lady Avery were settled and going out of his way to stop and chat with every member of the party. Except for her. Never once did he look her way. She unabashedly watched him, however. She noticed that he looked earnest as he spoke, and Sophie guessed he was apologising for his absence today. She hoped he was also thanking them all for their generous acceptance of his new guests.

Gradually, as was inevitable, the excitement began to wear down. Mr Chambers hid a yawn behind his hand and suddenly everyone realised the lateness of the hour. Lord and Lady Avery were persuaded to spend the night and were bustled off to their rooms. Reluctantly, people began to drift towards the house and their beds. Sophie couldn't blame them. It had been an amazing evening.

Any hint of fatigue fled, however, when she saw Charles at last making his way towards her. She smiled a nervous welcome as he drew near. 'Did you really call at Lord Avery's today?' she asked.

He didn't return the smile. His brow was drawn, his face serious as he took her hand. 'Sophie, I must ask you to join me in the library.'

She searched his eyes for some hint of what could be wrong. Had her meddling upset him further than she had expected? She could find nothing hidden in his expression except for grim concern.

'Please, my mother and your uncle will be there as well.'

'Of course.'

In silence the small group gathered in the library. Sophie had seen Jack Alden start to follow, but some signal from his brother had stopped him. Mr Alden had turned back to the party and asked the musicians to play a waltz, so that the remaining guests could dance under the stars.

Sophie sent a questioning glance at Lady Dayle, but the viscountess only shrugged, clearly as mystified as she. Only her uncle appeared to have an inkling as to what was afoot. He wore a strange grin as he watched Charles close the door behind them.

Charles did not look his way. Instead he came and sat by Sophie. She started when he took her hand and cast a guilty glance over at Lady Dayle.

'I discovered, several days ago, the name of the man who had been feeding stories of my past to the papers,' Charles said, 'However, it appeared clear that he was a lackey only, working at the behest of someone else.'

Lady Dayle sent a dark glance towards Sophie's uncle. 'Pray, don't keep us in suspense, Charles. Who was it?'

It was that look that did it; that finally connected all the pieces of the puzzle in Sophie's mind. The comforting smell of old leather faded away, the tense faces about her were forgotten. She was transported, sitting once again in the night air, feeling the relaxed comfort of Charles's embrace turn to a hard wall of tension. She heard the strain in his voice as he asked, *What was his name?*

'It was Mr Wren,' she said aloud, wondering. 'Was it not?' she whispered, coming back to the reality of the library and looking to Charles. She saw the confirmation and concern in his face, and turned hard eyes to her uncle.

He sat, apparently relaxed and unconcerned, but Sophie noticed that he was massaging the palm of his left hand with his right.

'I don't understand,' said Lady Dayle. 'Who is Mr Wren?'

'He is Cranbourne's man,' Charles answered.

Her uncle had at last decided to speak. 'Ridiculous. What would make you say such a thing, Dayle?' he asked, shaking his head. 'I know it sticks in your craw that I am heading the Board of Trade committee, but this is going beyond even your reputation for tomfoolery.'

'It is over, Cranbourne. It is time to tell the truth. It has been you all along. You arranged for that first piece in the *Oracle,* to discredit both Avery and I, and take us out of consideration for the post that you wanted. It worked well, too, did it not?'

'I do not know what you are talking about,' her uncle said. But Sophie saw the truth in his eyes, and something else too. Pain, perhaps, and fear. Good, she thought, letting her shock and fury have full head. He had been hurting her for years— but to find that he had been behind all the attacks on Charles?

She hoped the truth did hurt him. It was time he reaped a little of what he had sowed.

'It is too late to deny it,' Charles told him. 'You made a mistake. You should have stopped with the one story. I probably never would have found you out, and you would still most likely have had your chairmanship. But you didn't stop. You kept grinding the axe, seeking to destroy me. I wonder why?'

Sophie was aghast. She tried to catch Charles's gaze, to somehow communicate how incredibly sorry she felt.

'Of course I deny it. I have never heard such foolishness.' He stood. 'Lady Ashford is correct. You are a rag-mannered young fool.' His face twisted, and he teetered forward a step, but he recovered himself and sent a look of loathing towards Charles. 'You have no idea what you have done. You will pay for this night's work.' He stretched an imperious hand towards Sophie. 'Come, niece. I think it would be best if you and I departed along with the Ashfords.'

But Charles was on his feet as well. 'Do you think I will allow you near her? I don't think you understand, Lord Cranbourne. I know what you are. More snake than man. Cold-hearted and manipulative. Do you think I will see her future ruined for your own selfish ends?' His voice was cold, full of fury and disdain. 'These are people you meddle with, you miserable worm, not puppets on a string. We will dance for your pleasure no longer.' He pointed towards the door. 'You are correct, you will leave, but you will leave without Sophie. I will expose your treachery to the world if you even think to come near her again.'

'Just who do you think will be believed, boy? Whose word is better? And it would come to that, for you can prove nothing,' her uncle snarled. His face was pale and he looked to be sweating profusely.

'I have ample proof. Several damning witnesses, even confirmation from your own household. It should be simple enough to lay it all out before a magistrate.'

'No,' Cranbourne rasped. He was cradling his left arm. He took a step towards the door, but listed to one side and fell back.

'My tonic,' he pleaded. 'In my room.'

'Mother,' Charles said, the fury fading from his face, but Lady Dayle was already ringing for help.

Chapter Nineteen

A part of Sophie wanted to watch, to stand implacable in the face of her uncle's pain, exactly as he had done to her for years. She could not do it. She turned away, unable to look at him any longer, as Charles arranged for help, and sent for a doctor. She refused to watch as he was carried out by a brace of footmen. She acknowledged Lady Dayle's quick embrace, but did not turn from the bank of windows as the viscountess bustled off to see to the sick old man.

Beyond this room, the house was in an uproar. Guests clamoured to know what had gone wrong. The village doctor arrived and was ushered upstairs. Footmen and maids scurried back and forth with linen and water and simples from the stillroom.

Through it all, Sophie stood waiting. She waited to hear whether her uncle was going to live or to die. She waited for her wildly conflicting feelings to settle enough for her to know which of those outcomes would be more welcome.

Eventually the house grew quiet once more. Sophie heard

the doctor leave the house. She did not hear Lady Dayle approach until the viscountess was almost upon her.

'Sophie, darling,' she said quietly. 'Are you all right?'

'Is he...?' Sophie could not finish the sentence.

'No, dear. He is weak, but resting comfortably now.' She paused, and then laid a hand on Sophie's shoulder. 'The doctor says he cannot be certain, but he doubts whether Cranbourne has much time left. It could be a matter of weeks, he says, or months.'

Sophie did not answer. She could not sort through the myriad of emotions besetting her.

'He is asking to see you, dear,' Lady Dayle said gently.

'No,' Sophie said at once. Of one thing she was certain, and that was that she was not ready to face him yet.

'I fear you must. No matter what he has done, he deserves the chance to confess, to at least try to right some of the wrongs he has perpetrated. Before it is too late.'

Sophie shook her head.

'I think you need to hear it as much as he needs to tell it,' Lady Dayle insisted. 'And if you will not do it for him, or for yourself, then do it for Charles. I will send for him as well.'

Against her will and better judgment, Sophie allowed herself to be persuaded. She entered the room where her uncle had been taken, hesitantly, on Lady Dayle's arm.

He lay, looking thin and pathetic in the large bed. His skin tone had faded almost to the colour of the bed sheets. She could hear the rattle of his breath from across the room.

Charles and his brother entered the room behind her. They both looked as comfortable as she felt. Lady Dayle drew Sophie to the chair situated close to the bed and called her uncle's name.

His eyes fluttered open. He looked at once into Sophie's face and sighed at what he saw there. His gaze flickered to Charles, standing by the door, then returned to Sophie.

'Niece,' he said. She could barely hear him, his voice was so frail.

'Uncle,' she returned. For some reason it made him smile.

'Dayle is right,' he said. Sophie lowered her head. 'I just wanted you to hear why.'

Sophie was instantly angry. 'Do you look for forgiveness? This is not the theatre, where the villain is excused all on his deathbed just because he makes a pretty speech of contrition. These are real people, not actors, whose lives you have tampered with.'

'Not forgiveness,' he said quietly. 'I just want the truth to be known.' He paused for several breaths, gathering strength.

'Then why?' Sophie asked. 'Just tell us why.'

'I'm old,' he said simply. 'I've worked long and hard for this country, done the things that had to be done. The hard and dirty jobs,' he rasped, 'the sorts of things that are not celebrated in society's parlours. But it has all been clandestine, behind the veil, as they say.' He shrugged, a pitifully small gesture in the vastness of the bed. 'For a long time I was satisfied with that, happy even. Then I began to become aware that my time on earth is limited, and I suddenly realised that no one knew my name. Only a handful of people would ever know what I had done.' He looked at Sophie intently, clearly wishing for her understanding. 'I want them to know my name. Before I shuffle off this mortal coil I want to be acknowledged. I want my name in the history books, too.'

'But what has any of this to do with Charles?' Jack Alden demanded from his position at the door.

'Nothing at first.' Her uncle spared a glance for Charles, who had moved into the room and now stood implacably at the foot of the bed. 'Rapscallion turned politician—I didn't take him seriously. No one did. But he kept his nose to the grindstone, proved himself on small issues, until he began to be noticed, praised, held up as a bright future for the Party.' He was silent a long moment and only the sound of his laboured breathing filled the room.

'Your name came up too often, and then it came up for the appointment I wanted. You're young. You'll recover, despite your tendency to side with the ones with no power or influence.'

'But all those stories, the statue of King Alfred, the jockey at the Hampstead races, even I had never heard of half those pranks that Charles had played,' Sophie said. 'How could you have known?'

'He kept a file on me,' Charles said quietly. 'Going back for years. What I want to know is why?'

Cranbourne creaked with laughter. The sound made Sophie cringe. 'Good Lord, son, I've got files on everyone. If there is a dirty little secret in London, then I have it at my fingertips. But why you?' He cast a feeble grin. 'Because of a letter I received from an impudent pup years ago. Do you not recall?' He smiled at Charles's blank look, but it faded as his gaze drifted to Sophie. 'A letter from a sprout of a boy, telling me how a gentleman treats his family.'

'Oh my God.' Charles gave half a laugh himself. He turned to Sophie, something unreadable in his eyes. 'I had forgotten. I wrote, chiding him for his neglect of you. He never answered.'

'Neither did I forget,' Cranbourne answered with something of his old energy. 'I had a feeling you might be trouble. Kept an eye on you.' He nodded towards Sophie. 'It's like I told the girl, knowledge is power. How do you think we beat old Boney? Wellington might have whipped him on the battlefield, but it was behind the scenes that the real work was done. We whipped him there, too.' He finished with pride.

'It sounds like an expensive undertaking,' Charles said.

Cranbourne closed his eyes and nodded. 'A sight more expensive than you might think.' He stopped suddenly and his eyes opened again. Sophie did not understand the arrested look on his face. He stared for a long moment at Charles. 'I give you credit, Dayle. Never expected you to figure that out, too.'

It was all becoming too much for Sophie. All the pain, all the embarrassment Charles had suffered these last months. Her fault. She was reeling. Lady Dayle was softly crying. But Charles wasn't through yet.

'Sophie,' he said softly, trying to get her attention.

She shook her head, tried to gather her thoughts. 'I'm so sorry,' she whispered.

'No, I'm sorry, sweet, for there is more.'

More? God, how could there be more?

Charles looked at Cranbourne. 'Tell her,' he said harshly.

Her uncle looked away, refused to meet her eyes. Sophie shivered. It must be bad. 'What is it?' she asked Charles.

'I think he's stolen all of your money,' he answered grimly.

'What money?' She glared at her uncle. 'What is he talking about?'

Cranbourne's head tossed back and forth upon the pillows.

She stared, fixing on the motion, not the face of the man who had hurt them all so callously. 'Not all of it,' was all he said.

'Your parents left you money,' Charles broke in. 'It was to be a marriage settlement.'

Sophie was almost relieved. 'No, there was no updated will. I wasn't mentioned. Their estate went to the family shipping company. I, however, was given their shares in the company. I receive the dividends each quarter.'

'I don't know the specifics, but there was a large dowry. Eighty thousand pounds. If you do not marry before you are five and twenty, it goes to him.' He waved at her uncle. 'However, I suspect he's stolen it.'

'Not stolen,' Cranbourne whispered. 'Spent. Put to good use, for the good of the country. Do you think that bribes to the people close to Napoleon came cheap?' His voice was harsh, his breathing rattled louder now.

Eighty thousand pounds. Sophie thought of what she might have done with such an amount. Hospitals, schools. She thought of the difference it might have made to Mr Darvey, and all the men at the workshop back home. But then the words registered. Marriage settlement. It had never been hers, in any case.

'I don't need it,' she said with conviction. 'I've done well enough with what I have.'

'Yes, you have done marvellously well, dear,' Lady Dayle whispered through her tears, taking her hand. Sophie clung to her, drawing strength.

'Unfortunately he's robbed you of something more valuable than money,' Charles said grimly.

Sophie did not want to hear any more.

'Recall how he campaigned against me, here in town? Not just the papers, but the rumours, the whispers, the innuendo?' He met Sophie's eye. 'Do you remember what you told me about the aftermath of Mr Wren's visits? I think he's waged a similar war on you, in Blackford Chase. To make you unmarriageable.'

Surely not. Not even her uncle could have been so cruel. All the taunts, the rejection, the anguish of always being on the outside looking in. She couldn't ask, couldn't speak. She only stared at him, unspeaking.

'I don't regret it,' he rasped. 'It was the making of her. Look at her! The girl has spirit, strength.' His face contorted.

Lady Dayle stood, at last putting an end to this torture. 'That is enough, now,' she said. 'I will fetch your medicine, Lord Cranbourne. The rest of you, we will speak more of this later.'

Sophie left the room in a hurry, not stopping to wait for Charles. How could she face him, knowing what their friendship had cost him?

She did not return to her room. She could not bear the thought of being confined. The enormity of her distress forbade it. She had to be out, in the fresh air, where perhaps some of her emotional turmoil could leak away, bleed into the black heavens and leave her less burdened.

The kitchen door was locked again. She slid open the lock and stepped out into the night, aware of the vast emotional distance between those same simple acts last night and this.

She walked through the night, annoyed that the beauty of the evening had not faded, resenting the fact that everything could look so unchanged, when her life had been shattered so completely.

Unerringly her feet carried her the long distance to Lady Dayle's folly. The tears came as she stepped in. She stumbled to the nearest column and leaned against the cool marble. She gripped it while she sobbed, as if the force of her anger and grief might tear her away, and when the storm of crying abated she stayed, letting the beauty and serenity of it support and calm her.

She heard Charles's footsteps long before he arrived. But then he was close behind her. His body loomed over hers, so large and warmly masculine. He wrapped her in his arms, and she was safe in the warmth of his embrace again. She leaned back into it. All she wanted to do was forget. Forget it all, and stay here, secure in his arms forever.

'I am so very sorry,' he whispered.

She sighed. He'd held her in just this same way last night. The difference was, this time she knew how short the moment would last. He would leave. She would be left hurting. It was a pattern in her life that was becoming entirely too apparent. She straightened, stepped away, and put a little distance between them.

'What do you have to be sorry for, Charles? Nothing, except for the fact that you ever met me. It is I who am sorry. It seems I've been nothing but trouble since the beginning.'

'Don't think of it like that,' he said. 'Let's just be happy that it's over. We know the worst now, and can go on from here.'

'Over?' Her voice sounded strained, strange, like it belonged to someone else. 'It is hardly over. You can have your life back now. Reveal what he's done to you. Do it with my blessing.'

She stopped, cursing the devastating irony of the situation. The discovery of her uncle's perfidy was the answer to Charles's prayers, and the end to hers. For once scandal was going to work in Charles's favour, but it was going to tear her down along with her uncle, placing her for ever out of Charles's reach.

She tried to sound pleased for him, but even she could hear the hollow echo of her words. 'You'll be back on the path to the ministry in a matter of weeks, once the truth is known.' And back to the search for the perfect political hostess.

The tears were gathering force once more, she could feel them building up from the bottom of her soul. She turned away. 'Please, I need to be alone.'

'No, you don't.' He was coming toward her again, the image of tender concern. 'You don't have to face this alone.'

'I am asking you not to make this more difficult for me.'

'I'm trying to help, not make it more difficult. I know how you must feel. Let me help you.'

She felt a fleeting moment of anger. How could he even begin to know her feelings? Then she remembered—she wasn't the only one who had been betrayed.

But he had seen and understood her flash of emotion. 'No, you are right. There is no comparison to what he's done to you, and with such callous disregard. I could kill the man myself.' He drew close and this time she let him. 'I don't know how you feel. Tell me.'

She wrapped her arms around herself. 'I feel naked. Vulnerable.'

She could feel him smile against her hair. 'No, yesterday we were both vulnerable and alone. Then we came together, here in this very spot, and today we are together and strong.'

'How I wish that were true,' she whispered.

'It is true.' He took both her hands in his. 'As far as I'm concerned, last night's events are all that matter. We may have cleared up a lot of mysteries tonight, but when you cart away the rubble, it changes nothing.'

She gaped at him. 'Are you daft? It changes everything! It changes my past, and both our futures.'

'What's past is just that.' He dropped one of her hands and cupped her cheek. 'I've known your uncle was evil since the first day I saw you come crying down that forest path. Today isn't any different. The future is ours to shape.'

Ours. It had to be the most beautiful word in any language. She leaned into his caress. He gathered her close, pulling her in for a kiss. A soft, sweet, decadent kiss, full of visions of the future, full of promises. For a long moment she lost herself in it, let the heat and the lethal longing he stirred in her sweep away reality.

He broke the kiss and buried his face in her hair. His breath burned against her ear, sending a shiver down the length of her, igniting a slow burn of desire. 'No one has to know, if you don't wish it. We don't have to tell anyone what he's done.'

A splash of cold water could not have quenched her fire more thoroughly. Is that what he wished for? More secrets? More lies?

'No,' she said sharply. 'That is not an option we can consider.' She pushed away from him. 'Haven't you learned that lesson yet? I have seen what the weight of your secrets has done to you. Do you think I would add to that? Would you ask me to carry a similar burden?'

He stiffened, the oh-so-familiar mask dropped into place. 'I don't know what you mean.'

Sophie was growing more furious by the minute. 'You spout the words like you actually believe them. "What's past is past." Should I follow your words or your deeds, Charles?'

He didn't answer.

'You see, even now you shut me out. My life, my soul is bared before you, and still you close yourself to me. Even after all of this…' she waved an encompassing hand '…you still do not trust me.'

'You speak in absurdities. How can you say such a thing?' Now he was growing angry. 'You dare to speak of trust? When you went off half-cocked and pulled that stunt with Lord Avery and his wife?'

'I was trying to help them.'

'Yes, after *we* spoke of helping them. I said I would call on them, and I did, at the first opportunity. But it wasn't enough, was it, you interfering little minx? Did *you* trust *me* to handle it? No—you brewed up another of your hare-brained schemes and you came close to ruining them both for ever!'

'You know what I was trying to accomplish—for them and for us, too. But I'm not going to debate it with you now. This is just another distraction to keep me from the real topic. You are just building another wall to keep me out.'

'Stop it.' Now the anger in his voice was tempered with exasperation. 'You are just being fanciful.'

'Am I? No secrets, have you? Then explain it to me, Charles. Tell me just how you have come to believe that you killed your brother?'

Charles had once had the wind knocked out of him by a champion pugilist at Gentleman Jackson's. He had lain gasping like a fish out of water for a good fifteen minutes. But even that blow had not held the power of Sophie's words. He gaped at her, unable to accept that the truth had been uttered out loud.

'That is it—is it not? The truth you have laboured to hide? Or rather, that's the load of nonsense you have accepted as the truth.'

He stood, unmoving. He'd become accustomed to the swirling, unruly mess that replaced orderly thought and emotion whenever he stood in Sophie's presence, but this, this was reaching a new depth of chaos. He couldn't think, couldn't formulate a coherent response. He could only stand and wait for the surge of adrenalin to ebb, for panic and fear to recede.

'You don't know what you are talking about,' was all the response he could manage.

'Oh, but I think I do. I can scarcely believe it took me this long to unravel. It explains so much: the guilt, your talk of re-demption, and the way you cringe every time Phillip's name is mentioned. Once, at this very house, I asked if you wanted to turn yourself into your brother, when all along the truth is that you think you must replace him.' She moved and took up a position between him and the house, as if she expected him to run. 'I want to hear the reason why.'

Charles couldn't bear to look at her. He turned away, and swept both hands through his hair. He wished he could cover both his ears to block her out, the way he had done to irritate Phillip when they were small. Oh, God, Phillip. He missed him so damned much.

But Phillip was not going to rescue him from this situation, or any other, ever again. He breathed deep and reached for courage. He only hoped he had some.

'Fine,' he finally said. 'Only you could take this hellish night and wish to make it worse. I can see that you will not be satisfied until I am naked and vulnerable too.'

He began to pace. He couldn't hold still, couldn't believe he was admitting the ugly truth.

'You want to know why? Because it *is* the truth. Phillip came to me after Castlereagh offered him the assignment. He hadn't accepted it yet, and didn't know if he would.'

'And you encouraged him?' she asked softly.

'No—I taunted him. It was obvious he was wild to do it. He was actually thrilled that Napoleon had come back, because it gave him one last chance to get in the action. But Father had forbidden him to go. I laughed at him. Mocked him. Asked him if he meant to live under our father's thumb for ever.' Charles couldn't believe how much it hurt to say it, to remember it. He stopped at the far edge of the folly and stared out at the lake. 'He was so angry.'

'And you think that was the reason he decided to go?'

'The next time I saw him, he was preparing to leave. He came to say goodbye. If only I had known...' Grief choked off his words.

Sophie was behind him now. Her hands, so strong and capable for a woman, touched his shoulders, and slid around to embrace him. She laid her soft cheek in the middle of his back. 'Phillip was a good man. He did his duty, but he knew his own mind. He was only human. He chose to go because it was what he wanted, not because his little brother goaded him into it.'

'If you had seen his face. You can't know how it haunts me.'

'I know he would have been in his element. I imagine he was supremely happy in the time he was there.'

'I don't care—he shouldn't have been there at all. He shouldn't have died. He was the good one, the useful one, the one who would have become a great man.' He hung his head. 'It should have been me who died, not him.'

She circled around until she stood before him, her face aghast. 'How can you say such a thing?'

'I didn't. I didn't have to. My father said it for me.'

'Oh, Charles.' Her face crumpled, her lip trembled. Tears welled in her eyes. Charles felt like the biggest ass in the kingdom. She'd been through so much tonight and now here she was, grieving for him.

'How horrible. I wish I could give him a piece of my mind.' She wiped her eyes; he could see she was trying to pull herself together. 'I'm sure he regretted saying such a hateful thing.'

'The only thing he regretted was losing Phillip. He had been so proud of him. I don't think he could conceive of living in a world where his eldest son was no more. He didn't want to. When he contracted the lung fever, he didn't even try to get well. He just let it take him.' Charles did not want to remember the horror of those days, or his mother's frantic worry. 'He never forgave me.'

She stepped forward until their bodies were in contact. Her warmth and softness were a comfort. So was the hand that she slowly stroked through his hair.

'My poor Charles,' she breathed.

'That's not even the worst of it,' he whispered. 'When I heard the news about Phillip, I thought that I would die too. But do you know how I felt when my father died?' He took her by the arms, to be sure she looked him in the face, to be sure she saw the stark horror of the truth. 'Relieved,' he said harshly.

'I was relieved, almost glad, that I wouldn't have to see the bitter disappointment in his eyes every time he looked at me.'

He let her go. He felt empty, drained. 'There you have it. Now you know the worst, all the monumental failings of my life. But do you know, Sophie, as much as women value talking and sharing, I think there can be a point when two people know too much about each other.'

Now he was the one to draw away, to create a physical distance to represent the emotional room that he needed. 'We know the worst about each other now. You are afraid you will be hurt yet again, and I am just the selfish idiot to do it.'

There was sympathy and understanding in her eyes. He didn't want to see it.

'You are being too hard on yourself. You have been letting this gnaw on you for so long. Now that you have faced your demons, you can begin to heal. You must learn to make peace with yourself, Charles. Only then will you be able to move past this.'

'No. The only people whose forgiveness I need are dead.'

'Charles, please.'

'You'll never look at me in the same way again. I couldn't bear it.' He turned away. 'I can scarcely look at you now, knowing that you know.'

He was afraid she would press him. She didn't. For several long minutes, she stood silent. Then she squared her shoulders and breathed deep. 'You are wrong, Charles. There is only one person whose forgiveness you require. Your own.'

She came to him and laid her head on his chest. 'Tonight has been very difficult for both of us. I think we each have some serious decisions to make.' Her arms were around him, embracing him tightly. 'Let us both take some time and try to absorb all of this.'

She looked at him again, her face weary, her eyes serious. 'If you reach the point where you are ready to let go of the past and look to the future, then come to me.' Her voice dropped to a whisper. 'I will be waiting.'

She pressed a quick kiss to his lips and was gone.

Chapter Twenty

In the morning, the Ashford family was gone. So was Sophie. Mr Huxley was preparing to depart. And although, in Charles's view, Lord Cranbourne deserved nothing more than to be preparing to depart the earth for ever, the doctor declared him a little stronger today.

It was, perforce, a small group that gathered for breakfast. Charles forced himself to join them. Vaguely he wondered where the Averys were. He was in no shape to handle anyone else's difficulties. His own were stretching every resource he possessed. He got up and left the table before he ended up venting his despair.

By unspoken consensus the remaining guests began to prepare to return to town. They would all dine out for years on the story of this botched house party, Charles thought bitterly. He stayed out of their way and left them to their packing. Then he haunted the stables so he could stop Mr Mateo Cardea before he mounted up and left.

It worked. Charles stood in the bright sun and held the

horse's bridle while Cardea lashed his small portmanteau behind the saddle.

'I want to know what sort of hold he had over you,' Charles said.

Cardea did not pretend to misunderstand. 'He knew some dangerous details from my rash youth. Back then I thought privateering to be more glamorous than hauling cargo.' The man actually winked at him. Charles's snort echoed the horse's.

'Let us just say it was information that I do not wish a few of the people I do business with today to discover.' He shrugged. 'It was no hardship to go along with the old man. Besides keeping his information to himself, he offered me a handsome settlement. And who would not wish to be married to the beautiful Sophie?'

Charles clenched his teeth, but Cardea grew serious as he reached to shake his hand. 'You watch how you treat her. I have promised her that we will be a close family once again.' His grip grew stronger. 'I still know a few dirty tricks from the old days.'

Charles did not respond. He watched as the man mounted up and rode off.

Later in the afternoon, Charles stood at the library windows when Lord Avery entered the room.

'My wife and I are heading back into town, Dayle. We wished to thank you for your generosity. It's a sight more than I showed you.'

Charles would have spoken, but the man stopped him. 'You've given us a start. No doubt it is more than I deserve, but I thank you for it. We'll take it from here. I don't know how far we will get, but we'll make the journey together, and that's what matters.' He clapped Charles on the back. 'See you in Westminster.'

At last everyone had gone. Only Charles and his mother, and Cranbourne, still upstairs in his sick room, were left. Charles wandered the empty house, seeing Sophie in every corner, and knew how wrong he had been, about so many things.

He set off in search of his mother, and found her at last in the red drawing room. A bench had been pulled over and placed in front of the chimneypiece. She sat there, silently contemplating the portrait above the mantel.

Charles directed a wan smile at her and motioned for her to make room. Sitting next to her, he stared at the past and resolved to fix the future.

With a little sigh his mother let her head lean on his shoulder. Charles breathed deep, took her hand, and told her. He confessed it all. Everything about Phillip and his father and his vain attempts to make amends.

She cried. Each tear cracked Charles's heart open a little further. Then, being his mother, she scolded him, comforted him, and ultimately, forgave him.

Evening had come on. The servants, perhaps sensing that they were best left alone, had not come in to build up the fire. Charles did it himself, and then he leaned on the mantel and watched the snap and crackle of the flames.

'There is something else,' he said.

He told his mother about Sophie. From their childhood, to their more recent tempestuous relationship, to how he had allowed his guilt and self-loathing to spur him into pushing her away. Before he had done, he was the one with the tears in his eyes. He looked for her reaction.

She stared at him in fond exasperation. 'I would never have expected you to be such a nodcock, Charles. I swear, I will take back all my words of forgiveness if you do not get yourself after that girl,' she threatened.

'I will. I promise. But there is one place I have to go before I do.'

Charles went home. He had not been back to Fordham for more than a few hours since the day he had left, at fifteen. But, at last, he was home.

On the first day he visited Phillip's grave. He stood for a long time, just staring at the marker, then he sat down with his back against it and he talked with his brother. He laughed as he recalled the times of their childhood. He cried as he begged for his forgiveness. He told him all about Sophie and the muddle he had made of things, of his life. When the sun started to sink in the sky and the air grew chill, he stood, and he promised to visit again.

The next marker was his father's. Very gently he laid a lily at the base of the stone. His father had had a fondness for lilies. Maybe more than for his wayward second son. But Charles had to learn to let go of that resentment. 'Perhaps some day,' he whispered into the still evening air, 'I'll be able to do it.'

On the second morning he went straight to the forest after breakfast, to the tree where he and Sophie had first met. Charles stood at the base of the massive old monument and looked up into a maze of leafy green and gnarled brown. He took off his coat and grasped a branch.

It was not as easy as he had expected it to be, given the additional height he had gained over the years, but he made it almost to the top. It was the additional weight that kept him from getting as high as he used to do. He settled himself into the crook of a sturdy branch and he looked out over the green landscape of the forest.

Just the smell of the place brought back so many memories. He breathed deeply, absorbing the smell of loam and life, and remembered the surprise on Sophie's tear-stained face that first time they had met, when she had climbed up and found him here before her. He had climbed up here in a temper, he recalled, resentful of the increasing time his older brother was required to spend learning the workings of the estate. But he'd found the very best possible distraction for his sorrow. He smiled to recall that funny little face, the braids, and the pinafore she had left on the ground below.

He climbed down then, and revisited all their old haunts. There had been so much laughter, a few tears, and a bone deep trust. It had been a rich friendship, a balm to the soul of two lonely children. Looking back now, he could hardly believe he had left it behind when he had finally left home. He should have recognised the value of what they had shared.

The truly horrendous thought was that fate had given him a second chance at it and he had nearly made the same mistake. For a long time he sat in the gazebo where the pair of them had spent so many hours, and let the wind ruffle his hair.

Unbidden, his own words came back to him. He could hear them as clearly as if they floated past on the breeze. *He would sacrifice anything, do anything, to prevail.* That vow still held true, but it held a wealth of new meaning. He knew, now, what he must do.

Sophie had been right. He had needed this. He was ready now to move forward, to accomplish something with his life. With her.

Fate had given him a second chance. Charles only hoped Sophie would as well.

Chapter Twenty-One

The brush had drifted off the edge of the page. Sophie failed to notice for several long minutes, until her listless strokes resulted in a Prussian blue smudge on the edge of her draughting table.

'Ohh…' She tossed her brush away in disgust and began to search for the solvent.

A brisk knock sounded at her chamber door and Nell entered, carrying a tray. She set it down. 'Not again.' The maid sighed. 'Beggin' your pardon, miss, but p'raps you should concentrate on eating something before you try to work again. Else your table is going to look like little Edward has been at it.'

'Thank you, Nell. You may be right.' Sophie sat when Nell held out a chair, but she did not eat. She couldn't eat, she couldn't work, and she couldn't pull herself together enough to receive visitors or pay any calls. All she had accomplished since returning to Emily's London house, in fact, was sitting at her desk, staring out the window, and wondering if Charles was ever going to come to his senses.

She rubbed her temples. It was beginning to look as if he would not. She rubbed her eyes next. She refused to cry; she had done enough of that since leaving Sevenoaks. She refused to doubt herself too. The fact that Charles had not come to her was proof enough that she had been right.

'Miss?' Nell was standing before her, looking concerned. It was a nearly constant expression these past days. 'Will you let me pour you a dish of tea?'

'Yes, of course.' Sophie tried to smile. She accepted the cup, but forgot to drink from it. She must begin to make some plans for her future. She had received several flattering offers for design commissions. She could choose one of those. Mateo had reiterated his offer to take her home to Philadelphia. As a cousin only, he had said with a wink. She ought to at least consider it.

The tea had grown cold in her hand when Nell returned to the room a while later. Shaking her head, the maid took the cup from her and set it down. 'There is a visitor downstairs. For you, miss.'

'Oh, no. I'm not prepared to receive anyone, Nell. Please, just tell whoever it is that I'm not at home.'

Nell took her hand and pulled her to her feet. She began to tuck in her hair and straighten her gown. 'Oh, this one you will want to see, miss. Trust me.'

Bemused, Sophie went down. She knew by Nell's manner that it could not be Charles. Granted, she was not sure if the maid was more likely to be happy, if and when he did appear, or to be ready to knock him about the head with a chamber pot, but she definitely would not have remained so calm.

A strange man sat alone in Emily's drawing room. He stood as Sophie entered and executed a nervous bow.

'Miss Westby,' he said.

'Sir.' She made her curtsy. 'I am afraid you have the advantage of me.'

'I'm Mills, ma'am. I am editor of a paper, the *Augur*. Perhaps you will have heard of it?'

'Indeed I have.' She raised a brow. Surely this man had not come begging for a story? No, the staff would not let her be so harassed.

'Ah, good. Well, then you will be aware that I have had some dealings with Lord Dayle?'

Sophie's breath caught, but she merely said, 'No. I was not aware.'

'Oh. Well, I have had dealings with him, and he has asked me to deliver this.' He passed over a folded issue of his paper.

She glanced at it. The screaming headline took up half of the page.

Lord Dayle's Political Career at an End

Sophie gasped and looked up to question the man, but he had already gone. She unfolded the thing to read further.

It is rumoured that the much beleaguered Charles Alden, Viscount Dayle, has had his fill of scandalous slander and scurrilous attacks.

A source close to him reveals that he intends to eschew town life, desert his party, and his seat in the Lords. He will retire to his country seat, it is said, where he will raise bog berries and produce goat cheese, with the help of the multitudinous progeny of William the Goat.

Sophie laughed out loud. She snapped open the paper to read more, but found the remaining pages were blank. However, something did drop and land at her feet. She bent over to retrieve it. It was a sprig of lilac, and a sealed note. She broke the seal and spread the paper out.

You told me once that you knew all the pranks that I had played in my nefarious career. Prove it. Come now to the spot where I cavorted with Cyprian mermaids.

Cyprian mermaids? Ah, she knew the story it meant. Charles and the famous courtesans, swimming naked in the Serpentine.

'Nell!' she called, striding to the door. 'Fetch our wraps. We are going to the Park!'

'I just happened to have them right here,' Nell said, popping in from the hall and holding out Sophie's favourite pelisse.

Sophie laughed. 'You are a wretch, but I love you. Let's go.'

They set out. The sun hung high and a brisk wind blew threw the city streets again today. Sophie smiled and buried her nose in the fragrant lilac. She didn't notice the pair of heads peaking from the doorway behind her, watching her leave.

Sophie doubted whether she had ever walked faster in her life. They reached the Park in record time. She hurried toward the Serpentine. As she drew near she could see a lone gentleman standing on the banks of the pond. She left the path, lifted her skirts and began to run. He turned around…

And she skidded to a stop. It was Theo Alden. He was grinning from ear to ear and striking a dramatic pose. She stared, uncomprehending, until two facts simultaneously became clear: he was holding a sprig of lilac, and he was dressed exactly as Madame Dunyazade had drawn him. Sophie dropped her skirts and started to laugh.

'I am your vision brought to life,' he crowed. 'Magnificent, isn't it? All my friends are ragingly jealous.' He pointed and Sophie turned to see a crowd of Theo's dandified friends looking on. She waggled her fingers at them and they all waved back.

'Here you are,' Theo said. He handed her the lilac and pulled another thick sheet from his waistcoat. 'When you are a member of the family,' he said a little plaintively, 'will you design something else for me?'

Sophie was too busy breaking the seal to answer. Again there was just a short note.

I knew that one was too easy. Here is your next clue: Brew in the shoe.

She immediately knew what that one referenced: the tavern brawl at the Lady's Slipper. It had always been one of her favourites. She looked up at Theo with a grin.

'I'll design you an entire wardrobe if you will find me a hackney as fast as you can.'

He was off like a shot, running towards the corner gate. In a matter of minutes she and Nell were ensconced in a hired carriage and heading for the Strand. They clasped hands and grinned like fools at each other. But Nell dropped her hand and let out a little scream as there came a repeated thumping from the back of the vehicle, right behind her head. She recovered herself and put her head out of the window and looked back. When she ducked back in, her smile was back in place. She gestured for Sophie to do the same.

Several of Theo's cronies were hanging on to the platform on the back of the old carriage. Evidently above hitching a ride, Theo himself was right behind them in another hackney, his own head out the window just like hers. He was beseeching his friends not to fall off and beseeching his driver not to lose her coach.

The ride seemed interminable. Sophie pulled her head back in, but was tempted to put it back out and scream her frustration when traffic slowed their progress significantly. The Strand was even more busy than usual, it appeared, and the closer they got to their destination, the slower the going became. Farmer's wagons, dray carts and private carriages—the street was seething with frustrated traffic. Sophie quickly grew too exasperated to wait, and climbed out to walk. As she drew closer to their destination, the source of the problem became apparent.

A massive, shifting crowd surrounded the tavern they sought. The rough but happy men were singing and spilling into the street, blocking the flow of traffic both ways. She fought her way towards the door of the Lady's Slipper, but stopped when she saw what awaited her there. Sir Harold Luskison stood there, stationed behind the infamous shoe, passing out rum punch as fast as he could ladle it.

'Thank Heaven that you are here!' he cried. 'The tavern owner is irate and has threatened to have me arrested. Here, now,' he called to the men surrounding him, 'clear the way, men. The lady deserves a cup.'

Sophie made her way to him and he poured her a cup. She tasted it; it was deliciously hot and wickedly rich. Sir Harold thankfully handed her his lilac and note. He tossed her a devilish grin as well, stepped away from the steaming cauldron, and bellowed, 'It's all yours, gentlemen!' The crowd roared with appreciation. Sophie didn't hear it; she was perusing her newest hint.

After you have quenched your thirst, feed your mind. Here's your clue: I was born a poet, but was the only one to know it.

She paused. This one had her stumped. Frantically she searched her memory, but she could not recall anything in Charles's past pertaining to poetry. She shared the note with Sir Harold, but he only shook his head. Then Nell asked to see it. She looked it over and then looked up, her eyes bright with pleasure.

'Happen I know this one! I heard two footmen talking of it in Lady Dayle's kitchens. Lord Dayle dressed up like Byron and showed up at the Mayfair Ladies Byron Appreciation Society. He even read a poem before he was unmasked.'

Sophie slapped a hand to her head. 'I cannot believe I missed that one.'

'I don't think the Ladies liked the idea of it getting around. Several of them actually swooned before they found him out.'

'But where, Nell?' Sophie clutched her maid by the arms. 'Where did they meet?'

'At that fancy bookstore. Hatchards.'

Sophie pulled her into a tight embrace. 'I don't know what I would do without you, Nell! Quickly! Let's go!'

They backtracked to the cab and talked the driver into turning it about. The rum punch must have given out, because traffic began to move again. Sir Harold rode with them as well, this time. They lost some of the dandies to the lure of free liquor, but Theo and even some of the men from the crowd were still following behind.

Traffic in Piccadilly was busy as well, and Sophie thought they would never get through. She was near to bouncing on her seat in her excitement, but at last the cab pulled to a stop in front of the bookstore.

A smiling Miss Ashford stood next to the entrance, waving her sealed sheet of vellum. She wore the brightest smile Sophie had ever seen on her and had a tight hold of Mr Huxley's arm.

'Oh, Sophie—such news!' she called. 'Mr Huxley and I are betrothed!'

Sophie gasped. 'But how wonderful!'

'Here,' Miss Ashford said, handing her the paper. 'I wish you will be as happy as we are.' She leaned forward confidingly. 'We are going to tour the Lake District for our bridal trip.'

'I have always thought there needed to be a good map made of all those trails in Cumbria,' said Mr Huxley as he held out his lilac sprig. 'Tell your uncle that I am sorry things did not work out as he wished.' He bestowed a satisfied glance upon the beaming Miss Ashford. 'I think it all came out for the best, just the same.'

Her uncle was not the man foremost in Sophie's mind. This time the clue was just one sentence.

* * *

The King is blue once more.

Sophie looked up into a group of expectant faces. 'Westminster!' she shouted.

They had found him at last. Charles stood at the King's Entrance of Westminster, addressing another crowd. He had a huge bunch of lilacs in his hand and he was standing next to poor King Alfred. The statue had been moved from its position in the Hall and was indeed blue again, from head to foot.

The cab's door opened and Sophie descended slowly, staring in amazement. They were all here. Everyone. Lady Dayle and Emily and her family stood near to Charles. Mr Fowler, her publisher, actually dabbed at his eye with his handkerchief. All the girls who had performed at the masquerade were grouped to one side. Mateo stood with his arm around an openly weeping man—it was her Italian *stuccatore!* She recognised some of the men from her workshop in Blackford Chase, and Mr Darvey stood in the middle of them.

Only Charles was apparently oblivious to her arrival. He had continued with his speech. Sophie blinked back further tears at the sight of him. He was smiling at the crowd and he looked so tall and handsome. The sun glinted off the chestnut in his hair.

'…and so I do withdraw from the political arena. I have resigned from my committees and given up my appointments.'

Sophie gasped. Her heart melted, but then she stilled. Could he truly be giving up his political career altogether? She hadn't… She looked wildly about, wondering if anyone else knew what a sacrifice he was making.

'Oh, no, Charles.' It was Lady Dayle's voice protesting.

He laughed. 'Do not worry, it is a fitting end to a haphazard career, in any case. I am sure the government will sail smoothly on without this sometime rake and fribble.'

'But Dayle, you cannot have considered us?' someone called from the side of the crowd. Sophie looked over and saw a gaggle of reporters, pads out, taking notes. 'Our readers love you. They will be bereft.'

'Our editors will be even more so,' another said in a loud, theatrical lament.

'You'll have to find someone else to be your whipping boy, my lads.' Charles grinned. 'Haunt someone else's footsteps from here on out, for mine will be traipsing down a different, and far more complacent, path.' He stepped away from King Alfred and grew more serious.

'For a long time I have walked in shadow. I have held the darkness and decay of the past too close to my heart.' He gestured towards Sophie and directed that open, satisfied smile her way. 'It took a very special lady to pound that truth into my head.' He held out his arms to her and the crowd parted to make way.

Still in a daze, she advanced, spellbound by the lightness of Charles's voice and the brightness of his clear gaze.

'I've been lost,' he said simply. 'Never knowing just who I was, or what I needed. Now I do not claim to be completely redeemed,' he said with a rakish glance at the crowd, 'for I am afraid that is a task which will take the right woman years to accomplish.' He grinned as the crowd laughed along with him. 'But the process has begun. I am found, because one woman cared enough to search. We did not make it easy on each other, I assure you, but at the last I stand before you, all of our friends and family, not as Viscount Dayle, not even as Mr Charles Alden. I stand here, just a man, desperately in love with a woman.'

The crowd roared their approval and Charles beckoned to Sophie once more.

'I give you all the incredible woman who showed me how to find the sun again, how to hold on to the memories of the past, and let go of the pain, how to appreciate how blessed I am in the loved ones I still have. She has shown me that true generosity of spirit does exist in this world. She has demonstrated courage and fortitude and somehow, most miraculously, she has breached the barriers I had surrounded myself with and found something inside worthy of her love.'

He stepped into the crowd and walked toward her. They met in the middle. Sophie gazed at him in wonder. He handed her the bouquet, then, heedless of the many staring faces, he took her in his arms and kissed her long and hard.

The crowd cheered. He drew back and said to her alone, 'Some of those shadows will always be with me, I'm afraid. But I can see past them now, and it is clear that you are my future.' He touched her hair, ran a finger along the curve of her cheek. 'You will marry me, will you not?'

Sophie couldn't speak, couldn't believe it was true. She felt a sharp elbow in her back as Nell nudged her from behind, so she just nodded and kept nodding, for once in her life struck silent by happiness.

Charles did not appear to mind. He grabbed her up, whirled her around and claimed her mouth once more in a slow, most thorough kiss.

'She said yes!' someone nearby shouted, and a great roar rose up from the crowd. Laughing, the pair broke apart. Something soft landed on Sophie's nose and she looked up to see that everyone in the crowd had held a lilac and now they were tossing them in the air in celebration, surrounding them all in a soft, fragrant rain.

'A moment! Hold a moment!' The shouts, weak as they were, began to penetrate the noise of the crowd and to interfere with Charles's exultation. He tore his gaze from Sophie's shining face and glanced back towards the arching entrance way.

Cranbourne stood there, weak but upright, supported by a shorter man. Mr Wren, Charles presumed.

'I said, hold a moment,' Cranbourne said testily. Slowly the happy tumult abated and all eyes turned toward the man.

'I am the girl's guardian. She should seek my consent before she seeks to wed,' he said in a voice too frail to carry far. It carried far enough to rouse everyone's wrath, however. Hisses and boos met his statement and Charles saw his mother step towards the old man, her face as angry as he'd ever seen it.

'Why, you lowly little muckworm—' she began.

'A chance,' he wheezed. 'Just give me a chance to speak.' He waited until silence reigned once more. 'I do give my consent for Sophie to wed, but—' Everyone held their breaths. Charles struggled to hold on to his temper.

'I cannot condone Lord Dayle's retirement from service to the government. He is a good man. He has done nothing for which he need be ashamed.' Another cheer greeted this pronouncement. Charles just snorted. Sophie, however, was watching her uncle, and Charles knew what was about to happen when she tightened her grip on him.

'Lord Dayle has been under attack in the past months. He has been much maligned. Maliciously. He has been accused of many faults. Falsely. I know this to be true, because I am the one who perpetrated it.'

Charles looked to the left. The whole group of reporters was grinning and scribbling away as fast as their fingers would fly.

'It is I who am retiring from public life,' Cranbourne said. ' I hereby resign my positions, and although my word means nothing, now, I urge you to join me in my attempt to change Lord Dayle's mind.'

'What do you say, Dayle?' It was Sir Harold's voice coming from the back of the mob. 'The Tories stand in need of good men. Will you stay?'

Charles looked into Sophie's questioning gaze. 'I don't know,' he said to her. 'I was looking forward to finding new ways to make a difference.' He looked up and around at the grand buildings surrounding them. 'This was Phillip's path. Perhaps it will turn out to be mine as well. I just do not know.' He squeezed her hands. 'If I don't know what I want to do with myself now, there is one thing I do know for certain: that I want you beside me. For ever.'

Her dark eyes sparkled. 'You are free now. Free to follow whatever path you wish. There is only one absolute necessity in your future.'

He grinned. 'What is that, my love?'

'You must kiss me again. Now.'

So he did.

Epilogue

'I do not know just how your mother did it,' Lady Dayle said to the chortling baby in her arms, 'but look, there you are.'

She indicated the elegantly framed picture hanging just before them. It was the portrait that Sophie had drawn of her, when she had acted as Dunyazade, all those many months ago. The viscountess had adored the picture as soon as it had come from Sophie's easel, but it was only recently that she had noticed this remarkable likeness.

'I must admit, I thought you were losing touch with reality when you told me of this,' Emily Lowder declared. 'I was prepared to break the bad news to your sons that their mother was showing signs of senility. But you were right! It is the very image of the child.'

That long ago night, at Miss Ashford's, now Mrs Huxley's, masquerade, Sophie had indeed drawn Lady Dayle's secret dream: the viscountess surrounded by an unruly pack of happy grandchildren. Lady Dayle had adored it, and had had it framed and hung here in her sitting room. She had been admiring it once more just yesterday when suddenly the uncanny resemblance of the imagined child she held in the picture, to the baby currently residing in Fordham's nursery, had jumped out at her.

'It is unreal.' Emily exclaimed. 'How did she do it? Sophie could not have known, could she have?' She straightened, as if hit by a sudden thought. 'You've had the portrait of you and the boys moved back here from Sevenoaks, have you not?'

Lady Dayle nodded, puzzled. 'Yes.'

'Good, I want to get a look at it again.'

They went to the long gallery where all the family portraits were hung, taking the baby with them.

'Will he let me carry him, do you think?' Emily asked.

'He may, but will I?' Lady Dayle laughed. 'Oh, all right, but only because your own Edward is not here to protest.'

'Come here, you adorable bit of bunting,' Emily cooed. She dug her face in and covered his little neck with loud smacking kisses, making the next Viscount Dayle scream with delight.

'Here it is,' said Lady Dayle. They had reached the spot where the portrait had been restored to its former position. 'What did you wish to see?'

'I want to look at the image of Charles when he was younger,' said Emily. She stared at the painting, and glanced repeatedly at the boy in her arms. 'That's it,' she announced with satisfaction. 'She must have used the image of Charles as a boy for a model.'

'She could not have,' argued Lady Dayle. 'Sophie had never been here in the house that I know of. She never saw that portrait until I had it delivered to Sevenoaks.'

'Then how did she do it?' wondered Emily.

'I don't know, but perhaps it is better that we do not know.' She smiled. 'Hand him back to me now.' She took the baby away from her friend and held him up so he could see the painting on the wall. 'Do you see that boy there, the one with the wicked grin? That is your father, my boy.' She moved her hand. 'And that is your Uncle Phillip, right there. I'm sorry you will not have the chance to know him. He was a wonderful man and would have made a superb uncle.'

'Yes,' agreed Emily. 'He was just the type who would have lectured your parents endlessly about limiting the amount of sweets you were allowed, then he would have kept a pocket full of them just for you.'

'And this, you see, is your Uncle Jack. He is away right now, but will be home for the holidays.'

'Do you recall the day that we unveiled my drawing room? Who would have imagined, back then, that it would have worked out this way?'

'Oh, I don't know,' said Lady Dayle with a smile. 'I am sure that someone with a little imagination might have foreseen how happily it has turned out.' She kissed her grandson and looked back at the portrait. 'I do hope your parents do not wait too long to make the rest of that portrait into reality.'

The baby chuckled his agreement.

* * * * *

An Improper
Aristocrat

To Irene.
Her lessons were innumerable and invaluable. She
introduced me to the Romance genre and she showed me
every day in a hundred ways the sort of person I would like
to be. She was a true-life heroine in every sense of the word.

Prologue

The Valley of the Kings, Egypt
1820

From the shadowed walls of the desert wadi, the French-woman watched. Truly it was him—and from her hidden vantage point he lived up to every whispered tale making its way along the Nile. Her heart quickened.

He sat alone in his tent, scratching out notes by the weak light of his lamp. Narrowing her gaze, she studied him. Ah, yes. The light might be dim, but it illuminated a feast for the discerning female eye: a strong, chiselled profile, impossibly broad shoulders, rugged muscles straining the fine linen of his shirt.

He set down his pen and indulged himself in a lengthy, catlike stretch. Even in so unwary a pose she could sense his power, feel the pull of unwavering confidence and absolute masculinity. Inwardly, she smiled. This assignment, which she had objected to with such vehemence, was going to be no hardship at all.

She crept closer, moving carefully in the mix of rock and sand that littered the valley floor, mentally reviewing all that she knew of this renegade. The Englishman was a legend. He had discovered valuable antiquities in India, Persia and throughout the Orient. In the short time since his arrival in Egypt, he had already made some remarkable finds.

A great man, yes. But here, alone in the cool, dark hours of the desert night, just a man. And one who looked simply weary, and oddly content. Her lips curled wryly. Soon she would fix that.

Her quarry closed his ledger and rose. Stepping lightly, she approached the open tent flap. In one lithe movement she released the catch and stepped inside. Both the canvas and her cloak swirled satisfactorily at her feet.

The Earl of Treyford paused, caught in the act of peeling off his shirt. Fixing his unexpected visitor with an impassive stare, he reached for a name to go with the lovely face. 'Madame Fornier, is it not?' he asked, shrugging back into his shirt.

Her smile appeared to be one of genuine pleasure. 'Indeed. How flattering it is that you remember me, my lord.'

'I make it a point to know my rivals, *madame*.' Deliberately he did not return the smile.

'Rivals?' She pursed her lips. 'An ugly word, and one I'm not at all sure applies to our present situation.'

Trey didn't reply. The less he said, long experience told him, the quicker she would get to the crux of this late-night visit.

'My husband—you met him as well at *le docteur* Valsomaki's?'

At his nod, she continued. 'Fornier, he would be happy with your choice of words. Nothing more would he like than to be considered your rival. He tells himself and anyone who will listen that he is Monsieur Drovetti's foremost agent. But your accomplishments?' She raised a brow. 'He belittles them and says you have only been lucky in Egypt.'

She gave a sad shake of her head and reached up to loosen

the fastenings of her cloak. 'Jealousy steals the sting of his words. He has done nothing to equal your feats. I myself saw those figures of Sekhmet you shipped back to England. Very impressive, my lord.'

He inclined his head and watched as the last tie came undone. One lift of her shoulders and the cloak fell away. She stood proudly, her magnificent body skimmed by a shimmering, transparent shift. The effect was infinitely more arousing than even her bare skin would have been.

Trey merely nodded again. 'Thank you,' he said.

She advanced until she stood pressed up against him. 'There are other reasons that my husband envies you.' Her voice dropped to a husky tone that set his pulse to jumping. 'All of Egypt talks of your many lovers. They whisper of your ability to take a woman beyond herself and into a world of passion that few ever know.'

Against his chest he could feel the softness of her incredible gown and all the abundance it showed to advantage. Their gazes locked, then with a coy smile she snaked a hand inside his shirt, running her palm up and over the muscles of his chest. Moving slowly, she stepped all the way around him, trailing soft fingers across his arm and the breadth of his back as she went.

'Surely you were made for these harsh Eastern deserts,' she whispered. 'When first I came here I thought it foolish and arrogant that the men keep so many wives.' Her orbit complete, she pressed into the front of him once again. Trey knew she could be in no doubt about his interest. She cast a sultry look down at the throbbing evidence of it. 'But you…' she sighed '…you are the first, the only man to make me believe. You alone could do it, pleasure so many women, keep them satisfied and happy.'

She smiled up at him. 'Perhaps, in addition to your other talents, you will be the first Englishman to practise poly... poly...' She paused. 'What is the word I want? For marriage to too many wives?'

'Monogamy?' He returned her smile.

She laughed, a dark, throaty sound. 'It is a certainty that no woman would wish to share you. Already I hate all of those on whom you have practised your wiles. I want to tear their hair and scratch out their eyes.'

Her eyes met his boldly. With an unspoken challenge she pushed him gently back until his knees struck the cot. Searching and warm, her hands crept up, sliding slowly along his ribs, his neck, the line of his jaw, before pressing firmly down on his shoulders.

Trey allowed it, sitting on the cot and finding himself at eye level with her lovely bosom. He reached up and pushed aside the fabric, baring first one breast, then the other. 'So, we have established that your husband envies me.' Slowly he traced a finger around one dusky areola. 'And that you envy all the ladies who have come before you.' He teased the other now, circling both erect nipples in an ever-narrowing path.

He watched her shift restlessly, leaning into his caress. 'But what I wish to know, *madame*, is what Drovetti thinks.'

Her breath was coming fast, her pupils dilated with desire, and yet she smiled in appreciation of his tactics. 'The consul-general thinks only of winning the ancient riches of Egypt for France.'

She pressed his hands against her and again he obliged her, cradling the fullness of her breasts and running his thumbs over her peaks.

'And?' he prompted.

'And he thinks you are a talented Englishman with no love

for England.' She sighed with pleasure. 'I am to offer you a partnership.'

He laughed. 'Is that what you are offering?'

'That is what Drovetti offers.' She pushed him away and shed the gown, standing confident before him in all of her naked glory. 'This, I offer of my own free will, for nothing other than the pleasure you can give me.'

The smile still lingered on Trey's face. 'And if I accept the one, must I accept the other?'

Her only answer was a hungry look of intense desire. She leaned forward, straddled him on the cot and kissed him deeply. Burying his hands in her hair, Trey abandoned himself to his own inclinations. As was his habit—nay, his life's chosen philosophy—he seized the pleasures of the moment and left the inevitable trouble for tomorrow.

Unfortunately, trouble couldn't wait.

She knelt above him, her hands on the fall of his trousers, when the scream echoed along the craggy walls of the valley. Their gazes locked. Trey could read only puzzlement and alarm in hers as he grabbed her roughly by the arms. 'What have you done?' he demanded, his voice harsh.

'Nothing!' she cried. 'What is it? I must not be found here.'

Another shout. Cursing, Trey flung her away. He was out of the tent and running before the last chilling echo bounded off the rocky outcroppings. His partner's tent was dark, and, he realised after a quick search, empty. He stood a moment in the middle of camp. From which direction had the screams come? His feet and his gut knew the answer before his head, sending him pelting towards the closest tomb.

'Richard!' he shouted into the dark. 'Where are you?'

No answer. He ran harder, gravel and sand making the canyon floor treacherous, but at last he reached the spot. It was the first of eight tombs that had been discovered four years earlier by the Italian, Giovanni Battista Belzoni. Almost invisible during the day, now it was little more than a blacker maw against a background of darkly shadowed rock.

There, just outside the opening to the tomb, he found his partner sprawled against the rough, rock wall, a knife imbedded in his chest.

Trey gasped. 'No!'

He stumbled to Richard's side, frantically feeling for a pulse. It was faint, but present. His shirt was soaked in blood. Underneath him a dark stain was fast disappearing into the sand. Trey fumbled at his belt, and cursed himself for not bringing a flint.

'Richard. Who has done this?' He clutched the man with bloodstained fingers. 'Never mind. I'll go for help. Just hold on, damn it! Hold on!'

'No.' Richard's voice was faint, but insistent. 'Treyford, stay.' He lifted a feeble hand to the open neck of his shirt.

'Damn it to hell!' Trey cursed. 'Richard, was it the French? What have you got mixed up in?'

'My pendant,' he breathed. 'Bastards…heard you…ran off.' There was a long pause, punctuated by Richard's slow gasp for air. 'You take it.'

Trey bowed his head. The pendant, ancient and carved with old Egyptian markings, was Richard's most prized possession. His partner's breath rasped, sounding harsh and frightening in the dim light, but his fingers still fought to remove the piece. Trey closed his own hand over Richard's and gently lifted the chain from around his neck.

'Chione,' he choked. 'Give it to Chione.'

'I will.' The pendant was warm, but Richard's hand was cold.

'Promise.' Richard was emphatic. '*Promise* me, Trey.'

'I do promise. I will deliver it to her myself.' It was the least he could do to comfort his partner, who was as close to a friend as Trey was ever likely to get.

Richard's grip, when he grasped Trey's arm, was surprisingly forceful. 'My sister. They will come for her. Trey...help her.'

'Of course I will,' he said soothingly.

Richard's grip tightened. His breath was coming now with a sickening gurgle.

Trey squeezed his opposite hand. 'I give you my word.'

Richard's body relaxed. For a moment, Trey thought... But, no, Richard's hand was moving again, clasping his with grateful pressure.

'Sorry...take you from your work,' he whispered. Somehow he summoned the strength for a faint smile. 'Know you hate...to go home.' Richard's eyes closed. 'Protect Chione.'

'I...' Trey paused until he could go on with a steady voice. 'I swear to you, I will keep her safe.'

It was then, in the darkest time of the early desert morning, that Richard breathed his last, his hand still clasped tight in Trey's.

Trey stayed, crouched where he was, unaware of the passage of time, unaware of anything save the familiar ache of loss. More than a colleague, Richard had been the one person who understood what this work meant to him. Mutual interests, similar drives, complimentary skills; it had been enough to forge a bond of companionship and camaraderie. And, yes, of friendship.

Eventually their dragoman and some of the workmen arrived. Trey saw more than one of the natives furtively making the sign against the evil eye. Spurred on by the headman, a few hearty souls stepped forward to tenderly bundle Richard's body and prepare to carry him back to camp.

'Where is the woman?' Trey asked harshly when the dragoman approached him.

'She slipped away. I let her go.' Aswan cocked his head. 'Shall I find her?'

Trey shook his head. 'Do any of them know anything?' He jerked his jaw towards the milling men.

'I will discover it if they do,' Aswan said firmly. 'We go back. Latimer *effendi* must be prepared for burial. Do you come?'

Trey stared down at the pendant in his fist, then up into the lightening sky. 'No,' he said. The tide of anger inside him was rising with the sun. Grief and guilt and rage threatened to overwhelm him. He experienced a sudden empathy with the howling dervishes he had seen in Cairo; he wanted nothing more at this moment than to scream, to vent his fury into the deceptively cool morning air. Instead, he turned to the opposite direction than that which the workmen were taking, and headed for the ancient trail leading to the top of the cliffs.

It was little better than a goat path and required all of his focus, especially in the poor light and at the pace he was taking it. He was sweating heavily when he reached the top, and he stood, blowing against the cool morning breeze.

The sun was just topping the eastern cliffs, the sky above coming alive in a riot of colour. Trey ignored the incredible vista, looking away as the light crept across the fields and kissed the waters of the Nile. Stately temple ruins and the humble villages came to life beneath his feet. But Richard was dead.

Trey straightened, aware only of his own overflowing bitterness and the bite of the pendant in his grip. *This* was the reason Richard had been killed. Trey was sure of it. Richard had searched relentlessly for the thing since he had first arrived in Egypt, nearly a year ago. The day he found it, he had told Trey that the object filled him with both hope and dread.

Trey could see nothing to inspire such deep feelings. Shaped like a scarab, it looked almost alive in the rosy light of the burgeoning day. Until one felt the empty indentations— in the shape of the insect's wings—where at some time in antiquity thieves had pried the jewels out. Or until one turned it over to gaze at the underside, scored with the old writing.

Such defects had not lowered the value of the thing in Richard's eyes. He had strung it on a chain and never, as far as Trey knew, removed it since. Until today.

Trey ignored the stab of grief and fought to tighten his thoughts. He dragged his mind's eye back over the past months. Yes, it was true. All the strange little occurrences they had suffered had begun after Richard acquired the scarab. They were only small things at first: a few insignificant items missing, their belongings rifled through. Once an itinerary of antiquities that Richard had purchased for the British Museum had disappeared.

Lately, though, the situation had become more sinister. Their rooms had been ransacked and some of their workmen scared off. Richard had refused to discuss the matter, and had scorned the incidents as that which any foreigner might expect to endure in this harsh land.

Trey had not believed him. He had suspected that something more was going on, but he had trusted Richard to handle it. The boy was young, yes, but half-Egyptian himself. Like many of his countrymen he had appeared old beyond his years. He had handled himself with such dignity and their workmen with such ease; it had been easy to forget he hadn't much beyond a score of years in his dish.

And now Richard was dead. Trey should have pushed him, demanded an explanation. He hadn't. He had been too caught up in his work to spare it much consideration. Damn, he thought, letting the sour taste of guilt wash over him, and damn again.

He focused his rage at the pendant, glaring at the offensive thing, for a long moment sorely tempted to pitch it out into the abyss; to leave it once more to the ravages of time and the elements.

But he had promised. Given his word of honour to deliver the cursed thing to Richard's sister. A gruesome memento, in his view. And he had vowed to protect the girl. But from whom? Drovetti? Why would the French want the thing? Why would anyone?

He sighed. It didn't matter; he had promised. He would do it. He turned away and set his feet back on the path into the Valley.

Back to England.

Chapter One

Devonshire, England
1821

The ominous drip, drip of water echoed against the rough-hewn walls of the hidden chamber. It was true; the idol was here. It sat enthroned on its pedestal, bathed in a mysterious light that set its ruby eyes to glowing. Nikolas reached for it. Almost he had it, but something gave him pause. The glow of the eyes had become more intense. The idol was staring at him, through him, into him. He shook off the notion that the thing could see every stain ever etched into his soul. He reached again, but...

'Excuse me, lass.' Neither the impatient tones nor the broad Highland accent belonged to brave Nikolas.

With a reluctant sigh, Chione Latimer abandoned her rich inner world and slid back into her only slightly more mundane life. She set down her pen and turned towards the housekeeper. 'Mrs Ferguson, I am quite busy. I thought I had asked to be left undisturbed.' She had to suppress a flash of impatience. She had pages to write. There would be no payment from her publisher until the latest installment of Nikolas's adventures was in his hands.

'That ye did, and so I told the gentleman, but bless me if some of us dinna act as high and mighty as the day is long.'

A strangled sound came from behind her. The squat, solid figure of Hugh Hamlyn, Viscount Renhurst, stood right on Mrs Ferguson's heels.

'Lord Renhurst,' Chione said in surprise. 'Are you back from town so soon?' A quick surge of hope had her instantly on her feet, her heart pounding. 'Have you heard something then? Has there been word of Mervyn?'

'No, no, nothing like that.' He waved an impatient hand. 'My steward wrote me in a panic, some sort of blight got into the corn. I had to purchase all new seed for the upper fields, and since nothing momentous was happening in the Lords, I decided to bring it out myself.' His habitually harsh expression softened a bit. 'I'm afraid your grandfather's whereabouts are still a mystery, Chione. I'm sorry.'

Chione smiled and struggled to hide her disappointment. 'Well, of course, a visit from you is the next best thing, my lord.' She filed her papers away, then stood. 'Will you bring tea, please, Mrs Ferguson?'

The housekeeper nodded and, with a sharp look for the nobleman, departed.

'Now what have I ever done to earn her displeasure?' Lord Renhurst asked in amused exasperation.

Chione waved a hand in dismissal. 'Oh, you know how Mrs Ferguson's moods are, my lord.' She shot him a conspiratorial smile. 'I know the perfect way for you to get back into her good graces, though.' She led her visitor over to a massive desk centered at one end of the room. 'You know how she loves it when people make themselves useful.'

She indicated the large bottom drawer of the desk. It was wedged tightly askew and impossible to open. 'Could you please, my lord?' Only with a long-time family friend like the viscount could she ask such a thing. 'All the sealing wax is in there and I've desperate need of it.'

He rolled his eyes. 'I come bearing news and get set to servants' work!' Yet he gamely folded back his sleeve and bent over the drawer. He pulled. He pounded. He heaved. 'Why haven't you had Eli in to take care of this?'

Eli was the ancient groom, the only manservant she had left, and also the one-legged former captain of the *Fortune-Hunter*, her grandfather's first merchant ship. 'He does not come in the house,' Chione explained. 'He claims his peg will scuff the floor, but I think he is afraid of Mrs Ferguson.'

'Oh, for God's sake,' Renhurst huffed in disgust. His fashionably tight coat was straining at the seams, and a sheen of perspiration shone on his brow. 'We're all afraid of Ferguson,' he grunted. 'And you still have not told me what I did to end up in her bad graces.'

Chione smiled. 'It appears that Mrs Ferguson was, at one time, of the opinion that you were on the verge of marrying again.'

The viscount was startled into losing his grip. 'Good God. Marrying whom?' he asked, applying himself and pulling harder.

'Me.'

With a last mighty heave, the drawer came loose. Chione hid her grin as both the sealing wax and the viscount ended up on the library floor. He gaped up at her, and Chione could not help but laugh.

'Oh, if you could only see your expression, sir! I never thought so, you may rest assured.' He wisely refrained from comment and she helped him rise and motioned him to a chair before she continued. 'Can you imagine the speculation you would be subject to, should you take a bride of three and twenty? And though society's gossip is nothing to me, I could never be comfortable marrying a man I have always regarded as an honorary uncle.'

Chione tilted her head and smiled upon her grandfather's closest friend. 'And yet, although I've said as much to Mrs Ferguson, I'm afraid that, since you have no intention of marrying me, she has no further use for you.'

The viscount still stared. 'I confess, such a solution has never occurred to me! I know I've told you more than once that a marriage might solve your problems, but to be wedded to an old dog like me?' He shuddered. 'What if, against all odds, you are right and Mervyn does come back after being missing all these months? He'd skin me alive!'

Chione smiled. 'Mervyn himself married a younger woman, but he did so out of love. He'd skin us both if we married for any other reason.'

'You are doubtless right.' He sat back. 'Not every man in his dotage has the energy that your grandfather possessed, my dear. There is not another man in a hundred that would contemplate a second family at such an age.' He smiled wryly. 'So sorry to disrupt Mrs Ferguson's plans. I suppose now it will be stale bread on the tea tray instead of fresh bannocks and honey.'

'Perhaps not.' Chione chuckled now. 'But I would not put it past her.'

'Actually, I did have a bit of news for you, but before we settle to it, I must ask—where are the children?'

'Olivia is napping.' She smiled and answered the question she knew he was truly asking. 'Will has gone fishing and taken the dog with him. You are safe enough.'

The viscount visibly relaxed. 'Thank heavens. The pair of them is all it takes to make me feel my own age. Leave it to

Mervyn to spawn such a duo and then leave them to someone else to raise!' He smiled to take the sting from his words. 'When you throw that hell-hound into the mix, it is more than my nerves can handle.'

Mrs Ferguson re-entered the library with a clatter. She placed the tea tray down with a bit more force than necessary. 'Will ye be needing anything else, miss?'

'No, thank you, Mrs Ferguson.'

'Fine, then. I'll be close enough to hear,' she said with emphasis, 'should ye require anything at all.' She left, pointedly leaving the door wide open.

Lord Renhurst was morose. 'I knew it. Tea with bread and butter.'

Chione poured him a dish of tea. 'I do apologise, my lord. It may not be you at all. Honey is more difficult than butter for us to obtain these days.'

He set his dish down abruptly. 'Tell me things are not so bad as that, Chione.'

She gazed calmly back at him. 'Things are not so bad as that.'

'I damned well expect you to tell me if they are not.'

Chione merely passed him the tray of buttered bread.

He glared at her. 'Damn the Latimer men and their recklessness!' He raised a hand as she started to object. 'No, I've been friends with Mervyn for more than twenty years, I've earned the right to throw a curse or two his way.' He shook his head. 'Disappeared to parts unknown. No good explanation to a living soul, just muttering about something vital that needed to be done! Now he's been missing for what—near a year and half again? Then Richard is killed five months ago in some godforsaken desert and here you are left alone. With two children and this mausoleum of a house to look after, and no funds with which to do so.' He lowered his voice a little.

'No one respects your strength and fortitude more than I, my dear, but if it has become too much for you to handle alone, I want you to come to me.'

Chione sighed. The longer Mervyn stayed missing, the worse her situation grew, but still, this was a conversation she never wished to have. It was true, her life was a mess, and her family's circumstances were hopelessly entangled. It was universally known, and tacitly ignored, at least in their insular little village and along the rugged coast of Devonshire. Chione coped as best she could, but she did not discuss it. She was a Latimer.

She winced a little at the untruth of that statement. All the world knew her as a Latimer, in any case, and in her heart she was truly a part of this family. She would prevail, as Latimers always had, no matter how difficult the situation they found themselves in.

She stiffened her spine and cast a false smile at Lord Renhurst. 'We are fine, my lord. We have learned to practise economies. Now come, what news have you?'

'Economies!' he snorted. 'Mervyn built Latimer Shipping with his own two hands. If he ever found out what a mess it's become and how his family has been obliged to live...' He shook his head. 'I've spoken with the banks again, but they refuse to budge. They will not release Mervyn's funds until some definitive word is had of him.'

'Thank you for trying, in any case.' She sighed.

'Least I could do,' he mumbled. 'Wanted to tell you, too, that I went to the Antiquarian Society, as you asked.'

Chione was brought to instant attention. 'Oh, my lord, thank you! Did you speak with the gentleman I mentioned? Did Mr Bartlett know anything of use?'

'He offers you his sincerest condolences, but could only

tell me that, yes, Richard did indeed spend a great deal of time in their collection before he left for Egypt.'

'Could he not tell you specifically what Richard was looking for?'

'He could not.'

She closed her eyes in disappointment. Chione knew that Richard had been hiding something; something about her grandfather's disappearance, she suspected. Now his secrets had died along with her brother. Trying to ferret out the one kept her from dwelling on the other. But it was more than that. She needed to find her grandfather, and the sooner the better. She refused to consider what the rest of the world believed: that he was most likely dead as well.

'Bartlett did say that he spent a great deal of time with a Mr Alden. Scholar of some sort. He recommended that you speak with him if you wished to know what was occupying your brother's interest.'

Chione brightened immediately. 'Alden,' she mused. 'The name is familiar. Yes, I believe I have read something of his. I shall look through Mervyn's journals.' She turned to Lord Renhurst and smiled. 'Thank you so much. You are a very great friend, to all of us.'

The viscount blinked, and then sat a moment, silently contemplating her. 'You think this is something to do with the Lost Jewel, don't you?' he asked.

'I fear so,' she answered simply. 'But I hope not.'

'I hope not, as well.' His disapproval was clear. 'You are in a devil of a fix already, my dear, without adding in a lot of nonsense about pharaohs and mysterious lost treasures.'

'We might think it a parcel of nonsense, but you know that Richard believed in it. As does Mervyn.' To put it simply, they had *wanted* to believe. The men in Chione's family were adventurers in heart and deed. They craved travel and excitement as fervently as the débutantes of the *ton* craved young and single heirs to a dukedom, as constantly as the opium eaters of her mother's country craved their drug.

Chione cast her gaze down at her tea. What she craved were far simpler things: food for the table, a warmer coat for Will, the ability to pay her remaining servants' wages. But she would achieve none of those by drinking tea with Lord Renhurst.

'Do try not to worry, my lord. We shall muddle through.' Strategically, she paused and cocked her head. 'Listen, do you hear barking?'

The viscount's manner abruptly changed. He set down his dish of tea. 'Well, then,' he said briskly, 'we will scheme together to bring you about, but another time. I cannot stay longer today.'

Chione had to hide her smile at his sudden eagerness to be gone. 'Of course. Thank you so much for talking with Mr Bartlett for me.'

'Certainly.' He paused and a stern expression settled once more over his features. 'I've let you have your way so far, Chione, but I'm watching you closely. If I need to step in, I will.'

'I appreciate your concern, sir.'

He offered his arm, listening intently. 'Will you walk me out? I must be off.'

Chione resisted the impish urge to drag her feet. They stepped outside and she wrapped her shawl tighter about her shoulders. She breathed deep of the sea scent blowing strong on the wind. It was the kind of wind that brought change, her grandfather had always said. She closed her eyes and hoped it *would* bring change. She hoped it would bring him home again.

'Good day to you, Chione. We will speak again soon.' Lord Renhurst's groom pulled his phaeton up to the house and he hurried towards it. He skidded to a stop, however, when a horse and rider suddenly emerged from the wooded section of the drive.

The sun obscured her view, and Chione caught her breath, believing for an instant that she had indeed wished Mervyn Latimer home. The rider approached, and stopped in front of the house, allowing her to see that it was not the imposing form of her missing grandfather, but that of a younger man instead.

A man, indeed, and a specimen of the species like she had never seen.

Most of the men in the village were fishermen, gnarled from their constant battle against wind and sea. Lord Renhurst and her grandfather were older, and stout with good living. Her brother had always looked exactly what he had been—a rumpled, slightly grubby scholar. But this man… She gave a little sigh. He dismounted and she could not look away. He stood tall, broad and powerful. He looked, in fact, as if he could have ridden straight from the pages of one of her adventure novels.

As if he had heard her thoughts, he strode boldly towards the house. The closer he came, the faster her heart began to trip. He stopped and the skin on Chione's nape prickled, every tiny hair there standing at quivering attention.

'Good day,' he said to the viscount, who still stood in the drive. 'I am looking for Oakwood Court.'

His clothing looked as unusual as he. A coat of dark green, made of fine material, but cut loose, with a multitude of pockets. Snug trousers and scuffed, comfortable-looking boots. His linen was clean and his neckcloth a bit limp, as if he had been tugging at it.

'You've found it, sir,' Lord Renhurst replied. Chione thought he might have conversed further if not for a loud and happy bark that sounded suddenly nearby. 'Sorry, must be off,' he said as he edged towards his phaeton. Gravel crunched as the vehicle began to move, then the viscount twisted around on the seat. He looked back at her visitor and advised loudly, 'Good God, man, take off your hat!'

'Oh, yes. Of course.' The gentleman removed said article and turned to face Chione once more. He raked her with an assessing glance and his face softened a bit. 'Can you tell me where I might find Miss Latimer?'

Chione's mouth went dry. Gracious, but the man could not be real. He did not speak, he *rumbled*, with low tones that she could feel, echoing in the bones behind her ear, vibrating in the pit of her belly. His hair was too long to be fashionable, and dark. Nearly as dark as her own, in fact. Yet his eyes were the same colour as the cerulean sky overhead. It was a striking combination, especially when set off by sun-browned skin.

She swallowed and forced herself to gather her wits. 'Yes, I am Miss Latimer,' she said. But Lord Renhurst's last words finally dawned on her and made her realise how near the dog's barking had come. 'Oh, dear,' she said.

The gentleman was oblivious to the danger. 'Miss Latimer, it is a pleasure to meet you at last. I've come a great distance to find you.' He bowed. 'I am Treyford.'

The barking had grown louder still and had changed in tone. Chione could see the beast now, coming from the stables. She was no longer making noise for the sheer fun of it, now she was broadcasting a frenzy of doggy ecstasy.

'The pleasure is mine,' Chione strode down the steps towards her visitor. 'Pray, do excuse me.' She reached up and snatched the very fine beaver hat from the man's grasp just before the dog reached them. Then she turned and threw the thing away with all her might.

* * *

Trey's jaw dropped as his brand new hat sailed out to the middle of the gravelled drive. Good God, was the girl mad? Was this why Richard had been so adamant that Trey protect his sister?

He soon realised his mistake. The largest, ugliest dog he had ever seen came out of nowhere and pounced on the hat with a yelp of joy. The creature shook the thing as if to break it, tossed it in the air, growled ferociously at it, then settled down right there in the drive and began to tear into it with powerful jaws.

'I am sorry,' Miss Latimer said, 'but she would have knocked you flat in order to get it.'

The lady looked at him at last. He saw recognition in her eyes—eyes so dark they appeared nearly black. Slightly slanted, they were rimmed with the most astonishing eye-lashes he had ever seen.

'Treyford, did you say?' she asked. 'As in the *Earl* of Treyford? How nice to meet you at last! I feel we must know you already, so frequently did Richard mention you in his letters.' She cocked her head at him. 'But what a surprise to find you in England, my lord. I had thought you meant to stay and continue your work in Egypt.'

A shout from what he took to be the path to the stables distracted her, and Trey seized the opportunity to study the girl. She looked younger than he had expected. Richard had spoken often of his older sister and it had been obvious that they were close, her support a steady influence that Richard had relied upon. He knew she must be near to five and twenty, but she still looked little more than a girl.

She was also prettier than he had expected—a far cry from the strong-willed spinster he had imagined. Her skin was flawless, with a slight exotically olive tint, but still very pale in contrast to her dark eyes and even darker hair. Her face, finely moulded with high cheekbones, was set in a serious expression, as if she carried heavy burdens.

The shout came again, and Trey recognised her name.

'Chione! Just see what I've got!'

Her face had softened. 'It is young Will,' she said, as if that explained anything. 'Most likely covered in mud, but do not fear. I will not allow him near enough to ruin any more of your wardrobe.'

'Chione!' The boy came into view. He looked perhaps nine or ten years old, and carried a large open basket that bounced against his side as he ran. He was indeed slathered head to foot in mud.

'Beef, Chione!' he called in triumph. 'I was walking past the vicarage with my string of fish and Mrs Thompson called out to me. She vowed she had been longing for her cook's fish stew, and she asked me to trade. An entire joint of beef, can you imagine? I've got it right here!'

'How nice, Will,' Miss Latimer began, but a look of caution crossed her face as the boy drew near. 'Watch your feet. Careful!'

The warning came too late. The brim of Trey's beaver hat had come completely detached and lay directly in the boy's path. Even as her warning rang out, his feet became tangled and he went down heavily, the basket flying out ahead of him.

The cloth-wrapped bundle within took flight. Trey watched, prophetically sure of its trajectory even before it landed, with a splat, in his arms. He looked down at the stain that now managed to decorate both his coat and his linen, and then he glared at the disastrous duo before him.

Miss Latimer was solicitously helping the boy to his feet.

'My lord, we would be pleased if you would stay to dinner.' She indicated the dripping bundle in his arms. 'As you see, we shall be dining on roast beef.'

Chapter Two

Trey was in the grip of an excessively bad mood. He had travelled halfway round the world, only to end up in Bedlam. He had given his word, and so he had given up Egypt. And he had ended up in a madhouse.

It hadn't been his first impression. He'd left the village this afternoon, taking the coastal path as directed, and he'd thought this must be one of the most wild and beautiful spots on the Earth. Oddly enough, he found himself uncomfortable with the surrounding lushness. After the spare desert beauty of Egypt, this part of Devon appeared to be blessed with an embarrassment of riches: stunning ocean views of harbour and bay, woodlands full of gnarled trees, rocky cliffs, and charming dells bursting with early springtime displays.

Oakwood Court blended right into the undisciplined vista. The long, meandering drive left the coastal path and took one on a leisurely trip through a wooded grove, then abruptly broke free to cross a sweeping lawn. A traveller found oneself gifted with a stunning tableau of a many-gabled Elizabethan manor nestled against a rising, wooded slope. It was a distinctive old house, full of character.

Trey had never met Mervyn Latimer, Richard's famous

grandfather, who had won a cargo ship in a card game and turned it into one of the biggest shipping companies in England. Yet just by spending a short amount of time in his house, Trey felt as if he knew something of the eccentric old man. His larger-than-life presence fairly permeated the place, along with many fascinating objects that must have been collected throughout his travels.

And although the many curiosities hanging on walls, gracing the tables and filling the shelves of the house were interesting, they were as nothing compared to the arresting collection of human oddities he'd found here.

Directly after Trey's heroic rescue of dinner—the boy's words—his horse had been taken up by the groom. The wizened little man with a peg leg looked as if he belonged in the rigging of a Barbary pirate's ship. Yet he soothed the fidgety horse with a soft voice and gentle hands, and the skittish hack followed after him like a lamb.

Trey, in all his greased and bloodied glory, had been handed over to the housekeeper. A dour Scot if he had ever met one, she wore a constant frown, spoke in gruff tones, and carried heavy buckets of water as if they weighed nothing. Yet she worked with brisk efficiency and made sure he had everything a gentleman could ask for his toilet. Save, perhaps, clothes that fit.

She'd come to fetch him once he was changed into some of Richard's left-behind things, rasping out a crotchety, 'Come along with ye, then, to the drawing room.' He did, stalking after the woman along a long corridor with many framed maps upon the wall, and down a dark stairwell.

One notion struck Trey as they moved through the large house. There was a curious lack of activity. There were no enticing kitchen smells, no butler guarding the door, no footmen to carry water, no maids dusting the collection of bric-a-brac. Trey might be the black sheep of his family and a dark hole on the glittering map of the *ton*, but he had grown up in a substantial house and knew the kind of activity required to run it. The lack was somehow unnerving, and lent the house a stale, unused air. Somehow it felt more like an unkempt museum than a home.

Eventually they arrived on the first floor, and the house-keeper stopped before a richly panelled door. She pushed it open without preamble, stood aside and said, 'In here.' Without even waiting to see him cross the threshold, she shuffled off towards the back of the house.

Trey entered to find yet another room filled with the in-animate detritus of a well-travelled collector. And one animate specimen.

It was a child, of perhaps two or three years. Trey blanched. The only thing more inherently threatening than a respectable female was a child, and this one was both. She was very pretty, with long chestnut curls, but her heart-shaped face was smeared and her grubby little hands were leaving marks on the sofa she stood upon.

'Livvie do it,' she said, pointing down behind the piece of furniture.

Why the devil would a child be left alone in the parlour? Suppressing a sigh, Trey crossed the room to peer into the narrow space she indicated. The wall behind the sofa was smudged with what looked to be honey and a crumbled mess lay on the floor below. 'Yes,' he agreed with the solemn-faced sprite. 'You did do it, didn't you?'

She sighed and abruptly lifted both hands towards him.

Trey grimaced. 'I don't think so,' he said, shaking his head.

She only grunted and lifted her demanding little arms again.

Trey decided to take charge. Children responded to authority, did they not? 'Come down from there,' he said firmly. 'We shall find the irresponsible creature meant to be in charge of you.' He snapped his fingers and pointed to the floor.

The child's lower lip poked out and started to tremble. Great, fat tears welled in her brown eyes. 'Up,' she whimpered.

Hell and high water, were females born knowing how to manipulate? It must be a skill transferred from mother to daughter in the womb. Well, stubbornness was the gift his mother has passed to him, or so he'd been told many times in his own childhood. 'No,' he said more firmly still. 'Now hop down from there at once.'

The tears swelled and ran over, making tracks on her dirty cheeks. '*Uuuuuppp!*' she wailed, and her little body began to shake with the force of her sobs.

Oh, Lord, no. 'Don't do that,' Trey commanded. 'I'm picking you up.' Grimacing in distaste, he plucked her off the sofa, trying to keep her at arm's length. Quicker than a flash, more subtly done than the most precise of military manoeuvres, she foiled his effort and nestled up tightly against him.

Trey was suddenly and fiercely glad of the borrowed coat he wore. Underneath the chit's sweet honey smell lurked a more suspicious odour. 'Let's go, then,' he said, 'and find your keeper.'

The door opened with a bang and a distracted Miss Latimer rushed in. 'Oh, no,' she gasped, rushing forward to take the child.

'Shone!' cried the little girl. 'She-own! Livvie do it.'

'I do beg your pardon, my lord.' Miss Latimer strode back to the doorway and shouted in a most unladylike fashion, 'I've found her!'

The dour housekeeper arrived a moment later. She never glanced at Trey, but took the child and scowled at her young mistress. 'She's taken a plate of bannocks with her,' she said with a roll of her eyes, 'so there's no tellin' where we'll find the mess later.'

Miss Latimer shot an inquiring look at him. Trey had not the smallest desire to witness the fuss created should *that* discovery be made. He shrugged and maintained an air of innocence, and the young lady soon bundled the girl and the older woman out of the door.

Miss Latimer winced. 'I must apologise, my lord. Our household has been greatly diminished since Richard's death and Olivia *will* wander.' She continued on, but Trey was not listening. He knew he was glowering at her, but he could not help himself.

God's teeth, but he could not get over how beautiful she was. Her heavy, black tresses shone, as black as the moods that plagued him, as dark as any he had seen in his travels to the east. It was the perfect foil for her exotic skin, just exactly the tawny colour of moonlight on the desert sands.

Her eyes, framed by those lush lashes, agitated him. They were too old for her young and beautiful face. It was as if she had experienced too much sorrow, too much of the dark side of life, and it could not be contained. It spilled out of her, tinting her gaze with mystery, with *knowing*.

He realised most men would find her beauty fascinating, but damn it, this was exactly the sort of situation in which a man couldn't afford to give in to attraction. Women like this came with a multitude of strings attached, and Trey hadn't thrown off his own yoke of responsibility so he could take on someone else's.

He could see that his glare was unsettling her. He knew that she was at best unnerved, and at worst unhappy, at his presence. He did not care. He was unnerved and unhappy, damn it, so she might as well be, too.

He had come to England to aid an ageing spinster facing an undefined danger. He had been fully prepared to root out the trouble, deliver the damned scarab, and then quickly return to Egypt. There had been no mention of thick eyelashes and long ebony hair. He was not supposed to be dealing with children, and their flying joints of meat and their artful tears. In fact, the only danger here appeared to be to his wardrobe.

And the girl was still talking. Trey had the sudden, nearly irresistible urge to get up and walk out, to drop the scarab in her lap and to never look back. He suppressed a sigh at the thought, for he knew he could not do it. But damn Richard for getting himself killed and thrusting his responsibilities in his lap! He rubbed his temple and wished the girl would stop talking. He wanted to get this over with and get back to his work as quickly as possible.

Miss Latimer did stop, at last, as the door opened again and young Will, freshly scrubbed, bounded into the room, the dog at his heel. The boy dutifully made his bow and went to kiss her. The dog made a beeline for Trey, collapsed upon his Hessians, and gazed adoringly at him, tongue lolling.

'Oh, dear, I am sorry,' Miss Latimer said yet again. 'She has a hopeless passion for gentlemen.'

'Mrs Ferguson says she likes their accessories—particularly the ones made of hide or leather.' Will grinned.

'Will—take the dog outside.'

'She will howl,' warned Will. He turned to Trey. 'Morty likes you, Lord Treyford. Do you like dogs?' he asked ingenuously.

'For the most part,' Trey said, reaching down to scratch behind the beast's ears and lift her drooling head off of his boots. 'Morty?' he asked.

'Her real name is Mortification,' Will explained. 'Squire named her because he said he was mortified that such an ugly pup came from his prize bitch. I shortened it to Morty so her feelings wouldn't get hurt.'

'Will saved her life,' Miss Latimer explained. 'Squire was going to have her destroyed.'

'I gave my last guinea for her,' said Will. 'She's my best friend.'

Women, babes and puppy love. Good God. No wonder Richard had fled to Egypt.

'I've asked Mrs Ferguson to save a bone for her,' she continued. 'She will have it in the kitchens, so you may be left in peace, Lord Treyford.'

As if summoned by the mention of her name, the housekeeper appeared in the parlour door. Without ceremony she snapped her fingers at the dog. 'Come, you hell-spawned hound. Bone!'

Evidently the dog was familiar with the word. She rose, gave herself a good jaw-flapping shake, then trotted off after the housekeeper, casting a coquettish glance back over her shoulder at Trey.

The damned dog was *flirting* with him.

He looked up. The girl gazed back, expectation clear in those haunting eyes.

Trey faltered at the sudden, strange hitch of his breath. Something sharp moved in his stomach. This was, suddenly, all too much for him. Too much clutter, too many people. Hell, even the dog seemed to want something of him. Trey knew himself for a hard man, surviving in a harsh world. He lived his life unencumbered, with relationships kept to a minimum and always kept clearly defined. Servant and master, buyer and seller, associate or rival. It was simpler that way. Safer. Neither of those attributes, he was sure, could be applied to this family, and that made him uncommonly nervous.

The intense stare that young Will was directing at him only increased his discomfort. Suddenly the boy opened his mouth and a barrage of questions came out of him, like the raking fire of a cannonade.

'How long did it take to sail back to England? How hot is it in Egypt? Did you see any crocodiles? Have you brought back any mummies? Did you climb the pyramids? Were you afraid?' Red-faced, the boy paused to draw breath. 'Will you tell us over dinner? Please?'

Trey's breath began to come faster. He cleared his throat. 'Yes, well,' he said, trying to keep the harshness from his voice, 'actually, I've come to your home with a purpose, not on a social visit.' The boy looked mutinous, and Trey rushed on. 'I need a private moment with your sister, lad. I've a sort of…message, from Richard for her.'

The boy's expression cleared of its clouds. 'My sister?' he scoffed. 'She don't know enough words to have a proper conversation, my lord. Did you mean Chione?' He shot a devilish glance at the young lady, then turned to Trey, eyes sparkling as if sharing a great joke. 'Chione's my niece, not my sister!'

Now Trey was flustered, something that did not happen often. Niece? What sort of tangled mess had Richard dropped him into? He knew with certainty that there was only one answer to that: exactly the sort he had spent a lifetime avoiding.

Will was staring at him now. 'Didn't Richard tell you anything? He wrote us all about you. You see, my papa is Chione's grandpapa, so I get to be her uncle. And Olivia gets to be her aunt! Isn't that funny?'

It wasn't funny. It had been a long time since Trey had felt this awkward. But there was no way he could tell the boy how he had discouraged Richard's tendency to talk of his family, of anything other than their work. Trey didn't like chitchat. He liked focus, and determination, and hard work. He liked travel. Distance. Adventure. There was nothing wrong with that. So why was his stomach churning now?

He breathed deeply. It was too damned late to avoid this fiasco, but he'd be damned if he didn't extricate himself in record time.

Miss Latimer helped him take the first step. 'Will, why don't you run along and help Mrs Ferguson with dinner? Lord Treyford and I will take a stroll in the gardens. If that is acceptable, my lord?'

Trey nodded and watched as the boy started to protest, then hung his head. 'A pleasure to meet you, my lord,' he said, and turned towards the door.

The boy's dejected profile was impossible for Trey to ignore. He let loose a silent string of curses. But he was all too familiar with the heavy weight of childish disappointment. 'Hold, lad,' he said roughly, and the boy turned. 'Egypt is as hot as blazes. Yes, I climbed the pyramids, and, no, it was not the least bit frightening. I've been uncomfortably close to some crocodiles, too. Egypt is full of wondrous things.'

Trey closed his eyes. Just the thought of Egypt calmed him. He hadn't expected it, but the country had beguiled him. Time flowed differently there; he'd had a sense that the secrets of the past were just out of his reach, hidden only by a thin veil of mist.

'And the mummies? Did you bring any back?' The boy's eyes were shining.

'No, although I encountered plenty, both whole and in pieces.' He glanced over at the girl. 'Perhaps I will have time to tell you about it before I must go.'

'Thank you, my lord!'

Miss Latimer wore a frown as she rose to her feet. 'Just

allow me to stop in the front hall to fetch my wrap, and we can be on our way,' she said.

Good. Perhaps she was as eager to be done with this as he.

Chione wrapped herself well against the chill and led their guest outside, once again restored to her habitual poise. She should be grateful that he had made it easy for her to slip back into her normal, contained role, she told herself firmly, for she had been acting a fool since her first glimpse of Lord Treyford.

She had scarcely been able to help herself. All of that overt masculinity and absolute self-assurance touched something inside of her, stirred to life a part of her that she would rather be left slumbering.

And then she had heard it in his voice. That all-too-familiar longing when he had spoken of the wonders of Egypt. She knew that tone and exactly what it meant. *He was one of them.*

Like her grandfather, her brother, and even her father. Never happy where they were, always pining for something more exotic, more adventuresome, more dangerous. Or perhaps, just *more*.

That tiny wistful note that had crept into the earl's voice; that was all it took to effectively quench all of the flutterings and tinglings and ridiculously rapid heartbeats that had plagued her every time their eyes met.

An adventurer—just like the others. With that realisation she reached for calm, breathed deep and let the veneer of her assumed identity fall back into place. They stepped down into the formal garden and he grudgingly offered her his arm. She took it, then had to school herself not to gasp as a slow, warm burn started in her fingertips, flowed like honey through her, and settled in a rich puddle in the pit of her belly.

Perhaps she wasn't rid of all of those stirrings. Yet.

'You are very quiet, Miss Latimer.' Though his voice was rough, there was a hint of irony hidden in it. 'Not at all like your brother.'

Chione had to smile at that. 'No, indeed. Richard was many things, but quiet was not a label he was often burdened with.' She swept aside a low hanging branch and held it back invitingly. 'He was too full of life to keep quiet for long.'

He did not answer and they walked in silence for several moments. Despite her disillusionment, Chione could not but acknowledge her heightened awareness of his looming presence. It was more than the sheer size of him, too. The air fairly crackled around him, as if the force of his personality stamped itself on the surrounding atmosphere.

She wondered just what it was that brought him here. Not a happy errand, judging by his nearly constant frown, but really, who could blame the man? Since his arrival he'd had his hat eaten, his clothes bloodied, been entertained in the drawing room by a toddler and quizzed by a little boy. They should count themselves lucky he hadn't run screaming back to the village.

Chione was glad he was made of sterner stuff than that. 'Richard wrote of you so often,' she began. 'I know he held you in very high regard. Forgive me if I am rude, but I was surprised that you did not know of our…unusual family. Did he not speak to you of us?'

She had chosen poorly, perhaps, because his frown deepened. 'He spoke of you,' he said gruffly. 'And of your grandfather.' He paused. 'I should have asked sooner—is he still missing? Have you had no word of him?'

'No, not yet. Soon, I hope.'

'Do you still have no idea what might have happened to him, then?'

'On the contrary, there are many ideas, but no proof of anything.'

'It has been what? Two years? And yet you hold out hope?' He sounded incredulous.

'Not two years, yet, and indeed, I do have hope. I hope every day that this is the one that brings him home. My grandfather has been in a thousand scrapes and survived each one. He told me once that he meant to die a peaceful death in his bed, an old man. I believe he will.'

The earl looked away. 'Richard felt much the same,' he said.

Chione felt a fresh pang of loss at his words. Yes, Richard had understood. She blinked and focused intently on the surrounding wood. The forest was alive around them as the birds and the insects busily pursued all the industries of spring. She sighed. Life did go on, and Richard's responsibilities were hers now.

'I am happy to have the chance to thank you for the letter you sent to us, on my brother's death. It was a comfort to know that he had a friend like you with him when he died.'

For a long moment, Lord Treyford made no reply. The path had begun to climb and he paid careful attention to her footing as well as his. When at last he did speak, he sounded—what was it—cautious? Subdued? 'That is truly what I've come for, what I've travelled all this way to do. To speak to you about Richard's death.'

He fell silent again. Chione waited, willing to give him the time he needed. She harboured a grave feeling that she was not going to like what he had to say.

'Richard's last thoughts were of you,' he finally said. They had come out on a little ridge. A bench had been strategically placed to take advantage of the spectacular view. The earl motioned her to it and gingerly lowered himself beside her.

His gaze wandered over the scene. 'When one hears of

Devon, it is always the desolate beauty of Dartmoor.' He paused. 'It seems that nothing here is as I expected.' His gaze was no longer riveted on the view. Instead it roamed over her face, the blue of his eyes more than a match for the sky overhead. After a moment the intensity of his regard began to discomfort her.

She ducked her head and ruthlessly clamped down her own response. She breathed deeply, gathering her strength and reaching for courage. She raised her head and looked him in the eye. 'Tell me about Richard's death.'

It was enough to sweep clear the thickening tension between them. 'Yes,' he said. 'Of course.'

He reached into an inner pocket, drew something out. 'Just before he died, your brother asked me to give this to you.' He took her hand from where it rested in her lap and placed the object in it.

It was sharp-edged, and warm from the heat of his body. For several moments that was the sum of Chione's impressions, for she could not see through her sudden swell of tears. She breathed deeply again, however, and regained control of her emotions. As her vision cleared she got her first good look at the object.

Only to be seized by something uncomfortably close to panic. A wave of nausea engulfed her and she let the thing fall from her suddenly lifeless fingers.

Good God, he had found it.

Chapter Three

Trey watched, shocked, as Miss Latimer dropped the scarab as if it had seared her. She sat lifeless, eyes closed, fists clenched, neither moving nor speaking. He could see the sheen of sweat upon her brow. She really was frightened.

'Miss Latimer?' He grasped her cold hands and began to chafe them. Still she sat, frozen. 'Miss Latimer?' Already unnerved, he began to get impatient. 'Damn it, answer me!'

'Yes.' Her voice was faint.

'What is it?' Her eyes were opened now, but glazed, her focus obviously fixed on some inner torment. 'What ails you?'

There was no response. Trey bent down and retrieved the scarab, still on the chain that Richard had worn around his neck, and tried to press it into her hand.

'No,' she said sharply, shying away.

He closed his hand around it, feeling the bite of the insect's sharp legs. 'Richard's last wish was for you to have this,' he said roughly.

'I don't want it.' The words emerged in almost a sob. She clapped a hand over her mouth, eyes wide as if in horror at her own lack of control. Trey watched as she drew a deep breath and stood. 'Do you hear me, Lord Treyford? *I do not want it!*'

Trey was dumbfounded. Here was yet another twist to this horrifyingly convoluted day. He stared at the girl, wondering where the calm and remote young lady he had walked out with had gone. 'That is unacceptable,' he said flatly. 'I made a pledge to your brother that I would deliver it to you.'

She looked unimpressed.

'I gave my word of honour.' As far as he was concerned, that was the end of the matter.

Apparently it was for the girl, as well. It quickly became obvious that he had pushed her past the point of restraint. She stood poised, indignation in every taut line of her body, those incredible dark eyes glittering with emotion. 'I don't give a tinker's damn for your honour,' she ground out. 'Family honour, a man's pride, I've had my fill of it. It is all just fancy trappings and convenient excuses for doing whatever fool thing engages you, regardless of who you hurt or neglect in the process.' She cast a scornful glance over him. 'You keep it, Lord Treyford, and if by some miracle you do find the Jewel, then you may keep that as well.'

'Jewel?' Trey asked. He was getting damned tired of feeling like the village idiot, not understanding who was who or what was happening around him.

She let out a distinctly unladylike snort and turned away from him.

'Now, you wait just a moment. Keep it?' Hastily Trey got to his feet, trying to tamp down on the flickering rise of his own anger. 'Keep it, you say? If I had wanted to keep the cursed thing I would have stayed in Egypt,' he said, growing more furious with each word. 'I would not have abandoned my plans, given up my work, and tramped halfway around the world to this…' he swept his arm in an encompassing gesture '…this insane asylum.'

He rubbed a hand across his brow, dampened the flames of his temper, searching for patience. 'Months, this has cost me months.' With a sudden fluid movement, he thrust his arm out, dangling the scarab from its chain, forcing her to look at it. 'This thing meant something to your brother. It was so important that he spent his dying breath securing my promise to see it returned to you. And you ask me to keep it?'

For the briefest of moments he saw a stricken expression cross her lovely face, but then her eyes narrowed and her expression hardened. 'I know what it meant to my brother, and, worse, what it means to me.' She looked as if she meant to go on, but could not. Her spine straightened as she grappled with her emotions.

Trey was fighting the same battle, and losing fast. He glared at the girl, feeling helpless in the face of her irrational reaction, and resenting her for it. 'I promised Richard,' he repeated harshly. 'He lay in the sand with the life spilling out of him, and he took my hand and made me promise. To deliver this, and to protect you.'

'Protect me?' The sound that came from her was bitter, ugly. 'From what? The folly of trusting in selfish, egocentric men?' She raked him with a scathing glance. 'That lesson I have—finally!—taken to heart.'

She turned away, shaking with the force of the emotion racking her, and Trey could see the moment when she gained a measure of control. She turned, dashing the tears from her face, her voice once more composed. 'I apologise, sir, for taking my grief and anger out on you. I cannot… I need to spend some time alone just now. I trust you can find your way back on your own?'

She did not wait for an answer to her question. Trey stared in disbelief as she walked off, following the path farther into the wood. He stood watching her for several moments, debating whether to chase her down, before he glanced at the scarab in his hand. Turning, he walked back up the path towards the house.

He passed it by, going straight to the stables to fetch his horse. The wiry groom silently readied his mount, and Trey set out at a brisk pace, more than eager to put a stop to the most unsettling day he had experienced in years. He wished, suddenly and intensely, that he could send the scarab and a note and be done with the matter, that he could be free to make plans to return to his work.

The thought brought on a sudden longing for the simplicity of his time in Egypt. Long days, hard work, hot sun. It had been vigorous and stimulating. Hell, even the complexities of dealing with the wily Egyptian *kashifs* were as nothing compared to the chaos he'd unwittingly stumbled into.

There were too many things here he just did not understand. He had a promise to keep, it was as simple as that, but he could not quiet the worrisome thought that things were much more complicated here than they appeared on the surface.

Aswan had secured him a room in the village's best inn. The former headman—who had consented to leave Egypt and travel as Trey's manservant—expressed a substantial amount of surprise at his employer returning in a different suit of clothes from the one he had sent him out in. And though he was not usually the sort to chat with a servant, or anybody else for that matter, Trey found himself spilling the whole muddled tale as he stripped for a proper bath.

Now, as he gratefully sunk into the steaming tub, Aswan occupied himself brushing out Richard's coat. 'This vicar's wife, who made the trade with the boy,' he mused, his clever fingers making quick work of the task, 'she sounds most worthy. Should I wish to meet her, would it be frowned upon?'

Trey stared at the man. 'No, but why the hell should you wish to?' He regretted the harshness of his words when the Egyptian man raised a brow at him. 'If you do not mind my asking,' he said.

Aswan bowed. 'You may ask, *effendi*.' He returned to his work while he spoke. 'It is not often that one hears of a woman so generous and so wise as well. She accomplished her task, pleased the boy, and saved the young lady's face all at once.'

'Saved the young lady's face?' Trey wondered if there was some miscommunication at work here. 'From what?'

'From the discomfort of accepting charity. This is something of which you English do not approve, no?'

Trey sat up in the tub. 'Do you mean to say that that girl has been reduced to taking charity?' He experienced a sudden vision of the dusty, empty halls of Oakwood Court.

'Reduced? That is a good word,' Aswan said. 'Reedooosed.'

'Aswan.' His warning was clear.

'Yes, sir,' the man relented. 'It is common knowledge in the village that they are in trouble. The elder of the family, he is gone—no one knows where—yes?'

'Yes,' Trey said impatiently.

'His business—it goes on. There are the men who look after it.'

'Directors.'

'Directors. But the old man's own money, it is…iced? Froze?'

'Frozen? His assets are frozen?'

'Yes! And the family is left to support themselves until the old one is found. With Latimer *effendi* crossed over, it is difficult for them.'

Trey sank back into the warm depths of the tub. Well. That

explained quite a bit. Perhaps it also explained Richard's pleas for him to help Chione? Could her trouble be as simple as a lack of funds?

In any case, it gave him a clear reason to ride back out there first thing tomorrow. If Miss Latimer did not wish to keep the scarab, perhaps she would allow him to sell it on her behalf. After that, other arrangements could be set up to see the family through, at least until there was some word of Mervyn Latimer.

With hope, however slight, that his time in Devonshire might actually be near an end, Trey could at last fully relax. He heaved a sigh and laid his head on the back of the tub.

Poor Nikolas was still trapped in the tomb of the Ruby Idol.

Chione had fled to the library upon returning to the house, shutting herself in and the ugly truth out. Here she had sat at her desk, staring at the empty page before her, aware of how much more crucial that payment from her publisher had become, and yet unable to put a single word to paper.

She told no one the terrible news. Not yet. Mrs Ferguson brought her dinner in on a tray. Will came through seeking his lost atlas. Each time she pretended to be busy scribbling. They would know soon enough. Perhaps her household had accepted the truth long ago, along with the rest of the world, leaving her clinging to fruitless hope alone. Now, as the darkness grew around her and the house slipped into silence, she was forced to let that hope go.

He was dead. Her grandfather was dead. She had known it the moment she had seen that scarab. He had been obsessive about it and had worn it on his person always. In some way that she did not understand, the thing was tied up with the story of the Pharaoh's Lost Jewel. Richard, who had shared his unflagging interest in the ancient mystery, had believed that to be the reason that Mervyn Latimer kept the scarab close, but Chione had always believed it to be a symbol, a remembrance of his beloved son and of all the people he cared for, lost in the course of a long and dangerous life. For him to be parted from it, something catastrophic must have happened. But how had Richard come to have it? Why? A sound escaped from her, a rasping, horrible sound. It didn't matter. They were both gone and she was alone.

The place deep inside of her where her hope had been, her faith in her grandfather's ability to survive anything, was empty. But not for long. Pain, and, yes, anger and betrayal too, rushed at her, filling the hollow spaces, until she could contain herself no longer. She stood, unable to bear even the light of the single candle on her desk. She fled to the darkest recesses of the library, to Mervyn Latimer's favourite stuffed wing chair, and, flinging herself into it, gave in to her grief.

Long minutes passed as her inner storm raged, battering her with emotion. She cried for her grandfather, her brother, for her parents who had died long ago. She cried for the two children upstairs who were orphans now, just as she had been. She cried for herself. But gradually the howling wind of grief abated, leaving her spent.

Unflinching acceptance, warm approval, boundless love— these were the things her grandfather had given her, what she would never feel from him again. The thought loosed another painful, racking sob. He had taken her from chaos and given her security, happiness, a family.

Chione had been born in Egypt, to the Egyptian wife of Mervyn Latimer's son. But her parents had died when Richard was an infant, and Chione a child of only eight. She had recollections of them, of her mother's soothing hands and Edward Latimer's booming laugh. But she had other memories too, harsh and ugly memories that she had locked away, hidden from the world and even from herself.

She had no wish to bring them to light again. And for a long time there had been no need to, thanks to Mervyn Latimer. He had come to Egypt, carried both Richard and her to England, taken them in, and raised them with love.

Now he was gone and their roles were reversed. It was Chione who was left alone, with two children who had no one else to turn to. Chione was the protector now, and though the weight of yet another role might be heavy, it was one she would embrace. Not just because she already loved those children as if they were her own, but also because it was fitting somehow. Here was her chance to give back some of what she had herself been given. Acceptance. Family. Love. And if it came with a price, well, then, she was happy to pay it.

The thought had her rising, going back to her desk. She pulled out the well-worn letter from Philadelphia and spread it with gentle fingers. America, a land where people focused forwards instead of back, where new ideas were welcomed instead of shunned. She thought she might have flourished there, been of use, accomplished something truly worthwhile. A tear dropped on to the vellum, blurring the ink. Carefully, she folded it and put it away. Her dreams might need to be smaller now, but they would be no less important.

The untouched dinner tray still sat on the edge of her big desk. Chione saw that Mrs. Ferguson had placed today's post on it as well. Wearily she glanced at the notice from the butcher, a cordially worded reminder, which none the less explained why she had sent Will to fish for their supper today. She put it aside and picked up the next, and then she stilled. It was a letter from Mrs Stockton.

The woman was grandmother to Will and Olivia, though a

cold and self-involved one at best. Chione read the note quickly and with distaste. Yet another hint for an invitation to visit. The horrid old woman had shown no inclination to become involved with the children after their mother, her daughter, had passed on. She had even refused to see Olivia, the infant her daughter had died giving birth to. Her renewed interest in them had not come until after Mervyn Latimer had been gone long enough to cause concern—and when the possibility of his fortune passing to her young grandson occurred to her. Well, she would have a long wait before she received what she was hinting for; Chione had enough trouble without inviting it into her home.

Her home, yes. Her children, her responsibility, and not just now, but for ever. Chione straightened her spine and looked to her empty paper with new determination. She doubted the trustees would believe the scarab to be as definitive a sign as she did. Which meant no money coming in and no further hope of rescue, either. It could be years before they decided to release Mervyn's funds. Her writing had made the family a little more comfortable in the past few months. It would have to do more in the future. Dashing the last tear from her eye, she took up her pen and bent to work.

Nikolas had at last scrambled free of the collapsing tomb when she heard the noise. She dropped her pen and lifted her head, straining to hear.

Chione might not be a mother, but she had the instincts of one. She knew all the noises the old house gave forth as it settled during the night. She knew the far-off buzzing that was Mrs. Ferguson's snore. She hunched her shoulders each night against the gritty sound of Will grinding his teeth in his sleep, and she recognised the occasional thump that was Olivia falling out of bed. This sound was none of those.

Her candle had burned low, its pool of light spreading no further than the paper she had been writing on. Heart thudding, she left it and rose to slip into the hall.

The noise had come from upstairs. Chione paused long enough to cross to the wall where a collection of antique knives was hung. She slipped one from its mount, an ancient flint blade with an ivory handle. At the foot of the stairs she removed her sturdy boots, then silently padded up in stocking feet, instinctively avoiding the creaking spots.

Halfway up, she froze.

A muffled sound had come from below, from the direction of the kitchens. Someone was in the house. One person moving about, or two? It did not matter; she had to check the children first.

Chione eased on to the landing and trod as silently as she could into the hall. There was another, smaller noise that still sounded loud in the inky darkness. Her room, she thought gratefully, not Will's and not Olivia's.

But Will's room was nearest and the door was slightly ajar. She put her back against the wall right next to the door and listened. Nothing. Peeking in, she saw only Will, sprawled out fast asleep. But where was Morty? Her customary position at the foot of the bed was empty.

Chione found the dog a little way down the hall, bristling silently directly outside the closed door to her own room. Sending out a silent prayer, she crouched next to the dog and placed one hand on the knob. The ivory knife handle in her other hand had grown warm. She gripped it tightly, breathed deeply, then gave the knob a quick turn and thrust the door open.

Morty was through in an instant, emanating a dangerous

rumble as she went. A bark, a crash, a thump. Cautiously, Chione followed the dog in. Her window was open. Bright moonlight spilled through it, illuminating the shambles her room was in, framing the figure crouched in the window frame, and blinking wickedly off the long blade he held over Morty's head.

Chione didn't stop to think. She hefted the well-balanced blade and threw with all her might. The black figure grunted, then turned and went out the window.

'A very nice throw,' a deep voice said right behind her.

Chione gasped, and her heart plummeted to her feet. She spun around and fell back. Two large and capable hands reached out to steady her and she looked up, directly into the brilliant blue eyes of the Earl of Treyford.

Chapter Four

Trey waited until the girl had steadied herself before he released her.

'There are more below,' he said in a low voice. 'Fetch the boy, I'll get the girl. Where is she?'

He had to give credit where it was due. Miss Latimer did not bluster, swoon, or ask idiotic questions as he had half-expected her to do. 'Across the hall,' she whispered, and, taking the dog, turned back towards Will's room.

Trey crossed the hall and stealthily opened the little girl's door. He sent up a silent request to whichever deity might be listening, hoping that the babe would not squall when awakened. He need not have worried. Nerves of steel must pass with the Latimer blood, along with those incredible eye-lashes. Hers lay thick against her round, little cheeks, until he hefted her into his arms. Their one brief meeting must have made an impact, for she peered up at him, then tucked her head against his shoulder and promptly went back to sleep. He heaved a sigh of thanks and crossed back to the hall.

Miss Latimer was already there, along with a wide-eyed, young Will.

'We must move quickly and silently,' Trey whispered. He

shook his head when Miss Latimer would have taken the little girl from him. 'No, I'll hold on to her, unless we run into one of them. Then you take her and run for the stables.'

'Mrs Ferguson?' she asked.

'Is already there, with my man and your groom. They should have a vehicle ready when we get there.' Trey nodded and set out for the stairwell. 'Quietly, now.'

She reached out a restraining hand. 'No, Lord Treyford. This way.' She took a step backwards, and gestured farther along the hallway.

He might have argued, but Will grasped his forearm and hissed, 'Listen!'

Everyone froze. From the direction of the stairwell came a soft, ominous creaking sound.

Trey promptly turned about. 'Lead on,' he whispered. 'As fast as you can.'

They did move quickly, passing several more bedchambers before taking a connecting passage to the left. Almost at a run, they reached the end of that hallway in a matter of moments. Trey cursed under his breath. There was nothing here except a shallow, curved alcove holding a pedestal and a marble bust. Not even a window to offer a means of escape.

There was no time for recriminations. Trey's mind was racing. Could these be the same bandits who had murdered Richard? Was it possible they had followed him all the way from Egypt? If it were true, then they were desperate indeed, and he had to keep these innocents out of their hands. 'Back to one of the rooms. Are there any trees close to this end of the house?'

'No, wait a moment.' Miss Latimer was part way into the alcove. It was hard to discern in the near darkness, but he thought she was probing the wainscoting. 'Ah, here we are,' she whispered.

He waited. The dog gave a soft whine. There was a grunting sound from Miss Latimer's direction. 'Give it a push, Will,' she urged. 'No, there. Go on, hurry!'

The boy disappeared into the alcove, followed closely by the dog. Trey moved closer and could only just make out the outline of an opening in the curve of the back wall.

'In you go,' said Miss Latimer calmly. 'I will come behind you and close it.'

'Archimedes, is it not?' Trey said with a nod towards the bust. 'Someone has a fine sense of irony,' he whispered as he squeezed past her in the tight space.

He, in the meantime, had a fine sense of all the most interesting parts of Miss Latimer's anatomy pressing into his side as he passed. No, she was not the dried-up spinster he had expected, but apparently neither was he the jaded bachelor he had believed. One full-length press—in the midst of a crisis, all clothes on—and his baser nature was standing up and taking notice. Ignoring it, he moved past.

He had to stoop to enter the hidden doorway, and found himself on a tiny landing. Ahead he could barely discern a narrow set of stairs. Then the door slid home and the blackness swallowed them.

He reached out a hand. The other wall was mere inches away. If he had stood erect and unbowed, his shoulders might have brushed both sides of the passage. Suddenly she was there, close against him again, her mouth right at his ear. 'Archimedes fought and died. We shall run and live.'

Her words were in earnest. The situation was serious. And still a shiver ran through him as her breath, hot and moist, caressed his skin.

Trey muffled a heartfelt curse. His head was still bent in the low-ceilinged corridor, an awkward position made more so by the child resting against his shoulder. Danger lay behind and the unknown ahead, and he must face it saddled with a woman and two children. This was hardly the first scrape he'd found himself in, but it ranked right up there with the worst of the lot. And despite all this, still his body reacted to the nearness of hers. To the scent of her hair. To the sound of her breathing in the darkness. For some reason he did not fully comprehend, all of this infuriated him.

'Go,' he said in a low, harsh whisper. 'I'll be right behind you.'

She moved on silent feet down the narrow stairs. Trey followed, one arm cradling the child close, the other feeling the way ahead. At the bottom, the passage continued in a bewildering set of sharp turns. Several times Trey's trailing fingers found the empty air of a connecting branch, but Miss Latimer passed them by, moving forward at a good pace and with an air of confidence that he hoped was well founded.

Presumably the upkeep of the secret corridors was not high on the housekeeper's duty list. Cobwebs clung to his hair, stuck to his face, and soon coated his seeking hand. Dust, disturbed by their passage, hung in the air and tickled his nose. Desperate, he turned his face into his shoulder, trying not to sneeze. The occupant of his other shoulder had no such compunction.

How did such an immense noise come from such a small person?

The adults both froze, listening, hardly daring to breathe. Not far away, on the other side of the passage wall, sounded a triumphant shout.

Once more he felt the press of that lithe body, soft against his. 'We're near the upper servants' quarters,' Miss Latimer whispered. 'They will waste time searching them. There is another set of stairs just ahead.'

For just that moment, her scent, light and fresh, engulfed him nearly as completely as the darkness. But as she moved away and they began to descend the second stairwell, the air grew dank and the walls moist. They were moving underground.

'Where?' Trey growled quietly.

'The bake house,' she replied.

It was not far. In a matter of a few minutes they were climbing out of the clammy darkness, emerging into a small, stone building, still redolent with the rich, yeasty smell of fresh bread. Will stood on a box, just next to one of the high windows.

'There was a man at the kitchen door, but he went into the house a moment ago,' he whispered.

Trey turned on the girl. 'Who are they?'

'You don't know?' Her startled look was authentic, Trey judged. 'I have no idea!'

Perhaps not. He decided to leave the rest of that conversation for later. 'How far to the stables?' he asked, handing the child over.

'Not far,' said Will.

'Past the gardens and the laundry, beyond that grove of trees,' Miss Latimer answered. 'Perhaps a quarter of a mile.'

Trey suppressed a groan. It might as well be a league, with this ragtag group.

'We will stay off of the path,' he ordered in dictatorial fashion, 'and under the trees as much as possible. If you see anyone, drop to the ground as quick as you can, as silently as you can. We'll go now, before the sentry comes back to the kitchen door.'

Moonlight was streaming in the high windows; he could see the worry in Chione Latimer's eyes, though she had displayed no other sign of it. 'I'll go first,' he said. 'To the back of that garden shed.'

He paused, and caught her gaze with intent. 'If something

happens, go back into the passages and find another way out. Don't stay there, they will find their way in, eventually.'

Her expression grew grimmer still, but she only nodded.

Trey went to the door and opened it a fraction. He stood watching for a short time, but saw nothing, heard nothing except the usual nighttime chorus. The noise, in and of itself, was reassuring. Taking a deep breath, he plunged out of the door and sprinted to the shelter of the tiny garden shed.

Nothing—no shouts of alarm, no explosion of gunfire, no whistle of a knife hurtling through the air. He looked back at the seemingly empty bake house and motioned for his little group to follow.

They came, silent and swift. When they had reached him and stood, gasping in fright and fatigue against the old wooden wall, he felt something alien surging in his chest. Pride?

He pushed it away. Emotion, never a safe prospect, could be deadly in a situation like this, and besides, his stalwart band still had a long way to go. He took the child back again and nodded towards the nearby grove of trees.

What followed had to be the longest fifteen minutes in the history of recorded time, let alone in Chione's lifetime. Like mice, they scurried from one place of concealment to the next, always stopping to listen, to test for danger. They saw no one. Eventually they reached the stables. In the moonlight Chione could see that the great door stood open a foot or so. Morty, who had been sticking close to Will's side, suddenly surged ahead, tail wagging, and slipped in the building.

Chione sighed and hefted Olivia a little higher on her shoulder. She'd endured a maelstrom of emotions today, and now it seemed they were all coalesced into a heavy weight upon her soul. The scarab, she thought. It had to be that damned scarab.

She had barely set one foot in the door before she found herself enveloped in Mrs Ferguson's arms, the house-keeper's heavy rolling pin poking her in the side. For one, long, blessed moment, she leaned into the embrace. All she wanted was to just collapse, sobbing, into the older woman's arms, and not only because of the handle digging into her ribs.

'What did you mean to do—make the man a pie?' Lord Treyford asked the housekeeper with a nod at her weapon of choice.

'Wouldna be the first heathen I beat the fear of God into with this,' Mrs Ferguson answered, releasing Chione to brandish her rolling pin high.

'Speaking of heathens, that is my man, Aswan,' Lord Treyford said, waving a hand at the man standing watch near the door.

He bowed, and Chione's skin prickled. She handed the still-sleeping child to the housekeeper. It had been a long time since she had seen an Egyptian face. 'With you be peace and God's blessing,' she said in Arabic.

He bowed low, but did not answer. He looked to the earl. '*Effendi*, we should go now.'

They had everything ready for a quick escape. Will's sturdy Charlemagne had already been hitched to the pony cart. He was the last left; the other horses had been sold to finance Richard's trip to Egypt. Her heart heavy, Chione tried to ignore the empty stables, the stale atmosphere.

Would the house look as forlorn, when those men did not find the treasure they had come for? Would they destroy the place in revenge? Steal away Grandfather's collections as a substitute? Or, God forbid, set the house ablaze in their anger?

She stiffened her spine and raised her chin. Let them. All

of her valuables were right here. And tonight, they were under one man's protection. She looked for the earl and found him watching her. Inexplicably, she felt her spirits lift.

'Can you drive the cart?' he asked her. 'Aswan and I will ride.'

She nodded. He put his hands on her waist to lift her up to the seat, and Chione felt her hard-fought-for composure slip. She waited for him to release her, but his large grip lingered. One heartbeat. Two. Three. A swirling flood of warmth and unfamiliar pleasure flowed from his hands. It filled her, weighed her down, slowed her reactions, and very nearly stopped her mental processes altogether.

With difficulty she broke the contact, moving away from his touch, berating herself as she settled on the seat and took up the reins. Could nothing—not grief, danger or exhaustion—temper her inappropriate reactions to the man?

She turned to watch as old Eli helped Will and Mrs. Ferguson into the back of the cart and found that, yes—something could. Shock, in fact, proved most effective. 'Who is that?' she gasped. An injured man lay in the front of the cart, curled on to a makeshift pallet.

'Watchman,' Lord Treyford said tersely. 'His fellow came to alert us when they spotted the intruders lurking about. We found him out cold. Eli has seen to him.'

She stared as he took the lead of the village hack Aswan led forward. 'A watchman? Then you were expecting trouble?' The accusation hung unspoken in the air.

'No, not exactly,' he bit out, swinging up and into the saddle. He spoke again and the timbre of his voice crept even lower than his usual rumble. 'I promised Richard that I would bring you the scarab. When he begged me to, I promised to protect you. But truly, I thought it to be a dying man's fancy. Not for a moment did I believe that any danger connected with the thing wouldn't be left behind in Egypt. I never imagined the sort of trouble we've seen tonight.'

He made a grand sweep of his arm, indicating the stable, the wounded man, the cart packed full of her dishevelled family. 'I expected to come here and find Richard's spinster sister facing a civilised problem: a neglectful landlord, investments in want of managing, a house in need of shoring up. *Not* a girl barely out of the schoolroom, grubby children, flirtatious dogs and village gossip. *Definitely* not a hysterical tirade, secret passages and a narrow escape from armed intruders in the night!'

His mount, sensing his ire, began a restless dance. Seemingly without effort, he controlled it, bending it to his will even as he continued his tirade. 'The answer to your question is "No". Thanks in part to everyone leaving me in the dark—no, I was not expecting trouble. In fact, you have only Aswan, who had the foresight to suggest a lookout, to thank for our presence here tonight.' He glared at her from the back of his horse and finished with a grumble. 'Not that we were much use, in any case.'

Chione should have been insulted. She stared at his flashing blue eyes, his big frame emanating pride, anger and chagrin, and she was once more reminded of the exaggerated characters in her novels. The Earl of Treyford was prickly, harsh and bossy. He was also clearly angry with himself for not anticipating tonight's events and honest enough to admit that it was his servant's precaution that had saved the day—or night.

Though he might be the last to admit it, Lord Treyford was a man of honour. And she was not so easily subjugated as a restless mount.

Clearing her throat, she met his defiant gaze squarely. 'Then I extend my most heartfelt thanks to Aswan, my lord,' she said with all sincerity, 'for I am very glad that you are here.'

* * *

Her conciliatory tone mollified Trey, but only for a moment. In the next instant, he grew suspicious. In his experience women used that tone when they wanted something. Her wants did not concern him, only his own needs.

Unfortunately, he became less sure just what they were with every passing moment. Guilt and frustration gnawed at him, and he resented the hell out of it. He had years of experience behind him, decades of avoiding people and the tangled messes they made of their lives. And look what one day in the Latimer chit's presence had brought him to.

'Let's move,' he said as Aswan opened the door wide enough to get the cart out. 'Will says the track through the wood will bring us out on to the coast road. From there we'll go straight to the inn.'

Cautiously, they set out. The forest lay in silence; the few noises of their passage were the only discernible sounds. The coastal path was deserted as well, leaving Trey no distraction from the uncomfortable weight of his own thoughts.

There was no escaping the truth. He hadn't taken the situation seriously, had not considered that something like this might happen. The thought of that girl, those children and what might have been was unbearable.

Damn it   he was tired of being kept in the dark! What did everyone but him know about that wretched scarab? What was it about the cursed thing that could possibly have stirred these bandits to follow it halfway around the world? He didn't know, but he was damned sure going to find out.

To that end, and to the hopeful thought that the sooner he dealt with these sneak thieves, the sooner he could shake the Devonshire dust from his boots, Trey left his ragtag group in the care of the disconcerted innkeeper and turned his horse's head back the way they had just come. Fortunately, the first watchman had not been idle. He had a half-dozen men gathered, and though they were armed only with cudgels and pitchforks and one battered French cavalry pistol, they were eager enough. Trey gave them a terse set of instructions and they set out again for Oakwood Court.

But it was to no avail. The intruders were gone, leaving behind only a thoroughly searched house and a flattened juniper bush below the open window of Miss Latimer's chamber.

The taste of frustration was not one Trey was overly familiar with. Now he found it had a sour flavour that he did not care for at all, especially when he'd spent the last four-and-twenty hours having it forced down his gullet. So he was in a foul mood as he took to the saddle for what—his third trip today?— back to the little village of Wembury. Aswan wisely kept his own counsel and without a murmur took possession of the horses as they dismounted once again in the inn's courtyard.

The innkeeper, Mr Drake, had evidently been awaiting their arrival. Trey eyed the man with a bit of distaste; he found him rather dandified for a proprietor of a backwoods inn.

'Lord Treyford, your…guests have all been accommodated. I must warn you, though, that the boy has been put on a cot in your room.'

'Thank you,' Trey answered. 'Of course, you will apply all of their expenses to my account.'

'Yes, sir. Thank you, sir. I had wondered…'

Trey was sure he had. In fact, he was sure that the whole village would be wondering by morning. But that was the least of his worries. Was he going to have to wait until morning to get some answers? 'Are they all abed, then?' he asked.

'Aye, they are.' The man leaned in close. 'Had you any luck, sir?'

'Only the ill sort.'

'Bad news, that is, my lord.' He shot Trey a wry look. 'Today all the good citizens of Wembury will be a-twitter with the gossip. Tonight they'll be wide-eyed in their beds, sure that they will be the ruffians' next victims.' Sighing, the innkeeper shook his head. 'Every rusty blunderbuss in the county will be hauled out of storage, just like in those hungry, restless months after the war. Back then, old Jeremiah Martin shot his own brother in the arse, thinking he was a run-down Peninsular veteran come to steal his prized hog. We'll be damned lucky if no one is killed.'

Drake heaved another sigh, then slapped a hand down on the counter, startling Trey. 'Well, then, my lord, I've an extremely nice brandy laid out in the private parlour, should you like a nip before you retire.'

Trey hesitated only a moment. It was obvious that Mr Drake was not averse to a little soporific gossip. Suddenly, despite his usual scruples, Trey discovered he might not be averse, either. He needed answers, and he might finally begin to ask the right questions if he had a better understanding of the situation. And tired though he was, somehow retiring to a chamber with Will—and no doubt the dog—held little appeal.

The private parlour was more elegantly done up than one would expect, and the brandy was indeed very fine. Trey leaned back into the comfortably stuffed chair. 'I would like to think that discretion is one of the services my money will buy, Mr Drake.'

'Certainly.' He returned Trey's look with a sober one of his own. 'In this case, however, my discretion is of no use to you. The men who rode with you tonight, they will talk.'

Drake held up the decanter and, at Trey's nod, poured them each a second drink.

'Gossip, superstition, unlikely tales of the supernatural, and the mysterious,' Drake said as he settled back into his chair, 'they are all an integral part of the atmosphere here. The locals thrive on it, repeat it and embellish it.' With a lift of his chin he indicated the floors above. 'Your friends, they are favourites, both in the locals' hearts and in their whispered conversations.'

'But what the hell is a wealthy shipping merchant like Mervyn Latimer doing setting up his family here?' Trey nodded his head towards the ceiling. 'Shouldn't the lot of them be living in Plymouth, close to the shipping offices?'

Drake sighed and took a drink. 'Mervyn is a man who likes his privacy. Not easy to come by when you are famous twice over. In addition…' he leaned closer and lowered his voice '…there are rumours that the young lady has dealt with her share of snobbery.'

Trey raised a brow in question.

'It's her foreign blood, I suppose, although if you ask me it's a damned shame. A lovelier girl you couldn't ask to meet, in every way. But you know how dreadful people can be to an outsider. Here, in a smaller society, it is easier for her.'

'Not to mention that here the people are more needful of her grandfather's money?'

'That too. In any case, we've our own deep-water quay, and in his sloop Mervyn could be at his main offices quickly enough.'

Trey took a drink and thought a moment. 'It seems to me that the girl is a sight more needful of her grandfather's money than anyone else.'

'And so she is,' sighed Drake. 'But without proof of Mervyn's death—no body or any known catastrophe such as a shipwreck—the company remains in the hands of its board. Without his influence that group squabbles more than the local Ladies' Aid Society. So much so that the courts have ordered Mervyn's shares frozen pending investigation into the matter.'

'And who knows how long such an investigation will take?'

'Who knows when they will even begin, is the question.'

'So,' Trey mused, 'the girl is accepted here, but left near to destitution and still gossiped about?'

Drake flashed Trey a rueful smile. 'But who among us could resist—especially when you throw in such a topic as the Pharaoh's Lost Jewel?'

The jolt of excitement Trey felt had him sitting up a little straighter. Miss Latimer had mentioned a jewel, had she not, when he tried to give her the scarab?

'I don't know the legend,' he said, striving for a casual tone. 'What can you tell me of it?'

'Perhaps I would be better suited to answer that,' a sharp feminine voice said from the doorway.

It should have been impossible for a man of his age and experience, but Trey found himself blushing like a schoolgirl caught gossiping under the covers. Drake, however, seemed unperturbed, rising to greet the Latimer girl with his usual smoothness.

'Miss Latimer, I had thought you abed. Ah, it is not surprising that you should have difficulty sleeping after such a dreadful experience. Shall I warm you some milk, to help you drift off?'

Arms crossed, she leaned against the doorjamb, all injured dignity and unrelenting disapproval. 'No, thank you, Mr Drake.'

'Well, then, since you are awake…' he glanced at Trey with sympathy. 'A message was left here for you earlier. I shall just fetch it.'

He eased his way past her, but her disdain appeared to be focused firmly on Trey. He pasted on his most obnoxious look of unconcern and waved her into the room. 'Good, I am glad you are up. We have much to discuss.'

'Yes, so much that you decided not to wait for me, I see.'

Trey shrugged. 'Drake said you were abed. I merely meant to begin sorting out this mess.'

She glared, but held her peace as Drake returned, a sealed missive in hand. He handed it to her and shot Trey a mute look of apology.

Trey ignored him. A belated sense of uneasiness had him watching the girl instead. Who would be sending the chit a message here? A curious look passed over her face as she broke the seal and began to read.

'Something is not right,' he said. 'Who, besides the people in this room, or asleep upstairs, would know you are here?'

She did not answer. Trey glanced over at her. Even in the candlelight she looked bloodless. Her face was blank, her gaze fixed to the sheet she still held with trembling fingers. Trey had to suppress a sigh of exasperation. Lord, not again.

'What is it?' he asked. 'Miss Latimer?'

Mutely, she handed him the paper.

It was too much; too many emotions for a person to process in a single day. Chione found that her trembling legs would not support her. She sank into Mr Drake's abandoned chair and watched Lord Treyford read the note.

Le grand homme de la vague déferlante, he lives. He is in need of help. Find the coffer.

Alive. For a moment she was convinced that it was an illusion, a hallucination concocted out of her own grief and fear. But the proof was right there in Lord Treyford's hand.

Hungrily, she stared at it. Thank God, she had been wrong. Mervyn was alive.

'What is this? A man from the...surf? What nonsense is this, Miss Latimer?'

'*Great* man of the surf. Or something close to that. I think perhaps that part of it was originally in an island dialect.'

'*What* was in—?' His voice, growing loud again with impatience, suddenly broke off, and the look he gave her softened into a sort of exasperated pity. 'Miss Latimer, as much as it pains me, perhaps we should postpone this discussion. I fear the excitements of the day have been too much for you. Let Mr Drake show you back to your chamber.'

'No, I am fine. Do not fear, Lord Treyford. I have not come unhinged.' Chione's weary brain had finally processed the rest of the message. Mervyn was alive, but he needed help. How could she help him? She hadn't a clue as to where he was. And what was the coffer? All at once the fatigue that had swept over her was gone, lifted by her incredible relief, replaced by her anxiety, her need to be doing something, anything, to get to the bottom of all of this. She stood, then began to pace, from the fire to the window, and back again.

'Miss Latimer,' Lord Treyford began with a commanding rumble, 'sit down. I am a man of very little patience, and you have already consumed what small amount I possess.'

Chione swore she could feel his words resonating in the pit of her belly, and for some reason the sensation sent her restlessness spiralling even higher. He wore a tremendous frown and his knuckles were white where he clutched the note she had given him.

Her fingers shook as she went to extricate it. For a moment she was close enough to feel the heat and the aura of masculinity that emanated from him. 'I do apologise, but do you understand what this means? It means I was wrong. Mervyn is alive.'

He ran a hand along his jaw and up to his temple. When he spoke it was with the exaggerated patience one uses with a wayward child.

'I think, Miss Latimer, that it is time for you to sit yourself down and start giving me some direct answers.'

She opened her mouth to respond, but he held up a halting hand. 'No, don't talk. I am going to do the talking, you are going to answer only the questions I put to you. But before we begin, I am going to need another drink. Or two.'

He crossed over to a tray already set with a decanter and glasses. Chione sat in a chair in front of the empty fireplace and watched him toss one drink back immediately and pour himself another. When he returned, he held two glasses. He offered her one.

'Oh, no. I don't think…'

He held up his hand again. 'No. No talking and no thinking. Either is bound to get me in trouble. Take the drink, and just answer.'

He took the chair across from her and sat, staring at her with that broody frown that set her insides to simmering. Chione had had enough. 'Before I answer your questions, I have one of my own. Do you still have the scarab?'

He was startled enough to answer. 'Of course.'

She sat back in her chair in relief. 'I'm afraid I must apologise for my earlier outburst and tell you that I do indeed wish to have it.'

'Tonight would illustrate that you are not alone in that desire.'

She started to speak, but he cut her off. 'No, I do not want to hear protestations that it could have been something else that those thieves were after. We both know the truth. They wanted the damned scarab, and it's only dumb luck that they don't have it right now.'

Chione froze. Had his intentions shifted upon the discovery of the scarab's value?

It seemed he read her mind. 'I travelled here to bring the curst thing to you,' he growled, 'and so I shall. After you have given me what *I* need.'

Chione took a sip from her glass for courage. She managed—only just—not to cough and sputter as it went down. 'And what is it that you need, my lord?' Her saucy delivery might have had an impact if not for the brandy-induced wheeze at the end.

'Information,' he clipped. 'I want you to tell me just what the hell that scarab really is. Why Richard was killed for it, why you damn near swooned at the sight of it, why someone followed me all the way from Egypt, damn it, to try to steal it from you tonight.' The rumbling volume of his voice had raised a notch with each question.

Chione sat silent, considering. He might be curt, temperamental, cranky, even, but Richard had trusted this man. And he had proven himself worthy, keeping his word, abandoning his work, clearly against his own inclination. And tonight he had saved them all.

Chione was many things, but not a fool. She needed to find Mervyn and knew she would not get it done on her own. She needed help. And as much as it galled her to put her faith in yet another adventurer, she wanted his.

'Tell me about the scarab,' he said gruffly.

She took another drink of the brandy. 'For as long as I can recall, it has belonged to Mervyn. He wore it always—in a pocket, or on a chain. When I saw it today in your hands, I believed that it meant that he was dead.'

'Believed. Past tense.' He glanced toward the note she still held in her hand.

'Yes.' She raised her chin in defiance. ' I know you will think that I am foolish, but there is good reason to trust in that note.'

He didn't challenge her statement, or pursue her reasoning. 'Did you know that Richard was searching for the scarab?'

'Not really. He seemed genuinely thrilled to be going back to Egypt at last, and excited about his position with the Museum.' She looked away. 'I suspected that he was also searching for information about Mervyn's disappearance, but he did not confide in me.'

'Neither did he confide in me,' Trey said flatly. 'I do not know just where he found the thing. I do not know if the others who sought it in Egypt are the same ones who were here tonight. I still know nothing of importance, in fact. Yesterday you spoke of a jewel, but the jewels have long since been pried from the scarab. Tonight Drake talks of a Pharaoh's jewel. Tell me now, just what is going on here?'

'It is an old tale, an ancient legend.' Her throat tightened until she thought she might choke on the words, but she forced herself to go on. 'No one is sure just what the Jewel is. Some say it is a collar fashioned in the ancient style, made of gold and inlaid with hundreds of precious gems, others say that it is a huge diamond brought from the deepest Africa. I have also heard that it is an entire cache of jewels, stolen from a great king's tomb long ago.'

'Is the scarab part of the treasure, then?'

'No, the scarab is reportedly the key.'

'The key to what—the cache? Or is it a key such as you find on a map?' She could heard the impatience in his voice.

'Perhaps. I think someone once told Mervyn that the Jewel

itsclf was a map, one that would lead to a lost land of many treasures.'

'I see.' The earl's gaze wandered for a moment. She jumped when he snapped suddenly back to attention and barked out a question. 'What did you grandfather believe?'

'I don't know!' Her hands were clenched to the arms of the chair. 'I was never truly interested in the legend, not in the way that the men in my family were. Did you know that my father was killed because of that cursed Jewel?' She paused and swallowed, but now was not the time to reveal the truth of her family relationships. 'He was murdered just because someone believed he knew something of it! When you showed up bearing that scarab, I knew that Richard had met the same fate and likely Mervyn as well. Now this note says that Mervyn is alive! His fate may hang in the balance and I just do not know!'

Panic reached down her throat and stole her breath away. What if it was true? She had despised the legend, hated the light in her grandfather's eyes when he spoke of it, the excitement in her brother's tone when he talked of leaving, of chasing after a myth. She had resented the way the story grew, interfering with their lives. When talk turned to the legend, she had turned away. And she had been right. Her father had been murdered because of it; most likely her brother had been killed seeking it. But what if her ignorance also doomed Mervyn?

'Calm yourself,' Trey ordered. He refilled her glass. 'We shall sort it all out. Tell me what you do know.'

She breathed deep. Panic accomplished nothing. If there was one thing she had learned from her troubled early life, it was the value of a clear head in a time of crisis. She drank again and drew courage from the warmth the brandy spread through her chest. 'That is nearly all of it,' she said shakily.

'The legend is old. It came to Europe when Bonapart and his delegation of scholars and artists returned to Egypt at the turn of the century. There was talk then, that the scarab had been found, and brought to France.'

'It wouldn't surprise me to find that true. Many items went home with the French.'

'My father was with the English when they fought Napoleon in Egypt. He became interested in the tale and, of course, told his father. And once Mervyn Latimer shows as interest, the rest of the world takes heed. From then on the Latimer name became entangled with the tale, to the extent that many people whispered that the Jewel had been discovered and moved here to Devonshire.'

'Oh, hell.' It was true sympathy Chione saw in Lord Treyford's eyes. 'I can well imagine the shenanigans that have resulted from that rumor.'

'Yes.' She knew her tone was grim. 'There have been incidents over the years. Stowaways, treasure seekers hiring themselves on as footmen, suitors more interested in interrogating Grandfather than in impressing me, that sort of thing.'

'Good God.' He pulled a face.

Chione shrugged. 'I suppose it is the price for living with someone who is more a force of nature than a mere mortal,' she said. Suddenly there was no fighting the swell of tears in her eyes or the sting of grief in her throat. 'I'd pay it a million times over just to have him back now.'

Treyford looked truly horrified now. Chione struggled mightily to control herself, but she was so tired, and her emotions were close to the surface. A sob escaped her despite her best efforts.

The earl stood. He had not flinched once in the face of danger earlier tonight, but now he looked ready to bolt. 'Well, then. You've given me enough to think on tonight. Why don't you go on back upstairs and get some rest?'

A fog-like haze had crept into the room, clouding the edges of her vision. Chione realized how immensely tired she felt. He was right, she would rest. She stood—but immediately began to sway.

'Oh, for the love of…' he stepped forward and placed a steadying hand at her elbow.

'Thank you.' Chione looked up at the blurred form of the earl and sudden tears blinded her further. How she envied his strength, his unfailing steadiness. Treyford knew ugliness, had been immersed in the murky, fctid underbelly of the world. Evidence of it lived there, in his eyes. He'd experienced things that most of the people in her English life could not imagine—just as she had. So often she felt her experiences had set her apart, for ever alone, some part of her still the troubled, disillusioned little girl. For the first time, though, she recognised a kindred spirit. Even better, his was a hearty soul, one that had survived the darkness, conquered it. He was strong and resilient—just exactly what she wished to be.

'How wonderful you have been,' she began. A terrible feeling of guilt made her feel ill. She wished suddenly that she could tell him the truth about herself and her hodge-podge family. But what if knowing caused him to change his mind?

'Yes, yes.' He was not so brave in the face of her emotion— a look of true horror crossed his face now. 'Let's get you up to your room.'

His hand still at her elbow, he set out for the door. But Chione's feet refused to co-operate. She stumbled, only to be caught up hard against Treyford's muscled frame. Instantly her fatigue fled, replaced with a new, humming awareness. The eager, unruly side of her, the persona that she kept ruthlessly hidden, reared to sudden awareness. Through the fog that had descended over her brain Chione allowed herself, for an instant, to look, to touch, to feel.

Heat. Immense strength. Her face was pressed against his chest, her fingers curled tightly around his arms. Instinctively she clutched him harder, because all of a sudden the earth was sliding away beneath her feet.

His arm slid slowly and surely down her body, pulled her up and steadied her. She screwed her eyes shut and revelled in the warmth, the sheer closeness of his strong, solid form. He cleared his throat and she sighed. The scent of him—sweaty male mixed with something foreign and exotic—faded just a bit as she lifted her head and gazed into his stormy blue eyes.

'Are you all right?' His face was set in grim lines.

She nodded.

'I'll take you up.'

He held her close as they navigated the stairs. How long since she had felt like this—truly safe? It made not a whit of sense, but undeniably she felt so, sheltered in the curve of his arm. At her door he stopped.

'You need to sleep.' He said it gruffly. An order.

She found she didn't mind. 'Yes, there will be the children to deal with in the morning.'

'Goodnight, then,' he said.

'Goodnight, my lord. And thank you.'

His relief as he left was obvious. Trying not to feel hurt, Chione opened the door and took herself in to bed.

Chapter Five

Trey came awake when the afternoon sun slanted into the tent and struck his face. It surprised him. He rarely slept during the afternoon rest that Egypt's fierce climate forced on every working man and beast. He pinched the bridge of his nose and thought the men must be enjoying the unusually long reprieve.

Then his hand fell back and hit the soft pillow he rested on, and he knew. England, not Egypt. He threw his legs over and sat upright, feeling the familiar wave of impatience, the pressing need to be moving—on to the next site, the next adventure, or perhaps just away from the ties of the past. Any of the above would suffice.

He reached for his trousers—and froze as yesterday's tumultuous events rushed him, along with the bitter realisation that his stay in Devonshire was likely far from over. Oh, to be sure, there was still that tingling of excitement, deep in his stomach, that came with the prospect of a mystery. He never could resist a challenge, and the riskier it was, the better he liked it. But it was one thing to pit himself—brain, bone and sinew—against an adversary. It was quite another to pitch headlong into a fight he still did not understand, and another thing again to wade into a fracas involving women and children.

And such a woman. Gorgeous, intelligent, strong. The sort of woman who stole a man's breath away, and then began to systematically strip him of everything else he held dear. A temptation even to Trey, who knew better.

What the hell time was it anyway? Where was Aswan? He rose and finished dressing, his uneasiness growing as he ventured forth from his room. The inn was quiet. Too quiet. Only a day's experience of the Latimer family had him expecting some sort of continual upset. But there was no sound of a dog barking, no children shouting, no angry cries from terrorised kitchen staff, nothing.

And no one. The taproom was deserted, as was the parlour. Finally he found Drake in the kitchen, debating the seasoning of a beef stew with the cook.

'Ah, Lord Treyford! You have awakened just in time. You will be first to test the stew and tell Henri that it needs a dash more thyme.'

It smelled heavenly. Trey's stomach rumbled, but he looked away from the dish that the cook set on the table. 'Not just yet, thank you. Where has Miss Latimer got to? And the children? I cannot believe they did not wake me earlier.'

'The young lady? She took her family back to Oakwood first thing this morning. Your man tried to awaken you. When he could not, he decided to accompany them himself.'

'Back—this morning?' Trey choked. 'Damned lot of fools! What if the thieves come back? What if they are watching the house?' He strode out of the kitchen and headed for the front door, calling for his horse as he went.

'But, my lord—' Drake was hurrying behind him '—they took the watchman you hired, and your Aswan as well.

We've heard of no trouble, only received orders for supplies and requests for a carpenter and a housemaid. They are surely unharmed!'

Not for long, Trey thought grimly. He threw the saddle over his mount's back himself. *Not for long.*

Chione had a nose fashioned from an old stocking. She had two large ears made of sturdy grey bombazine, a heavy passenger who kept striking her with his short sword, and, before her, a terrified Roman child barricaded behind an overturned chaise. She also had an audience, although she was sublimely unaware of it.

'*Hannibal am portas!*' shrieked the little Roman girl, resplendent in her toga.

'That's *Hannibal ad portas*, Olivia,' said Chione-the-elephant. She tried to hide her fatigue behind a crisp tone. 'And it was not only the children who feared such a dangerous enemy. The grown-up Romans were terribly frightened when Hannibal climbed over the Alps. It was a brilliant strategy, but he lost thousands of men on the dangerous journey.' Her passenger's shield struck her in the back of the head once again. Chione abruptly sat up, sending him tumbling to the carpet. 'I'm afraid you are just growing too heavy for this, Will.' Hands at her hips, she stretched her tired and aching back.

'Chione!' he complained. 'Surely Hannibal never fell from *his* elephants.'

'He rarely retreated in battle, either, young man, but look how well that served us yesterday,' said a familiar, deep voice from the doorway.

Chione gasped and tore off her long nose before turning. Lord Treyford stood there, amusement and annoyance warring in his icy blue eyes, Morty pressed lovingly to his knee. A rush of heat flooded her. Belatedly she reached up to snatch the ears from her head.

There were times when Chione mourned the loss of her Egyptian heritage, more when she missed the love and guidance of her mother. But there was one thing she had learned at her Eastern mother's knee and had used to her own advantage as she grew, and that was the value of an inscrutable demeanour. It leant an air of mystery and control that gave her an advantage. Right now she sorely needed one.

So she went with the tried and true. She ignored her mortification, and reached deep to find a semblance of composure, for she thought she would rather die than allow the Earl of Treyford to guess how he affected her.

Certainly Will, at least, appeared oblivious to her embarrassment. He had already laid aside his weaponry and greeted the man. 'I wish I could have faced those men last night head on, like Hannibal,' he grumbled, brash with a ten-year-old's sense of invulnerability.

The earl took up his sword to examine it. 'Hannibal had a force of over six-and-twenty thousand, and was fully prepared for many of them to die,' he said with an experimental slash of the air. 'You were part of a much smaller force, and I don't think even one of them could be regarded as expendable.'

Will grinned. 'You are right, of course, sir.'

Chione had recovered her composure enough to become annoyed. 'I have a suspicion that Lord Treyford might be one of those fortunate few who finds himself always in the right, Will.'

He failed to rise to the bait. 'Very often, I do, in fact.'

'Just like my father,' Will said knowingly. 'He always said that if Archimedes of Syracuse was so smart, he would have got the people out while the Romans were still occupied with their sea assault, instead of waiting for them to besiege the landward side. I guess we proved him right.'

'We did. Certainly Archimedes showed us the way last night.' He handed Will his sword back with a nod of approval and the first approximation of a smile she had yet seen from him.

She sighed and swept back a stray lock with tired fingers. He was most likely relaxed because he was here to bid them all goodbye. His servant, Aswan, had accompanied them today, and had been a tremendous help, but he had also mentioned— more than once—his employer's eagerness to be gone.

It had been a blow to hear it. Chione had left the servant and then spent a good part of the afternoon pounding spilled ashes out of rugs, wondering why all the men in her life suffered the uncontrollable urge to run away. With each strike she had meted out a metaphorical retribution. Her grandfather. *Thwack.* Her brother. *Thwack.* And now Lord Treyford. The resulting flurry had the rugs clean in a trifle.

It had been therapeutic exercise. She was in a better frame of mind now. In fact, she thought she might have siphoned off some of the earl's impatience, for that was precisely how she felt right now. There was much to be done, and she had a pressing eagerness to get on with it all. Much of the house still needed to be restored, guards would soon be arriving to be interviewed, and she must begin making arrangements for the search for Mervyn. But beyond a doubt, her greatest need was to bid adieu to the Earl of Treyford. He fractured her concentration, distracting her at a time when she could scarce afford it. What she wanted was his help, and if she wasn't going to get it, then it would be a relief to take back the scarab and be done with him.

And if she repeated that to herself a dozen more times, she might well come to believe it.

'Will,' she began, 'why don't you take Olivia to the kitchens? When Mrs Westcott arrived today she had a pudding and basket full of biscuits. I'm sure the two of you could coax something out of her.'

It was a sure ploy, for Will was a walking appetite. His eyes lit up and he reached for his sister's hand. 'Come along, Olivia. Biscuits!'

Treyford pried the dog's head from his knee. 'And take the dog, please!'

'Come along, Morty. Bone!'

The three of them trooped out. Chione sighed and turned back to the earl.

Her heart began to pound. All of the emotion, all of that focused intensity, had immediately resurfaced. It shone with unblinking fervour in his eyes, emanated from him as he stalked towards her across the room.

Chione was no strategist, but even she recognised the advantages of retreat. She stepped behind the overturned chaise. Pride forbade any show of weakness, however, so she strove for nonchalance as she flipped it right side up.

He only raised a brow and kept advancing, until his legs came up against the piece and only the narrow expanse of worn cushion separated them.

'Come along, Miss Latimer, rest!' he said in echo of Will's wheedling tone.

She raised her chin. 'Hardly fitting or amusing, sir, since I am neither a child nor an animal.'

The heat of his gaze was nearly palpable as it raked her dishevelled form from head to toe. Despite herself, Chione felt a flush rise to colour her cheeks as the earl slowly shook his head. 'No, you are neither, although I am in no need of a reminder.'

He paused and she struggled to keep her blush from intensifying. 'In point of fact, you are by far the most managing, frustratingly independent woman I've had the misfortune to encounter. You reject me, my help and the scarab soundly, you dispatch a sneak thief in the night all on your own, show us all the route to safety, and then return here, without waiting for me or anyone else, to start the clean up yourself.'

His tone was one of grudging admiration, but he ruined it when he pointed an imperious finger at the chaise. 'Now sit— before I am emasculated any further or you ruin your sterling reputation by passing out. You are as pale as a ghost and nearly trembling with fatigue.' He seized her hand and pulled her around the chaise.

She fetched up close against him, so close that she could feel the heat of his body. She caught herself inhaling, hoping to catch the spicy scent of him, but he let go and gestured for her to sit. 'Did you sleep at all last night?'

Mute, Chione shook her head and sat.

'I thought as much.' He sighed. 'Your lesson was charming and obviously effective, but could it not have waited?'

'The children were restless,' Chione shrugged. 'They are anxious too, and it is reassuring for them to carry on with normal activities in a time of stress.'

'Perhaps they would have been less stressed had they been still safe at the inn,' the earl suggested.

'We have been safe enough,' Chione bridled. 'Your watchmen assured us that all was clear before we left the inn.'

'You should have cleared it with me,' he growled.

'You would not awaken. There was much to be done.' And nothing left to be said. If he was going to take his leave, she wished he would proceed. Perhaps then her jittering, jumping insides would be still, and *she* could be the one to get on with her life.

'Still, a day in the village, even a day confined to the inn, would have been better for the children than returning here and seeing the ransacked house.'

Sarcasm must be as contagious as impatience. 'Ah, I had forgotten your vast experience with children, my lord. Yes, we should have spent the day frolicking while their fears grew apace.' She grew serious. 'Those two children know what loss is. It is far better for them to face a hard truth, rather than to fret and worry and allow their imaginations to take flight.'

Her explanation only appeared to annoy him more. He was pacing now, but he turned back, exasperation evident in the glint of his eye and the rigidity of his frame. 'Could you not simply relax for one day? Could you not give yourself a few hours to recover and your friends the chance to help you with your burdens? Good God, Miss Latimer, what is it that you are trying to prove?'

That had her out of her seat like a shot. His accusations struck true, but she would never allow him to see it. 'I am trying to prove nothing, my lord, only trying to do what must be done. It is no great insult to be called a managing female. It is who I am, what I do. I manage.' She crossed her arms and sniffed. 'Someone must.'

His expression went from exasperated to merely wary. 'Yes, someone must, and I would say you've done a damned fine job with a lamentable set of circumstances. But—'

'Thank you.' Chione had no intention of letting him say anything more. 'Mrs Ferguson and I *managed* to get much accomplished today, in putting the house to rights, and in arranging a permanent set of guards for the estate.'

He looked uncomfortable. 'Yes, we did not get a chance to discuss that note last night, did we? Perhaps now—'

'No, we did not. Nor did I get the chance to retrieve the scarab from you. You do have it with you, do you not?'

'Yes, I have it—'

'Good.' Chione drew a deep breath and tried to throw off both her fatigue and the knife edge of irritability that this man seemed to draw out of her. 'It seems we are for ever arguing. I do beg your pardon and I thank you most sincerely for all that you have done.' She held out a hand and with effort kept it miraculously steady. 'May I have the scarab now?' She gave a little laugh and tried to mean it. 'The relief you will feel at being done with it must only be exceeded by your desire to be quickly gone.'

He pulled it from a waistcoat pocket and willingly handed it over, but he wore a frown as he did so. Chione ignored it, concentrating instead on the scarab. 'The chain is not familiar to me—might it be yours?'

'No. It is in the same condition it was in when Richard gave it into my keeping.'

Chione turned the thing around and around in her hand. Something was nagging at her.

'I admit I am glad to finally see the thing in your hand,' he said.

She could not look at him. 'Yes, your duty is dispatched. Now you may be on your way.'

'Forgive me if I am mistaken, but that sounded remarkably like a dismissal.'

Chione looked up in time to catch the dangerous glitter growing in his blue gaze. 'No, of course not,' she said brightly. 'It is only that Aswan told us how eager you are to return to Egypt.' She forced herself to smile. 'I do wish you the best of luck in your work, Lord Treyford. Perhaps, if you wouldn't think it too improper, I might write to you some time in the future and share the tale of how this all comes about in the end?'

'Write to me?' He sounded incredulous. 'Hell, no.'

She lowered her gaze. 'I am sorry to presume.'

'I'm sorry you do too!' It was almost a shout, but Chione did not startle this time. She rather thought she was becoming immune to his unpredictable spikes in volume.

'Did you expect I would just drop that in your hand and traipse on my merry way?' he raged. 'Shall I offer you my congratulations on a lucky escape from unknown bandits and hop the next ship to Alexandria?'

That was exactly what she had expected—and exactly what she had spent the day alternately dreading and wishing for.

'Was that not your plan?' she whispered. She pooled the scarab's chain into her fist and held her breath.

'No, damn you, it was not!'

He looked truly affronted now, and Chione realised that while she had been so wrapped up in concealing her own feelings, she had wounded his.

'I am so sorry—' she began, but before she got any further the parlour door swung open. They both turned to face a grimy Mrs Ferguson. 'Viscount Renhust has come to call,' she announced. 'Again.'

Trey was so furious with the Latimer chit's presumptive dismissal of both him and his character that he actually missed the housekeeper's words. Yesterday he would have wept with joy to hear such a casual dismissal. Yesterday he would have kissed Miss Latimer's little, ink-stained hand and been out of Devonshire before nightfall.

But that was yesterday. Today was different, and he refused to consider the notion that anything more than her precarious situation made it so.

Then the housekeeper noted his presence and addressed him directly.

'Ye're here too, are ye? Good.' An older gentleman swept past her into the room and she pointed a finger at him. 'Keep an eye on that one, will ye? He bears watching.' And then she was gone.

The gentleman looked startled to find another man in Miss Latimer's parlour. He gave Trey an appraising glance and a cool nod before turning to the girl.

'Chione, could you please explain just why the servants are abuzz with talk of thieves and midnight raids? The entire coastline is in an uproar. Rumours have you all kidnapped or dead and the villagers under siege from merciless marauders.'

Trey snorted.

'Events have unfolded swiftly.' The girl stepped forward and took the man's arm.

'It would appear so,' he grumped. 'And I've had an irate letter from Mrs Stockton, too. She asks me to intervene on her behalf. It would appear she's willing to send Will off to school.'

'I've already declined such an offer,' Chione bit out. She shot a glance Trey's way. 'And we've more urgent matters to discuss. If I might present you to Lord Treyford?'

But Trey was feeling angry and ill used and incredulous. 'Introductions?' he snorted. 'I have had my fill of this madhouse. In less than a day I've been attacked by the dog and your dinner, prodded, shouted at, dismissed, and been caught up in a night-time raid by treasure-seeking bandits. Now you insult my honour, disparage my intentions and expect me to sit down to tea like some London milksop?'

'But I didn't, I thought...' the girl sputtered.

'Come now,' chided the gentleman.

Trey ignored him. 'There are six kinds of trouble afoot here and no time for tea parties! As much as you—or I—might bemoan it, the fact is I made a vow.'

'Treyford, did you say, my dear?' Scorn fairly dripped from the other man. 'That does explain it. I'd heard you had the wardrobe of a scarecrow and the mouth of a fishwife.'

'Lord Renhurst!' scolded Chione.

'Renhurst?' Trey repeated. 'You do have the advantage of me. I've never heard of you.'

'Gentlemen, please,' she pleaded. Into the following moment of silence came a soft whine. They all turned to the doorway. There stood little Olivia, with the trailing end of her toga in her mouth, and Will, kneeling, restraining an eager Morty, who obviously wished to join in the fracas.

Trey immediately pulled in on the reins of his temper, but the sight of the children had an opposite and far more spectacular effect on Chione Latimer. Suddenly the quiet, competent young lady was gone and in her place stood a hot-tempered virago.

'Enough!' she cried with a stamp of her fetching little foot, and Trey felt something ease inside of him. He hadn't realised he'd been waiting for something to shatter that implacable calm. Flashing eyes and fiery indignation suited her far more than that air of dutiful resignation.

He had to hide a smile as she pointed at the trio in the doorway. 'You three—up to the nursery and stay there until I come for you.' Two pairs of eyes widened, a tail tucked, and they were instantly gone.

'And you two—' She rounded on Renhurst and Trey with a molten-eyed stare worthy of an ancient Gorgon. Renhurst merely scowled back at the girl. Trey, however, felt the effect of her gaze, hardening in traditional male fashion. He turned away in an attempt to hide it.

She wasn't having it. She marched right up to him and glared into his face. 'Lord Renhurst is here because I asked him.' She spun on her heel and focused her anger on the viscount. 'Treyford is here because *Richard* asked him.'

'Richard?' That brought the other man to attention.

'Yes.' She glared at them both. 'My brother is gone, but I have a chance to save Mervyn, and I'll not let your petty squabbling get in my way.'

She turned those incredible eyes on Trey and he thought her gaze might have softened a bit. 'I am sorry if I injured your feelings.'

Before he could scoff at such a notion she poked a finger square in the middle of his chest. It startled him, but not as much as the warmth that spread from that small contact. It rippled outward and then quickly moved south to contribute to his growing discomfort.

'I know you hoped to deliver the scarab and be gone, but you also said you'd made a vow to protect me. I hope you meant it, because I'm going after my grandfather.' She paused, drew a deep breath and something dark moved in her gaze. Fear? Guilt?

'In a way,' she said, 'your help was Richard's last gift to me, and, by God, I'm going to accept it.'

Trey noted the determined set of her shoulders, caught the hint of pleading that she tried to hide. He acknowledged the rush of desire that this woman roused in him, and the other, more dangerous currents she stirred in his soul. All of his life he had courted danger, craved risk, lived for excitement, and not once had he experienced such a strong sense of foreboding. But what choice did he have, truly? Not one. So he nodded his head and gave himself over into the hands of impending doom.

Chapter Six

Chione let out the breath she hadn't realised she'd been holding. He was going to stay. She shushed the niggling part of her that still resisted putting herself into the hands of yet another thrill-seeking wanderer. She pushed away again the lingering guilt she felt at not revealing the truth about her family relationships. Without a doubt her chances of finding Mervyn had just dramatically increased; she couldn't take the chance of revealing he was no blood relation at all.

Lord Renhurst's shocked tones pulled her back to reality. 'Did you just say he delivered the scarab?'

Chione breathed deep and turned to face the viscount. 'I did. You see, somehow Richard found Mervyn's scarab. Lord Treyford brought it to me.' She pulled the piece from her pocket and watched the conflicting emotions cross his face.

'But, Mervyn wouldn't… If this has left his possession…'

'I know exactly what you are thinking,' she said, 'but, truly, all is well.'

His mouth set, Lord Renhurst reached for the scarab. Chione held it out to him, but was once again distracted by the chain. No, it was the clasp that bothered her. No simple hasp, it was an unusual, cylindrical shape. She pulled it back for a closer look.

It opened easily enough, but unevenly, so she was left with a small, solid, cuff-like disc in one hand and the long, slender cylinder that it fit into, in the other. She frowned. Why should such a short disc require such a long barrel?

It was then that she saw the tiny etching on the disc.

She gasped, 'Look!'

'What?' Both men were on their feet now.

'That mark—it's mine. My name, I mean.'

Treyford stood behind her, peering over her shoulder. She could feel the heat of him against her back, and lower. It settled around her, upon her, found its way inside to send a flush to her face. 'All I see are three wavy lines.'

'Yes, three parallel lines. It's meant to look like water.'

'Your name is water?' Treyford sounded sceptical, and she stepped away.

'No, her name is Chione—it means "Daughter of the Nile".' Lord Renhurst looked troubled.

'It is the mark I used when we played as children, having adventures, making up stories, sending secret messages.' She glanced at Lord Renhurst and gave a faint smile. 'Richard's was a pickaxe, and Mervyn's was a row-boat.' Excitement built inside of her. 'Don't you see? It's a message from Richard, but what could it mean?'

Chione had a sudden thought, and slipping the scarab from the chain, she put the artifact back in her pocket and examined the cylindrical piece once again. She gave a cry of triumph when she spied a thin seam encircling it, but nothing happened when she probed it with her fingernail.

'Here, let me.' Treyford had pulled a knife from his voluminous coat. She handed over the chain and he pried at the tiny line.

Chione was hovering so close she thought she heard the soft click when a hidden latch gave way. Inside the seemingly solid compartment rolled back and Chione froze when a small, white piece of paper fluttered out and to the floor.

With a look of pure disgruntlement, Treyford knelt and handed the rolled paper to her.

There was one word written on it—*Alden.*

Fighting back tears, Chione met the earl's gaze. 'I was wrong,' she whispered. 'This was Richard's last gift to me. Hope.'

It was a fitting gift from her brother, and one that Chione sorely needed during the hectic planning that followed. It served her well as she persuaded, cajoled, negotiated and threatened, until she had everything arranged to her satisfaction.

First both of her reluctant supporters needed convincing that Mervyn was indeed alive and in need of rescue. Neither of the two was inclined to put any faith in the note that had been left for her at the inn.

'You don't know who sent it,' said Treyford. 'It could have been the thieves, or someone working with them.'

Even Lord Renhurst was obstinate. 'I've known Mervyn Latimer for thirty years, and never heard him called something so ludicrous as Great Man from the Surf.'

'But don't you see,' argued Chione, 'that is exactly what makes this all the more believable. Almost no one knew of that name. He didn't want it mentioned. Ever.'

'Why not?' they both chorused.

Chione flushed. 'He was embarrassed. It was given to him by primitives off the coast of South America. He had stopped at one of the more remote islands to trade, and take on water and supplies. His long boat ran aground on a shoal at the mouth of a cove. Mervyn, impatient as ever, dove in and swam the rest of the way to shore, much to the amazement of the natives. They said they had never seen a man as strong as a mountain, with skin and hair as white as the caps of the sea.'

'I understand the name, then, but why the embarrassment?' asked Treyford.

Chione's colour deepened. 'Because the native chief agreed to trade, but he wished a favour in return.'

'What?' Both men were fascinated now.

'He wanted his first wife to have a child with hair the colour of the surf and eyes the colour of the sky.' Chione did her best to shrug her own discomfort off as immaterial. 'So you can see why he wished the story to be kept quiet,' she said earnestly. 'Only someone intimately acquainted with him would have known that name.'

Fascinated, yes, but they were not convinced. Chione despaired of changing their minds, until inspiration struck. 'Eli was there,' she said. 'Ask him.'

As Eli still would not set foot in the house, they all three trooped to the stable. They found the old groom lovingly brushing Lord Renhurst's big bay gelding.

'Eli,' Treyford called. 'Who is *Le grand homme de la vague déferlante*?'

The old man looked to Chione, and she nodded.

''Tis Master Mervyn,' He grunted. 'But if ye be calling him that when he returns, he'll be running you off the place.'

With that hurdle cleared at last, Chione unexpectedly encountered a more tenacious one: the universal conviction that she should stay at home while someone else travelled to speak to Mr Jack Alden.

'I can travel to London and back far more quickly without you,' said Lord Treyford.

'Alden may be a scholar, but he is the brother of a viscount,'

Lord Renhurst informed them. 'He'll be far more likely to speak freely with a proper gentleman.'

'Ye won't be going nowhere without a proper chaperon,' stated Mrs Ferguson flatly. 'And I'll not be standing by while the lot of ye run off, leaving the bairns in danger.'

The housekeeper's was the only argument that Chione heeded.

So it was that, after much debate and countless revisions, a plan was devised and settled upon.

First they would circulate the rumour that Chione was in need of funds and planned on selling the scarab.

'No one will have the least trouble believing that,' sighed Chione.

They put it about that Lord Renhurst was going to travel to London to make the transaction for her. Treyford, in the meantime, told everyone he encountered that he was returning shortly to Egypt and his work.

It was hoped that any trouble would follow Renhurst, who would travel armed to the teeth, with his groom, one watchman disguised as his valet, and another acting as a post-rider. The viscount assured Chione that the four of them could dispatch any attackers. They would travel on full alert, at a leisurely pace, leaving plenty of opportunity for mischief. In fact, he was so confident in his own success, Renhurst wrote ahead to make arrangements for the miscreants to be held in Tavistock, where he would wait for Chione and Treyford to meet him.

Treyford would make a show of his departure, but would double back to Oakwood Court in the night. He and Aswan would stay hidden in the house, just in case the attackers were not fooled and staged another assault on the house. If all appeared clear, then he and Chione—and a chaperon, inter-jected Mrs Ferguson—would leave Aswan, Eli, extra guards and Mrs Ferguson with the children while they met up with Lord Renhurst and then travelled on to speak with Mr Alden.

Leaving the children troubled Chione desperately, though she knew it must be done.

'Why not ask Mrs Stockton to come for a stay?' asked Renhurst once when she was fretting. 'She's a blood relation, I'm sure she'll be happy to help.'

'Absolutely not,' Chione stated in a hard, flat voice. 'I'll stay home myself, or drag the children along to London, before I ask a single thing from that hateful woman.'

Treyford looked up at her in surprise, but she refused to meet his gaze.

After a moment's reflection, Lord Renhurst nodded. 'I can't say I blame you.' He sighed. 'She's scarcely a model grandmother to those children, and I know that she's shown you her worst side more than once. But her mean streak wouldn't be your biggest problem in any case. Once she'd got herself ensconced here at Oakwood, I'd wager you'd have the devil of a time getting her to leave.'

Chione racked her brain and considered at least a hundred different scenarios, but finally had to concede that the children's staying behind was the best alternative. The realisation did nothing to ease her anxiety, however. So when she found herself briefly alone with Lord Treyford, she didn't hesitate to question him.

She was trying to haul a portmanteau unobtrusively to the carriage house, where Treyford was keeping the preparations for their journey hidden. He stood in the doorway, watching the children tumble on the lawns with Aswan. Shrieks of childish laughter rang out as Aswan played the stalking bear to Will and Olivia's Red Indians. Yet the peace of the scene could not soothe Chione's troubled heart.

'Learn-cloth?' asked Aswan.

'No, *loin*cloth,' said Will.

'*Loin*cloth,' the Egyptian repeated, nodding his head.

'I know you are fond of him.' Chione paused beside the earl, indicating the servant and hoping she would not offend Treyford. Aswan appeared to be a perfectly dutiful servant, but he set her nerves on edge. More than once she had felt the heavy weight of his gaze on her, but when she looked, he was always well occupied. 'I need to know that Will and Olivia will be safe. Are you absolutely certain of Aswan's loyalty?'

Treyford nodded his understanding, but kept his eyes on the laughing trio before them. For once Morty had abandoned him and was darting among them, barking madly. 'I trust Aswan implicitly and without hesitation,' he said. 'He has grown attached to the children. I believe he would lay down his own life to protect them, just as he almost did once for me.'

Chione could not hide her curiosity. 'What happened?'

Treyford shrugged. 'Cairo is a dangerous place. I had a gorgeous—and valuable—tomb statue to sell. Word must have spread.'

Chione could not hide the spasm of pain she felt at the mention of the treacherous Egyptian streets.

'Miss Latimer…?' He paused in his story.

'I'm sorry.' She waved a dismissive hand. 'Please, continue.'

But he hesitated. She looked up and into the dark intensity of his searching gaze.

'Please finish,' she asked. 'Will, especially, has been through so much, and we cannot know for sure it would be safe for them to come.' She closed her eyes a moment and clenched her jaw. 'They need Mervyn back, for so many reasons. I must find him, and as much as I appreciate your help, and Renhurst's, I *know* that I should be the one to talk with Mr Alden.' She opened her eyes. 'You must understand how difficult it is for me to leave them.'

Treyford nodded and looked away, back towards the revellers on the lawn. Even in her distress, Chione felt the loss of his regard, as if someone had placed a screen between her and the scorching heat of a fire. She could only be grateful.

'We were caught unawares in the narrow streets of the *Hasanain*,' he began. 'It is a Turkish neighbourhood, in the northern section of the city, occupied by merchants for the most part, and we were not expecting trouble. I should have known better. Life is held far cheaper than gold in that part of the world.' His low, dispassionate tone sent a shiver down her spine.

He rolled a shoulder, as if she had jogged the memory of an old blow. Chione stared. He had shed his coat again, and, as usual, his neckcloth was askew and his waistcoat partly unbuttoned. As he moved, she could see the rippling movement of muscle beneath the soft linen of his shirt. She began to grow warm again, but this time the heat grew from inside.

'I was occupied fighting the biggest Turk I have ever seen. I swear, the man's thighs were as thick as stumps and he had fists like rocks.' He turned then and locked his blue gaze with hers. 'Most level-headed Egyptians would have run, leaving the infidel to his fate. Not Aswan. He stayed, and when I finally finished off that giant, Aswan was dispatching the last of the others. *Four* others.'

He shook his head. 'I've seen more fighting in my life than I care to recall, but I've never seen anyone move so fast, or strike so hard.' His eyes lost focus for a moment, as if he were looking back through the mists of time, then he turned away. 'Aswan is someone you want on your side, Miss Latimer.'

Chione didn't reply. She just stared at his profile in the lengthening shadows while her mind's eye conjured a dramatic, dusty, violent scene half a world away.

'You're not bad in a fight yourself,' he recalled her with a glance askance. 'I should have complimented you before. That knife throw was impressive. Who taught you? Mervyn?'

'No, it was my mother.' She shot him a sad smile. The thought of her mother, of her own burden of secrets, only emphasised the gulf between them. 'A young girl's life is held cheaper than most, in the East. She taught me well to protect myself.'

'A good thing.' He nodded his approval.

Chione wished his approbation didn't warm her quite so much. The story he had told, however, much occupied her mind. She didn't question him further, but later, in the solitude of her room, she wrote long into the night. Before she snuffed her candle and rolled wearily into bed she had completed the next instalment of her story and Nikolas had found a sais, or groom, to accompany him on his travels.

The next morning she recruited Mr Drake into their scheming. He readily agreed to check on the children, and promised to do his best to keep anyone from realising she was gone.

Old Eli, trying to lighten her spirits, even pledged to sashay about the grounds in one of her gowns. Chione laughed at his antics along with everyone else, but she noticed that the earl's smile never reached his eyes. Neither, she suspected, did her own.

At last the time came, and everything was set in motion according to plan. Renhurst departed. Treyford pretended to depart. He came back deep in the darkest part of the night and sequestered himself and Aswan in the unused butler's suite. Chione was left alone to wait.

What she yearned to do—and would not—was to go down to the servants' quarters, to allow Treyford's blunt confidence to bolster her own. Even an ear-bursting disagreement with the earl might come as a welcome distraction.

'Why don't you visit Trey?' Will asked. He had been down to the servants' quarters regularly, and found it odd that Chione had not.

'It is Lord Treyford to you, young man.' Chione said.

'Lord Treyford, then. You haven't been to see him even once.'

'Will, come here to me.' She pulled the boy close and spoke in a grave tone. 'You are old enough to understand that this is no game. The danger is real.' She raised a brow in question and he nodded solemnly. 'No one must realise that the earl and Aswan are here. I want to find your papa, and so does Lord Treyford. By staying hidden, he is taking his role seriously, and so you and I must do the same. We must go on as if they are not here, and everything is normal.'

Will sighed. 'Yes, Chione. But normal is boring and Trey has hunted tigers and dug up mummies!'

Chione knew by the light in his eye that Will would be back down to talk with Lord Treyford. She also knew, despite the yearning in her breast, that she would not.

Though she might fob Will off with talk of duty and danger, the truth was that she was a coward. The earl both fascinated and frightened her. She was uncomfortable with his effect on her, afraid of the ease with which he awakened the *djinn* that lurked in her heart.

For so long she had struggled to bury the passionate, unruly side of her nature. The un-English part. She'd succeeded mostly, tucking away the demon inside of her, along with the dreadful memories of how she had come to be, and the guilt she felt at living a lie.

Then Treyford showed up, easily the most un-English aristocrat she'd ever heard of. He appeared driven by unknown torments of his own, and showed every sign of being as addicted to adventure as the men in her family. And yet it was his uniqueness that spoke to her, and his solid, unhesitant assurance that puzzled her. How did he achieve the one, in spite of the other?

She didn't know. She only knew that something in him reached right down to the hidden part of her soul and whispered it awake. Except that Chione did not wish it to awake, for what would she do with it once Treyford was gone?

And gone he would be. Once Mervyn was found—as she prayed he would be—her tenuous hold on the earl's loyalty would be lost. He would be free and eager to go back to his own pursuits. As would she, Chione reminded herself. The children would be safe and happy, and she would be released from all the worries of the past year.

So Chione waited, and she threw herself into her writing. It was, after all, much easier to craft a hero from fancy and whim than to mould one out of the stuff of real life.

Chione was not the only one chafing at the delay. Trey thought he might go mad in the over-stuffed butler's rooms. If the long boring hours trapped among a profuse assortment of decorative pillows and delicate knick-knackery didn't turn him into a Bedlamite, then the sheer frustration that came with inaction would finish the job.

For hours he paced, from the sole window looking over the kitchen garden, through the sitting room, into the bedroom and back again. Like the fire in the grate, Trey had always been a creature of restless motion, flickering from one task to the next. It was a lesson he'd learned early, and well. Never stay put long enough to put down roots. They invariably became ensnarled with others', and once they had you it was over. If their creeping tendrils did not strangle you, then they blasted you, with demands or criticism, until nothing was left save a dry and withered husk.

Men often exclaimed over the dangers of the life he had led. What they didn't know—could never understand—was that he welcomed such dangers. They were tangible, and thus conquerable. It was with people, and their hidden passions and inexplicable behaviours, where the truest danger lay.

And Chione Latimer was as dangerous a case as he had ever seen. A fixer. Someone who could not resist involving herself in other people's messes, jumping in where angels feared to tread. As a case in point—just look at the ragtag group that made up her household. Or the children. Based on Renhurst's remarks, they had other family. Surely she could have managed more easily had she sent the children to them.

Trey had fully expected, therefore, that Miss Latimer would take advantage of his forced confinement. There was plenty wrong with him, in most everyone's eyes. He'd thought it highly unlikely that the girl could resist the chance to try to fix him.

He'd been wrong. Perhaps he was not worth the trouble, or perhaps he was too difficult a case for even Miss Latimer's skills, for she never so much as poked her nose in the butler's quarters.

It was a relief not to have to fend her off, Trey told himself. Just as it would be a relief to be done with this trip to London. The girl was grasping at straws. His job was to see her safe until she realised her hands were empty. Then he would settle a generous stipend upon the girl and he would be done with her, and all the entanglements of her messy life.

Done, except for that tiny, niggling doubt, that small part of him that wondered why she hadn't been tempted to fix him, too.

* * *

Trey was entertaining that very doubt, contemplating that very question as he stood at the window, watching the fading light. In just hours they were to make their late-night departure. Some small sound alerted him, and he turned to find her silhouetted in the door. His heart stopped, then began to race. He saw the trouble in her dark eyes.

'What is it?' he asked.

'There is a rider coming fast up the drive,' she said. 'I think it is Mr Drake.'

It was Drake. Trey waited as Miss Latimer went to meet him. With the door partially open, he heard Drake enter the main hall and sensed the urgency in his voice. She brought him straight in.

'I have had news that may affect your plans,' the innkeeper said without preamble.

The girl stilled. 'Has something happened to Lord Renhurst?'

'No, no.' Drake's tone was one of reassurance. 'I've had a letter from a friend.' He shrugged. 'It may mean nothing, but I thought you'd better decide.' The innkeeper shifted, and scrubbed a hand through his hair. 'It seems a bit silly, now, but…' He breathed deeply. 'I've a friend who runs the George, at Exeter. We've a friendly rivalry, you understand—we vex each other on purpose and exchange news, and such. He's crowing—bragging about his good fortune. He's let all his rooms for the entire week, right along with all the others thereabouts.'

'How nice for him,' Trey said drily.

'I'm getting there, sir,' Drake said. 'Seems there has been a hue and cry that way among the scholarly set. Historians, antiquarians and the like. A great many of them have gathered to debate the authenticity of a new relic—something to do with old King Alfred.'

'But what does it mean to us, Mr Drake?' Miss Latimer puzzled.

'I just thought—if the scholar you are off to consult is at all interested in that sort of thing, he may not be in London at all—but as close as Exeter.'

The girl's eyes grew round as she absorbed the implication. 'Exeter,' she breathed. She rose and rushed out of the room.

Trey exchanged a sardonic look with Drake, but she was back in an instant, a pile of journals in her hands. 'Yes, Mr Alden has written several articles on justice during the time of Alfred the Great, and one on his translations. Surely he would be at such a gathering!' Eyes shining, she embraced the innkeeper. 'Exeter is only two days' travel. We can be there and back within a week!'

Drake's face was flushed, but he was smiling. 'Thought that might be the case.'

Trey was smiling too. Oh, yes, this was ever so much better. He saw the moment when the rest of it hit her. Her smile faded, and she sat abruptly down. Unerring, her gaze sought his.

'But what of Lord Renhurst? He's gone to Tavistock. He'll be expecting us.' She turned back to Drake. 'We cannot wait. What if Mr Alden should leave Exeter? Who knows where he might go from there.'

Trey shrugged. 'I'm afraid you'll have to reconcile yourself, Miss Latimer. It looks like it will be just you and me.'

Chapter Seven

The world outside the carriage window lay silent. Ahead only the faintest tinge of pale blue flirted with the horizon, hinting at the coming day. Inside the carriage the darkness still lay thick and heavy, a fact for which Chione could only be grateful. All of her resources were fully engaged at the moment, wrestling a demon no longer content with its imprisonment.

It was a reckoning Chione had known was coming. She had marked Lord Treyford as dangerous at first sight, when he had vaulted off his horse at Oakwood and strode towards her, eating the ground with his warrior's stride. And she had been right. Every encounter with the man had disarmed her further.

She'd been careful for so long. Kept the fiery part of her soul leashed so tightly that for long periods of time she forgot it. Not so now. No matter how she resisted, the earl had been busily knocking holes in the fortress hidden inside her. The creature inside that fortress was awake now, and quivering with anticipation, for the object of its interest reclined, sublimely unaware, just inches away.

He wasn't supposed to be in the carriage at all. He was supposed to be up on the box. Lord Treyford had emerged from the servants' corridor dressed as a coachman in coarse homespun and a worn greatcoat. Not a very successful disguise, in Chione's opinion, since the rough clothes clashed with his supremely confident manner and only emphasised his powerful form. But he had pulled on a pair of gloves and announced his intention of shortening the journey by taking his turn at driving. Chione had waited for her breath to come back, then had nodded her vigorous agreement and climbed gratefully into the coach with her new maid.

Jenny Ferguson, niece to Chione's housekeeper, had jumped at the chance to act as Chione's maid and companion on their journey. Unfortunately, Jenny had never travelled past the outskirts of Wembury, and never at all in a closed carriage. They had barely reached Knighton before the girl turned green. Up she'd gone into the fresh air and the company of the well-favoured and unattached driver, and down had come Lord Treyford, into Chione's worst nightmare.

Her eyes kept straying to him, despite the darkness. But the demon inside her didn't need to see. She sensed him, revelled in his looming presence.

Chione thanked all the powers that be for the darkness, for it took a deal of time for her to conquer her foe, time for her to quell the quivering, hollow excitement in her belly and calm the runaway beat of her heart. Yet she persevered.

This…attraction she felt for the earl, it could only be a momentary distraction. Nothing could come of it—how well she knew that! No, other women might think of attracting such a man, might dream of becoming his countess, but not Chione. The heavy burden of her past forbade such a future. Her life was about other things. She had accepted that fact, embraced it.

Her determination only grew with the dawning day. She waged her silent battle, and by the time the sun had climbed high enough to illuminate the carriage interior, she had triumphed. She took out a book to keep herself occupied, and her fingers did not even tremble. Much.

At first Trey was content with the new arrangement. He and the driver could still trade off, and they would each have a chance to rest out of the elements. But whoever had said there was no rest for the wicked must have had an insight into Trey's thoughts. In the darkness, his awareness of his companion seemed a living thing. Her scent, as fresh as rain in the desert, enveloped him in an almost tangible embrace, and he caught himself straining to hear the soft sound of her breath. As the sun rose he abandoned his plans to sleep and gave himself over to watching Chione Latimer instead.

She looked serene in the soft morning light, her lovely face as timeless as the depictions in the Temple at Karnac. For a time he was content to admire the tawny smoothness of her skin, to trace with his eye the graceful curve of neck and cheek, to watch for the lush flutter of her eyelash as she read.

But after a while he began to feel restless. Fidgety. Like a six-year-old who tugs the curls of the girl he admires, Trey had a sudden yearning to ruffle Miss Latimer's calm.

He leaned over to peer at the leather-bound book she held.

'Preparing a lesson?' he asked. 'I do hope it is not something of Homer's. In my opinion, Olivia is too young for man-eating monsters. Not to mention all those conniving suitors of Penelope's. And the seductions.' He paused. 'On second thought, Miss Latimer, I believe *you* are too young for Homer.' She laughed and he held out a hand. 'Perhaps it would be better if I kept that for you.'

She grinned and sparkled up at him as she closed the book with a snap. 'Sorry to disappoint you, my lord. It's only a diplomat's account of the Ottoman Empire.' She cocked her head to one side. 'Plenty of avarice and intrigue in Constantinople, though, so perhaps you might enjoy it at that.'

Trey gave a theatrical shudder. 'Constantinople? Wretched city. Perhaps you would do better to stick with Homer after all.'

A pink flush stole over the girl's cheeks. 'Oh, it's not for the children.' Trey could tell she was striving for nonchalance. 'It's just a bit of research for my stories.'

Her manner—perversely—awakened his curiosity. 'Stories?'

'Yes.'

He raised a brow. 'Bedtime stories? An article for the local paper? Journal entries? I confess I'm at a loss.'

Her flush had turned to the full-fledged burn of embarrassment. 'I should have thought—that is, I assumed someone would have told you.' She raised her chin a notch, as if daring him to judge her. 'It's no secret. I write adventure stories.'

It was not what he had been expecting her to say. But he was learning to expect the unexpected from this girl. She was beautiful, strong, independent. Unsettling. *Dangerous*, whispered the wary, uncompromising part of him. He ignored it.

'Adventure novels?' he asked. 'As in, the serial stories? Like those Nikolas serials? What are the titles—*The Emerald Temple* and *The Scroll of the Sapphire Slave*?'

'Yes.' She nodded. 'Those.'

He was impressed despite himself. 'That sort of thing is very popular. The Nikolas stories in particular. In my travels back to England I was aboard ship with several enthusiasts. They were reading to pass the time, trading copies and talking incessantly of what might happen in the next installment.'

He paused and realised that the note of finality in her voice had meant something. It took him a moment to figure it out.

'Those? You wrote those? You mean to say *you* are A.

Vaganti? You wrote the Nikolas series—about the world-travelling adventurer?'

Her face still rosy, she nodded.

Trey stared at the girl sitting across from him. In her prim spencer and plain travelling dress, her hands folded on her book and her blush intensified by the soft morning light, she was an irresistible mix of exotic siren and innocent maiden. She was a conundrum, was Richard's sister, and he was a fool. He stared a moment longer, then he threw back his head and laughed.

She bristled. 'Laugh if you will, but it's kept us warm and fed this winter.'

He struggled to stop, to attain an attitude of detachment as his gaze lingered on her indignant expression. 'My dear girl,' he snorted, 'pray, don't take offence. I only laugh because half my fellow passengers aboard the ship home were convinced that *I* had penned those novels!' He laughed long again. 'Oh, the whispered rumours! They swirled about me like fog. They had themselves convinced that I was returning to England only to deliver the latest story to my publisher.'

She laughed. 'I sent the next instalment to *my* publisher just yesterday. I thought to use the time to plot out the next.' She cocked her head and grinned at him. 'Although I see how the mistake could be made—you do resemble Nikolas, somewhat.'

'So I've been told.' Trey shook his head. 'When I think how those passengers would react, could I tell them that their beloved A. Vaganti is a mere slip of a girl…'

Her grin faded. 'I dare say they would be disappointed.'

But his rusty sense of humour had got a hold of Trey, and he would not let her mood deflate. 'Only to learn that the author who writes such swashbuckling tales gets her research from books.' He allowed the tiniest hint of mockery to invade his tone. 'I know Richard shared your grandfather's thirst for adventure. Aren't you afflicted with the family trait as well? Aren't you pining to get away—to get a taste of what you describe so well for your readers?'

Once again she surprised him. Instead of zinging him with a witty rejoinder, she visibly withdrew. Her body language tightened and her gaze grew shuttered. 'Yes,' she said sombrely, 'there are a few places I would like to see. Paris, perhaps, or Rome. I would like to experience for myself the raw energy of America. But for the most part, my passions vary widely from the rest of my family's.'

Trey leaned in close and pitched his voice low, just a notch above a whisper. 'It must be the enforced intimacy of our tête-à-tête, Miss Latimer, but I find myself quite interested in hearing of your passions.'

She didn't respond to his teasing. For a moment she didn't respond at all. The delay gave Trey time to wonder just what he was doing. In his urge to unsettle Chione Latimer, what was he doing to himself?

'Perhaps I will share mine, but only if you will reciprocate.'

Trey shrugged, trying not to show how the notion unsettled him. 'Fine, although I take leave to censor my answers to fit a young lady's ears.' He smiled. 'What is it you wished to know?'

'When did you know that you wished to spend your life adventuring? Your estate is in the north, is it not? What spurred you to leave the familiar behind and explore the mysteries of the world?'

He spent several long moments composing his answer. He'd been joking earlier, but he found that a bit of censoring was indeed in order. Not to protect her, however, but him.

'When I was nine years old, I received a present from my uncle—my mother's brother, a younger son who had joined the East India Company. I'd never met him, and truly, I don't recall if he had ever sent me anything before that, but that year, being an accurate judge of young male sensibilities, he sent me a shrunken head and a gorgeous book on the islands of the Caribbean.'

She laughed. 'I would imagine you were entranced.'

'Completely. I studied everything I could on the region. And what was not to love? Voodoo and pirates and tribal beauties—it was all wonderfully exotic.' And so completely unrelated to the rest of his life. 'We struck up a correspondence that lasted until his death. The next year, he sent me a family of carved elephants and the book was about India.' He quirked his mouth at her. 'And that was how it all began. Now it is your turn. I know your brother burned to make advances in the archaeological world. All of England knows of your grandfather's ambition to explore all the unknown places left on our ever-shrinking world. But I wish to know—what are your dreams, Miss Latimer?'

She, too, took her time in answering, and he wondered if it might be for the same reason. 'I want to make a difference, Lord Treyford.'

He leaned back. 'A difference?'

'Yes. Of all people, you should understand. You've travelled so far, seen so much. Like Jenny, most people cannot see outside of their own small lives.'

Trey had an uncomfortable idea where this was going.

'Misery, hunger, want, hopelessness, they abound in the world,' she continued. 'I want to help. Is that something you can at all understand?'

He thought of the downtrodden beggars in India, doomed by and from their birth; he pictured the miserable slaves he had seen in the East, remembered the dirty children scurrying about the streets in cities from Calcutta to Cairo, to London itself.

'Yes,' he said.

She glanced away, but not before he saw the sadness, the pain she tried to hide behind long lashes and quiet competency. His own good humour fled completely, replaced by something more dangerous as he watched her gaze unseeing out of the window.

'My mother was an Egyptian. Did you know?'

He nodded and she went on.

'When she died, Richard was still a babe, and I was not much older. We were alone, frightened, hungry, tired.' She shot him a quick glance and a wry smile. 'I would suppose an earl would have no idea what it means, to feel so helpless.'

'You would be wrong.' The words were out before he knew it.

He didn't want to see the curiosity in her gaze, or the compassion. Luckily she looked away again, at the uncanny brightness of the morning.

'I hated it,' she said with sudden intensity. 'I was so angry, and I felt so betrayed.'

She sighed and sat silent for several long moments.

'Then Mervyn Latimer came. He saved us, gave us everything important in life: love and peace, family and hope. He brought us out of darkness, into the light.' She looked his way once more. 'I dare say you know what I mean, then?'

Trey couldn't breathe. How had they arrived at this place, from the lighthearted banter they had shared earlier? He had the sudden urge to lash out at her, to make her angry so she would forget what she had asked, what she might learn. But that would be running, something he'd been doing for so long, and look where it had got him, right where he had never wished to be. And he had a strange disinclination to diminish himself so, in her eyes. So he screwed up his courage and he said, 'No. I'm afraid no one ever rode to my rescue.'

This time he was the one who turned away. He didn't want to see her reaction.

He imagined it, though. He imagined the pity in her eyes even as he heard her struggle to keep her tone neutral. It made him want to howl.

'We were lucky.' It came out nearly as a whisper. She paused and her voice grew stronger. 'Mervyn is a great man. Richard and I were not the only ones whose lives he has changed. I mean to be like him. I want to help others as I have been helped.'

Trey blinked. Once again she shocked him with the unexpected. She'd suffered loss, pain, hunger, betrayal and yet she wished to help? He thought that Mervyn Latimer must indeed have been a saint, to have raised such a girl.

'I haven't done it yet,' she continued. 'I haven't accomplished much. But I have plans. Once Mervyn is found, I shall make a difference.'

He turned abruptly. 'Don't belittle what you have done. You've touched many people's lives and made them better. The children, the villagers, even that circus troupe that you call servants.'

Her eyes widened. 'Thank you. That is extremely kind of you to say. Except for the circus part, of course, but I promise I won't tell Mrs Ferguson.'

'It's the truth, damn it.' Her modesty irritated him.

She shrugged. 'I do appreciate the compliment, it's only, when I think of all the good that Mervyn has accomplished…' Her voice trailed off.

'Your grandfather is a wealthy man. Such will always have

influence in the world. It's easy for him. While you...' Trey raked an appreciative gaze over her well-armoured form '...are undeniably a woman.'

'In a wealthy man's world?' she asked tartly.

'Exactly. I confess it freely, although it's not the thing to admit—but I've always been grateful that I was not born a woman.'

She gave him exactly the same sort of once-over that he'd just given her. 'As are we all.' She smiled.

Trey felt the weight of that look all the way down to his toes. Lord, why did it have to be this innocent girl who made him feel so hot and addled?

'You are right, though, that being a woman will make my goal that much more difficult to reach. Worse than being a woman, though, is being an outsider, belonging to neither of the worlds I have inhabited.' She sighed. 'Commerce, politics, even society, they are the quickest ways to philanthropy, and they are closed to me.'

Trey raised a brow. 'So your sphere of influence is smaller. It means only that you help in smaller ways, one person at a time, and who is to say which is more valuable?'

Her eyes lit up, her countenance softened. She smiled—and the world was alight. Unconsciously, Trey leaned forward, wanting to bask in her brilliance.

She ducked her head a little, still looking at him through the fan of her dark lashes. She was gorgeous. Fearless. With a start, Trey realised that the carriage had begun to slow, but he did not care. He yearned to touch her, to take in some of the light she shone into the world.

As if possessed of a will of its own, his hand rose, brushed her cheek, traced her ear, and caressed the slender column of her neck. He leaned closer still. Her eyes were wide, startled.

His slid slowly closed, even as he captured the fullness of her lower lip between his own.

She made a sound, a squeak of surprise, but she did not pull back. Not relinquishing contact, Trey eased across and into the seat beside her. Instinct, or perhaps something more dangerous, had taken hold of him. He gathered her close and pressed a soft kiss on her jaw and buried his face into her smooth, fragrant nape.

The carriage drew to a halt, but he barely took notice. She trembled underneath his hand.

The door opened. Trey blinked and drew back. Frustration swamped him, but at the same time he was oddly grateful for the rescue.

'We've nearly reached Modbury, my lord,' the driver announced. 'Thought we'd water the horses and give the ladies a chance to stretch their legs.'

Slowly, Trey pulled away. He rose and climbed out of the carriage before turning to look Chione Latimer in the eye. 'Your grandfather would be proud of you.'

She made a sound of protest, but he cut her off.

'Your brother, too. You're a fool if you can't see the good you have wrought. A bigger fool, even, than I.'

Before she could respond, he turned on his heel and strode away. So open, and so naïve. She was indeed a pretty, open-hearted fool. He had to wonder if he had ever in his life been so optimistic.

He suppressed a snort. No, he had been born a cynic, and all the formative events of his life had proved the extreme practicality of it. It was this sort one had to worry about, the trusting ones who inevitably got hurt.

He had to keep his distance, watch his step. It was becoming very clear just how easily he could be the one to do it.

Chapter Eight

Lord Treyford did not return to the coach. He took up the ribbons when they got back underway and allowed the driver to rest. As the sun grew higher and the day grew warmer, Chione was able to open the carriage windows. Jenny, who said she could manage the interior as long as she could feel the wind on her face, joined her.

Chione felt nothing but cowardly relief. Treyford had touched her. She rather thought he had kissed her. She put her fingers to her lips. Could you call that a kiss? The nearest thing to it, in any case, and she had let him. Worse, she had wished for more.

With a sigh she dropped her head in her hands. A great, colossal idiot—that's what she was. She'd put herself into the hands of yet another man who would eventually disappear on her, and then she'd nearly kissed him.

Warning bells should have been pealing when he'd touched her. Instead she had lost herself in the low rasp of his voice. Just being in his presence had become a risk. Something about him inspired her heart to open, even as her mind screamed for her to stop. She'd exposed herself, revealed things that she had never discussed with anyone. And he had understood, accepted and even encouraged her.

Her reaction had been instantaneous. She had drunk it in—like water to her parched soul—and immediately begun to crave another taste.

The trembling that beset her had nothing to do with the jolting carriage and everything to do with the insidious effect that Treyford had on her. So dangerous—for where would it stop? Chione had secrets that must be kept, but even now she could feel herself craving the warmth of his regard, the heat of his touch.

No, it was better to stay away. A relief not to have to deal with his overpowering physical presence. Her attraction to the man was a burden, but one she must bear for only a short while. Once Mervyn was found he would be gone. Until then distance would serve her, where her control had not.

So she watched Jenny hanging out of the window and she willed herself not to relive those unsettling moments. Instead she occupied herself with fretting about the children and wondering how Lord Renhurst was faring. Certainly they had seen no sign of trouble; she couldn't help but worry about what that might mean to the viscount. But an hour or so later she had worried herself out. It seemed a futile exercise while trapped in a carriage. She'd brought along Mervyn's journals and she set herself to whiling away the afternoon hours looking for a clue to what the coffer might be.

To no avail. There was no mention of a coffer, the scarab, or even the Pharaoh's Lost Jewel. If you relied solely on Mervyn's journals, you would not even know that such a thing existed. Chione wondered if she might have more luck with Richard's journals, but all of his effects had not yet arrived from Egypt. She must remember to ask Lord Treyford if he knew what had become of them.

She would ask him at their next stop. But she would ask only that. Distance was key.

She never got the chance. Treyford set a gruelling pace. They travelled late into the night, not stopping until Totness for a few hours' sleep.

The next morning she and Jenny had a hurried breakfast in their room and were hustled right back out to the carriage. This time when the girl objected, it was the coachman who came down to switch places, and Chione knew that the earl had reached the same conclusion as she. He was doing his best to stay far away from her.

He succeeded admirably well. They stopped twice to change horses, but in both instances Chione barely caught a glimpse of Treyford. The pace he set continued, relentless but efficient. They rolled into Exeter just as the second evening of their journey faded into night.

Fortunately their destination was easily found. Exhausted but grateful, Chione climbed down from the carriage, instinctively looking for the earl.

He stood with the horses, giving instructions to the ostlers. As the tired animals were led away, he approached. Chione kept her countenance calm, but could do nothing to stop the frantic beating of her heart.

Avoiding her gaze, he took her arm. 'Bring the girl,' he said, voice low, 'and let us search out this friend of Drake's.'

As it turned out, there was no need. A short man, round as a child's ball, came beaming from the taproom before they had taken a step.

'Welcome, welcome!' he called. Breathing heavily, he hustled right up and shook Treyford's hand with enthusiasm. 'An honour it is to have you at the George, sir, ma'am.' He nodded to Chione. 'I've my best private parlour set aside for you. Come in! Come in!'

'I'm afraid you are mistaken...' Chione cast a helpless look at Treyford as the portly little man took her arm to lead her away.

'Not at all!' he insisted, and keeping up an endless stream of prattle, he dispatched Jenny upstairs and led Chione and Treyford along to a cheerful room, lit by a welcoming fire.

Then he shut the door and his officious manner fell away.

'My lord Treyford,' he bowed. 'Miss Latimer. Welcome to the George. My heavens, but you have made good time!'

'But, sir—' Chione was perplexed '—how did you know to expect us?'

'Our crafty friend Drake, of course. He sent a rider ahead to warn me, but I must tell you that he beat you by only a matter of hours! I've only had time to rearrange a few rooms—no easy matter with all these historians descended upon us.'

'Thank you for your efforts, Mr Cedric, is it?' Treyford had finally spoken up.

'Just Cedric, please, sir. Just Cedric.'

'Cedric, then. Also, I must thank you for your earlier discretion. I assume Drake has filled you in on the particulars of our mission?'

'Only the essentials. And there is no need to thank me. Do anything for a friend of Drake's, I would. Well, then...' he rubbed his hands together '...it's a Mr Alden you're looking to find, is it not? I've sent my own nephew out to make inquiries. Shouldn't be long before we hear something from him.'

Chione could see that Treyford looked ready to object.

'Very discreet, of course,' Cedric said with a raised hand. 'He's a smart boy—knows when to talk and when to listen.'

Treyford shrugged. 'You've made this very easy on us, Cedric.' He cast a glance askance at Chione. 'Miss Latimer's maid should have her bags unpacked by now. Would you mind showing her to her room?'

Chione bristled. 'Thank you, Cedric, but I've been confined to the carriage for the last two days. I find I'm not quite ready to be confined to my room.' She glared at the earl.

'No, of course not,' Cedric agreed. 'So long a journey—and not a decent bite to eat between here and there, I'll wager. You must be famished. My good sister is the cook here, and she is preparing something special for you both. I'll just go out and see to it.'

'Thank you.' Chione ignored Treyford as the little man left. Chin high, she took a seat near the fire. Distance was one thing, but such a high-handed dismissal was another. He'd been the one to run his hands over her, after all. Now he acted as if she were diseased.

'Miss Latimer—' he still hadn't quite met her eyes '—I feel I must apologise. My actions earlier were inexcusable.'

'Which actions?' She knew she sounded testy, but that was precisely how she felt. 'When you kissed me in the carriage or just now, when you dismissed me from your presence like a child?'

'Both, I must suppose.' He shot her a wry look.

'Oh, very well,' she conceded. 'I must take some of the blame as well. It must have been the long empty hours.' She shot him an apologetic grimace. 'Truly, it is not often that I immerse myself in such maudlin sentimentality. I'm sorry you got dragged in.'

'Dragged in, but not under.' He moved at last away from the door, and Chione could see his expression grow serious. Still he did not take a seat, but remained standing, watching her steadily.

'There is something…intangible between us, Miss Latimer. It does us no good to deny it.'

Chione froze in her chair. Still he stared. Waiting.

Slowly she nodded, feeling the heat rush to her face.

'So let us acknowledge it, and thereby disarm it. We both know it is there, but I think we both understand it would be folly to act upon it. We have a job to do. It will go easier if we can be comfortable with each other.'

He was right. She should be grateful he had addressed the problem. How many men would think to lighten such a burden by offering to share it? She was indeed grateful and relieved as well. But somewhere deep inside of her she was forced to acknowledge an unmistakable wave of disappointment, a curious sense of opportunity lost.

'Are we in agreement, then?'

Once more she nodded. She couldn't have spoken even had she wished to.

'*Et voilà!*' called Cedric as he backed into the parlour, pulling a laden cart behind him. 'Now you shall see how a good English cook trumps Drake's Henri any day. My sister has created a spread that will put anything served in Devonshire to shame!'

He began to pull the covers off of the dishes. 'Eat up, my friends. You will need your strength tonight. My nephew has returned.'

Chione glanced at Treyford, than back to Cedric, the question unnecessary.

'Your man is here. Across town, at the New Inn.'

Trey and Miss Latimer followed the boy through the dark streets of Exeter without incident. None the less, a foreboding prickle had inched its way along his spine. Now, safe in the small lobby of the New Inn, it hadn't dissipated. Instead it settled—a tense throb of awareness—smack between his shoulder blades.

He could not be sure of what it meant, but long experience

assured him it didn't bode well. Trey scrubbed his brow in frustration. Then again, perhaps his instincts were befuddled. He glanced across at the woman who'd accompanied him. She was more than capable of driving a man to distraction. And for the first time he was showing himself susceptible to a woman's wiles.

He cursed and began to pace, restless as a caged cat. The boy, at least, had been settled happily into a warm nook in the kitchen. A good thing, since this was taking so long.

The man they had travelled to see was here, mere feet away. Simple enough to climb a few stairs and knock on the door. But no. This was England, where the obsession with social graces made him want to scream. Instead—because he failed to carry so useless an object as a calling card—he'd had to sweat over a carefully worded request, hand it over to a lackey, and wait for a reply. And wait. And wait.

He crossed over to the window, standing well to the side so he could not be seen. Thankfully there was nobody to see outside at the moment, either. 'What the devil did you mean to do in America?' he asked without looking at his infuriatingly calm companion.

'I beg your pardon?' Still she was unruffled.

'Drake told me that before Mervyn disappeared, you meant to go to America. What did you mean to do there? Travel?'

'Yes.' She didn't elaborate, just gazed at him with some curiosity. 'Have you ever been there?'

'No.'

'I think I would have liked it. Americans are very forgiving, I believe. There your past is not as important as your willingness to work, to better yourself.'

Her words increased his agitation. 'You don't need to better yourself,' he said gruffly. 'You are fine as you are.'

'Thank you,' she said, but raised an ironic brow. 'But I think that you understand the wish to begin again? To start anew with the past wiped clean?'

He didn't answer. He started to pace again.

'Stop fidgeting,' she murmured. 'You'll draw attention to us.'

'It's the middle of the damned night,' Trey snapped. 'Who is there to see?'

'You never know who might come in.' She shrugged. 'And we don't want to leave a lasting impression on the clerk.'

'We're making a morning call at midnight,' he began. 'What sort of impression—?' He stopped. Voices outside, faint, but drawing nearer. Damned if the girl wasn't right.

He crossed quickly over and pulled her into a shadowy corner just as the door opened. A cool waft of air preceded a riotous group of young men into the room. Trey bent low over the girl, shielding her from their gaze with his body. 'Laugh,' he said, his face perilously close to hers.

'What?' Her eyes were wide with alarm.

'Laugh,' he whispered the harsh command. 'Like the sort of woman who should be out alone with a man at this time of night.'

Still she did not comprehend. Speechless, she just stared at him, her pupils dark with surprise, and, if he was any judge, with sudden want.

So Trey did what he must. What some part of him had burned to do since he'd first laid eyes on her. He pulled her hard against him and seared her with his kiss.

For an endless, nerve-racking moment she froze, rigid in his arms. The men behind him had caught sight of them. Whistles and catcalls rang through the small room. Someone shouted some ribald advice and she must have caught on.

Suddenly she answered his kiss. She curled her small hands

over his shoulders and pressed herself fully against him. Underneath his mouth, she began to inexpertly move hers.

The dam holding back Trey's desire burst. A flood of passion overwhelmed him. He asked for more, kissed her harder, demanded her surrender. She yielded, and he urged her lips apart.

The men had moved on, but Trey didn't stop. Couldn't stop. She fit against him, soft curves hugging his hardened frame perfectly. He surged inside her mouth, entwined her tongue with his, taught her to kiss him back with long sinuous strokes.

'Ah-hem.'

With a superhuman effort Trey pulled his mouth from hers. She blinked up at him, her expression a gratifying whirl of disappointment and desire. Reluctant, he stepped away.

She staggered, swaying on her feet. 'I think we just left intangible behind,' she said.

Trey only grimaced and gripped her tighter.

'What do we do now?' The question emerged on a whisper.

'We talk to your scholar,' he growled.

Together, they turned to face the waiting clerk.

They'd awakened the man. Jack Alden answered the door in a dressing robe, trousers, and spectacles. He hadn't bothered to comb his hair.

'Lord Treyford,' he said, opening the door wide. 'Do come in.'

Trey stepped in and Alden spied the woman hanging behind him. 'Oh…' he tightened the belt of his robe '…I wasn't aware you'd brought a friend.'

'I thank you for agreeing to see us, Mr Alden,' Trey said. 'May I present to you Miss Chione Latimer?'

The man raised a brow. 'Indeed you may, my lord.' He shut

the door and, with a gentleman's grace, bowed over the girl's hand. 'What a great pleasure, Miss Latimer. I was well acquainted with your brother.' He kept the girl's hand clasped in both his own. 'Allow me to offer you my condolences. We lost a great mind when he passed on. And I lost a good friend.'

'Thank you.' She inclined her head, regal as a queen. And every bit as lovely. Trey saw the open appreciation in the other man's gaze and his fists grew tight. 'I am very glad to meet you,' she said.

'Please, sit down.' There was a chair next to the small fireplace. Alden settled the girl into it and waved Trey to take the wooden chair at the small desk. He perched himself upon the rumpled bed.

'This does explain a bit,' he said to Trey. 'I couldn't imagine what the Earl of Treyford wished with me when the boy brought your note. I had not even heard that you had returned to England, but I would have thought you would be in London, what with all the furor over the exhibition of Belzoni's Tomb.'

'Oh, has he opened it, then?'

'To great acclaim. It sounds more like something you would be interested in than this King Alfred chicanery. I didn't think that English artifacts were what appealed to you.'

'Not as a rule.' Trey lifted a shoulder.

'Forgive us for approaching you at such an odd hour,' Miss Latimer broke in. 'But it is an odd situation we find ourselves in.'

Alden grinned. 'Not surprising for a member of the intrepid Latimer family.'

Trey saw the slightest frown crease her brow.

'No, unfortunately not.'

The scholar must have seen it too. 'Forgive, me, I meant

no disparagement. Richard shared some of your family's colourful history. It must be a challenge, that sort of legacy.'

'Every family has challenges.' She raised her chin in that stubborn way she had. The sweet familiarity of the gesture hit Trey hard and unexpectedly. 'Does not yours, Mr Alden?'

He laughed. '*Touché*, Miss Latimer. Mine does indeed, and my family's peccadilloes are nearly as notorious as your own.'

Trey saw her relax. He wasn't relaxed. He was knee-deep in exactly the sort of trouble he'd spent his life avoiding. He stared at the brave set of her shoulders, the serious expression on her face, and he told himself that all was well. He'd caught himself in time. He would escape unscathed, before either of them got hurt.

'And I'm certain you would do anything to protect your family, notorious or not?' she asked Alden with a raised brow.

'Of course,' he responded at once.

'As would I, sir. Which leads me to exactly why we have come in search of you.'

Trey listened as she spun her tale, and he answered several questions that Alden had regarding his work with Richard Latimer. He watched the other man closely, sure that he would scorn such a convoluted account of artifacts, bandits, coded messages and hidden clues. He was wrong. Mr Alden proved an attentive listener throughout. When the girl had finished, he sat back in his chair, took off his spectacles and wiped them absently. For several moments a dead silence hung thick in the room.

Finally she stood. With one hand on the mantel and her earnest gaze fixed on his abstracted face, she asked, 'Have you any idea what your name on that slip of paper might mean, Mr Alden?'

'Yes…' he put his spectacles back in place '…I believe I might.'

She sank back into her chair. 'Thank heavens,' she said in a near-whisper. 'Please, tell me what you know.'

'I think it is more a matter of what you know.'

Trey glanced sharply at the man, but he was already continuing.

'After Richard received the position with the British Museum, we spent a good deal of time together as he prepared to leave.' He looked to Trey with enthusiasm. 'I don't have your experience, of course, my lord, but I do find Egypt fascinating. I have the complete *Description de l'Egypte*. We pored over it and several other works I have in my collection.'

'Did he ever mention Mervyn's scarab to you?' asked the girl. Eagerly she pulled the thing from her pocket.

'He didn't.' Alden's expression flared with interest. 'May I?'

'Of course.'

He took it and inspected it closely. 'Amazing,' he said. 'But, no, Richard did not speak of it. He was remarkably interested in one thing, though.'

'What?' She sounded breathless. Trey was more than a little interested, too.

'A legend. An ancient tale, he said, about an architect's daughter...'

'And a tomb robber!' she breathed.

'So you know it?' Trey noted a particular intensity in his eyes as the scholar asked the question.

'Oh, yes. Mervyn used to tell us the tale often when we were children.'

'I've never heard of it,' Trey interrupted. 'Will you tell it?

She laughed a little self-consciously. 'Oh, it's just another ill-fated romance. There's no historical importance attached to it.'

'Please, I'd like to hear it again as well,' encouraged Alden.

She nodded. She sat a moment, gaze downcast, and when she looked up there was a faraway look in her eyes.

'It begins with an architect in ancient Egypt, a man who helped design the secret tombs of the pharaohs. He was well favoured and a member of the wealthy bureaucracy. He had a daughter, both learned and beautiful. When she came of age he decided to make her an advantageous marriage.'

Trey watched a flush of colour grow in her countenance. She sneaked a quick glance in his direction. He watched her steadily and nodded for her to go on, inwardly cursing the heated reaction that innocent gaze wrought.

'The girl had her own ideas about marriage, as young people often do. She had met a charming and handsome boy, the nephew of a provincial ruler. He pursued her and she loved him madly. It was a respectable alliance, so the father agreed and the marriage was made.'

She breathed deep. 'They were happy for a time. The architect's daughter was already with child when she made a terrible discovery. Her husband was not who he said he was. It was all a lie. He was actually from a notorious…' she paused and glanced at Alden '…family of tomb robbers. He'd only used her to discover secrets from her father. Secrets about the pharaoh's tombs.'

This time she looked at Trey openly and with a challenge in her eye. 'Mervyn always stressed that she was a very intelligent young lady, and now she was an angry one as well.'

'A dangerous combination,' acknowledged Trey.

'The architect's daughter did not let on that she knew her husband's secret. All the agony she felt at his betrayal was kept hidden. She waited and she plotted. When he made his move she was ready. She tricked him, and trapped him in the tomb he meant to plunder.'

She blinked. Trey could see her gathering herself, pulling back from where the story had taken her.

'So she locked him in with the treasure he had betrayed her for?' Trey thought it a fitting end for the scoundrel.

'No, she took the treasure. Or part of it. She kept it for her daughter.'

'Yes,' Mr Alden agreed, 'and according to Richard the treasure was passed down for many generations of daughters.' He leaned forward, failing to hide his serious expression behind his spectacles. 'What happened to the architect's daughter, Miss Latimer?'

'The legend does not say.' She cocked her head at him. 'Richard and I used to discuss it, though. He always said she would set herself up as a wealthy widow and remarry.'

'And what did you think?'

'I'm sure I don't know.'

'You must have had a theory,' he pressed.

'It's just a legend.' She gave a sheepish little shrug. 'Oh, very well. I once told Richard that I feared that she would hold on to her anger. That she never let herself love again. I told him I believed *that* would be the true tragedy.'

Her answer appeared to energise Alden. He stood. 'Richard was extremely intent on finding any reference he could about that legend.' He walked to the desk and ran his hands along a stack of books there. 'We discussed it at length.' He turned with one of the books in his hand and fixed Chione with a direct look. 'One night, very late, he begged a favour of me. He said if his sister ever came to me, I was to ask her about the legend and most particularly I was to ask that last question.'

Trey was suddenly alert. 'Did he fear an impostor?'

'I can only guess as to his motives—he didn't explain. But it must be so.' He knelt before the perplexed looking woman.

'I am very glad you gave the right answer, for now I have something to give you.'

'From Richard?' Tears brightened her eyes.

'Indeed. He asked me to keep it close always. But now I may give it to you.' With great solemnity he placed the book in her lap, then opened it.

It was hollowed inside. Trey heard her gasp even as he rocketed out of his chair.

Tucked away lay a shining golden box, perhaps four inches in diameter. She lifted it and they both exclaimed aloud. Hieroglyphs encircled the top edge and each surface featured brightly coloured pictures done in skilled relief.

'They are from the legend,' Chione cried.

Trey saw that it was true. Each side of the box illustrated a scene from the tale she had only just recounted. Most disturbing was the image on the lid: a woman sobbing, leaning on one side of a massively ornate door. On the other side was depicted only darkness.

'But where did Richard find it? Why didn't he tell me?' Sorrow warred with anguish in her voice.

'He would not tell me where it came from,' Alden said. 'I do not believe it had been in his possession for very long, but I cannot say for sure.' He lowered his voice to a whisper. 'Open it.'

Tears streaming down her face, she did. She gasped again and reached inside, pulling out a large, gleaming emerald.

'It's beautiful,' she breathed, cradling it in her palm. Her eyes met Trey's and she held it out to him.

He took it, noted the weight of the thing and the unusual shape.

'The scarab,' Trey rasped. 'Where is it?'

'Here.' Alden passed it over.

Trey turned it so that the head of the insect faced the girl. Very lightly he settled the emerald into the empty space on the right wing. It fit perfectly.

'What does it mean?' she asked in a whisper.

'I don't know—' he raised his head and looked her directly in the eye '—but it looks as if there's one more to find.'

Chapter Nine

Chione heard the undertone of excitement in Treyford's voice, saw the gleam in Mr Alden's eye and was abruptly brought back to her senses.

'That's all well and good,' she clipped, 'but hardly relevant to the issue. Mr Alden, please do not think me ungrateful. I thank you for the service you have done both Richard and me—but Treyford and I are not seeking the Pharaoh's Lost Jewel. I've come hoping you could shed some light on my grandfather's disappearance.'

'I wish I were in a position to do so,' he said, obviously chagrined.

'Did Richard mention nothing about Mervyn's disappearance?' Chione could hear the desperation in her own voice. 'Did he never discuss any ideas he might have had? Anything about where Mervyn might be?'

'We spoke of it, of course. I remember he mentioned that your grandfather was last seen on Malta?'

'Yes,' she said, hoping for more.

'That's not a very helpful clue, is it? I remember Richard saying he might have left there and gone anywhere in the Mediterranean.'

Her shoulders slumped, but she refused to give up. 'I've often thought that Richard was hiding something. I wondered at the time if he sought that position with the museum so that he might find a way to look for Mervyn. He wouldn't ever admit it, but he didn't precisely deny it.'

'He never mentioned such a thing specifically to me either,' Mr Alden said, his tone slow and thoughtful. 'But I did notice more than once that he attacked his search with renewed vigour when the topic of his grandfather came up—almost as if it motivated him.'

Chione saw Treyford's quick frown. 'What are you suggesting?' he asked.

'I just wonder if the two aren't related.' The scholar's gaze was distant, but he continued to speak with methodic thoroughness. 'Let us just organise our thoughts for a moment. First we have the scarab—Mervyn's prized possession, you say?'

Chione nodded.

'And it is widely associated with the mystery of the Pharaoh's Lost Jewel. Then we have this lovely little box...' he ran a caressing finger along the edge of it '...relating an ancient tale unknown to most, but familiar to Mervyn and your family. And the jewel inside is undoubtedly linked to the scarab.' He nodded towards the artifact, sitting with the emerald still nestled in place. 'So it follows that perhaps the tale is linked to the mystery of the Lost Jewel.'

'You think the emerald is the Pharaoh's Lost Jewel?' Treyford sounded as sceptical as Chione felt.

'No. I'm beginning to believe, though, that the treasure in the legend, the one the architect's daughter passed on to her daughter, might be.'

'It makes sense,' agreed Treyford. 'But still that leaves us with more questions than answers.'

'And none of them gets me any closer to finding the coffer, or Mervyn,' complained Chione.

'I disagree,' Alden said smoothly. 'Look closely. Mervyn is the central figure in both cases. He is the one who binds it all together.'

'What are you saying?' she whispered.

'If we want to find Mervyn Latimer, we're going to have to solve the mystery of the Pharaoh's Lost Jewel?' Treyford asked. In his tone she could hear an odd mixture of anticipation and resignation.

Mr Alden nodded. 'It may be so.'

Everything in Chione wanted to reject the idea. She'd spent her life ignoring the mystery, resenting the toll it had taken on her family. Both her father and her brother had died while pursuing the Lost Jewel. The thought of taking up the chase repulsed her. But what if it were the only way to save Mervyn?

'Even if you are correct, Mr Alden, I have nowhere to go from here. No clue to lead us closer to a solution. Unless there is something else you can tell us?'

'I'm afraid not,' he answered. He knelt before her again and took her cold hand in his.

It didn't help. She felt empty, dejected. She raised her eyes to Treyford, but he appeared equally as lost.

'What do Richard's journals say of this?' asked Mr Alden finally. 'He kept detailed notes of all of his research. Have you consulted them?'

A brief stab of hope flared to life. 'I have not. I do not have his journals.' She looked again to Treyford. 'The same thought actually occurred to me yesterday during the long drive. So much has happened, I forgot to ask you. Might you know what happened to the journals?'

Treyford frowned. 'You should have received Richard's effects a month or more ago. It took me several weeks to plan the journey to England and prepare to leave my work, but I had his things sent on ahead.'

'I did receive a few boxes of gear and books,' Chione recalled, 'but no journals and not many personal items. Is it possible that not all of the boxes have reached us? Were they all posted together?'

'I do not know for sure. Aswan packed them and saw to the shipping.' He shrugged. 'We can ask him when we get back to Oakwood.'

Even such a small step helped Chione to feel better. At least it lent her hope for further progress. 'All the more reason we should be getting back quickly.' She stood, happy to have an excuse for decisiveness again. 'Mr Alden, I don't know how to thank you.'

He stood as well and pressed the lacquered box into her hand. 'The pleasure has been mine. I cannot tell you how happy I am to have met you at last.'

Chione blushed at the frankly appreciative look he gave her.

'You are all that Richard boasted of and more,' he said warmly.

'Thank you for being such a good friend to him,' she said. 'I hope I may count you as mine, too?'

'I insist upon it,' he said.

Treyford stepped in and distracted the scholar by offering his hand. 'You know the direction of Oakwood Court, should you recall anything else?'

'Indeed I do.'

Chione saw a glint of humour in Mr Alden's eyes. She looked to Treyford, but he did not appear to share it.

'I wish you both the best of luck,' the scholar said.

* * *

The warning sting was lodged in the base of Trey's neck again. He kept his step light and his senses on alert as he hustled them both back through the darkened streets. But he struggled to keep his thoughts focused. They kept determinedly wandering back to the chit at his side.

Bad enough that he'd kissed her. Truly kissed her, this time. Yes, he'd had an excuse; a couple in the midst of a tryst was the only sort who would be regarded as an ordinary fixture in such a situation, and the act had also hidden their identities quite thoroughly. No, what bothered him was how much he had enjoyed it. Immensely—Good God, but he'd enjoyed it immensely. It was a sad truth— one virginal kiss from Chione Latimer had rocked him more thoroughly than even the most erotic nights spent with the skilled women of the East.

Once she had entered into the spirit of the thing, Chione had melted into his embrace. He'd branded her with the heat of his desire and the sweetness of her innocent need had flowed into him, filling up cracks and crevices he hadn't known were empty. When that pox-ridden clerk had interrupted them, Trey had literally wanted to throttle him.

Heaven help him, but he knew better. He knew firsthand the dangers that came with allowing that sort of passion to rule your life. He'd seen with his own eyes the bitterness that comes when it inevitably fades, and he'd made a vow never to find himself in such a miserable spot. And yet, even knowing the futility and risk of such a thing, still he longed to kiss her again. God help him, but he wanted more.

She'd bewitched him. With her beauty, yes, but beautiful women were found the world over. Chione Latimer had so much more. Passion, loyalty and the rare ability to give of herself. She was unlike any woman Trey had ever met. Certainly she bore no resemblance to his vacuous, self-absorbed mother.

Her defence of her family had touched him tonight. Always, and in defiance of seemingly insurmountable odds, she placed their welfare ahead of her own. She cared for them, laboured for them, strived mightily to keep the remnants of her happy home together.

But at what cost? He thought of her longing to start anew in America and wondered what other dreams had Chione sacrificed for her family. Had she hoped to meet a man there? One who would not mind an Egyptian mother and a notorious family? One who would offer marriage?

He thought of the smitten look on Alden's face tonight and frowned. Why not? Trey might have forsworn a legshackle, but any number of other men would be lucky to take a woman like Chione Latimer to wife.

Trey's own temperament was without doubt the wrong sort to ever contemplate a lifelong commitment. Every significant relationship in his past had proven that he was capable of neither giving nor inspiring that sort of devotion.

In contrast, Chione appeared to be designed for it. She was far too lovely to wither away a spinster, too full of warmth to remain for ever childless. It was a certainty that no child of hers would ever question his mother's love.

Perhaps, then, that should be his goal, though even the thought of her with another man caused both his fists and his stomach to clench.

Perhaps, then, it was time that they both faced a few hard truths.

No matter the physical response she evoked, and perhaps especially because of the other, more complicated feelings she inspired, nothing could come of it. The sooner they finished this wild goose chase, the sooner he could be gone, away from temptation and the futile contemplation of what could never be.

And the sooner she could move on as well. Before long she must face the fact that Mervyn was beyond their reach. Perhaps Trey could help convince her it was time to think of herself as well as her family.

Abruptly he realised that the street had ended, spilling them into the wider area of the marketplace. It was deserted, the open spaces forlorn in the faint moonlight. Trey steered Chione to the shadows behind the empty stalls and together they circled quietly towards the George.

He breathed a sigh of relief when they entered the courtyard of the inn. Back safe. He spared a brief thought for Renhurst. Since he and the girl had gone unmolested, he had to assume that trouble had indeed followed the viscount. He hoped the man was up to the challenge.

The yard of the George was quiet, the galleries empty. Trey steered Chione towards the stairs, but as they reached the first step he paused. Before he could talk himself out of it, he grasped her arm and pulled her to a stop.

'Miss Latimer, I will, of course, ask Aswan about the whereabouts of Richard's journals, but I hope you realise the likelihood that they will contain anything useful is extremely low.'

She frowned up at him. 'We don't know that. You heard Mr Alden; he said Richard kept detailed notes.'

'Did Mervyn's journals contain anything helpful?'

She didn't answer.

He sighed. 'It's a long journey back. We'll both have plenty of time for contemplation. I hope you will begin to realise that we are nearing the end of your quest. You've done your best, not even your grandfather could fault you. But soon it will be time to think about a new chapter in your life.'

'I don't understand.' She gazed up at him. 'You want me to give up?' She pulled away, every line of her broadcasting her incredulousness. 'I thought you understood what Mervyn Latimer means to me. I can't give up. I won't admit to failing him.'

'You haven't failed him. Can't you see?' Trey was in uncharted waters here. Lord, he hoped she would throw him a line. 'You've done your best for him, for his children, even for his faithful servants. But you must know when it is time to stop. Stop and think—have you done what's best for you?'

She looked utterly blank. 'I have no idea what you could mean.'

'Mervyn loved you no less than those children. Wouldn't he want what is best for you?' He straightened. 'In any case, it seems doubtful that you can continue on much longer the way you have been.'

'Treyford, it's been a long day.' She began to fish in her reticule for her key. 'I'm not even sure what you are talking about, and I'm too tired to argue with you.'

But Trey had to finish this now. He might never get up the nerve for such a conversation again. 'I am talking about thinking in new directions. I want you to think about doing what is best for everyone—including yourself.' He was fast becoming exasperated. 'I heard Renhurst mention the children's grandmother. Where does she reside?'

'In Portsmouth.' She sighed. 'Why?' He saw comprehension at last in her eyes, followed quickly by anger. 'Do you think to tell me I should give Will and Olivia over to her?' She laughed, but it was an ugly, bitter sound. 'Never, not as long as I draw breath.'

'What reason could you possibly have…?' He paused. 'Oh. Unless…. Is she poverty-stricken as well?'

'Poverty-stricken?' she gasped with indignation, but then she flushed. 'No, she is comfortable enough.'

'Then your reason is?'

'She might have pounds and pence, my lord, but she also has all the warmth of a snake. She is cold and distant and demanding. The children don't know her, nor is she truly interested in them. What interests her is the money they might bring her way. What she hopes for is influence. Enough influence over the children so that she might gain some control of Mervyn's shipping company and estate.'

'Is it so bad a trade? Let me play devil's advocate for the moment. What of nannies and governesses and tutors? Will could go to school, make friends of a similar age.' He wanted to touch her, hold her tight, force her to listen. Instead he gripped his hands tightly at his sides. 'He wouldn't have to fish for his supper.'

'He wouldn't have anyone to love him, either!'

Trey snorted. 'I assure you, many an English child has survived without love. It is practically an unwritten rule, is it not? It is the established custom among the wealthy to ignore their offspring until they are of age.'

'Just because it is done does not make it right. Yes, do look at the children of the aristocratic and the wealthy. How do they turn out? Selfish, for the most part, and lazy. They don't contribute anything to the world around them.'

They had been speaking in whispers, but her voice raised a notch as she grew more vehement. 'Yes, every child deserves security, but emotional security is just as important. We must feed their bodies, their minds and their souls as well. Then they can grow confident, trusting, ready to give back to the world they inhabit, rather than just taking.'

'But must it be you?' Trey asked. 'Are you the only one who can do this for those children?'

'No,' she said and now it was triumph ringing in her tone. '*Mervyn can.* He raised me with love and caring. They deserve no less. Do you understand at last why I cannot just abandon this search for him?'

'I do understand why you feel that way,' he huffed. 'But you must eventually face the facts. There is a very real possibility that Mervyn is dead and we will never know why or how.'

He turned and walked away a few steps in frustration. 'The more I hear, the more I cannot accept that you must sacrifice so much of yourself. I never said you must abandon the children. They deserve a happy home and the chance to realise their potential—but so do you. Will you be content dedicating yourself to their needs and ignoring your own?'

He could see in her stare that she was no closer to comprehending him. They came at this issue from absolute opposite ends of the spectrum. But then her head went up and he saw her eyes narrow in suspicion.

'Are we talking of my needs or yours, my lord?'

'Excuse me?'

'I'm beginning to suspect that it is your freedom you worry about.' She stepped closer and lowered her voice. 'Those children are a gift, not an obligation. Perhaps you are unable to see that. But then, not everyone is as eager to escape responsibility as you are.'

Her words stirred to life the embers of old wounds. 'Would you care to explain that statement?' he asked carefully.

She lifted her chin. 'You are an earl, a peer of the realm,' she said with a flourish of her hand. 'Surely you have lands, estates, a duty to the people who depend on you, and indeed to the laws and subjects of England.' She stepped closer still and glared directly into his face. 'When were last at your seat, my lord? Do you know the condition of your tenants? Are they thriving? Suffering? Have you once sat in your place in the House of Lords or concerned yourself with the difficulties facing this nation?'

Rage flickered along veins, fuelled by ancient hurts he'd thought long buried. He closed his eyes. Idiot. When would he learn? A pretty face, a sweet smile and he'd done what he'd known he should not. He'd got involved, offered opinions, took a step into the chaos that swirled around this slip of a woman.

Silent, lips braced against the torrent of angry words that threatened, he walked back to the stairs. Gesturing, he waited for her to proceed ahead of him.

She went, and kept quiet until they reached her room. There she turned to him, her back against the locked door. 'Don't worry, Treyford,' she said in a subdued voice. 'I will not hold you any further. You've more than fulfilled your promise to my brother, and you've been a tremendous help to me. I thank you.' She raised those incredible eyes to his and, like the first day he'd met her, he could see once more sorrow and pain reflected there. 'When we get back you must feel free to make plans to return to your work.'

Trey turned to go. He took a step towards the door of his adjoining room. Then he stopped. He shook his head. Why, with this woman, did he always act against his instincts? He turned back. Already she fumbled with her lock.

'Miss Latimer.'

Her furtive movements stopped, but she kept her face to the door.

'I have a fine and trustworthy man of business. He hires estate agents and caretakers and the myriad number of people required to look after my interests. They all fare far better under his kind and interested guidance than they would ever do with me.'

He breathed deep. 'I am a hard man. I admit it. Hell, most of the time I embrace it.' His sigh was long and heartfelt. 'Tonight, however, I find myself regretting it.'

She turned to face him, her expression blank.

'I hope you will believe me, Miss Latimer, when I tell you that tonight, for once in my life, I was not looking out for my own self-interest.' He raised a brow in self mockery. 'If I appear ignorant and bumbling, it's because it is what I am. I have no experience in caring for anything except my own sorry hide. I'm unsure how to share concern or offer advice.' He allowed the bitterness he felt to creep into his voice. 'And since I do it so ill, I don't plan to repeat the attempt. Please forgive me.'

He turned away. But he hadn't taken more than a step when she caught his hand, held it close, cradling it against the warmth of her bosom. He could feel the rapid beating of her heart; see the uncertainty in her face.

'I'm sorry,' she whispered. 'I don't know what it is. In your company I lose…something.' Her head tilted back and she stared upwards, as if searching for answers in the dark recesses of the corridor. 'I don't know why, I only know I am not myself when I am with you. Or maybe it is that I am more myself—and it frightens me.' She ducked her head back down, staring at their clasped hands for a moment, before raising her gaze finally to his. Behind the dark curtain of her lashes shone both remorse and something close to despair. 'I shudder to think of the things I have done since I've met you. I've shouted, lectured, practically blackmailed you into doing my bidding, and now I've attacked your character.'

Never in a thousand years would Trey dare tell her how

similarly she affected him. He reached out and ran a finger along the exotic bones of her face. 'That's not all you've done,' he said roughly.

She put her hand up to his, encircled his wrist with a fragile grip, and leaned her soft cheek into his caress. 'No,' she whispered, the word thick with emotion, 'not all.'

Everything inside Trey screamed for him to drop his hand, back away and run. All the perils he'd faced in a long and adventurous life were as nothing compared to the danger represented by Miss Chione latimer.

Again, instinct failed him. His heart was pounding, his breath coming fast. He answered the mute appeal in her eyes by closing his own. He slipped his hand further, buried it in the ebony tangle of her hair and covered her mouth with his.

Fire. It was the answer to all of her uncertainties, the reason why her body inevitably betrayed her mind when Treyford was near.

Djinn were creatures of fire. As humans were created from earth and the angels of air, so *djinn* craved heat and warmth and flame. Something inside Treyford—his soul, perhaps—blazed with the heat of his passions: for life, for the past, for his work. But right now she knew that the highest flame inside of him burned for her.

It escalated, calling irresistibly to the *djinn* Chione had buried so long ago. And she answered. She remembered what he'd taught her earlier, slanted her mouth and returned his kiss, hot and demanding.

Foolish. Chione well knew the dangers of exposing herself, acknowledged the risk of giving in to such undisciplined passion. But all the gods help her, she just didn't care. Parting her lips, she invited him inside. The thrust of his tongue sent her need spiralling out of control. *Yes.* She was wild with wanting, fierce with it. She reached up, wrapped her arms around him, pulling him even harder against her. Extraordinary heat, exotic scent, the hard feel of his body pressing her against the door. Heaven.

He tore his mouth from hers and traced her jaw with his kiss. She arched into him as he seared the sensitive skin of her neck with his hot, seeking mouth, marking her as his. Chione shuddered. *God, yes*—she was his. The hidden part of her had always known it. The rest of her was swiftly reaching agreement.

His fingers were hard at work, frantically unfastening the many buttons of her pelisse. Desperate for his touch, Chione reached up to help. In a moment it was done, and his hands were inside, cradling her, caressing her, teasing her nipples into hard, eager peaks. Her breath exploded from her as he bent down and suckled her, right through the many thin layers of her gown and her undergarments. The heat, the wetness, the hard flick of his tongue, all of it combined to shoot molten rivulets of desire through her body, stealing her breath, weakening her knees.

He must have sensed her unsteadiness. He ran a caressing hand over her hips, and down her leg, lifting it gently until it was curved about his hip. He leaned his body into hers, pressing her into the door, lending her stability even as he rocked the hard length of his erection against her.

Chione moaned. The unfamiliar position opened her body in the most intriguing way. She felt at once eager and excruciatingly vulnerable. But there was no turning back now. His hand was inching its way in tiny, teasing circles towards the most intimate part of her. She arched into him, bracing the other foot and settling her shoulders firmly against the hard support of the door behind her.

Without warning that support disappeared. Chione tumbled backwards into her own room as the door was snatched suddenly open from within. Too surprised even to cry out, she landed hard on her back.

A great whoosh of breath left her lungs. Aghast, she stared up, saw hands reaching for Trey, pulling him away before the door slammed home once more, shutting her away from him. She gasped, fighting for air.

Strong hands grasped her quickly from behind and crushed her back against a massive chest. One hand clamped firmly over her mouth, gagging her with the strong smell of garlic and tobacco. Panicked, she struggled for the room to breathe, for freedom. Her captor barely noticed. Just like that she was caught, without a struggle, without even a cry of alarm. If Chione hadn't been so frightened, she would have been disgusted.

Such was not the case on the other side of the door. She could hear grunts, a crash, then a repeated thudding sound, as if somebody's head was slamming repeatedly into a wall.

Her captor listened as well. He still held her fast with only one arm—the other he trailed over her breasts, down her belly. 'I am to bring you unharmed,' he rasped in her ear. 'Hassan has ordered it to be so. Disobedience is dangerous, but if you fight me, I will be happy to forget what I am told.'

He spoke with a heavy accent. Chione bucked away from his searching grasp, her mind racing.

'I am going to take my hand away. If you scream, I will enjoy making you stop.' He squeezed her even tighter for a moment before he eased his hand away. Then his hand gripped her wrist and cruelly twisted her arm up behind her back. 'Do not scream.'

She shook her head.

Something heavy hit the door with a great crash. A small,

high window let in just enough moonlight for her to see the wood rattling on its hinges. The man leaned around Chione to take up a piece of rope. The move gave her a first look at him, but he wore both a turban and a cloth wrapped around his face.

As he released her arm a gasp of relief escaped her. Both her wrists, though, were caught tight in one of his massive hands. He turned her so that she faced him, still gripping her hard. 'Tonight the interfering Englishman dies.' She could hear the satisfaction in his voice. 'Nothing will save your lover now.'

Chione shook her head and strained away, a sudden idea growing. 'No,' she said. 'He is a demon—he cannot die!' She pulled away, not towards the door, but away from it, towards the back wall of the tiny room. 'Do not let him in here! He is an *ifrit*!'

He was startled enough to let her go. *'Ifrit?'* Then he gathered himself. 'Impossible! He is English. What do the *inglizi* know of the *ifrit*?'

Chione glanced fearfully at the door again. 'He knows the secrets of the ancients. Perhaps they have given him his powers.' She cowered into the corner. 'Do not let him in! He has the eye! You have angered him greatly. We will be dead in an instant.'

The doorknob rattled. The entire door shook again. 'Chione!' Her name rang out in a powerful bellow.

Her captor had forgotten her. All of his fearful attention was focused on the door. Chione grabbed the water pitcher. No—too light. As was the basin.

'Ifrit or not, he can be killed,' he muttered. With swift and deadly precision he moved to one side of the doorway, his sword out and gleaming in the low light. 'We will see how he likes the taste of my steel.'

With a tremendous crash the door fell in. Treyford strode

over the wreckage. Chione screamed a warning. He jumped aside only just in time to avoid the heavy downward stroke of the sword. The blade did not rise again. Instead its owner followed it down, landing sprawled across the wooden door, pieces of the heavy porcelain chamber pot scattered around his head like a halo.

Chapter Ten

Hᴉs chest heaving, Trey looked up from his fallen attacker
and straight into Chione Latimer's distressed gaze. All the
colour had drained from her golden complexion. Almost
without thought he reached out a comforting arm to her.

She didn't respond. Eyes wide with horror, she was staring
down at her handiwork. 'Is he…dead?'

Trey squatted next to the prostrate man. 'No. He'll be fine,
except for one hell of a headache.' He rested an arm on his bent
knee and shot her an amused glance. 'Prehistoric knives and
chamber pots,' he said with a shake of his head. 'Remind me
to stay in your good graces.'

Her shoulders sagged. Alarmed, Trey jumped up and
enfolded her in his arms. 'My God, are you all right?'

She nodded weakly against his chest. 'Are you?' she asked
faintly. 'I thought…I was afraid they had…'

'No,' he soothed. 'I'm fine.' From somewhere he dragged
up a reassuring grin. 'Besides this fellow, there are two more
outside. One is knocked out cold. The other was tossed down
the stairs by a nice strapping lad who saw the fight, didn't like
the odds and came to my aid. The rest of them fled once
everyone began to stir.' He sighed. 'We'll have to come up

with something better next time. Picking them off one by one is hardly effective.'

'Next time...' she began, but then she stopped. 'Wait! He said his orders came from Hassan. Do you know him?'

Perplexed, Trey shook his head. 'No. An enemy of your grandfather's, perhaps?' He looked down at the man sprawled on the floor. 'He's crafty, whoever he is. Do you suppose they followed us and Renhurst too?'

She stepped away and looked up at him again with frightened eyes. 'The boy—Cedric's nephew!'

For half a second, Trey's heart stopped. He stared at the crowd beginning to mill outside the door and shouted 'Cedric!'

'Here, sir!' the answering call came. 'Vandals!' Cedric's voice spat, growing closer. 'Thieves and rogues. Nothing to worry about now,' he blustered to the gathering people. 'The constable will deal with this lot. Tie 'em up good and tight, boys!'

'Cedric!' Trey called again.

'Yes, sir!' The crowd parted. 'Here I am.'

'Your boy, Cedric,' Trey said in a lower voice. 'Has he made it home?'

'Home safe, sir.' Trey breathed his relief and noticed Chione's matching sigh.

'And his packages are safe as well,' Cedric continued. 'All taken care of.'

'Thank you, Cedric,' Chione breathed. 'I could never have borne it, had anything happened to him.' She shuddered. 'And thank heavens you had the notion, Treyford, for him to take the artifacts and slip away before us.'

'Yes, well, I have a slippery mind,' he said wryly.

'Sir!' Cedric's barkeep was kneeling over the man Chione had struck. 'This one's starting to stir.' He grinned. 'Shall I give 'im another bash in the noggin?'

'Let's just get them to the constable, lads,' Cedric said.

'Heaven knows what he'll do with them,' Trey said. 'Find out what you can from them—but I doubt it will be much.' He paused, suddenly struck by a notion and spoke an Arabic phrase out loud. 'Chione, doesn't something in that mean gold?'

She thought a moment. 'Box of gold? No, I think golden box.' She looked his way with dawning horror. 'Do you mean that they knew of it?'

'Damn. It sounded so. Certainly I heard those words more than once.' He huffed in frustration. 'Either they heard all that we said or they know more than we do about this damned mystery.'

'But if they heard—they'll be after the journals. They'll head back to… Trey, the children!'

Bleakly, Trey turned back to the innkeeper. 'Cedric, rouse your stables. We'll need the coach. We'd best be off right away.'

Their need to travel quickly eliminated all but the most cursory conversation. Chione confessed to herself that this was a relief rather than a hardship. She needed time alone to think, to gather her wayward feelings into some semblance of order, and, most importantly, to pack away again the passionate aspect of her nature. The curious thing was that she didn't find herself trying very hard. At last she reached the conclusion that, for good or ill, Treyford had irrevocably awakened her unbridled half. Her sensible self very much feared that it would be for ill, but the *djinn* was out of the lamp now, and there was no forcing her back in.

Many times in the past her passions had manifested themselves negatively. Anger, jealousy, betrayal—Chione had sometimes frightened herself with the intensity of her feelings. Painful experience had taught her to resist the seductive pull of her fiery nature. It was nothing like that now. This time she had something truly pleasurable to focus on.

Scenery slipped by unnoticed and afternoon stretched into evening as Chione's thoughts lingered on the Earl of Treyford. With flushed cheeks she relived the heat of his lips, the exquisite feel of his hands on her body. He'd touched her everywhere and it hadn't been enough. Even now she quivered as she remembered his fingers playing her like a harp, sending lush vibrations to her very core. He'd been at once firm and tender, and she had been nothing if not eager.

She forced herself to consider the wisdom of dwelling upon the sweetness of those forbidden moments, when she knew full well that hurt lurked just around the corner. Without a doubt Treyford would be leaving. Chione had enough experience with men of his character to know that he would be gone sooner rather than later. Hadn't she already thought that. Treyford was like the men in her family—exactly the sort of man she had pledged not to become involved with. Could she forsake her own vows and leave herself open to that pain again?

At last, as the light faded, the coach rolled to a stop. Chione and Jenny Ferguson had the chance to stretch their legs while the horses were changed. Treyford had pushed himself hard, driving for such a long stretch, and once they were ready to get under way again, positions were switched. The coachman climbed back on top. Jenny decided to brave the cold night air for a chance to keep him warm. Treyford, clearly exhausted, crawled into the coach and shot Chione a weary grin. 'We're near to Trusham, and making good time,' he'd said hoarsely. In mere moments, he'd been asleep.

Only Heaven knew how. Chione smiled at his unknowing form, curled up awkwardly on the opposite bench. They'd hit a particularly rough stretch of road and the jerking of the carriage was anything but comfortable. Treyford had his head propped in the corner, but with each new bump his head slipped lower, until finally his chin would hit his chest and he would startle, bouncing back upright to start the process over again.

Chione at last took pity on him. Timing her movements with the jostling of the carriage, she slipped over to his bench, slid up next to him and eased his head over on to her shoulder. For a moment all was well. Then she encountered the same problem. Every bounce sent his head sliding down and towards her bosom. Fighting laughter, she gave up. She moved further away and gently settled his head comfortably in her lap.

Ah. The weight and heat of him felt good. She heaved a sigh, relishing the wide curve of his shoulder pressed against her hip. This was not fire, but warmth. It felt comfortable, intimate.

The rhythmic rise and fall of his chest soothed her, while at the same time the stir of his breath against her skirts excited her senses. Chione felt oddly suspended, caught in a moment out of time. Outside the chill wind blew and trouble awaited. But here existed peace and warmth. Sanctuary.

Without conscious thought her hand raised, her fingers hovering over the thick tangled length of Treyford's hair. How she longed to touch him. She wanted to run sensitive fingers over his ear, along the bristly line of his jaw. And more—she wished she could touch his soul, soothe his skittishness, ease away all of fate's tangles that lay between them.

Unbidden, her mother's voice echoed in her head.

'Stay free, if you can, of passion that exists without a deeper foundation.'

How well she remembered the love, the concern that had hidden behind the warning. Her father had been dead by then—murdered by a villain seeking knowledge of the Lost

Jewel—and the frantic flight her mother had embarked upon with two children cut short. Eshe had been captured, bartered, sold, tossed around like meat at a butcher's stall. Chione and the toddling Richard had been left in the street like dogs.

But Chione was her mother's daughter. She'd heard where the men had said they meant to take Eshe, and doggedly she'd followed, her baby brother in tow. Her mind instinctively shied away from those horrid days. Mostly vague impressions remained—endless heat, pitiless eyes, the incessant crying of her hungry brother. Only two truly sharp memories remained to haunt her dreams; the first time she had stolen a loaf of bread to keep them from starving, and the kind smile of the farmer and his wife who had taken them in, fed them and given them transport to the small city of Asyut.

There she'd succeeded in tracking down her mother, ensconced in the household of a Frank, a foreigner. Eshe had cried over them and praised her daughter to the heavens for her strength. The Frank hadn't minded them, as long as they stayed out of his way, and they had all settled quickly into a routine. Chione had been happy to mind her brother all day, keeping mostly to the gardens, and she'd curled up contentedly with him on a pallet in the kitchen during the night. But the evenings belonged to the three of them, those precious hours between the foreigner's dinner and the time he took himself—and her mother—to his bed.

It was in the evenings that they talked, of common things, and of life, and of dreams. That night Eshe had been combing Chione's hair with long slow strokes when the sharp knock on the door and the perfunctory summons had come. Chione had taken the sleeping Richard into her arms and asked the question that had been haunting her.

'Does he hurt you, Mother?'

Her eyes had been cast down to the floor. She'd been afraid to see the truth of it in Eshe's eyes. But a calloused finger beneath her chin had forced her to lock gazes with her mother.

'*I do not give him the power to hurt me, young one.*'

Chione had not answered, only wrapped her baby brother tighter in her arms. Eshe had correctly interpreted the gesture.

'*Do not confuse what he does to me with what I had with your father. Your father and I, we had a great love—the sort that poets sigh over and all the world aches for.*'

Her tone had been fierce, but then her gaze had drifted away from Chione, concentrating on something that her daughter could not see.

'*No, my dear one, this Frank does not hurt me, but neither does he move me. We feel nothing for each other.*'

She'd grown silent for a moment and pensive.

'*Perhaps that is the danger, though. Memories of your father—they fill my heart with joy. What this man does is empty, heartless. He does not harm me, but perhaps he does...bring me down, rip me from the heights I shared with your father.*'

The impatient call had come again. Her mother had gone then to answer it, but turned back as she reached the door.

'*You are strong, like me, little one. Some day you will also be a lovely young woman. I tell you now to stay strong, Chione. For my sake I hope you will remember that desire is nothing without finer feelings. Without love, it cannot lift you to the heavens.*'

With Treyford Chione did indeed feel lifted to the heavens. What if he was the only one who could take her there? No other man had ever affected her so profoundly. Her eyes drifted closed. What would her mother think of a passion in which the deeper attachment was only one sided? No doubt she would scorn such a connection.

Chione sighed. She was less inclined to do so. What she felt for Treyford, she was beginning to realise, was true. But she must also face his fundamental truth. The earl was unable—or unwilling—to return such feelings.

She sighed again.

'You are not going to cry, are you?'

Though his voice was soft, Chione jumped. 'How long have you been awake?'

He shifted around until he could look her in the face, though he didn't lift his head from her lap. 'Since you moved over here.' His smile was tender.

'You're a rogue.' But she said it without heat. 'I'm sorry— you need your sleep. I only sought to help.'

'You did help. I think this has been better for me than sleep.' His gaze was smouldering, his tone concerned. He reached up and tucked a wayward lock behind her ear. 'What were you thinking of, that made you feel so sad?'

She flushed a little. 'My mother. I was remembering something she tried to teach me. Something I don't seem to have learned very well.'

The shadow of some strong emotion passed over his face. 'At least she made the attempt,' he said. 'That counts for something.' He twisted back around into his original position on her lap. 'You don't mind, do you?' he asked quietly. 'It's been a long time since anyone really touched me.'

'I don't mind,' she whispered. His words set off her longing once more, and the aching need to comfort him. But Chione knew that he would not welcome such emotions. She thought instead to lighten the atmosphere. 'I don't think I believe you in any case. Richard alluded to your many conquests in a few of his letters, you know. I confess, at the time I always wished he would include some of the details.'

'None of them were worth the ink,' he said shortly. 'Tell me, what was your mother like?'

She smiled. 'Amazing. She was incredibly alive. Vibrant with it. Perhaps you know what I mean? Richard was the same, living each moment to its fullest.'

'I do know. I think that is perhaps the first thing that drew me to Richard. He was the only partner I've ever worked with, you know.' He sounded pensive. 'The only person I could tolerate in such constant contact.'

'Eshe, my mother, was impatient with people as well. Did Richard tell you that she ran away from her family as a young girl?'

'No, he didn't.' He sounded intrigued. 'That's most unusual for an Egyptian girl, is it not? Do you know why she left them?'

'All she would ever say was that they refused to live in the world. She was determined to learn more of it before she settled down to marriage and family.' Chione stopped, unwilling to follow the thought any further.

The silence stretched out for long moments. A comfortable, companionable silence. Chione jumped a little when he broke it.

'And what was it that had you so melancholy? What was it that your mother tried to teach you, and failed?'

She realised that when he spoke, she could feel it. And somehow it was the most intimate thing she'd ever experienced. Vibrations travelled from him directly to her thigh and further, unsettling her almost as much as the question itself.

She swallowed. 'So many things. She was a very wise woman.'

'As is her daughter.'

Chione knew he meant it. There was a strange sort of intimacy to this position—bodies touching, but unable to read each other's expression. Without facial cues Chione had to rely on his tone and the total relaxation of his body against hers. She sensed how rare this was for him. It was without a doubt a first for her. It was also freeing, as if she could say things she might otherwise not, forge ahead with questions that any other time she would have hesitated to ask.

'And your family?' she asked. 'Did your mother labour as fruitlessly as mine—trying to impart the mysteries of life?'

He tensed, and she could sense the struggle he tried to hide. She kept quiet and after a moment he continued.

'Unfortunately, my mother was not as wise as yours.' He paused. 'Wisdom has never been counted a fashionable accomplishment, you understand.'

'Was she a great society lady, then?'

'For a number of years, yes.' He shifted a bit, but didn't turn. 'Are you not familiar with the Stafford family scandal?'

'No. Indeed, I didn't know there was one. I do apologise.'

'I thought everyone in England knew of it.' His tone was bitter.

Perhaps that explained his distaste for his homeland. 'I am a merchant's daughter, living in the wilds of Devonshire. Society's gossip is nothing to me.'

'It is a sordid little tale, in any case.'

A lock of his dark hair had snagged on a button of her pelisse. Gently she untangled it. Unable to resist any longer, she gave in to the intimate atmosphere and her own temptation. Blissfully she dug her fingers in and chased the highlights through the thick layers that drifted across her lap.

Treyford let out a sigh of intense pleasure and went

boneless against her. For several long minutes silence reigned as she indulged them both.

'She used to do that, you know. I always loved it.' His voice hummed against her, low and reflective.

'Before she went down to dinner, or out for the evening, my nurse would take me down to her. She was always so beautiful, in her rich gowns and sparkling jewels. She would smile at me, hold me close a moment and stroke my hair. I always thought she smelled like an angel.' His words sounded meditative. 'She was happier, then, when I was very young.'

'What changed?' Chione asked in a near whisper.

'Everything. My parents had had a volatile courtship, a grand passion. My mother had been meant to marry another. She was not officially betrothed, but the understanding existed. But then she met my father. They fell instantly in love, and they were not discreet. Her father ended up having to pay reparation to the other man, but I suppose he thought nabbing an earl for a son-in-law was well worth it.'

He sighed. 'I don't know what happened. I was young. One minute I lived in a happy home, the next I did not.'

'How sad.'

'Yes, it was sad, and somehow…frightening. I don't recall specifics, you know. It is all jumbled into an image of horrendous accusations, loud voices, scurrying servants and endless sobbing.'

His voice trailed away and Chione thought he had finished, but in a moment he began to speak again. A chill went down her spine as she realised how his voice had changed. He sounded hollow, detached, as if he spoke of something that had happened to someone else.

'The last fight was the worst. They caught me unaware. I had brought some of my painted soldiers downstairs to the drawing room, hoping my mother would come in eventually. I remember the glorious battle I had set up. The French were arrayed on the bench by the pianoforte, the English, of course, had the high ground on top of the keys. Victory for our boys was imminent when at last my mother did come in.'

It was several long moments before he went on. 'She didn't see me through her tears. She went to the sofa in the far corner, almost as if she were hiding. I understood why a moment later. My father followed her into the house. He passed the drawing room by at first and went upstairs. But soon he was calling her, screaming her name. So angry—I had never seen him in such a rage. I hid beneath the pianoforte while they argued. It was…ugly. I huddled there, feeling as if each vicious word tore another piece of my world away.'

The image horrified Chione because she knew precisely how it felt. How painful it was to have security and comfort ripped away. How hurt and anger sometimes rushed in to fill the empty spaces of your heart and left you for ever changed. Her own heart ached for that devastated little boy and for the bitter, wary man in her lap.

'I found out later just why he was so angry. My mother had taken up with my uncle—his own brother.' His shoulders hunched a little, the bones digging into her thigh. 'I imagine you know what a travesty that is considered by the English.'

Chione did know. She could imagine the resulting scandal-broth.

His chest rose and fell on a massive sigh. 'My mother packed her things. She came in for moment to kiss me goodbye. She said she would send for me, and then she was gone. I never saw her again.'

Sadly, Chione thought that the lessons Treyford's mother had taught him were not the ones she might have wished.

'My father died a few weeks later. An accident,' he said bitterly. 'I was left to the care of my uncle—the same uncle who had torn them finally apart.'

His voice trailed off. Chione sensed there was more to the story—but she doubted she would ever hear it. She closed her eyes and let her head fall back. Even this little bit of information illuminated much about Treyford's character. He manipulated his life so that he would never again be that vulnerable little boy. Who better to sympathise with that than her?

It became suddenly easier to understand his moods and his restlessness. Incredibly, it was largely her doing. She had him well and truly trapped and he retreated emotionally because he could not do it physically.

His breathing had deepened, the rise and fall beneath her hands had become more rhythmic. Chione thought he had finally fallen asleep. In a burst of clarity she realised how difficult it had been for him to reveal so much about himself. It touched her, but it also reminded her of the bitter truth. Treyford might give in to a moment's passion, but that was likely all he could ever give.

He wanted her; that she could not question. But Chione doubted whether he could bring himself to pursue her—not without encouragement. By her reckoning, this left the ball firmly in her court, but also left her to answer one burning question. Could she accept his desire knowing that nothing more would follow?

Chione rather thought she could. Her heart rate ratcheted at the thought of finishing what they had started. Yes, it was unconventional, but truly, it was almost a relief to have no expectations beyond the physical. Treyford was not likely to ask awkward questions. A man with secrets of his own; he was unlikely to probe hers. It would be liberating, really. She would be free to relax as never before. No need to reveal the ugliness of the past, no need to sustain her consuming role, no need to feel guilty about living a lie. She could unleash her passionate nature with impunity. Treyford would not be around long enough to be harmed by it.

She rested her gaze tenderly on the tousled head in her lap, felt the tension in the shoulder her hand rested on, and she knew. For the first time she would forsake Eshe's sage advice. She would savour what the fates allowed her. Perhaps it would turn out to be nothing more than the desire Treyford poured over her with his touch. For certain it would be short lived. But she was going to reach out and take whatever he felt he could offer. It might not be the grand romance that her parents had, but, like her mother, she would have memories for the cold and lonely times ahead.

Trey had drifted off under the ministrations of Chione's clever fingers. He awoke some time later to find her gone back over to the other bench, Ferguson's niece huddled there with her, and the carriage stopped for another change of horses.

Purposefully not meeting Chione's eye, he scrambled out of the carriage, circled around the back, then stood there in the cold morning air, scrubbing his hands over his face and cursing himself for a fool.

He winced when the driver came up from behind and gave him a friendly slap on the back. 'Sleep tight, my lord?' he asked with a wink. 'Or did ye take advantage of the dark as I did with wee Jenny?'

'Should have done,' muttered Trey.

But the driver looked suddenly chagrined. 'My apologies, sir. I didn't mean no disrespect to Miss Chione.' He straightened. 'Nor to my Jenny. T'was naught but a kiss or two we shared, and my intents is honourable.' He grinned. 'Mrs F. would be having my hide, otherwise. And 'tis clear that neither of them is *that* sort o' girl, iff'n ye knows what I mean.' He ended with a broad grin and sauntered off to check the traces.

Trey watched the man go and envied him his certainty. The only thing Trey could be certain of was his own idiocy. And perhaps of the fact that somewhere buried under Chione Latimer's calm and competent exterior, there did lurk *that* sort of girl. Exactly the sort of girl to set his blood afire and make him forget all the principles that had governed all of his adult, blessedly unfettered life.

After a nod from the driver he climbed up on to the box, took up the ribbons and eased the fresh horses from the crowded inn courtyard. Once they had left the town behind he let them go and found his thoughts straying right back where they didn't belong: on the ever-more-prickly problem of Chione Latimer.

Yes, he'd long suspected that a well of passion existed underneath her tranquil exterior. He'd enjoyed teasing her occasionally, pricking her temper, rousing her to a spirited debate. But, good God, he'd never imagined she might gift him with such an uninhibited response, and he'd been shocked at the tower of answering passion her hunger had unleashed in him. He'd sprouted a hammer between his legs, iron hard and clamoring for her grip. Hell, he'd been so lost that he'd almost taken her right there against the door.

Unintentionally, his hands tightened on the ribbons. One of the horses threw up his head in protest and Trey forced himself to ease up. Madness. Outright idiocy. What else could one call it? Ravaging an innocent girl on English soil ranked right up there with the stupidest and most perilous things he'd ever done. And not just any girl, but one caught up in exactly the sort of tangled web of relationships that he abhorred.

By God, he should be grateful that those thugs had been lying in wait. Had it been Cedric who interrupted them, it would be Trey stuck in a trap of his own making instead of three stubbornly mute bandits mouldering in the constable's strong room.

And then, last night he'd compounded the problem, exceeding even his own capacity for stupidity. Good God, he hadn't mentioned his mother to a living person in nearly twenty years. The ease he felt with Chione, the comfort he took in her touch, her conversation —it grew ever more addictive. And dangerous.

Marriage. It was what she probably contemplated, what he might have been forced to—what, if he had any honour at all, he should consider even now. He shuddered. Only his high regard for her allowed him to even entertain such a thought.

Such a marriage could never be anything but a trap. For her as well as him. Trey was not capable of giving the sort of intimacy she would expect, nor could he bear to be stuck in any one place for long. England would be the death of him in mere months. Neither could he ask a well-bred girl like Chione Latimer to give up her family, or subject her to the hardships of his itinerant lifestyle.

No—a union would be misery for one of them at the start and a disaster for them both before long. How could it not be, when resentment and petty jealousies came on the heels of the best alliances? How much worse would it be for a pair so mismatched? Trey was not eager to find out. He'd had a lucky escape. He would make the most of it and get away while the exit still lay clear.

Chapter Eleven

The memory of the rest of that journey would not be one Chione cherished. Frightful scenes drifted through her mind's eye: the house looted or burned, the children held hostage. Her nerves were in a ragged state when at last they pulled up the drive to stop in front of the house. Eagerly, Chione peered through the open window and breathed a heavy sigh of relief. Everything looked to be in order from the outside.

But then the carriage door opened to a familiar leering grin instead of to Eli's welcoming smile and Chione's heart dropped to the gravel below.

'Higgins, you are here,' she said stupidly. Mrs Stockton's impertinent footman. But if he were here, then that meant…

'Aye, miss, but not for long.' Only slightly lower he muttered, 'With any luck.'

Chione ignored the impertinence. The cloying taste of dread lay heavy in her mouth as she hurried into the house. She didn't even wait to speak to Treyford. A threat to her family had indeed manifested itself, but it had come from an entirely unexpected source.

Inside all lay quiet. The downstairs rang empty and

deserted. Even the kitchen was vacant. Panic rose as she raced up the stairs to the schoolroom. Afraid of what she would *not* find, she eased open the door.

They were there. Chione sagged in relief to see Mrs Ferguson grouped at the window with Olivia and Will. Then her brain began to function again and she took in the reality of the little tableau.

The housekeeper held a bowl and a rag. She sat next to the boy on the sofa, bathing the reddened wheals that crossed his thin shoulders. Will's face was turned away from her. Next to him, on the floor, sat Olivia. She stroked his hand, a look of profound sorrow on her little face.

A whisper of a sound—some dreadful cross between fury and sorrow and regret—escaped her. Olivia's sharp ears caught it. At once her head came up and her eyes lit with joy.

'Shone!' she shouted. In an instant she had flown across the room and flung herself into Chione's arms. 'Shone! A bad lady came! She hurt Will.'

Will's head had whipped around. He sat up, manfully fighting back tears. 'It's Grandmama, Chione,' he said thickly. 'She arrived the day after you left.'

Clutching Olivia close, Chione quickly crossed the room and enveloped the boy in a careful embrace. Swallowing heavily, she asked, 'What happened, Will?'

He couldn't answer. He buried his face in her gown and shook with silent sobs.

Mrs Ferguson answered for him, the thunderous look on her face growing even darker. 'She accused him of shirking his studies,' she spat.

'I didn't!' Will erupted with red-faced, boyish indignation. 'I only went to help Eli in the kitchen gardens. I saw him struggling with the seedlings from my window.'

'She did *this*,' Chione said in a dangerous voice, 'because you helped in the garden?'

'No—she called him in for a lecture when she saw him out there,' the housekeeper said. 'Said he needed to learn what is suitable for a boy of his station.'

'A boy of my *fortune*—that's what she said.' Chione had never heard so scathing a tone from her dear Will. He'd lost his innocence, his precious faith in the world, and she ached with guilt even as she mourned its loss.

He looked pleadingly at her now. 'She said that Papa is dead, and that I must learn to act as befits his heir. I told her he's not dead! He's missing—but he'll come back! She said I was insolent and had to learn not to talk disrespectfully to my elders.'

'And she struck you?'

'No,' interjected Mrs Ferguson. 'She had her woman do it.' She shook her fist. 'Aswan put a stop to it, but I swear—t'ain't finished. That one will soon know what comes from beating an innocent child! I'll break her fine, haughty nose for her, see if I don't!'

Will leaned back into Chione's embrace. Searchingly, he looked into her face. 'He'll be back, won't he, Chione? Papa's coming back, isn't he?'

'I pray so, Will.'

'The bad lady locked Livvie,' Olivia piped up. Her tone was proud.

Chione stroked her hair. 'Locked you, my darling?'

'Had a right fit about little Miss's wanderin',' Mrs Ferguson said darkly. 'Said she was too young to be outta the nursery. Locked her in, and with no nurse!'

'I can well imagine the state of the nursery.' Chione tried to summon a smile, but it wouldn't come.

'She's dismissed Eli, Chione!' Will said, still distraught. 'And she tied Morty up in the stables.'

'Has she, then?' Chione could hear the danger in her own voice. 'Well!' she said. She kissed both children and stood. 'I think it is time I greeted our guest.'

'What will ye do?' the housekeeper asked.

'How many times has the old woman told me I was no better than a spiteful stray cat? Now I have it in mind to show her my teeth.'

'Chione, dear! Do sit down. How glad I am to see you back.'

Chione had found Mrs Stockton in the suite of rooms that Mervyn had shared with his second wife—Mrs. Stockton's daughter, Marie. She'd obviously made herself at home. Ribbons, feathers and something that looked like cattails covered the table in front of her and the floor close by.

'I think I shall stand, Mrs Stockton.'

The woman had aged in the years since Chione had last seen her. Always slender, she looked painfully thin now, almost skeletal, with bones protruding through fine skin. She shrugged one prominent shoulder now. 'You will suit yourself.' She held up the bonnet she was trimming. 'How do you like it?' She sighed in satisfaction. 'I do believe I could have made a smashing milliner, had Mr Stockton not snatched me up to make me his bride.'

Chione did not reply and the other woman looked up at her. The chiselled lines of her face had deepened, but the dark eyes burned just as intently.

'Oh, do sit,' she said, 'otherwise I shall have a crook in my neck.' She sighed deeply and frowned, deepening the grooves that lined her mouth. 'There's no use ringing for tea, not in this house, but *we* can at least be civilised. I don't mean to complain the minute you return—but your servants! Such a stubborn, prideful lot. Four days I've been here and not a word would they speak of where you'd gone or when you'd be back.'

'Why are you here, Mrs Stockton?'

She smiled, but the expression was a stark contrast to the cold glitter in her eye. 'My dear Orville insisted!' she said with a wave of her hand. 'My son is technically head of the family now, Chione.'

'Perhaps he is head of your family, ma'am,' Chione retorted. 'He has nothing to do with mine.'

'You know he holds your interests close to his heart, my dear. And of course he wished to hear of his dear sister's children. He thought that now you've had a taste of dealing with all of this on your own, you would be willing to accept a little help.'

She set down the bonnet and sat back in her chair. 'Orville is quite the fashionable young man now, Chione. Did you know that his closest friend is the son of a baronet?'

'No, I did not.' Chione's tone conveyed how little she cared.

Mrs Stockton narrowed her gaze. 'He could have his pick of any number of *ton*nish young ladies, you know. But he thinks only of you.' She leaned forward. 'My dear, he is ready to share your burdens.'

'Thank you, but I can manage my burdens on my own. You may wish to write and tell him I said so before you begin to pack your things.'

The woman stood. 'I should have known better than to expect good manners from you.'

'Yes, you should have, when you barge in where you know you are not welcome.' Chione raised her chin. 'What claim do you have on manners? Angling for an invitation is not the same as receiving one.'

'You left me no choice. A good thing it is, too, that I did not wait. For what do I find but you gone—who knows where!—and my grandchildren left in the care of servants...' she lowered her voice to a malicious whisper '...and *heathens*!'

'Will and Olivia were well looked after by people who genuinely care for them. I understand this is a difficult concept for you to comprehend.' Chione allowed some of the spite she felt to leak into her words. 'In addition, our friend Mr Drake agreed to look in on them every day during my *short* trip.'

'That jumped-up innkeeper? I sent him on his way quick enough.' She folded her arms and stared down her long nose at Chione. 'Have you no idea what sort of acquaintance is suitable for these children? They have a place in this world and it is time that they learned it.'

Chione snorted, a distinctly unladylike sound. 'Perhaps a viscount will be considered suitable, ma'am? Lord Renhurst has been close to our family for years. He also pledged to keep watch on the children if he returned from his business before me.'

'Yes, yes, he was here,' Mrs. Stockton said dismissively. 'I received him civilly enough, but it quickly became clear that, though his title is respectable, he is not the sort that will do us any good. He speaks more like a farmer than a man of society and influence.'

She huffed her exasperation. 'Listen well, girl. Mervyn Latimer robbed me of my chance when he stole my beautiful girl away. But he's gone now, and I've heard how my grandchildren have been forced to live.'

Chione bit back her anger. 'We have done well enough.'

'Ridiculous!' the old lady spat. 'Look at this place!' She gestured about her. 'But then I shouldn't have expected you to comprehend me.' She raised a superior brow. 'Even a dusty, deserted house and a diet of porridge is a step up for you, isn't it?'

Chione cringed.

'Will should be in school by now,' the old woman intoned, 'keeping the sort of company that will do him good later in life. Just look what Oxford did for Beau Brummel, or look what Joseph Banks did with his father's money and a good education!'

She turned her back on Chione and strolled back to her place at the table. Picking up the unfinished bonnet, she said, 'Things are changing. Boundaries are not what they used to be. Will some day will be head of an immense shipping company, but he could also be so much more. The boy has wealth, and good looks. All he needs are connections.' She tossed her head proudly. 'One of my own dear friends just happens to know a member of the board of admissions at Cambridge. Think of it, Chione. There is no telling how far he could go.'

'With you trailing right along in his footsteps, no doubt.' Chione could not hide her disgust for the woman and her ceaseless ambitions. 'I am sorry that your plans for Marie were thwarted, sorry that Mervyn Latimer was not high enough on the social scale to satisfy you. But those two loved each other. They were happy.' Her shoulders slumped in defeat and she turned away. 'I am sorry that was never enough for you.' She took several steps towards the door before turning back with a hardened gaze. 'Just pack your things and go. I will not have you using these children for your own gain.'

'Hold on a moment.' Mrs Stockton's mollifying tone had vanished. Now her voice rang with command. 'I am not finished with you, young lady.'

'I am finished,' Chione threw over her shoulder.

'Perhaps you will be, before I am through.' The bitter old woman pressed her lips tight in irritation. 'Do you think I shall sit back and let you decide the fate of my grandchildren?'

'It is what you have always done before,' Chione replied flippantly.

'I haven't wasted my time alone in your house, Chione,' Mrs Stockton said, gloating. 'You will accept Orville's suit and you will bow to my wishes concerning Will, or I will expose you.'

Incredulous, Chione turned. '*Expose* me?' The worst of her secrets were buried deep. The chances of them being unearthed now were highly unlikely. But an ominously cold spot of fear rolled down her spine and made her stop.

'That is what I said.' Mrs Stockton crossed to a delicate lady's desk near the window and withdrew a stack of papers from a drawer. Crossing back, she flung them triumphantly on the worktable, heedless of the fripperies underneath. 'You will do as I say or I will tell the world that it is *you* writing these vulgar little serial stories!'

The small knot of fear inside of her relaxed. 'Will you?' The corner of Chione's mouth turned up.

'Yes, I will! What do you think will happen when your readers discover it is a *girl* stuck in the back of beyond penning their sensational tales?'

'Well, I imagine it might cause quite a stir.' Chione shrugged. 'One might even call it a scandal.' She paused and tapped her teeth with a finger. 'I should think that everyone who has never read one of my stories will suddenly want to. My readership will double, even triple, perhaps. My publisher will renew my contract. I'll receive more money, and, if I'm lucky, perhaps a bit of acclaim.'

She narrowed her eyes and took a menacing step towards the evil old woman. 'Then I predict I will feel an urge to stretch my talents. I think I shall wish to pen an article for the society pages.'

Chione raised her brows in question. 'What do you think your lofty friends would say once they heard of your father's wig shop, Mrs Stockton? What will they think of a merchant's wife's plans to lift herself as far and as fast as she can? Will they shake their heads at a woman who goes where she is not invited, stays when the mistress of the house is not at home, disparages her acquaintances, and dismisses her servants? Will they offer the cut direct to the woman who locks a little girl alone in a room and has a young boy beaten on the flimsiest of excuses?' Almost casually she reached out and picked up the sheaf of papers. 'Shall we find out?'

Her opponent was white-faced, but far from beaten. 'How dare you threaten me, you insolent little guttersnipe? My father might have been a wigmaker, but he was a loyal, solid Englishman. We cannot say the same of your dark-skinned heathen mother, can we, my dear?' She crossed over to the door connecting to the bedchamber and opened it. 'Reynolds,' she called, and her sturdy dresser came into the room. 'Go out and call for Higgins. I have put up with this chit for quite long enough. The two of you will take her up to one of the servants' rooms in the attics and lock her there.' She sneered at Chione. 'The tides have turned, young lady. You will do as I say or I will leave you locked up there until you agree. If that fails, then I shall lock Higgins in with you for a day or two, and then we shall see what becomes of your high-and-mighty airs.'

She laughed at the shock that Chione knew showed in her face. 'It is over. Who shall come to your aid? Your housekeeper?' Her smile broadened.

'I shall,' came a deep, reassuring rumble from somewhere behind her.

There had never been any real chance of the old woman succeeding in her threats. Chione knew that. Yet she also couldn't deny the nearly overwhelming relief that flooded her at the sound of that voice. Trembling a little, Chione turned to see Treyford approaching. He took her arm in a steadying grip and together they turned to face the surprised Mrs Stockton.

'Who are you?' the woman demanded.

'I am a witness to your failings, Mrs Stockton,' he answered easily. 'I suggest you follow the lady's advice and pack your things.'

'Chione,' the old witch said imperiously, 'I demand to know who this man *is*!'

Chione had to clear her throat. 'He is a colleague of Richard's—' she began.

'I am a friend of Miss Latimer's,' Treyford interrupted. 'One of many who might have thwarted your scheming, I might add.' He eyed Mrs Stockton with distaste. 'But since you seem to place a value upon these things...' He drew himself up, his face like thunder. A little flutter went through her as the sheer size and strength of him struck Chione anew. 'I am the Earl of Treyford, madam.'

The older woman flinched and abruptly sat back down.

'And now I shall have a turn at making demands,' he said in a dangerously low voice. 'I demand that you gather up your possessions and your damned impudent servants and be out of this house within the hour. I demand that you set your scheming mind permanently away from this woman and her charges.' He drew a hand across his mouth as if wiping away a bad taste. 'By God, but you make me sick. What right do you think you have to come into this house, making threats and doing harm to those two innocent children?'

'What right?' she answered weakly. Then she straightened her spine. 'I have a blood right! I am the grandmother of those children.'

'A grandmother who hasn't seen the boy in years? Who by all accounts has never before laid eyes on the girl?' Treyford scoffed. 'I should think you have waived any rights you might once have had.'

The woman's servant stepped forward and whispered something fervently in her ear.

'What?' Mrs Stockton's eyes widened, first in horror, then in sudden delight. Chione saw it and a foreboding chill grew in her breast.

'Yes, now I recall it,' the old woman cackled. She stared intently at Treyford a moment, then her expression turned to one of scorn. 'Well, I find I do not care an iota what you think, my lord. I cannot believe I did not make the connection right away. Treyford! A name that lives in infamy. The original scandal was a disgrace, of course. But you have only added to it, have you not? Rapscallion! Rake! Wanderer! Adventurer!' She turned a sneering expression on Chione. 'Exactly the sort I would expect you to take up with.'

She stopped with a gasp and an unholy glee dawned in her eye. 'Is *this* who you have been gallivanting about the countryside with? Oh, good heavens, but you could not have gifted me with anything more perfect! And to think that I meant to sacrifice my Orville…' She breathed deep and a small, triumphant smile played about her lips. 'But now there is no need! You've ruined yourself with this rakehell!'

But Chione had heard enough. She was trembling in fury. 'Stop right there! I will have no more of you or your insults. Get out of this house. Now!'

The hag laughed in triumph. 'Gladly! And I will go straight

to the nearest magistrate.' She gestured to her maidservant and
sauntered to the connecting door. 'Those children will be mine
before the day is out!'

Chapter Twelve

Trey watched the door close on the scheming old hypocrite before he glanced down at Chione. Startled, he reached and took her hand. 'Chione?'

She was no longer trembling. Instead she stood, pale and unnaturally still. 'Chione, are you all right?'

She breathed deep and held it a long moment.

'Yes,' she said, turning to go. Outside the doorway she braced a hand on the wall. Following, Trey could see that her gaze was unfocused.

'Chione?' he asked again.

She looked at him. 'I thought about what you said, Treyford, long and hard. I considered the possibility that you were right, and Mervyn is gone.' Her breath hitched, but it was not quite a sob. 'And still I knew we had to continue. Much as I hated the thought of chasing after the treasure, I knew we were doing the right thing. Even if we found the worst, at least the children and I would know. We could grieve and move on—without being caught up in an endless cycle of hope and despair.'

Trey winced. Those troubled eyes—why did they always stab him to the quick? A single tear spilled over her lovely face and Trey shifted restlessly on his feet.

'I convinced myself—I was secure in the knowledge that we've been pursuing the right course, the only course. And I was wrong! I've accomplished the very thing I've been fighting all along!'

'It will be fine, Chione,' Trey soothed. 'I'm sorry I ever caused you to doubt yourself. Now that I've met the woman, I'm sorry I ever brought her up. We won't let her take the children.' He frowned. 'Not after what I heard today.'

'I never even stopped to consider that she might use such a thing against me, or ever even know we'd gone. And she doesn't even know the worst of it! What if she discovers the rest?' A note of hysteria crept into her voice. 'I've lost them, Treyford! She'll take them and it is all my fault!'

She turned on him with surprising swiftness. 'And it's your fault, too! You and Mervyn and Richard, and even my father! All the men in my life who talk of far-off lands, exotic and mysterious, when all along the true appeal is just that it is far away!' She gripped his arm with surprising strength. 'Well, I've had enough! You've all swept me into this nonsense and look what has happened! I love those children, Treyford. I can't bear to lose them!'

Trey had seen Chione face hardship and danger without a flinch. She'd faced this entire ordeal with scarcely a tear. Now, for the first time, he saw her control snap. Terror washed over her in an almost visible wave. Her body convulsed, her fingers digging tighter into the muscle of his arm before slipping away. Trey watched, helpless, horrified, as she sank, sobbing, on to the floor.

Despising his own weakness, he stood frozen a long moment. He couldn't think past the terrifying sound of her grief. Finally he shook himself free of inertia, reached down and scooped her up. Cradling her shuddering form close, he strode down the hall. 'Mrs Ferguson!' he called.

No answer. He called again, pacing up and down. He had no idea where to take Chione and she was in no condition to tell him. Still awash in tears, she had curled herself into his embrace, a pitifully small, heartbreakingly despondent bundle in his arms. Finally he went to the stairwell, took a deep breath and again called the housekeeper's name.

As the last echo faded there came the sound of a door slamming on the next floor up.

'Quite the pair o' lungs on ye, haven't ye?' he heard her call back. The housekeeper reached the landing above and poked her head over the rail. She caught sight of Chione and gasped. 'What did the wicked auld baggage do to her?' She beckoned. 'Quick, before the bairns see her.'

Trey was already walking up the stairs. 'She's threatening to take the children,' was all he had to say. 'The local magistrate, who is it?' he asked.

Her face grew even graver. She held Chione's door wide to allow him to enter with his burden. ''Tis Lord Renhurst...' she paused, then added significantly, 'but ye canna count on him to side with Chione. He was more than a bit liverish when he got back, and talking of finally doing his duty.'

He laid Chione tenderly on the bed. She turned away, still curled into a ball. Trey sighed. Just when were they going to get a bit of luck to go their way in this mess? By his calculations they were long overdue. 'Where the hell is Aswan?' he asked the housekeeper.

Perching herself on the bed next to Chione, she shrugged. 'Haven't the faintest. That one stays gone for hours, then pops up where there was nobody a moment before.' Her thick fingers were running tenderly through Chione's hair.

'If you see him, tell him not to disappear again. I have need of him.'

He turned to go, but she stayed him with a calloused hand on his arm. 'What will ye do?'

Trey knew what he wanted to do. He wanted to run, as far and as fast as he could.

'I don't know,' he answered and turned away.

How had he got here? To a place where people looked to him for answers, expected him to right the wrongs in their lives? This was exactly why he had *left* England.

Viciously he kicked the front door open and headed for the stables. It was too late for him to run. He was embroiled, entangled. Damn Richard for sending him right back where he never wished to be.

The doors of Renhurst's impressive home were opened by the butler and Trey was escorted to Renhurst's spacious study. The older gentleman stood braced behind his desk, a frown upon his face and his arm done up an elegant black silk sling.

'Treyford,' he said without a smile. He did not come out from behind the desk, instead indicating that Trey take the seat across from him. It was at that moment that Trey truly began to worry.

'Renhurst,' he said, with a nod in greeting. 'I must assume that you met up with our miscreants as well? Is it serious?'

'No, damn you, it's not my arm that's serious.'

'What happened?' Trey asked carefully.

'The bastards made their move in Chudleigh. I was there waiting for you, and wondering just what was taking you so cursed long.' Renhurst frowned and took his seat. 'Woke up in the dead of night to find one of the devils searching my bags. Picked him off with my pistol, but was overrun by a regular swarm of them. Good God, what a mêlée! My groom knocked a couple out and your hired man sunk his knife in one. Then the inn roused and they retreated. Took their wounded with them, but left us the gun-shot one. Had to pay to have him buried outside the churchyard.'

'We had nearly the same sort of trouble,' Trey said, sinking into his chair.

'And Chione? Is she well?' the viscount asked sharply.

'Yes, of course, she is fine.' He quickly outlined all that had happened.

When he had finished, Renhurst leaned forward in his chair. 'And is that *all* that occurred?'

Trey stared. 'Of course.'

The viscount sat back. 'Because I tell you, Lord Treyford, that I was not pleased to receive your message and learn that the two of you would not be meeting me as planned. I was even less pleased to hear that the pair of you would be journeying in another direction altogether. Alone.'

Trey straightened and glared at the man. 'We were not alone. Just what is it that you are insinuating, Renhurst?'

'I'm insinuating nothing. I am telling you outright that I am as angry as a wet hen.' He sank back into his seat and cradled his arm. 'Lord, I am too old for this. What was I thinking, letting the pair of you embroil me in such a mess? Clearly this is more serious than we have believed.'

'It is serious,' Trey agreed, 'but not insurmountable. And we've other trouble that must be dealt with first. The Stockton woman is running mad in Chione's home. We've got to get rid of her.'

'Yes, I am aware. It's all part and parcel of the entire foolish situation.' He shook his head. 'Clearly I have been remiss in my duty. I've let Chione's pretty ways—and my own foolish hope that Mervyn might just show up—sway me.' He glared at Trey. 'Well, that's done now. One way or the other, I mean to see the girl settled.'

Before Trey could ask just what he meant, a sudden commotion in the hall outside distracted them both.

'Don't be ridiculous, you oaf, of course he will see me.'

With a sinking feeling, Trey recognised the querulous voice.

Mrs Stockton's slight form appeared in the doorway. She carried a satchel under one arm. When she saw Treyford she stopped dead, causing the butler to nearly run her over. Then she looked to Renhurst. 'I will have my way, my lord, or I swear I will take this all the way to Chancery Court.'

'Oh, do come in, Mrs Stockton,' Renhurst growled. 'I've already been looking into this matter. Chancery Court *should* take up this sort of thing, but since Mervyn has not been declared dead and the children are neither orphans nor wards, it falls into my jurisdiction—and I swear by all that's holy, I'll have it ended today.'

'It is your duty to give me those children, Lord Renhurst.' The woman minced into the room, moved the other chair at the desk as far away from Trey as possible and sat, her bag at her feet.

Renhurst cleared his throat. 'Now then—' he began.

'Hold a moment, my lord.' Trey stopped him. 'You need to send for Chione. She has a right to be here.'

'What the girl has,' Mrs Stockton interjected, 'are my grandchildren. And I want them.'

'No, Treyford is right,' Renhurst agreed. He rang for the butler and instructed him to send someone to fetch Miss Latimer.

'She's probably halfway here by now, in any case, the interfering chit,' sniped Mrs Stockton.

'Enough of that,' warned Renhurst. 'This is an official proceeding. Your spite has no place here.'

'Well, surely you have seen the way they are living,' the

woman protested. 'All alone in that dusty tomb of a mansion with only two decrepit servants? It is a situation of which I cannot approve.'

'It's a bit late to be voicing that opinion now,' Renhurst objected, 'when you might have done something about it any time in the past two years. You've never had them for a visit, or come here to see them. Not so much as a Christmas ham have you sent, and believe me, it might have been put to good use!'

'I could not interfere while it was still possible that Mervyn might return,' she retorted. 'But now that it seems that the old dastard has met a fitting end—' She stopped at the look of sudden anger on the viscount's face. 'That is, you must know that I've never felt welcome! Even now I am here uninvited and have been treated most rudely!'

The magistrate rolled his eyes.

'I tell you, I came here with the best of intentions. My son Orville meant to offer for the girl, then they would all be under my...ah, our, protection.'

Trey started when Renhurst nodded in agreement.

'That is, actually, not such a bad idea. I've long told the girl that a good marriage would be the simple solution to her problems.' He glanced askance at Trey. 'That opinion has only been strengthened by recent events.'

Trey sat forward, but the viscount had turned back to Mrs Stockton, a speculative expression in his gaze. 'It does seem as if you've left it a little late, though. The girl's been struggling on her own for some time now. And I've never heard of any special regard between her and your son.'

'Orville is young. He was not ready to take a bride before now,' Mrs Stockton said primly.

Renhurst's fingertips met in a steeple in front of him. 'Orville Stockton? It seems as if I'd heard that name somewhere. Yes, I recall it now, some contretemps with Lord Sharpe's daughter, eh?'

'A mere misunderstanding,' she said hurriedly. 'My Orville sent me here in good faith to offer marriage, only I arrived to find Chione mysteriously gone and the children left in highly questionable hands. Not a word would anyone tell me of where she had gone, and when I searched the house, I found this!'

She pulled a stack of papers from her satchel, on top of which sat a bound copy of a set of serial stories.

Renhurst took them. Upon looking them over, he laughed. 'All this tizzy because the girl reads adventure stories? It's hardly surprising considering her family history, and, in any case, I confess I've read 'em myself on occasion.'

'If you will examine the papers closely, you'll see that she does not read them. She writes them!' Mrs Stockton declared damningly.

His brow furrowed, Lord Renhurst made a closer examination. 'Hmm. By George, I believe you're right.' He looked up, met Trey's gaze, and laughed. 'So that's how she's been doing it? And she never said a word!' His eyes crinkled further. 'I suspected she had begun to sell off Mervyn's things.'

'It's no laughing matter, it is a disgrace!' Mrs Stockton said, outraged. 'The girl has practised a deception on the public, and I dare say, on her neighbours and her community as well.'

The magistrate frowned at that. 'Well. It's not exactly seemly for a woman, but hardly fatal, either. Especially for girl in her circumstances.' He leafed through the volume for a moment. 'She does a dashed good job of it too, I say.'

Mrs Stockton sat silent, clearly taken aback. Obviously she had expected the viscount to be more repulsed at her revelation.

Trey spoke up. 'From what I understand, Chione only took up writing to keep food on the table and clothes on the children's backs.' He frowned at the old woman. 'It's a step she might not have had to take if Mrs Stockton had shown some interest or support before now.'

'What would you have me do?' Mrs Stockton had resorted to a pitiable role now, it seemed. 'My beautiful daughter gone before her time, and my annuity from Mervyn Latimer halted?'

'It is my understanding that you have a very generous inheritance from your late husband. Had you wished, I'm sure you might have seen your way to helping.' Renhurst's disgust for the woman rang out clearly now.

'And Mervyn Latimer might have kept his personal finances clear of Latimer Shipping's,' she spat back. 'My Harold worked too hard to see his money go to—' She stopped suddenly.

'His grandchildren?' Renhurst asked.

The woman's face twisted. She could obviously feel success—and her chance at Mervyn Latimer's company— slipping through her fingers. 'None of this changes the fact that Chione Latimer has proven herself no better than a lightskirt! The girl has ruined herself!' She pointed a bony finger in Trey's direction. 'With him!'

Renhurst cast a disapproving frown at him. Trey merely glared at the woman and gave a sad, little shake of his head. How had he ended up here? Perhaps the Egyptians had been correct. Perhaps his quest to uncover the past had offended the ancient gods. Perhaps this situation he found himself trapped in was their revenge—tangled relationships, half-truths, chaotic events—his own personal version of hell on earth.

He'd brushed the notion of the gods' displeasure aside when he'd first heard it. After all, the smirking native who had proposed it sat tending a fire built from scavenged bits of his own ancestors and their sarcophagi. But it might bear a bit of rethinking, given his current circumstances.

Before he could speak, however, there sounded yet another commotion in the hall.

The door opened and Chione came in, brushing past the long-suffering butler. 'Miss Latimer, my lord,' the man said with a speaking look at his master.

'Yes, yes, it's fine, Hodge,' Renhurst said with a roll of his eyes. 'But no one else, do you hear? I don't care if 'tis Liverpool himself come to tea.'

'Very good, sir.' The door closed with a click in the dead silence of the room.

Chione hadn't moved. She stood stock still, looking taken aback at finding the lot of them there before her. Trey caught the smallest droop of her shoulders, saw the incremental widening of her gaze. For a moment he feared her reaction. He watched with baited breath, knowing that an emotional outburst would cause the worst sort of damage.

But she recovered. Trey watched, transfixed, as her chin lifted, her shoulders went back and she stood, the very image of determination in the face of adversity. In that moment he suffered an elemental shift. She faced down her enemies, as beautiful, proud and remote as an Egyptian goddess come to life, and Trey knew deep in his soul that he would never again be the same.

This, then, was the reason he found himself here. On shaking knees, he stood. Belatedly, the viscount did too.

'I hope my arrival comes before you have all decided my fate,' Chione said. She sounded completely self-possessed. Trey suddenly wished he felt as steady as she sounded.

'Oh, do sit down, Chione,' Renhurst grumped. 'When a complaint like this arises, it's my duty to listen. You're here now. You'll get your say.'

Trey pulled a seat into the spot between Mrs Stockton and

himself. Chione took it, and cast a contemptuous glance upon her relative.

Mrs Stockton returned her cold regard. 'I was only just telling the magistrate of your disgrace, Chione.'

'My *what*?' She raised a disbelieving brow and Trey breathed a sigh of relief. Thank the gods for intelligent women. If Mrs Stockton had expected a tearful, repentant Chione to make her case for her, she'd underestimated the girl.

'Oh, no,' the older woman snorted. 'Don't think you'll be getting out of this, dear girl.' She turned to Renhurst again. 'The girl has been gone for days, and not a word would anyone breathe about where she might be. Today she waltzes in, dishevelled as a common port whore, in the company of a man renowned for his womanising and itinerant lifestyle!' She paused to breathe deeply. 'I won't have it! I do not wish those children exposed to her moral decay. I want them out of that house and turned over to me today!'

Chione's tawny skin had paled, but she glared at Mrs Stockton with murder in her eye. Trey barked out an incredulous laugh and Renhurst turned to him, his brow raised in question.

'Lord Renhurst knows where Chione has been and why, you wicked old baggage. He helped us plan the journey! As for her being ruined, we took along Ferguson's niece as a companion.' He turned to Renhurst. 'Can you imagine that anything objectionable could befall Miss Latimer under the watchful eye of a Ferguson?'

The old woman looked disdainfully at Trey. 'Are you daft, man? A hired maid is not a suitable companion.' She directed a baleful glare at the magistrate. 'And in any case, you can't trust her word. The girl will say anything that her family tells her to say!'

'This is Devonshire,' Renhurst objected. 'Not London. Not

Portsmouth. Do not think to paint the good local people with your own dirty brush, Mrs Stockton.'

'Chione is practically penniless,' the woman said flatly. 'The children dress in little better than rags. They eat peasant food, and little enough of it. Worse, she fills their head with nonsense. After all this time, she is telling those children that Mervyn Latimer is still alive.'

Renhurst appeared surprised. 'That is perhaps not the best course, Chione.'

'Such a thing is not beyond the realm of possibility,' Chione said. 'My lord, the children and I remain cautiously optimistic. Is there a crime in that? Even if we are wrong, you may tell me which is worse—believing in a lost cause or being beaten for it?' She sent a hate-filled look in Mrs Stockton's direction. 'I wish you could see Will's back, sir. He looks like a sailor caught pilfering rum, not a boy hoping his father still lives.'

'It's true,' Trey affirmed. 'And in a decision such as this, I think you should be made aware of Mrs Stockton's propensity for harsh punishments. I myself heard her threaten Miss Latimer this morning. She said she meant to lock her in a room with her footman for a few days. As a cure for your high-handed ways, was it not, Miss Latimer?'

'Of course, I didn't mean it,' fluttered Mrs Stockton. 'I merely meant to frighten the girl.' She shrugged and turned to appeal to Renhurst. 'Perhaps she cannot help it. You've had experience with her. Surely you know how she is; always going beyond the line of what is pleasing for a young, *English* lady.'

Chione gasped. Trey sat up straight in his chair. Lord Renhurst banged a hand on his desk.

'I'll have none of that sort of talk here, madam. Miss Latimer has been known to us all since her girlhood. She's never acted anything but a lady.' He raised a hand as the older woman started to protest. 'No, I've heard enough. I'll decide the salient points of this issue.'

He stood and went to one of the mullioned windows. For several long minutes the room filled with an oppressive silence while he gathered his thoughts. Finally, he spoke.

'This is a most uncomfortable decision to be forced to make. The welfare of the children must be paramount.' He turned to face the motley crew assembled before him. 'It is clear that I have been remiss in my duty. I should have seen this situation resolved long before now, but I suppose it was easier to assume that all was well enough.'

He cast an ironic look over their little group. 'Until today I have never heard a word spoken against Chione Latimer.' His face softened when his gaze moved on to Chione. 'Without doubt she has already demonstrated years of loving concern for Will and Olivia.'

He cast a disparaging brow upon Mrs Stockton. 'You, madam, have only demonstrated your own churlish small-mindedness today. And yet...'

He crossed to the desk and sat once more, a frown of concern clear upon his brow. 'Mrs Stockton does have the re-sources needed to care for two children. I hope she has a level of maturity that could guide her,' he said with a meaningful look. 'And I'd hazard a guess that she harbours some ambi-tions for the children—' He held a hand up as Chione made a sound. 'No, Chione, that is not necessarily a bad thing.'

'It is when it is not tempered by love for them, my lord,' Chione said, very pale.

He compressed his lips thoughtfully. 'You may be correct about that. But you may also rest assured that I intend to take a special interest in these children, until news of Mervyn Latimer is uncovered, or until they come of age. This is a difficult decision, and I must give a thought to their future to help me decide.'

'No,' whispered Chione.

'Your own future is uncertain, Chione. Despite my belief in your best intentions and conduct, I cannot deny that your reputation will suffer once word of your journey gets about.' He cast a disgusted look at Mrs Stockton. 'As it no doubt will.'

The woman suppressed a confirming smirk. Trey suppressed a stab of hate and something that felt remarkably like fear.

'There is no notion of what might have happened to Mervyn,' Renhurst continued, 'and no end in sight to the squabbling that has beset the directors of his company. Your attempts have been valiant and praiseworthy...' he gestured to the pile of manuscript pages '...but Mrs Stockton can send Will to school. She can dower Olivia. She can see to their futures.'

Chione had begun to shake. An eerie calm had descended over Trey. Very deliberately he reached over and took her hand.

She shook him off. 'Please,' she whispered.

'The situation cannot continue. It would be best if you married, Chione,' the viscount said flatly. 'Would you consider taking Orville Stockton?'

'You cannot be serious,' she said.

'I am deadly serious. Enough to have even given thought to Mrs Ferguson's wild scheme of marrying you to me. I can do no less to see Mervyn's family settled.'

'There is no need for these theatrics.' Trey's voice emerged firm and calm, an accurate reflection of the total calcification of his soul. 'If Chione's prospects are the only thing keeping you from granting her custody of the children, Lord Renhurst, then you may rest easy.' He raised her hand in his. 'You may all wish us very happy, for she has already consented to become my wife.' Trey felt Chione stiffen, heard her quick intake of breath, but he dared not meet her eyes. He stared hard at Renhurst instead. 'I trust the prospects of the Countess of Treyford should be more than adequate to provide for two children?'

Profound relief showed on the viscount's face. Mrs Stockton looked ready to explode.

'Of course, of course!' Renhurst agreed. 'I confess, I had hoped it would turn out to be so! The perfect solution to all the various difficulties of the thing. May I be the first to congratulate you both?'

Trey inclined his head. Mrs Stockton made a strangled noise that everyone ignored. Chione sat frozen and silent.

'Well, then! I do pronounce that legal custody of William and Olivia Latimer be given to the Earl of Treyford and to Miss Chione Latimer, the soon-to-be Countess of Treyford. Such a decision assures the children of both a loving home and a secure future. And so I do order it be done.'

Renhurst stood then, and crossed over to a bell pull. 'Now, we must have something to toast the betrothed pair,' he said happily.

Trey stood. 'I appreciate the sentiment, but if we have finished, I have some pressing business to attend to.' He cocked a brow at the viscount. 'Will you see Chione home for me? I know she would like to fill in the details on the outcome of our travels.'

He fixed a piercing eye on the still dazed Mrs Stockton. 'Chione is to be my wife. Olivia and Will I regard as my own until Mervyn Latimer is found. I protect what is mine, madam. I trust you will be gone from Oakwood within the hour.'

He bowed over Chione's hand without ever looking her in the face and then strode from the room.

Chapter Thirteen

Chione sat by the fire in her bedchamber, drying the heavy cascade of her hair, staring at the flames with a leaden gaze. The welcome heat combined with the hardship of travel and the emotional turmoil of the day; together they should have been an irresistible burden, pushing her towards sleep. Yet her mind refused to rest.

She has already consented to become my wife. The words—the lie—echoed relentlessly in her head.

With one sentence Treyford had routed them all. Then he had left and no one had seen him since.

Chione had never been so shocked in her life as when he had baldly made his announcement. She was still surprised and intensely grateful. He had not run off and left her to face her difficulties alone, although she strongly suspected that was exactly what he had wished to do. He had saved her, saved the children, and only she knew how great a sacrifice he had made. She could not rest until she saw him, thanked him, told him how sorry she was for the pain such a step had caused him.

With some dismay she thought back to her resolution to

accept whatever sort of emotional liaison that Trey could offer. Whatever else might come of it, she feared this impromptu engagement would put an end to that. Chione knew with a certainty that Treyford would now be closed against her. He'd been spooked, and even if he did go through with the betrothal, and—her mind whispered the word—*marriage*, then she strongly suspected that he would be gone within months. He'd go back to his adventuring, and she would be left alone, again.

Part of her recoiled at the idea; it was most assuredly *not* what she had hoped for. She sighed. It only reinforced the folly of permitting herself to dream.

A larger part of her mourned the lost opportunity with Trey, pined for the warm connection, the sense of intimacy that had begun to grow between them. She could not deny, though, that it was a price she was willing to pay. He'd gone so far past any expectation that either she or Richard had had of him. She would do her best to ease his anxieties, tell him she was ready to deal with this situation in any manner he wished.

So she sat while the fire died down, her hair dried, and her nerves balanced on a knife's edge. And still he did not come.

Trey left Thornton Castle on foot and walked the coastal paths of Devon for hours. He fiercely ignored the beauty of the landscape, focusing all his attention on the violence of the Atlantic crashing into the cliffs so far below, allowing the endless conflict to reflect his own emotional turbulence. Unfortunately, it could not do much to ease it.

Trey breathed deeply and tried to calm himself. He'd faced far worse in his life. He'd escaped not one, but two Turkish prisons, outmanoeuvred a malevolent pasha bent on making him a eunuch, and once he'd narrowly escaped being sacrificed to a primitive tribal goddess. Surely a mere slip of a woman could not lay him so low.

Truthfully, there was a part of Trey that thrilled in excited expectation at the thought of marrying Chione. She was so profoundly unlike any of the women he had known before. Not an innocent, nor yet a seductress. She had an unearthly self-assurance, a quick wit, an appreciation for the absurdities of life and the courage to fight against the injustices. If ever there was a woman he could trust—it was she.

His heart rate ratcheted up again and he knew he'd reached the crux of the matter. This was the thought that had him quaking in his boots. He didn't think he could do it—let her in. He'd been alone his entire life, by preference, purpose and design. He didn't know how to trust.

But he wanted to. And that was the thought that truly terrified him.

It was a long walk back to Oakwood Court, but not long enough for him to sort out his conflicted feelings. When he arrived it had grown late and the house lay in darkness. Trey thought everyone was abed until he got to the stairs. There he found Aswan, with Olivia in his arms, both admiring a portrait of an extravagantly dressed Tudor gentleman.

Olivia's little finger pointed to the painting. 'Codpiece,' she said.

'Cod peeese,' said Aswan. 'Codpiece.'

'Good God,' choked Trey. 'What are the two of you about so late?'

Olivia looked about in delight. 'Draybird!' she cried, holding out her arms imperiously.

Trey took her from his servant. 'Olivia,' he said in greeting, 'how is it that you cannot get my name right, nor half your family's, and yet you know the correct terminology for a codpiece?'

She nodded and pointed. 'Codpiece.'

'I suspect I shall have to speak with your brother about this.'

'The little miss wanders at night, *effendi*,' Aswan said, unruffled. 'I watch her.'

'Yes, I understand how thoroughly you have guarded these children, Aswan, and I thank you.'

The Egyptian bowed. 'It is an honour, *effendi*.'

The girl yawned and laid her head on Trey's shoulder. He handed her over. 'Is Miss Latimer abed?'

Aswan nodded. 'She is in her bedchamber, but not yet asleep.'

Trey raised a brow.

Aswan let loose with a rare, shining grin. 'I watch. I also listen.'

'I'll keep that in mind,' Trey said, clapping him on the back.

Trey hesitated outside Chione's door a moment, gathering his courage before he knocked.

Once he did, the portal opened immediately and she looked out, her brow clearing as she saw him. Trey had to suppress a smile. Only a woman of Chione's great beauty could look so tempting in a frayed dressing gown wrapped tight up to her chin. Then he swallowed. Good Lord, her hair was down. It fell straight, shining dark to her waist. A powerful wave of lust hit him at the sight and he had to fight to concentrate on her words.

'Treyford!' she said. 'I am so glad to see you back. I had begun to worry.' She paused, regarding him with a long steady gaze, then deliberately she stepped aside and motioned him in.

He returned the thoughtful regard, acknowledging her decision to admit him into her room and all the potential ramifications of it. Swiftly he made his own choice and stepped in. It was the least he owed her.

'What?' he asked lightly. 'Did you think I'd do myself in rather than marry you?'

She smiled. 'Actually, I considered it, along with any number of other vividly morbid scenarios.' She shrugged. 'It is one of the drawbacks of being a storyteller. It seems I'm always imagining the worst possible outcome of any given situation.'

A fire smouldered in the grate. Exhausted, but acutely aware of their isolation, Trey dropped into one of the chairs before it. 'We'll make a good match, then,' he said, 'because I am for ever imagining a way *out* of the worst possible outcome.'

She took the other chair. Trey couldn't take his eyes off of her hair. It hung, thick and glorious, glinting in the dim light. A fall of velvety night sky brought to earth. His fingers twitched.

'Shall we?' she asked, and the tension in her voice brought him back to attention. 'Make a match of it, that is? I thought perhaps you only said that to rout Mrs Stockton.'

'Did it? Rout her, I mean?'

'Oh, yes.' Her tone rang with no little satisfaction. 'When you walked out I thought she would have an apoplexy. I've never seen anyone so red in the face. Nor heard such vitriol spilled. She's not happy, but she's gone.'

Trey frowned. The healthy glow of her skin was nearly as distracting as her hair. 'But if we did not marry, if the old witch discovered the betrothal was a sham, she'd be right back here. With twice the spite.'

She sighed. 'Very likely.'

'Well, then.' Trey sat, shoulders slumped, heavy with exhaustion. His conflicting emotions were tearing him in two. Residual fear lingered on one side, along with the conviction that Chione deserved so much better than anything he could give her.

But the other side—oh, the other side of him thrummed with nearly irresistible desire. It pooled heavily in his loins and at the same time whispered temptingly in his ear. He was very much aware of her, perched nervously on the matching chair. They were here, alone together in the dark of night and, somewhat absurdly, they were betrothed. She wasn't dressed, yet she'd admitted him to her bedchamber and now she sat, gazing at him with her siren's eyes—a fascinating mix of knowledge and innocence, need and nervousness.

'Treyford.' Her voice was gentle, as if she knew what writhed inside of him. 'I wish you to know how very grateful I am. I hope you realise that I never expected—'

'I do,' he interrupted. 'It was not your doing.'

'I want you to know I'll do whatever I can, handle this in any way you wish. We can declare that we don't suit, or I shall say that I've found another—'

'Stop,' he whispered. 'Let the world believe as they wish. I don't care. But between us, let's have the truth.'

Eyes wide, she nodded.

'The truth is, I don't know what I wish for. Nor, I suspect, do you. How can you when you are caught up in such circumstances? Let us agree that the betrothal will stand until we find Mervyn…and then we will discuss our options.'

'Thank you,' she said quietly.

He let loose with a sharp bark of laughter. 'God, don't thank me. It's a bad bargain you're getting at best.' He sighed. 'I suppose that I should have thought of it at the outset of all of this, but…' A terrible sadness washed over him. 'The issue is not what I wish for, Chione, but what I—' He sank his head in his hands, then, distraught, he forced himself to look up, to face her. 'I can't do it,' he whispered. 'I can't be the kind of husband that you deserve.'

Her breath caught. Above the worn collar of her wrapper he could see her pulse begin to jump. For a long moment she stared, then abruptly she shook her head. 'You've done so much for me.' Determination flared in her eyes. She stood, crossed to him and knelt at the foot of his chair. 'There are some things that perhaps I should tell you, but I do not want you to worry, Treyford.'

Trey couldn't help himself; he reached out, touched an ebony lock of her hair, followed it down past her curves. Then he brushed a caress across her cheek. 'So soft. So incredibly beautiful.' He took his hand away. 'I can't bear the thought of hurting you, Chione. But I will. It is inevitable.'

She gazed at him through the lush curtain of her lashes, reached out and took his hand. 'I won't ask for what you cannot give.'

Her words sprang a lock hidden inside of him. Somewhere, buried deep, a lonely weight shifted from his soul. She understood, at least partially. Perhaps she only said the words out of gratitude, but right now *he* was the grateful one—thankful for her insight and the caring generosity of her spirit.

Wordless, he gripped her arms and pulled her into his lap. She gasped again, her breath coming quickly as he settled her firmly across his thighs. Trey ran an appreciative gaze over her flushed cheeks and widened eyes. She looked a little frightened, but more intrigued. He groaned as she wiggled her rump experimentally, then bent down and covered her mouth with his.

Insistently, urgently he kissed her, claiming her with his mouth and with his tongue. She opened to him, following where he led and moulding her mouth to his. Her arms curled up behind his neck, her fingers sending shivers down his spine. Greedy, he wrapped her in his embrace, drank deep, and sucked the clean scent of her into his lungs until he thought he would gladly drown in it.

She felt tiny when he ran his hands along her sides. How could she be so fragile and so strong at once? For she was tougher than he, he knew it for a certainty. Deeper he kissed her, thrusting with his tongue and fighting off the clear, cold truth. God, he was a fool. All along he'd worried that he would not be able to let her in. Now harsh reality hit him hard. The truth was he didn't know how to keep her out.

He pulled back. In the dim light of the dying fire the look she gave him was soft, accepting, welcoming. Suddenly he stood, taking care to keep her close. 'I wish I were different. I wish I could be what you need.' He groaned and stooped down a bit, resting his forehead on hers. 'God help me, I most especially wish I did not want you so damned much.'

She smiled. 'I am glad you do, for where would that leave me?'

Trey stared. 'Do you want me, Chione?'

'I…I do.' Her gaze faltered and fell away. 'Perhaps I should not, but I cannot help myself.'

Heart pounding, Trey put a finger to her chin and pulled her face back to his. She came easily, closing her eyes, pressing herself against him and lifting her mouth to be taken. He obliged them both, driving deep, needing the taste of her to force out every niggling fear and doubt. And it worked. She clung to him, matching kiss for kiss, until he thought their souls must be touching.

Finally, impatient, Trey tore his mouth away, moving on to the sweet hollow beneath her jaw. Chione let her head fall back and he took advantage of the opportunity, snaking loose the tie of her wrapper and pushing the garment from her shoulders until it sank to a puddled heap at her feet.

She wore a simple shift beneath, cut low with slender straps, baring her long neck and a delightful expanse of golden flesh. Beneath the fine linen her nipples strained, already taut against the soft fabric. He filled his gaze with her, and then his hands. His heart rate quickened, and at his temple a pulse began to beat.

With a groan he reached down, swept her off her feet and into his embrace. Chione squeaked, then nuzzled his neck, pressing soft kisses beneath his ear. Growing bolder, she licked her way along his jaw. His mind raced as they reached the bed, imagining all the other places he wanted her tongue, and he nearly exploded right then and there.

He set her down on her feet and she breathed his name. 'Treyford.'

Slipping his fingers beneath the straps of her shift, he leaned in close and began to run a slow caress up and down, from her shoulder to the enticing softness of the top of her breast. 'Chione,' he said, low and urgent, 'I want you to call me by my name.'

Her eyes had closed in ecstasy at his teasing touch, but now they flew open. She smiled and crept warm fingers up his chest, then began to slowly undo the buttons of his waistcoat. 'Trey,' she said softly.

'No.' His hands stilled. 'My real name.'

She stopped. 'I'm afraid I don't know it.'

'I know,' he said simply. 'Not many people do. For a long time I've preferred it that way. But I'm going to tell you,' he said huskily, 'because when I bury myself inside you I want to hear you call my name.'

His words made her tremble. 'What is it?' she whispered.

'Niall,' he said.

Her fingers spasmed into his waist. 'What?'

'Niall.'

'How do you spell it?' she asked, her eyes wide.

He told her.

'And you do not pronounce it in the northern way? Neal?'

'No—my mother thought it more original the other way. I gather my father was not fond of it.' He tensed a little. 'Does it bother you?'

'No,' she said slowly, 'it is only that—do you remember when Renhurst told you the meaning of *my* name?'

'Yes. Chione—daughter of the Nile. It is beautiful.'

She smiled. 'Thank you. That is a widely accepted translation of the name, but Eshe, my mother, always told me that she meant the older translation for me.'

Trey waited.

She flushed. 'Lover of the Nile.'

He laughed and her blush deepened. The flush of colour entranced him. His desire rushed back, so fast and hard it took his breath away. He kissed her again, but this time it was a long, slow plunder. His hands circled restlessly over the swell of her breasts and then he couldn't wait a moment longer. He pulled at the worn, old shift impatiently and heard a tearing sound as he swept it over her head.

'My shift!' she cried in dismay.

'I'll buy you a hundred,' he growled, 'but I have to see you.'

Lord, but she was beautiful. Full, high breasts, each crowned with dusky, wide areolas and tipped with a tiny nub of nipple. The contrast enthralled him. He reached out, ran his flat palm over them and, when she gasped with pleasure, he squeezed her nipples gently between his fingers.

'Oh, good heavens,' she said.

He smiled, then paused, trying to remember if sex had ever been so light-hearted, so *right*. Purposefully he sat her down upon the edge of the bed. He knelt in front of her, as she had done earlier, and set his mouth to her breast. She gasped and arched to him, and for long, untold moments he suckled her, first one breast, then teasingly moved to the other, until they were both breathing hot and fast and nearly undone with desire.

At last Trey could wait no longer. With one last teasing flick he let Chione's nipple slide away and he stood. 'Move back to the middle of the bed,' he urged.

She complied, the dark curtain of her hair falling forward and covering her like a silken cloak. Trey began to undress with eager fingers, his gaze feasting all the while on her enchanting curves, her luscious long legs and the dark thatch of glistening curls at their apex.

In turn, Chione's gaze followed his fingers, and her obvious fascination with his body made him surge even harder yet. When his hands went to the waist of his trousers, her expression changed slightly. She was still intrigued, but there was something defiant there, too.

'You do not mind if I…?' He gestured to his trousers.

Her chin went up. 'I'm not scared.'

'Good God, no. I just wanted to be sure…' He trailed off.

'I'm sure,' she said, rising to her knees and coming closer. 'In fact, I wish to help.'

He jumped at the light touch of her fingers on his belly. 'I think I'm the one who's scared,' he said. He ran his hands down the silky skin of her back and over the sweet curves of her behind. 'You are a goddess,' he whispered, 'an ancient dream come to life.'

At last she found what she sought. The woollen fall of his trousers was pushed aside and he sprang free. A low, appreciate grumble tore its way out of him as she stroked it with delicate, searching fingertips.

'My God,' he groaned. 'You're everything I've been afraid of my entire life.'

She smiled—the self-satisfied smile of a woman discovering her own sensual power. Then she grasped him with her other hand. Trey gritted his teeth, rocked back on his heels and let her explore until he could take no more.

'My turn,' he said, climbing on to the bed and pulling her down beside him. He trailed a finger down her quivering body, parted her swollen folds and slipped into hot, slick paradise.

Now she moaned in pleasure as he stroked her, spreading, rubbing, teasing her to breathlessness. Her fingers tangled in his hair as he suckled her again and let his fingers work magic. When he at last slid a finger into her she cried out in helpless surprise.

'Niall,' she gasped, and the sound of it was a hot brand to his heart. 'You are making me want…need…something.'

Trey kissed her again and laughed low. 'Don't worry, Chione. I'm going to give you what you need.'

He braced himself above her and kissed her hard. Her head went back when he parted her velvet core. Gasping again, she writhed in wild abandon as he eased himself against the slick heat of her desire.

God. He had to slow down, to bide his time. He had meant to pleasure her to the brink of madness before he sought his own, but her artless, uninhibited response was driving him there instead. There could be no waiting.

Carefully he eased into her. It was the brink of heaven he was poised upon, nirvana, every sort of bliss ever imagined by man. But beneath him Chione had stilled.

'All right?' he croaked. God help him, but it was all he could manage.

'It hurts,' she said, frowning up at him.

'I'm sorry.' He could feel her body adapting around him

as she shifted beneath him. There was no help for it. He groaned deeply and slid home.

'Yes,' she moaned, arching her back. 'That's better. Please.'

He answered her inarticulate plea, moving slowly, stroking high and long, building the ache and the longing, destroying doubt and fear. At first she merely hung on, wrapped around him and clinging like a vine, but then she began to understand the rhythm. She braced herself and thrust up to meet him, tilting her pelvis and inviting him in. Trey's urgency grew, his hunger swelled until it was bigger than he or she, and instead became something beyond themselves, something they could only experience together.

Trey couldn't wait. He reached down to where their bodies joined and found the secret nub of her pleasure. The effect was instantaneous. Her eyes flew open and her body tightened around him. He thought his heart might burst with the effort of holding back.

'Let go, Chione,' he urged hoarsely. 'Just let it happen.'

'I don't…I don't know…if I can.'

'You can, you will. We'll both go together.'

And she did. Her body shattered around him, milking him with the strength of her rapturous response.

It was beyond bearing. He was harder than he'd ever been in his life. No matter how many times he'd done this before, with Chione it was different. She'd changed him, bound him with ties that he had never wanted, but which somehow freed him to find new heights of exquisite passion. He let loose, driving into her with abandon until his climax took him by storm. For endless moments he rode the wild currents. Gradually they gentled and he drifted down, floating peacefully into a rolling wave of contentment.

Chapter Fourteen

Chione awoke slowly the next morning, boneless and warm. Naked. And alone. A stealthy rustle sounded somewhere behind her and then the soft click of a door. She sat up, but Trey had gone.

Telling herself firmly that he was making a nod to the proprieties and not running away, she burrowed back beneath the covers. For several minutes she lounged, reliving the glories of the night before. It had been eye opening and amazing, but, despite her brave words, she had been a little frightened.

When Trey had urged her to let go, her first thought had been that he didn't know what he was asking. Somehow it had become more than just loosening a natural restraint. He'd been asking her to abandon a role that had saved her life. And it was a role, a persona that she had adopted to fit with her new life: calm, resolute, restrained. A good little English girl, whose name was the only exotic part about her. She'd thought she couldn't let it go, for it would leave her open, vulnerable, exposed.

Then the truth had hit her. She could, because Trey had already seen past the facade. He was the only person who had ever looked deeply enough to glimpse the emotional, uncertain, volatile creature within, and from the very first he had accepted her, welcomed her, pushed her out of hiding and into the cold light of day.

It was her, the real Chione that Trey had been making love to. The Chione who had scolded, scorned and rejected him. The Chione who had turned to him in her hour of need, trusted him, kissed him, talked with him. Loved him.

So she had done it. She had let go and allowed Trey to take her to the heavens. It had been a lovely trip.

But now her feet were firmly back on earth, and unease began to set in. Last night she'd done what her practical, grounded self had sworn never to do. She'd given herself to an adventurer, linked her fate to an emotionally distant man who was likely to always be gone—in head, in heart and in fact.

And he still did not know the truth about her. In Exeter he had scolded her for putting her family's interests ahead of her own. How would he react to find that she wasn't truly part of this family? Could he understand how ties of love and gratitude bound her as tightly as those of blood? She was afraid to find out. What if it angered him enough to abandon this uncertain betrothal?

The thought spurred her into activity and she leaped out of bed to wash and dress. But mundane activity could not banish her distress, or change reality. She was at war with herself and required a greater distraction.

She breathed deeply and left her rooms. She thought she would take breakfast with the children. Just knowing it was a possibility soothed her. This was why the emotional turmoil was worth it. Will and Olivia were safe now, their futures secured. It was enough. It had to be.

Trey's manservant was leaving the nursery playroom as she approached.

'Aswan,' she called as he closed the door behind him.

Always she felt a little uneasy around him. He rarely spoke to her, but she knew that he watched her a great deal, and with a startling intensity.

'Aswan, have you spoken with Lord Treyford this morning?'

'I dressed him,' he replied. 'But there was little enough speaking.'

'Oh. Do you know where he is now?'

'He has gone to the village with young Will. He says only that he will require a mount since we are to stay a while longer.' Undeniably there was a question in his gaze.

'Yes, well. I am sorry that Lord Treyford did not give you the news himself,' she began.

'News?'

'Yes. We—Treyford and I—are betrothed.'

'I do not know this word. Bee-trothed.'

Chione could feel heat rising to flush her cheeks. 'We are to be married.'

'Married?' For the first time he met her gaze squarely, eye to eye. 'Mated?'

A little intimidated, Chione nodded.

'So,' he said in a musing voice. Then he collected himself and gave a little bow. 'May I wish the…young Miss Latimer much happiness?' He turned and started down the hall. Chione could hear him muttering under his breath. She called out to him again.

'Aswan, did Lord Treyford speak to you about my brother's journals?'

He turned back, curiosity alight in his face. 'No, young miss, he did not.'

'Treyford told me that you were the one who packed Richard's possessions and had them shipped home. We were wondering if you could tell us if perhaps some of the boxes have not yet arrived? I never received his journals and some of his other personal effects are missing as well.'

He took a step back towards her. 'I have seen the boxes in the *effendi*'s rooms. I hope the young miss will not mind, but I noticed that one or two were not there. I thought perhaps you had kept them close to you—' he watched her '—or perhaps that the thieves had taken them. But you say that you have never received these crates?'

'No. Everything I have received is there.'

An indecipherable gleam shone in his eye. 'Ahh. Yes. I will investigate this, young miss. You have my word.'

'Thank you. There is no regular post in Wembury, but the man who travels to Knighton twice a week to the post office might be able to help you.'

'Thank you.' He bowed once more.

'And, Aswan, I wish to thank you for the care you have given the children while we were gone.'

He looked as if he might speak, but then he bowed again, abruptly turned and left. Chione watched him go, and then she entered the playroom.

She was still there, reading to a drowsy Olivia, when Will and Morty returned, a look of suppressed excitement on the boy's face.

'Good morning, Will.' Chione spoke low and gestured to the nodding child in her lap. 'Did you and Lord Treyford enjoy yourselves?'

'Oh, yes, Chione!' he answered in an excited whisper. 'Trey let me help choose his mount—a strapping, good-natured grey—and he says that it is time I had a horse of my own!'

'Did Lord Treyford return to the house with you?'

'No. He sent me on home alone. He said he had business

to attend to.' Will had grown more solemn. 'Trey told me that he means to marry you, Chione.'

'Yes,' she said with a semblance of a normal tone. 'I think we will all be very happy together, don't you?'

Slowly, Will nodded. He walked over to the window seat where Morty had retreated and perched beside her. 'Does this mean we'll stop looking for Papa?' he asked. His fingers ran idly over the dog's ears.

'Of course not,' Chione replied, surprised. 'In fact, I think Lord Treyford is the best person we could choose to help us, don't you?'

'Yes, I suppose that is right,' he said a little more hopefully.

Chione could see that he was still unsettled at the idea of yet another change in his young life.

'I'll tell you what,' she said, shifting the sleeping Olivia in her arms and standing carefully. 'Why don't you practise your sketching by drawing us Lord Treyford's new mount? Then, when you are finished, we'll have another look at the *Aeneid* and you can tell me what you remember of the Trojan Horse.'

As she'd hoped, the resumption of such an ordinary occurrence as lessons soothed him. 'All right,' he agreed. 'Do you know, Chione, that Trey was mightily impressed that I already knew so many of the finer points to look for in a saddle horse? That's what he said—mightily impressed.' His chatter continued as he took out his sketchbook and Chione breathed a sigh of relief as she went next door to put Olivia down.

The first thing Trey noticed when he entered the parlour that afternoon was that horses were still the dominate topic of Will's conversation. He sat next to his sister, who was astride a rocking horse, her mouth full of buttered muffin and her eyes as big as saucers as Will regaled her with what sounded like the tale of the Trojan Horse.

'Imagine your horsey fifty times as large, Livvie,' the boy enthused, 'and stuffed to the brim with fierce warriors!'

'Ooooohh,' breathed Olivia.

'Ye watch what ye be fillin' her head with,' Mrs Ferguson grumped from the fire where she was toasting the muffins. 'Odds are it'll come spillin' out at the least likeliest moment.'

Morty noticed his entrance before anyone else. The dog got to her feet with a happy bark and came to welcome him. Trey gave her a thumping greeting and let his gaze slide past the dog to Chione.

She betrayed herself with only a slight start and a faint colouring of her cheeks. Trey smiled at her and acknowledged the housekeeper and the children. He had gleaned before that this heavy tea more often than not served as dinner for the family so when Chione gathered herself enough to ask him to join them, he accepted.

He took a hot muffin from Mrs Ferguson with thanks and tried to conduct himself normally—a nearly impossible task. Like a boy in the grip of calf-love, he hadn't been able to get the image of Chione out of his mind all day. How was he supposed to converse like a gentleman when he had an intimate knowledge of the beauty beneath that stark grey gown and a nearly constant urge to run his hands over it?

He'd awakened early this morning with a need to escape, to breathe free air and spend some time alone. But he'd changed his mind when he'd found Will gingerly descending the stairs. Fury had flared fresh as he watched the boy's careful stride and he'd immediately invented an errand to distract him from his pain. To Trey's surprise, he'd enjoyed himself almost as much as Will had. The boy was clever, eager to learn and apparently quite horse-mad. When he'd begun to tire, Trey had sent him home and had gone on alone to meet with Drake.

There had been much news to exchange with the innkeeper, little of it good. Trey had thanked him for his help with Cedric and filled him in on their trip. Grimly, he had heard what Drake had to report. Locals were talking of strangers in the area, some with questions about the Latimers. Mervyn Latimer's sloop appeared to have been broken into. Drake had sent a few of the guards Trey had hired out to scour the hills around Oakwood. He had taken Trey to view what they had found.

Trey had stood in the sheltered nook and looked out at the clear view of Oakwood Court. The spot was well used. And, according to Drake, it was one of several, each with a different perspective on the house below. Trey had poked at the log dragged over as a seat and felt a spasm of worry.

'Hassan,' he had mused. 'Who the hell are you?'

He'd been in danger more often than not, it sometimes seemed, but this was different. This threat was like quicksilver, slipping through his fingers each time he got a grasp of it. Like a nebulous cloud it hung over the woman and children he had just made himself irrevocably responsible for. He'd remembered the captivating mix of Chione's fragility and strength beneath him last night and the stick he'd been exploring with had snapped in two.

'Did you bring the grey home tonight?' Will's question broke in on the memory.

'Yes, I did.' It took an effort for Trey to get himself focused on the present. 'The gelding is ours now, all right and tight. Perhaps after tea you would like to come with me and make sure he's comfortably settled?'

'Oh, yes,' the boy agreed, eyes shining.

Trey looked to Chione. 'I didn't find Eli in the stables when I got back.'

He noticed her breathing quickened as she answered. 'Aswan took him off this afternoon.'

Trey raised a brow in question.

'I talked with him about the journals this morning.' She shrugged. 'Perhaps they went off to the post office?'

'I'll heat some water so ye both can have a bath when ye get back,' Mrs Ferguson interrupted. 'There's no need for the pair of ye to smell of horse, too.'

Trey laughed. 'Thank you, Mrs Ferguson.'

The housekeeper heaved herself to her feet. She directed a sharp look at Will. 'Don't dawdle in the stables. I'm puttin' the water on to heat.'

As she left Chione leaned over and placed a hand over his. 'Thank you,' she said softly. 'For everything.'

Trey ran his gaze over her face and didn't reply. For a long moment they sat, simply watching each other, enjoying the mounting tension, until a brisk knock sounded on the parlour door. Eli poked his head in.

'Aswan's got a parcel for ye, Miss Chione. Where do ye be wantin' us to put it?'

'Good heavens, but that was fast,' she replied.

'Is Aswan with you, then?' called Trey.

The door opened wider to reveal the servant standing there. 'Yes, *effendi*.'

'I'll need to speak with you when you are done with that.'

'Yes, *effendi*.'

'However did you find it so quickly, Aswan?' Chione asked, rising and going to investigate the box he held.

'I merely began looking in the right place, young miss.'

'The right place would o' been at the post,' grumbled Eli.

'They said there that they gave this over to a woman a week or so ago. A woman who said she was travelling on to Oakwood.'

'A woman?' Chione asked. 'More of Mrs Stockton's meddling, no doubt.'

'I don't know,' Eli said doubtfully. 'Were it she, she would have brought it here to open it.'

'Where did you find it then?'

'We asked in some o' the pubs in Knighton. Found a young scrapper who spotted a fire lit at his granddad's empty fishing shack. No one there when he arrived, but he found some things that sounded like what we were looking for. He took what hadn't been put to the fire yet and sold them to the pawnbroker. We got back what we could.'

Trey saw Chione look uneasily at Aswan's expressionless face. Then she glanced back at him. He nodded imperceptibly in her direction.

'Thank you so much, both of you,' Chione said. 'Will you just take it along to the library? I'll get started right away.'

Trey stood. 'Come along, Will. We'll drop off Olivia in the kitchens. She can help Mrs Ferguson while we are out in the stables. Aswan, I'll speak with you when we get back.'

Chione gratefully followed the men to the library. This was just what she needed—something to keep her mind occupied. She was very happy not to have to sit in her room tonight and wonder if Trey would come. And if she repeated that to herself, she might just come to believe it.

Chione opened the box with eager hands. She stilled when she discovered the objects lying loosely wrapped at the top. Two miniatures: one of Mervyn Latimer and one of his lovely wife, Marie. Both were smoke stained. Tears gathered as she drew the paintings out, but she fought them back.

A few of Richard's journals were indeed underneath, along with some of his drafting equipment and a singed book or two.

She did cry, then, for all that she had lost and perhaps a little for all she feared she might never gain. But shortly she dried her eyes. She took up the latest of Richard's journals, settled herself comfortably on the worn chaise, and set to work.

Chione told herself it was natural to begin with her brother's budding relationship with Lord Treyford, but she couldn't deny the eagerness with which she sought out any mention of his name. They were few enough at first. Richard had begun this new journal as he set out for Egypt. The first pages were filled with short notes regarding the journey; the first entries of any length began when he reached Alexandria.

The excitement with which her brother had returned to Egypt surprised her. He had thrilled to each new sight, sound and experience. Just reading about their homeland filled Chione with a vague dread. She skimmed ahead, looking for a mention of Trey.

At last she found it; a brief mention of Richard's first meeting with the infamous earl. A few pages later, a slightly longer description of their decision to work together. Disjointed bits about their trip up the Nile followed, but when they reached Thebes and established a more permanent base in the Valley of the Kings, the entries became more detailed.

Chione drank in several descriptions of Richard's growing respect for Trey. She smiled when Richard approved of Trey's treatment of their workers and laughed when he once despaired of the earl's reluctance to discuss anything personal.

She grew more serious when she discovered several mentions of Richard leaving their site for a day or two, searching for something that he never named outright. She knew it must be the scarab when she found the entry written just a week before his death.

Found s. today. Nearly shamed myself by crying like a woman. But will not give in to despair. The thief who sold it to me could not—or would not—say where he obtained it. I did learn that C. G. B. is in Egypt. Coincidence? Will watch him closely.

Chione drew a shuddering breath. It had to have been the scarab. But who or what was C. G. B.? A similar entry a little further on only raised more questions.

Drovetti in Thebes today, and in the company of C. G. B. Neither happy to see me. I am getting close.

Even more troubling was Richard's last entry.

Drovetti knows. I will find him.

Chione stared at the words for a long time. The last words Richard wrote before he had been killed. He'd been close to finding Mervyn, she knew it. And he'd been killed because of it.

'Have you found something?'

Chione jumped and looked up to find Trey standing in the doorway. His voice sounded soft, but a hard glitter shone in his blue eyes as he closed the door behind him and entered the room.

'Something, yes, but not what we need.' She sighed. 'It's frustrating. Richard's notes are very cryptic. I think I know what he means, but I can't be sure.' Heart pounding, she waved him down to sit beside her and showed him the last entry.

'Drovetti?' he asked. 'Drovetti knows what?'

'Where Mervyn is, I had supposed.'

Trey looked sceptical. 'I highly doubt it, Chione. Drovetti is the French consul in Egypt. His focus is firmly on besting England's consul-general, Henry Salt. Drovetti spent the months when I was there travelling the Nile looking for more treasures to send to France. Unless Mervyn is sitting on top of an impressive artifact, I can't see him caring one way or another.'

Chione did not argue with him. 'Did you speak with Aswan?'

'I did. Our Egyptian is a man of many resources, my dear. It appears that while the bandits have been watching us, Aswan has been learning a bit about them.'

'Are you sure that is all that there is to it?'

'Completely sure. You know, Aswan came to our dig with Richard. He always seemed devoted to the lad, and he's shown you and the children the same devotion.'

'I can't deny how wonderful he's been with the children.' Still, there was something more to Aswan's story, Chione knew. Perhaps she would begin to watch the servant as intently as he watched her.

She picked up another journal. 'This one covers the time before Richard left for Egypt. It mentions Mr Belzoni more than once. Have you ever met the man?'

'The circus strongman turned intrepid traveller?' Trey looked amused. 'From what I saw he is quite a skilled excavator. He certainly beat Drovetti to some prize antiquities, but, no, I have not had the pleasure. Why?'

'It looks as if Richard spent time with him in London before he left. I think he felt as if they had a good deal in common. Belzoni gave Richard advice on how to handle himself in Egypt. He even gave him some letters of introduction to smooth his way. It appears that in return, Richard helped him catalogue his artifacts and prepare them for exhibition.'

Trey squinted in remembrance. 'Yes, Alden did mention that Belzoni's exhibit had opened to great success, didn't he?'

'I had forgotten!' Chione suppressed a shiver of excitement. 'Could he be the C. G. B. that Richard mentions? Do you think we should go to London and speak with him ourselves?'

'We might. Let's give you a chance to get through those journals first, though.' A grim look passed over his face. 'I know I scoffed at the notion of finding anything in these before, but now I'm asking you to do your best, Chione. This mess is far from over.'

Cold dread seized Chione as he told her what Drake had shown him today.

'They are not done with us yet,' he finished.

She straightened, allowing anxiety to coalesce into determination. Gripping Richard's journal tighter, she shot him a blazing look. 'I'll find it.'

The flare of approval in his eye warmed her. 'That's the spirit,' he said softly. 'We're not done with them yet, either. And while you are looking, we'll all have a chance to adjust to our new—circumstances.'

The 'we' he used caused her heart to trip faster.

Reaching out, he put his hand over hers. His finger traced a tiny circle on her skin. 'I couldn't ask earlier,' he breathed. 'How do you feel?'

'Fine.' She breathed deeply and confessed, 'Scared. Confused.' She did not reveal the predominant emotion she'd clung to all day. *Hopeful*. 'How do you feel?' she asked with a twist of her mouth.

He laughed. 'I've been bombarded with more emotions in the past twenty-four hours than I think I've experienced in my life,' he said a little helplessly. 'But right now?' His circling finger began to creep up her arm. 'Lost. Found.' He'd reached her shoulder and he began to lean in, his eyes fixed ruthlessly on her mouth. 'Desperate to touch you again.'

Her eyes widened just as their lips met, then slid closed on a moan of homecoming. His questing fingers found her breast and she leaned into the caress, wordlessly asking for more and knowing with a sudden certainty that that was what Trey meant to her. Home. Her other half. For most of her life Chione had known something was missing. She'd thought it must be her heritage that made her feel so, or the dark secrets of her past. She'd tried so hard to be what she was not, seeking to hide her insufficiencies from the world. But all along she'd only been missing him.

Trey deepened his kiss and Chione's ability to form a coherent thought vanished. This time she banned fear and gave herself over to simply feeling.

He kissed her sweetly, with a tenderness that replaced last night's urgency and incredibly, aroused her even more. His fingers moved lightly over her; butterfly wings that sought out buttons and ties until he had her bodice down, her stays undone, and her shift about her waist. And all the while he kissed her. Deep, soul-stirring kisses, nipping, teasing kisses, and every sort of kiss in between, until he had her leaned over the low back of the chaise and her naked breasts thrust up at him entreatingly. Her nipples were hard, yearning for his touch, and at last, with a look of rapture, he took his mouth from hers and worked his way slowly down.

An eternity later his mouth closed over her nipple. He gave her aching breasts the same treatment he had given her mouth. He licked, laved, sucked, and even bit her with a gentle pressure. Chione wanted to scream. A molten trail of pleasure, of endless, joyous *need* trickled from his mouth to pool between her legs.

She couldn't help it. This was Trey—her Niall—making her feel so right. Passion built inside of her until she had to give it voice or die. She gasped, shuddered, and moaned his name aloud.

He raised his head and met her gaze with a blazing blue triumphant one. 'God, Chione, I wish there were words for what you do to me.'

For a moment she shared his triumph, marvelling at how giving him pleasure intensified her own. Then she forgot everything as he raised the hem of her gown.

The heat and the longing she felt grew as his fingers travelled past her stockings, over her garters and on to the naked skin of her thigh. He touched her centre and she was lost.

She was wet, drenched with need, and soon so was he. His fingers slid like magic over her most sensitive spots and the tension inside of her loomed suddenly large.

But then his hand disappeared from where she needed it most and he slipped down from the chaise to the floor. She whimpered her confusion. His movements were jerky as he pushed her skirts up further and his voice sounded hoarse when he spoke. 'Wider,' he urged. 'Open your legs, love. I have to taste you.'

Her body obeyed before her mind could wonder and his questing tongue soon answered in any case. Chione gasped. 'Niall—what are you…?'

'Shh.' He eased her back down. 'Let me, Chione.' He flashed her a wicked grin. 'I promise you'll be glad you did.'

She was. His tongue was hot and it went unerringly to all the places that craved it. He teased her unmercifully, far past the point of restraint. Chione's hips bucked wildly and she buried her fingers in his hair, clutching him hard and surrendering all control until she exploded in a thousand different directions.

She came back to herself abruptly when Trey loomed above her, filling her to the hilt in one hot, hard thrust. She cried out, holding him tight with arms, legs, and muscles she hadn't even known she'd had.

'Hang on,' he said in a strained voice above her. 'This isn't going to take very long.'

It didn't. And this time, after the explosion, Chione very much feared that a few of her essential pieces had unknowingly bonded with his.

Chapter Fifteen

Chione breathed deeply. The half-forgotten smell of warm honey and dates drifted to her on the breeze. She'd forgot how astonishingly cool and clear the morning air could be in Egypt. With a start she realised where she was. Or where she wasn't. In the garden of the Frank, outside the home of the man who had owned her mother.

A dream, she told herself firmly, staring down the gravelled path that led to the house. *It's only a dream.* Suddenly Trey was on the path, stalking towards her. This was not the languid, satisfied man who had walked her to her rooms and kissed her thoroughly goodnight a few hours ago. This Trey looked angry, resentful. She caught a brief flash of hurt on his face before he reached her and stopped, an icy glare spearing her to the soul.

'You could have told me,' he rumbled, his resentment echoing like thunder. 'Why didn't you tell me, Chione?'

She came awake with a jerk, and drew a shuddering breath. Her mother had told her that her mind would speak to her in dreams. There was no mistaking what it was saying. It didn't feel right to share her body and not her whole soul. Chione just did not want to hear.

Seeking distraction, she climbed out of bed and threw back the curtains. The softer, early morning light of Devonshire flooded in, obliterating her vision of Egypt. She wished that the spectres of her past could be so easily forgot, and her guilt in not sharing them with Trey. Taking up one of the journals that she'd brought to her room, she settled in the window seat.

She was working her way backwards and now was ready to give her attention to the journal that chronicled Richard's thoughts as he prepared to leave for Egypt. The tone in these pages was more eager expectation than grim determination. The familiar easygoing voice at once comforted her and made her miss her brother all the more.

She sharpened her eye and read closely when she first saw Jack Alden's name, but she could find no mention of Mervyn, Richard's search for information on the legend of the architect's daughter, or of his acquisition of the golden box.

There was rather a long section on his meetings with Mr Belzoni. Her brother appeared to have been very impressed with the former strongman and his ambitions. Belzoni wrote out several letters of recommendation to various *kashifs* and others he thought might be useful in Richard's work, and in return Richard seemed to have helped him catalogue his artifacts. Stuck in the pages were copies of several inventories that her brother had written out. The first one appeared to be a list of objects with short descriptions. Despite herself, Chione was interested.

Mummified fingers
    Forty-three in all. Belzoni reports the remainders of the
    bodies have disintegrated into dust.

Papyrus
Lavishly decorated, three and twenty feet long—
the longest
in Europe!

Some of the objects were marked; these appeared to be the ones that Belzoni meant to include in his exhibit. She had to assume the others would be sold. She was folding the lists to put them aside when abruptly she stopped.

She gasped. It was true; she'd seen her name, at the bottom of the first list.

Wooden Statues-Two
Each four feet high, with a circular hollow, as if to hold a
scroll or papyryus. Chione might be particularly interested
in what the scroll contains.

The mark was there. The statues were in London—in Belzoni's exhibition.

Chione was out of the window seat so fast she tripped over the small pile of journals. Scrambling to her feet, she tore out of her room and into the hall. When she reached Trey's room she did not stop. She burst through the door, surprising both Trey, who stood in front of a long mirror, and Aswan, who was handing him a starched neckcloth.

'I've found it!' she gasped. 'We've got to go to London!'

They were travelling again, but in a completely different manner from the first trip Chione had taken with Trey. Instead of four people in a fast-moving coach, they had a caravan the size of a regiment and nearly enough people to form one.

Chione had absolutely refused to travel without the children again. Both Eli and Mrs Ferguson had refused to be left behind. Jenny came to help with Will and Olivia and to keep an eye on the coachman. Aswan held sway over the large number of armed outriders that Trey had hired.

There could be no attempt at stealth this time, not with two carriages, a luggage wagon, Will's pony and the dog. But though they were a large group, they were not unwieldy and they made surprisingly good time.

Chione could not help but notice how much happier Trey appeared since they had left Oakwood Court. The challenges and excitement of travel suited him. He lost the faint hunted look he had been carrying and appeared completely relaxed. The obvious change only added to Chione's burden of guilt. Clearly Trey was not a man meant to be tied down.

Just as clearly, she was not a woman who could slide easily into the role of countess. One look around at their rag-tag entourage proved that, as did Chione's ever-increasing worry about her past. Her mind kept wandering back to her confrontation with Mrs Stockton, to the cold stab of fear she'd suffered when the harridan had announced that she'd discovered Chione's secrets. She hadn't, of course, but what if, in seeking revenge, she stumbled across the truth? It was unlikely, but not impossible.

Chione wondered repeatedly if she shouldn't just tell Trey about herself right out, but her imagination won out over her resolution every time. She would picture his shock, imagine seeing shame in his eyes when he looked at her instead of warmth and desire, and she would delay. As the trip continued, it became easier to push back her vague feelings of dread and focus instead on keeping Olivia from falling out of the open carriage window.

For their last night on the road, Trey stopped his little caravan in Maidenhead. He chose Mr. Lovegrove's Red Lion rather than the more famous Bear Inn, for he thought all the coaching traffic in and out of the Bear might provide an opportunity for their adversaries.

The tang of freshly oiled tack mixed with the solid smells of horse and hay as Trey inspected the hacks available for hire. Across the way Eli groomed the tired grey with loving hands and Will slipped Charlemagne a carrot and a quick caress. Morty had curled into a contented ball near the door, but Trey was aware when her head perked up. She sampled the air and gave a soft woof.

Trey exchanged glances with Eli, then nodded meaningfully towards Will before he stepped away from the job horses. 'Will,' he said casually, 'I thought I saw Charlemagne favouring a back foot when you put him away. Why don't you check it out and give all of his shoes a good going over, too? I'm going to speak to the stable master about this pair of chestnuts.'

The boy agreed and with a last silent warning look to Eli, Trey crossed to the stable door, where the dog now stood at attention. It had grown dark and the stiff breeze had driven nearly everyone indoors. As Trey watched, an ostler took a horse from a newly arrived traveller near the inn's main door. As the boy and the horse grew closer, Trey saw the dark figure of a man finish speaking with Lovegrove. Yet instead of following the innkeeper inside, the newcomer turned towards the stables.

Trey ducked into the shadows and called for the dog to

follow. She came willingly, yet stood alert at his side. The ostler passed into the stable. The man still came on. Trey murmured a stern command and stepped into the light.

The stranger stopped short. 'Treyford! Here you are, then! I've caught you at last!'

'Alden,' Trey said in surprise. 'Jack Alden.' He stood still while the scholar thumped him enthusiastically on the back. 'What are you doing here?'

The man took Trey's arm and pulled him towards the stable door. 'I've come to warn you.'

'Warn me?' Trey soothed the dog, who had begun to bristle when Alden took hold of him.

'Yes, you and your companions are being followed.'

'Oh?' This Trey already suspected, and, in fact, hoped was the case. He just wanted to get his little caravan safely installed in London before their adversaries struck. When the situation escalated again, he wanted to have the upper hand. 'What is it exactly that you've seen, Alden?'

The scholar breathed deeply. 'I'll start at the beginning, then, so you won't think I've gone off half-cocked.' He smiled. 'I'm on my way back to London. My brother's wife is due to present him with a child soon, and I expect I'll be needed to provide him moral support. Or at least enough brandy to get him through her ordeal.'

Trey managed a smile.

'In any case, I had left Exeter and stopped for the night in Glastonbury. On settling the bill the next morning, I heard a man mention your name. Very casually, to be sure, but it was clear he was hoping to find out if you'd passed through there.'

'Did you know this man?'

'He could have been anyone's lackey, save for his unusual

accent. The innkeeper had no information for him. I paid my shot in record time and followed him outside.' Alden's tone grew more serious. 'A rag-tag group waited outside, such as I've never seen. But it was seeing their leader that made me decide to follow.' He eyed Trey carefully. 'I suspect, with a career like yours, you've made an enemy or two, but I confess, were it me, I'd think twice before crossing such a man.'

'Tell me,' said Trey.

'Two score and ten, perhaps? Difficult to tell behind the impressive beard. He was dressed as immaculately as any English gentleman, and sported an elaborate turban. Don't take me for an old woman, Treyford, but it was his eyes that were most disturbing. They were dark, but somehow…flat. Inhuman, I could almost say.'

The mysterious Hassan? Trey wondered. 'And that was in Glastonbury?'

'Aye. Ten or so of them, near as I could tell. They've trailed carefully behind you ever since. Until this afternoon. I overtook them in Twyford. They were gathered at the King's Arms and it looked to me like a council of war. I'd say you'd better prepare yourself for some trouble.'

A surge of anger and frustration welled in Trey's chest. So close. They were but a day's short travel from London. He stood a moment, indecisive. Should he gather his odd regiment together and run? Or was this it? Had it come already to a last stand? He bit back his irritation. He needed time.

'You know,' Alden said slowly, 'what you need is a distraction.'

'It would be ideal,' Trey agreed tersely, 'but how?'

'Most of these men appear to be Egyptian, or Turkish perhaps. By all accounts they are a superstitious lot.'

'They can be,' Trey agreed.

'Perhaps we can spook them, give them a little something to worry about? And you could use the delay to get your people out of here.'

Trey grinned. 'I like the way you think, Alden.'

The man smiled back, ruefully. 'Yes, well, I have to say, life has been quiet since my brother settled into domesticity. It will be good to shake things up a little, and, I confess, I look forward to putting all that study to a good use.'

'Well, I'm happy to oblige,' laughed Trey. 'I'll send my man Aswan with you. If anyone could put the fear of ancient gods and modern Englishmen into their souls, it'll be the pair of you.'

His tired and bedraggled caravan arrived in London early the next morning. Despite their exhaustion, the children hung out the window, enthralled by the teeming streets, the tall buildings, the joyful noise and noxious smells of so many people and animals living cheek by jowl. Will, in fact, seemed almost disappointed when they reached the more genteel environs of Soho Square. Trey supposed to an eager boy's eyes it lacked the dangerous romantic appeal of London's more treacherous districts.

'Not to worry, Will,' Trey called. 'London has more than its share of adventures for you to get into.' They came to a halt in front of a suitably impressive home. Trey dismounted and slapped the grey affectionately as Eli came over to take it in hand.

The ornate door still stood closed. Trey put down the step and handed the women and children out of the carriage. Jenny and Olivia stood hand in hand on the pavement, gaping at the handsome row of townhouses. Will and Morty faced the other direction, both staring longingly at the grass and gardens in the Square.

'May I take Morty over to stretch her legs?' asked Will. 'She doesn't like being confined to the coach.'

'We're none so fond of it either,' muttered Mrs Ferguson as she accepted Trey's help in descending.

'Of course, Will,' Chione answered, 'but you'll have to wait until we can get the key.'

'No need.' The boy gestured at another lad crossing the street, ball in hand. 'We'll just tag in with him.' He set off, the dog frisking at his heels.

'Oh, dear,' Chione said, surveying the still silent house. 'I do hope Pilkens got the letter I sent ahead.'

'I only hope the old barnacle's still alive,' Mrs Ferguson said. 'He always was an odd duck, I don't figure close to two years sittin' in an empty house has done him any good.'

'Now, don't you begin by pestering him,' Chione chided. 'I offered the poor man the chance to come to Oakwood Court when we closed this house up.' She raised a brow at her housekeeper. 'Strangely enough, he declined.'

'I said he was odd, not stupid,' Mrs Ferguson answered. She picked up her bag and laboured up the short stairs, Jenny and Olivia following.

Trey laughed and exchanged a glance with Chione. Seconds ticked by while the rest of the world receded. For this moment they were alone, alive and enjoying the inevitable pull, the intangible call of desire. Not urgent, just the private joy of a promise to be fulfilled. Then the coachman called for Trey and the spell was broken.

Chione looked across the square to where Will had gone and then back at the house.

'Go on in,' he told her. 'The outriders are waiting for me. I'll deal with them and the luggage and keep an eye on Will.'

She smiled. 'Thank you.'

Trey sent a couple of his hired men to the mews with the remaining riding horses. The others he set to unloading baggage. He shared a quick word with the coachman and went to the front to check the straps on the lead team. Calling a reassurance, he walked down the street side of the coach and team.

That was when he saw it—a grubby hand at the end of a reaching arm, snaking from beneath the baggage wagon to snatch a small portmanteau.

Trey did not react. He finished his conversation with the driver, then strolled down to the cart. He stopped very casually next to the large front wheel, bent down, reached right through the spokes and grabbed the scruff of the boy underneath, who was quietly trying to creep away with his prize.

A startled yelp rang out and a massive struggle ensued. 'Get off me!' The boy flailed like a fish on a line, but Trey pulled him in close to the wheel, reached his other arm around and hauled him out and over to the curb.

The scrawny lad glared at Trey and at the gathering circle of curious men. Obviously deciding that resistance in the face of such odds was futile, he abruptly ceased struggling and changed his tactics.

'Don't turn me in, guv,' he pleaded, his eyes welling with unshed tears. 'I wouldn't a nicked it if me bruther didn't need 'is medicine.' He sniffed. 'Comes turrible dear, it does.'

Trey laughed. 'Little brother needs medicine, eh? That's one I haven't tried myself. Full marks for inventiveness, lad.' He kept his hold on the boy and squatted down to look him in the eye. 'That bit work often for you?'

The dirty creature shrugged. Trey noted how thin the shoulder in his grip felt, nearly as insubstantial as the patched and worn jacket that covered it. 'What's your name?'

His answer was an unintelligible mumble.

'What's that?'

'I said, it's Bartholomew,' he spat.

'Ah.' Trey gazed down at his captive thoughtfully. 'Church orphanage, was it? Born in August?'

He nodded.

'Well, it could have been worse. Had you been born in October, you might have been named after St Jude.' He ran his gaze over the boy again. 'Are you still living there?'

He looked away.

'Where are you staying, lad?'

The boy shrugged those thin shoulders defensively. ''Ere and there.'

'You might be able to help me, then. I need a likely lad while we are here in London. Someone with their wits about them, someone who knows the streets and has a watchful eye. He'd have to know when to keep quiet and be able to blend into the background, perhaps even be willing to do some fetching and carrying. Do you know anybody who might fit the bill?'

He gave Trey a measuring look. 'Is yer business above board, or shady-like?'

'Strictly above board, I swear.'

'Too bad,' the lad scoffed. 'I got a few contacts.' He heaved an exaggerated sigh. 'But iff'n ye be needin' someone right away, I s'pose I could do it for ye.'

'That would be convenient,' Trey agreed. 'Tell me, do you have a brother or are you on your own?'

A slight shake of the head was all the answer he got.

'I'm going to let you go, then. You can run off, if you like. But there's a warm bed in the stables and a shilling a day to be had if you take the position.'

His eyes widened. 'I'm yer man, guv!'

'The name's Treyford. And if you work for me, there's to be no more "nicking" anything. Are we agreed?'

He nodded.

Trey tossed him a coin. 'Run on back to the stables and tell the man with the peg that I've given you the job. He'll see you settled.'

The boy pocketed the coin. He looked Trey over and shook his head. 'Ye must be daft, yer lordship.' With a cheeky wink he was off, running down the street to make the turn that would take him back to the mews.

Trey grinned at the watching men. 'Let's get this unloaded quick, then, before I get taken in again.'

Laughing, they went back to work. Trey turned, and saw Chione still poised on the top step. He'd had no idea she'd witnessed the incident, but even from here he could see her tremulous smile and the tears trapped in her thick lashes. He paused, drawn up short by her unexpected reaction, but she only nodded at him, turned and went in.

Trey shrugged and went back to work. When the baggage was unloaded, he left the opening of the house to Chione. He quickly arranged a watch schedule for his men, and then he set off for Piccadilly.

Belzoni's Tomb had closed for the day. Trey was unable to wangle his way into the Egyptian Hall, but he did purchase tickets for the following day, and after parting with a good bit of coin, he managed to 'discover' the explorer's town address.

Unfortunately, the rooms in Bayswater were empty. Trey left a polite note asking if the Italian explorer could meet with him at his exhibit the following day. He walked back to an employment agency along the Strand, where he persuaded the owner to delay his dinner to go over his files of household servants.

* * *

What with one thing and another, it was once again late in the evening when he arrived back home and most of his motley crew had gone to bed. His watchmen were alert, but reported no signs of trouble. Trey climbed the stairs with weary feet, only to pause on the second floor and wonder where he was to go.

Fortunately he'd only been there a moment when a door down the hall opened. Chione backed out with a quiet tread. She turned, saw him and gifted him with a tired but brilliant smile.

Trey's heartbeat ratcheted up alarmingly. He looked away, a little wary of the intensity of his response.

'Brace yourself,' she whispered as she came closer. 'Incredibly, our entourage has grown again since you left.' She stopped, very close. He could smell the sweet scent of her hair. 'We've a new cook bedded down next to the kitchen, a nursery maid in with Olivia…' she nodded towards the door she had just left '…and a chambermaid upstairs, who, she says, the employment agent threw in for good measure.' She tilted her head. 'And of course, there is your urchin asleep in the stables.' She paused. 'It's a scary prospect, is it not?' Her tone was sympathetic, but there was a definite challenge in her raised brow.

She was teasing him. And she was right; the thought of being responsible for even more people should have bothered him. The fact that she knew it should have bothered him even more. Perhaps later it would. Now all he could think of was the taste of her mouth, the soft slide of her skin beneath his. He pulled her in close and kissed her, hard and demanding, using his rising excitement to blot out any incipient anxiety.

It appeared her mind ran in a similar direction. She fisted her hands in his hair and kissed him back with matching ferocity.

When finally he released her she reached up, cupped his cheek with her hand and turned him, forcing his gaze to meet hers.

'Thank you,' she said fiercely. 'Thank you for everything you did for that boy today.'

Puzzled at her reaction, he nodded. 'One person at a time, remember?' he asked.

She did. She smiled through watery eyes and something inside of Trey gave way, crumbling before the emotion he saw there. She stood on her toes, pulled his face in to hers and kissed him with soft lips.

He groaned and they were gone, mouths and hands roaming wildly. Trey felt that in some way Chione was offering him something more than her body. He ran his hands over her back, pulled the sweet curve of her bottom tighter to him and wondered if he had the courage to take it.

He never got the chance to answer the question. A door opened and long, loud throat-clearing commenced, interrupting their embrace.

'Betrothed ain't married!' chastised Mrs Ferguson. 'Both of ye get to yer rooms. Alone!'

They broke apart. Laughing, Chione slipped away. She stopped, pointed him towards a door and gave him a little push. Obediently, wondering just what the hell he'd got himself into—or more importantly, what Mrs Ferguson had got him out of—Trey went.

Chapter Sixteen

A brisk wind invaded London early the next morning, clearing the fog and making the way clear for a glorious, sunny spring day. Unfortunately, neither Trey nor Eli had the opportunity to take pleasure in it. They sat in a coffee house in Piccadilly, across and down a bit from the Egyptian Hall. The exhibit had only just opened. Mrs Ferguson and Trey's new protégé had just entered.

Trey looked and saw a hackney carriage pull up in front of the Egyptian Hall. As he watched, Chione and Will climbed out, both dressed in plain, serviceable clothes. He had to admit, they did look like a boy and his governess out for a morning's romp. They approached the pillared entrance of the Egyptian Hall and Trey stood.

In a leisurely fashion he and Eli made their way across Piccadilly and towards the Hall. The bright morning light did not flatter the place any more than last evening's dusk had. Certainly it stood out from its neighbours, with its pylon shape, its stucco front and its figures of Isis and Osiris flanking a first-floor window. If the statues were more Greek, and the overall design only vaguely Egyptian, then Trey was sure that the average Londoner would scarcely know different.

Ah, but the inside was another matter altogether. Belzoni had obviously gone to much trouble and expense to remodel the entire place. They entered the first area, which the programme proclaimed to be 'The Room of Beauties'. The flickering gas light burned low, the atmosphere was hushed. It was meant to convey the moment that the strongman had first entered the tomb, likely the first person to see these sights in three thousand years. The room was large, nearly twenty feet long, Trey guessed, and a very close approximation of the real tomb. Every wall was lined with gorgeous figures in relief, just as in the Valley of the Kings.

Although the hour was early yet, a good number of people were inside, taking in the wonders in nearly mute fascination. Trey separated from Eli as planned. As he moved farther into the room he spotted Mrs Ferguson ensconced on a bench next to a mummy case, knitting in hand. The boy Bart stood next to her, completely absorbed in the grisly figure. Trey smiled wryly. The mummy was not nearly so horrifying as the thought of what Mrs Ferguson might do with a set of knitting needles.

He could see no sign of Chione or Will, and though he took his time exploring the dark shadowed corners, he did not see a wooden statue with a hollow back. Signalling to Eli, he moved on to the next room.

This was an even larger area, named the 'Entrance Hall' by the Italian. Four pillars, adorned with scenes of Pharaoh being welcomed by the gods, dominated the centre of the room.

Still Trey did not see Chione. Carefully he made his way through the crowd. He edged his way past a group of people and gave a violent start. A woman stood in the corner, poised over a glass case filled with medals and decorative ornaments. A woman with dark hair and beautiful, intense features. Not Chione. Madame Fornier.

His stomach churned and his mind flashed back to the image of her standing naked before him, his hands roaming over her flesh. Flushing right to the roots of his hair, he glanced about, searching for Chione. He breathed a little easier when he did not see her and debated his next move.

All of his instincts told him that she did not belong here. The lady's presence was entirely too coincidental. He would have to approach her. Pasting a smile on his face, he advanced in her direction.

'Madame Fornier,' he said in a low voice. She did not look pleased to see him. 'What an unexpected delight. I had not heard that you meant to leave Egypt.'

His caressing tone had reassured her. She smiled into his eyes. *'Ah, Monsieur le Earl!* I did not think to see you in London,' she purred. 'Alas, many things have changed since last we met.' She shot him a quizzical look. 'I heard of your partner's death. A sad blow.'

'Yes,' Trey agreed, suddenly curt.

'We, too, have suffered misfortune. My husband—he has fallen from Drovetti's favour. And so we have been forced to take up a new business venture.'

'I am sorry to hear of it,' Trey said. 'But I hope your new position is as…satisfying…as the old?'

She moved a step closer. Trey kept his gaze locked with hers, though he knew they were in danger of attracting unwanted attention.

'Oh, no, my lord,' she spoke in a whisper now and with a pout on her lovely face. 'Only to you will I confess that I have not been satisfied at all since our last encounter.'

Trey raised her hand to his lips. 'Now that is a tragedy indeed.'

She watched him through half-lidded eyes. 'Perhaps you will help me with this trouble?'

'Perhaps I shall.' He took a step back and resumed a more normal tone. 'But, please, tell me of your new business.'

She sighed. 'My husband has entered the service of Captain Batiste. Perhaps you have heard of him? He is a well-known traveller and has shown an interest in Egypt as well.'

'I'm sorry I have not, but I wish you much success.'

'Thank you,' she simpered. She gestured to the exhibition around them. 'Monsieur Belzoni does not know what a great service he has done us. So many people have arrived early in London for the coronation. Belzoni's book and now his exhibit have once again stirred a great interest in Egyptian artifacts. We have done very well, selling some of our collection at a good profit.' She glanced about, slightly irritated. 'I was to meet a potential buyer here today, but I am afraid he has decided not to keep the appointment.'

'How rude…' Trey smiled lazily '…and how incredibly stupid.'

'I shall not wait any longer.' She tilted her head and smiled. 'But that does leave me with a great deal of free time this morning. Perhaps, if you are free also, we could spend it together?'

'I am heartbroken to say that I have an appointment also this morning, and it is one that must be kept. Would you forgive my refusal and grant me the privilege at another time?'

'For you? Of course. Our lodgings are in a dreadful area of Shadwell, but my husband is very rarely there.' She leaned in and pressed her bosom against him intimately as she kissed both his cheeks. 'I promise, should you visit, I will make you very comfortable indeed. *Adieu, Monsieur le Earl.*'

'Goodbye, *madame.*'

He watched her take her leave. She sashayed right past the combined force of Mrs Ferguson, Bart and Will, who all stared as she went by. Trey waited a few moments before he approached them himself.

'I take it you saw the lady?' he asked.

'Cor, guv! Who didn't?' Bart said appreciatively.

'I want to know where she goes from here, Bart, but I do not want her or anyone else to know you are trailing her. Can you do that?'

'Easy,' he scoffed.

'Do you have the money I gave you this morning?'

The boy nodded.

'After her, then. And be careful, lad. Do not get yourself in trouble. If something doesn't look right, leave it, and get yourself home quick.'

'Aye, guv.'

He turned to go, but Will put a hand on his sleeve and turned to Trey with pleading eyes. 'Please, Trey. I want to go too.'

There was more in his face than just a boy's lust for adventure. Mervyn was the boy's father, after all. After a moment's hesitation Trey glanced wordlessly at Bart.

The former street urchin knew what he was silently asking. He glanced at Will and he nodded.

'Fine, then, but Eli will go along.' Trey sighed. 'If something happens to you, your niece will skin me alive.'

'Thank you,' said Will fervently. Eli nodded at Trey and then they were gone.

Trey turned to Mrs Ferguson. 'Do you know where in blazes Chione has got to?'

The housekeeper nodded and gestured with her chin. 'She's making friends.'

Trey turned and saw an immensely tall man framed in an arched doorway, talking to someone in an animated fashion. By the height and breadth of him, it could only be the infamous Belzoni himself. The large man took a step aside and Trey caught sight of his audience. Chione, very pale, stared back at him with narrowed eyes.

'The *ushabti* figures of blue faience are indeed very beautiful,' the Italian explorer said as they entered what he called the Entrance Hall. 'We also found some of wood, and stone. There were an immense number of them stored in a room with the slaughtered carcass of a bull.' He chuckled. 'Clearly, with so many of the little servant figures buried with him, Seti did not intend to waste his afterlife on manual labour.'

'Who could picture Pharaoh fetching water or cooking a meal?' asked Chione inanely. Her brain had ceased to function the moment she had seen that strange woman pressing herself obscenely against Trey. She'd known he'd had a multitude of women in the past, but somehow she'd been so preoccupied with the search for Mervyn and dealing with the present reality of her unexpected betrothal that she had just pushed the idea of the future away. She was very much afraid that a glimpse of it had just hit her hard. She clenched her fists. She fully planned to hit back.

But not at this moment. She was here with a purpose. Now she had to concentrate on finding her brother's clue. Chione focused her attention back on Belzoni and his conjecture on what a pharaoh's lift might have been like. He paused when she laid her hand on his massive arm.

'Mr Belzoni, I see Lord Treyford across the room. Shall I introduce you?'

'Of course,' he agreed readily.

Trey had already started towards them. They met in the centre of the four pillars.

'Lord Treyford,' Chione began, 'may I introduce Mr

Belzoni? He has been showing me some of the *ushabti* figures he found buried in the tomb.'

The great Italian bowed low.

'Richard Latimer spoke of you often, sir, and praised your collection of antiquities so highly that we could not possibly stay away,' Trey said.

'Ah, I have already offered the lady my sincerest condolences. Richard was a kind boy and an excellent scholar.'

'He spoke of the extensive work you did, copying the reliefs of the tomb in wax and reproducing them here. What a huge undertaking that must have been. Would you do us the honour of escorting us through yourself?'

'It would be my pleasure.' The big man did seem truly delighted. 'We must go upstairs to the galleries to see the true sequence from corridor to burial vault. But first, have you seen the models? I have the Second Pyramid and also Abu Simbel.'

Chione trailed in the men's wake, listening to Trey marvel over the Italian's stories of his explorations and the insights that had led him to so many discoveries. Her own attention was divided. She kept her eye out for the wooden statues, and for Eli and Will and the rest of them. She glimpsed the housekeeper, but her interest in the men's conversation peaked when Belzoni began to talk of his feud with the French and even with England's own consul in Egypt, Henry Salt.

'In your travels, sir, have you ever made the acquaintance of my grandfather, Mervyn Latimer?'

'No, miss.' The Italian shook his head. 'I did not have the pleasure. Your brother mentioned his many exploits. He sounds as if he was a great man.'

Chione ignored his use of the past tense. 'Did Richard ever speak to you of his interest in the Pharaoh's Lost Jewel?'

Belzoni stroked his chin. 'Once. We had a lively debate on the subject.'

'And will you share your opinions, sir?'

'Of course.' He glanced at her thoughtfully. 'I will tell you what I told your brother. The pharaohs of Egypt have been robbed of thousands of jewels over thousands of years. What is one more? No—if there is such a treasure—and I have my doubts—then I would guess it is something more valuable than gemstones or gold.'

Trey looked sharply attentive. 'Such as?'

'An important scroll, perhaps? A map to the tombs in the Valley? Or a key to finally translating hieroglyphs? An Egyptian once told me he had heard it was a map to a lost city of treasure, but he was a thief, himself. Who can tell which is the truth of it? I would guess it must be something out of the ordinary for the legend to persist so long.'

'That is a very interesting theory, Mr Belzoni. I shall think on it.' Trey glanced at Chione before continuing. 'In his journals Richard described some of the amazing artifacts he helped you catalogue. I've seen some of the most interesting ones he wrote about, but haven't seen two wooden statues he mentioned—hollowed out to hold scrolls? Are they included in your exhibit?'

'Yes, of course. They are not so magnificent as my statues of Sekhmet. I hope you will not be disappointed.'

Chione's heart began to race as Belzoni led them to a shadowy corner of the gallery. There stood the statues, just exactly as Richard had described. Two sheets of rolled papyrus had been tucked into place. Trey walked around them, eyeing them critically.

'Not very fancy, perhaps, but definitely useful, are they not? Especially to a royal scribe or some such person.' He looked to their host. 'I have not seen your Sekhmets, sir. Where are they?'

'Downstairs. They are truly lovely. I shall take you there.'

'If you will excuse me, gentlemen, I think I would like to finish admiring these reliefs you worked so very hard on, sir.' Chione struggled to keep her tone even.

Trey nodded. 'We will meet you downstairs when you are finished, Miss Latimer.'

'Of course.'

Struggling to stay calm, Chione strolled on. She watched the gentlemen exit downstairs, then had to wait until an obviously courting couple followed. Finally, her pulse racing, she went back to the statues.

Glancing furtively about, she drew out one sheet of papyrus. It was blank. Uttering a prayer, she reached for the second. She unrolled it carefully, and nearly collapsed in relief when she glimpsed her brother's handwriting.

To find the coffer, Chione must face her greatest fear.

Clutching the scroll to her, she slumped against the wall.

Trey was standing with Belzoni when Chione came downstairs. He took one look at her pale face and drawn expression, uttered a sound of concern and hurried to her side.

'Did you find it?' he asked quietly, reaching out a steadying hand.

'Yes.'

'You have it?'

She nodded.

'Mr Belzoni,' Trey said as the explorer approached, 'I am afraid that Miss Latimer is feeling unwell. Unfortunately her carriage is not due back for quite some time. Do you think you could procure us a hackney?'

'Yes, yes, certainly. There is a bench right here, my dear young lady. Please sit while I see to it.'

'Thank you, you are so kind.' The look she gave Belzoni was truly grateful. 'I suppose, after the trials of our journey, I should have rested today. I was just so eager to see your treasures, sir.'

The explorer beamed. 'But it is not worth risking your health, my dear. I hope a rest will put you to rights.'

It was not long before Trey was able to bundle her into a hackney carriage. They bade their genial host goodbye and pulled away, but Trey had given the jarvey orders to wait at the corner. In just a moment, Mrs Ferguson climbed in.

'Where is Will? And Bartholomew? And Eli?' Chione said, looking around from the corner she had curled herself into.

Trey explained.

'You sent Eli to watch over them? What if he can't keep up?' She looked paler still, and suddenly furious.

'Bart knows what he is about,' Trey said.

'And young Will deserves a chance to do his part,' Mrs Ferguson piped in.

'I warned them both about not taking chances,' Trey continued. 'They will be fine.'

Chione looked even more upset at being overruled, but she turned away. She sat staring out of the window while the rest of them exchanged silent glances. Trey began to wonder if perhaps she truly was ill.

'Well…' Mrs Ferguson eventually broke the silence '…what of it? Did you find what you were looking for?'

They looked to Chione, who never turned from the window.

'May we see it, Chione?' Trey asked gently.

She pulled the tightly rolled papyrus from her pelisse. Trey read it, and then passed it on to the others. They all stared at each other once more in puzzlement.

'But what does it mean?' Mrs Ferguson finally asked.

'I think only Chione can answer that,' Trey said.

'I don't know!' she finally burst out. 'I have no idea. Damn Richard! How could he bring us so far and not be clear in the end?'

'Must be something,' the housekeeper said pragmatically. 'A childhood fear? Something he would ha' remembered? Snakes, maybe? Or spiders?'

'No, I've never been frightened of such things,' she answered irritably. 'Richard would know that. I don't understand. Perhaps someone else switched the scrolls.'

'Who?' asked Trey. 'If those thieving bandits had discovered and interpreted the clue, they would not have bothered to leave a fake. They'd have taken the damned coffer, whatever it is, and gone back to Egypt.'

'Well, there's been no sign of them,' she returned. 'Perhaps that is what happened. I don't know.'

In fact, Trey had indeed had word of their adversaries. Last night Aswan had frightened a year off of the life of one of the guards by 'risin' out o' the dark like a haunt in the dead of night.'

The former dragoman had come bearing good news. As with most predators, the bandits had focused on their stealth and their target and never once considered a threat from elsewhere. He and Alden had turned the tables on the bandits and now the hunters had become the prey.

One by one, the scholar and the Egyptian had begun picking the villains off. Aswan knew multitude ways of silencing a man, and they now had four of the thieves tucked away with Bow Street, and full knowledge of where the rest of the increasingly nervous band was quartered.

Unfortunately, Trey did not feel that now was a fortuitous time to share that information with Chione. He watched her face redden with embarrassment and even anger when Mrs Ferguson cast a dark look his way and suggested that men were what frightened Chione most.

'That makes no sense at all,' Chione snapped.

'That boy always did love a puzzle,' the housekeeper moaned. 'Why didn't he just tell us straight out where the damned thing is?'

'He left a clue only Chione could decipher,' Trey said. 'Otherwise anyone at all could have come along and found what we have searched so hard for.'

'I don't wish to discuss this,' Chione bit out. 'I need time to think.' Trey could not ever remember hearing her use such a sharp tone.

The carriage fell silent, but they did not have to endure the uncomfortable atmosphere for long before they arrived in Soho Square. Chione stalked into the house without uttering a word to anyone. Ferguson followed. Trey retreated to the stables to wait until Eli returned with the boys.

'The woman went straight to a boarding house in Shadwell,' the groom reported. Trey told him what had occurred after he left. They sent the boys back to the house, then stood in the courtyard of the mews and shook their heads at the capriciousness of women.

'Can't recall when I've ever heard of Miss Chione in such a taking,' mused Eli. 'Don't look good, does it?'

'If it is her greatest fear that has her in such a mood, I'm not sure I want to face it either,' Trey agreed.

Eli sighed.

'Wait—' Trey stopped, struck by a sudden thought. 'Eli, have you ever heard of a Captain Batiste?'

Slowly the old salt turned, surprise alight in his face. 'Aye. Knew him as well. Where did you be hearin' o' him?'

'From the lady you were following. Did you know her? Madame Fornier, or her husband? They were minor agents for Drovetti in Egypt when I was there, collecting antiquities for him.'

'No, never heard o' the pair o' them. But Gustavo Batiste? He's a bad character.'

'How so?'

'Mind if we sit?' Eli asked, pointing to a bench along the wall.

They crossed over and settled on the bench. 'Ah,' Eli sighed, 'that's better. Batiste,' he mused. 'Hadn't thought o' him in donkey's years. Used to captain one o' Mervyn's ships, he did. They were friends, o' sorts. Had a lot in common. He loved exploring new places, being first somewheres, jest like Mervyn did. But they had a fallin' out. Mervyn fired him. Furious he was, but he got him another ship and struck out on his own. They were rivals afterwards, even though Batiste could never really compete on the same level as Latimer Shipping.'

'What did they argue over, do you know?'

'Man was a slaver. He was runnin' with a light crew, havin' converted half the crew quarters to slave holds. Mervyn found out when one o' Batiste's men came to him. Turns out Batiste was dumpin' the poor buggers overboard whenever they spotted a ship of the line, to keep from paying the fines—right steep they would a' been, too, at a hundred pounds per head. Lordy, I ain't never seen Mervyn so mad as he was that day.'

'He does sound a nasty character.'

'Aye, best avoid him,' Eli said, rising and heading away to his room.

Trey slowly followed him into the house. He could not help but wonder what the Forniers might be doing for such a man as Eli had described. Their presence here at this time made him extremely uneasy. Things were coming to a head, Trey could feel it. He had to find a way to get Chione talking about her greatest fears.

Chapter Seventeen

Something had happened to Chione when she had read her brother's words on that papyrus. The creature inside of her—the *djinn* who had left her hiding place behind and begun to blossom under Trey's careful tutelage—had roared in sudden anger and fright, and then promptly disappeared.

Chione had been left feeling suddenly small and alone, burning with a strange combination of terror and hateful defiance. When Trey had spoken so gently to her in the carriage she had wanted to scream at him, to jump from the moving vehicle and run until her breath gave out and she lost the dark swirl of emotion churning inside of her.

Instead, hours later, it still churned and Chione did not know how much more she could take. She'd gone straight up to her room and although she had been glad to hear of Will and Bart's safe return, she had refused each gentle nudge to come down. Now the afternoon had lengthened into evening and the house gradually grew quiet. Chione slipped into the darkening corridors and began to prowl.

From the family bedrooms to the attics, past the kitchens where the servants were having their dinner, and even to the wine cellars, she stalked. She could not contain herself or the terrible anxiety besetting her. Window to window, room to room, she watched and waited and tried desperately not to think. She saw the guards changing shifts, one at the front of the house, one at the back. She nodded and kept going. She found Olivia in the stairwell and firmly tucked her back into bed in the nursery.

Inevitably, and at last, she found Trey. Or he found her. He ran her to ground in the dining room, a location she capitalised upon by keeping the long table between them.

Clearly, this exasperated him. 'Enough, Chione,' he barked. 'You're as edgy as a cat. We need to talk.'

'I don't wish to talk.'

'Yes, that is becoming increasingly clear. The real question here is why don't you wish to?'

'Because I am exasperated and frustrated, that's why,' she answered sharply. 'You know how I feel about the Jewel.' She struggled to keep the anger out of her voice. 'It dangles there, just out of reach. Men chase after it, dancing to its tune like puppets. And after a lifetime of vowing to ignore the song, I gave in. I started the dance and now the music has suddenly stopped!'

He raised a brow. 'So you are ready to give up looking for Mervyn? Just like that—you'll accept that you'll never know what happened to him?'

'No! Of course not.' She sounded unreasonable. She didn't care—she *felt* unreasonable, and she didn't know if she was more annoyed with Trey or herself. She turned away from him, running her hand along the sideboard.

'That does seem to be what will happen if we don't puzzle out that clue.'

'It's not a clue—it's an unanswerable question! How could Richard do that? Lay the blame for failure so firmly at my door?' Pain gripped her, and a sorrow so profound she thought she might crumple to the floor beneath its weight. But there was resentment inside of her too, and anger, and they gave her the strength to stay on her feet—and on her side of the table.

'No one is blaming you, Chione. We haven't even tried to answer that question yet.'

'I have tried. I've racked my brains all day. I cannot recall any silly childhood terrors. I'm not afraid of water, heights or dogs. *This* is my biggest fear—not finding Mervyn. After that would come fear of losing the children, but you've taken care of that. If I had to choose another, it would be not having enough money to care for all of us, but you've dealt with that as well, haven't you?' She gave a belligerent wave of her hand.

'Perhaps that is it, then,' he said quietly, leaning his hands on the dining table. 'Perhaps you fear losing control. But I am not a conventional man, Chione, nor are you in any way typical. I am not going to dominate you. I would never even wish to.'

She gave a bitter laugh. 'You couldn't be more wrong if you tried. Haven't you learned that most basic principle, even in all of your travels? Control is an illusion, Trey. It doesn't exist. All we can do is hang on, do our best, and pray that some good will follow the bad in this life.'

He looked surprised, but not angry. 'Is that really how you feel?'

'It is what I know. What I've known since I was eight years old and my world fell apart.'

He pushed away from the table and she started, moving back a step. She didn't know what was wrong with her. This was Trey—she knew she could trust him. But she also knew that if he touched her she would fall apart.

He stared at her as if he could see the strain ripping its way through her. Abruptly he sat down. 'Let's just talk then, all right? We'll speak of an entirely different subject.' He waved at the chairs along her side of the table. 'Sit.'

'I was wondering,' he began, 'if you had found a mention of a Monsieur or Madame Fornier in Richard's journals?'

'Madame Fornier?' she asked testily, sliding into a chair. 'Is that the woman who draped herself all over you today at the exhibit?'

'Yes, have you heard of her before?' His voice was frustratingly even.

'No, nor have I seen her mentioned in Richard's journals, but I haven't made my way back through all of them.'

'What of a Captain Batiste? Eli tells me Mervyn knew him. It seems the Forniers are working for him now.'

'Yes, I know of him,' she said. It was difficult to think, to focus on anything outside her own misery. 'He is a merchant captain. He used to work for Mervyn. They had a friendship, a partnership of sorts, but it went bad. I was young, but Richard told me that Batiste was jealous of Mervyn. He wanted what Mervyn had and he wanted it without delay. Eventually it ate away at their relationship.'

'Yes, Eli told me the story. It was just a thought. Something doesn't feel right, and I'm trying to figure it out. I'm not comfortable with that particular lady being in London right now.'

'Why not?'

He gazed at her steadily for a moment before answering, 'Because she was in the camp the night that Richard was murdered.'

Stunned, Chione jumped to her feet. 'What? Do you mean that woman murdered my brother?'

'Sit!' he commanded. 'Hear me out. No, I do not mean any such thing. In fact, I know most definitely that she did *not* kill Richard. But I'm beginning to wonder if she might not know who did.'

She was still on her feet. 'What would a Frenchwoman be doing in camp in any case? And how could you possibly know that she didn't do it? Perhaps she was after the scarab and the Lost Jewel, you can't know.' She paused. 'Unless...'

He stared back at her, silent. Anger and humiliation surged through her. She was tempted, oh, so tempted to jump over the table and smack the determinedly calm look from his face. But she didn't. 'I see,' she said icily.

'No, you don't. She came to me with some half-cocked story of an offer from Drovetti. And you forget, although she was in the camp at that moment, Richard was not. He had gone to one of the tombs. To meet somebody?' Frustration cracked through his implacable facade at last. 'I don't know, because for the longest time, nobody bloody well told me anything!'

She didn't reply. She couldn't. All she could see in her mind's eye was that woman pressed up against Trey—while Richard faced death alone in a rocky canyon nearby.

'I hadn't even met you then, Chione. I had no idea what you and Richard were involved in, let alone that she might be involved in it, too.'

'And today?' she asked nastily. 'I did not see you protesting when she flirted so baldly.'

'Today I was trying to get information from her. I couldn't let on that I suspected her of anything, or I would have learned nothing.' He paused. 'And I am going to have to try again.'

Chione turned to leave the room.

'Running?' Trey asked unpleasantly. 'You've been running all day, Chione, ever since you saw that clue. Don't you think it's time you stopped and faced whatever it is that has unsettled you so?'

Fighting tears, she kept going.

'Please,' he said tiredly, 'this is far from over, Chione. I have had news from Aswan.'

She paused and he began to talk. She was shocked to hear what Alden and Aswan had been up to. She turned back and glared at him. 'I don't *want* to hear any more. All I want is Mervyn back. I don't want to deal with this any more. Let them have the damned jewel, as long as they leave us alone.'

'They won't. It's gone too far, now. It's all mixed up in one intangible mess.' He came around the table. This time she didn't move. He took her hand. The usual spark of sensation, that indescribable jolt she experienced every time he touched her, threatened to shake her out of her self-imposed numbness. Ruthlessly, she squashed it. She did allow him to lead her across the hall, to the family parlour. A fire crackled in the grate, casting shifting shadows over the room. Trey pulled a chair close to the flames and she settled into it. He brought one over for himself, and positioned it so it faced the fire as well. Together they sat, staring into the flames, the smoke-tinged air settling, like a trance, over them both.

'Eventually, you will have to talk to me,' he said quietly. 'But for now, just listen. Perhaps it will help if you hear what *my* greatest fear is.'

She shook her head, but he paid her no heed.

'I told you that my mother left. She had a horrendous argument with my father, and then she ran away. She left him— us—behind, preferring to live in disgrace with his brother.'

He paused, but she said nothing. She couldn't decide if she was more afraid he would stop, or afraid he would go on.

'What I didn't say, what almost no one knows, is that my father went after them. He got himself raging drunk and chased them. He was gone for two days. When he came back he shut himself up in the library and drank some more. He stayed in there, and stayed drunk, for over a week. I was not allowed to see him, but one night I woke up—and found him staring at me in my bed.'

Chione could see him swallow before he continued.

'"She didn't love me," my father said to me. "Not the way I loved her." He took a swig from the bottle he held in his lap. "She didn't love you either, did she? Not enough. Not enough to stay, not enough to take you with her." Then he was quiet a long time. I think I cried, but he didn't seem to notice. "Be glad," he said eventually. "You'd be dead too, then." He stood, but he didn't leave. He just stood there a long time, looking down at me, but not really seeing me. Finally he gave a massive shudder. "Her eyes are open," he said. "But she can't see me any more." Then he turned and left.'

Trey sighed, but Chione sat frozen in her chair. 'A couple of days later,' he said, 'we received word. The two of them had been in a carriage accident. Tracks showed that another vehicle had forced them off the road and down a steep embankment. My uncle was grievously wounded. My mother was dead. It had taken a while for them to be identified because my uncle had been unconscious for days. The next day my father had an accident of his own. He and his horse went over a cliff, one they must have been by a thousand times. No one questioned it, but we all knew the truth.'

Finally, Trey turned his gaze away from the flames. He stared at her with pain in his gaze, and a hardness that frightened her, but she could not look away. Tears welled in her eyes and she struggled to keep them from overflowing.

'For a long time my greatest fear was that my father had been right. That my mother hadn't loved me, as my father obviously hadn't. What if I was unlovable? What if no one *ever* loved me? Eventually, though, I stopped being afraid. In fact, I began to hope that that was indeed the case. What had love done for my parents? Killed my mother. Made my father weak? Certainly. Turned him into a murderer? Perhaps.'

He looked away again. 'So I scorned the idea of love. Certainly I did not find any reason to doubt my conclusions. Although I lived for the letters from my mother's brother, I couldn't say he loved me. We had never even met. And my other uncle, the one whose custody I was put into? The one who destroyed my parents? I rarely saw him. He sent me a birthday present once, too. Just one. A riding crop, supple and gleaming. Included with it was a note to my tutor, giving him permission to use the thing to beat the arrogance out of me. Which he did. Regularly.'

Chione uttered a soundless protest, but Trey's gaze remained fastened on the fire.

'I was sent away to school before long. If you know anything about Eton, you know that affection and love have no part in the curriculum. I kept my head down, I did well at my studies and I continued the correspondence with my travelling uncle. When I was done I wished to go to him, rather than attend university, but my guardian wouldn't hear of it.'

'So I did what I was told. I waited until I reached my majority. I waited until all the foldcrol was done and over with and all the privileges of my rank were passed to me. Then I took that riding crop that my uncle had sent to me all those years ago, and I thrashed him with it—to within an inch of his life. I left England and I never came back, until I came to you.'

The tears were streaming down Chione's face now. Trey looked at her and his hard, set expression softened.

'And here, at last, I found evidence that I had been wrong,' he said. 'Here was love and comfort. Here was a family devoted to each other, willing to sacrifice for each other. Here you were, Chione. Everything I never wanted, but had to have. And once again, I was afraid.'

'Stop,' she whispered. She knew what he was doing—telling his secrets so that she would be obligated to share hers. He didn't understand. She could not do it. She'd lived with her secrets for too long. They defined her, had indeed become a part of her. If she gave them up… She shivered, unable to even finish the thought.

'Don't you see?' she cried. 'This is it, what I fear the most. This—intimacy. You sharing your secrets and wanting me to share mine.' She halted on a sob.

'Why, Chione? Why are you afraid?'

There was a huge lump in her throat. It was going to choke her. She'd thought that Trey was safe, but she'd been wrong. She never should have agreed to the betrothal. She had to put a stop to this. Deliberately she hardened her features. She would take a page from Trey's book and strike first. Hurt him before he could hurt her further.

'You're ruining everything, Trey,' she said fiercely. 'Do you think that I didn't know that about you? That I couldn't sense your reluctance to be open? I welcomed it. It freed me. Even when we became betrothed, I didn't worry too much, fool that I was. Don't you see? I don't *want* to be burdened with your secrets. I don't want to burden you with mine. And it's all going to hell now. You're letting in things that will destroy us both.'

She swallowed hard and continued, determined to put an end to this. 'You learned the right lesson as a boy. I've finally learned it now. Emotion destroys. Look at your parents. Look at mine. Love always comes with a price, whether it be heartbreak or mistrust or eventually hatred.' She laughed harshly.

'Even friendships are not immune, and professional relationships suffer too if emotion enters the scene. Look at Mervyn and Batiste.'

She stood, looking down at him with narrowed eyes. 'It's too late now. I was wrong to pull you in.' She took a step away from him, towards the door. 'The betrothal is at an end. It might be better if you leave now.' She walked out, heading for the stairs before he could speak, before he could have a chance to call her back.

Trey sat, stunned. Silently, he watched her go. A black cloud of anger and disbelief filled the room and descended over him. For a moment he wallowed in it. Wasn't this exactly the blow he had been expecting? Hadn't he known it would be a mistake to get involved, to allow himself to hope? And even though he'd expected the hurt—hell, he likely deserved it for going against all the principles of a lifetime—it didn't make the stab to his heart any less devastating. As he stared at the empty doorway where she had disappeared, the temptation to follow her suggestion, to get up and leave, nearly overwhelmed him.

But hiding away from pain was the course that had led him here. He had just watched it lead Chione out that door, too. Trey was canny enough to notice when he was rapped over the head with one of his own tricks. She had lashed out at him to distract him, to protect herself. She was still hiding. From something in her past? Something terrifying that reached right down into the core of her, judging by the change in her demeanour and just how much she was willing to sacrifice rather than expose it.

He puzzled it over, but could not guess what it might be. He thought perhaps that Richard's journals might give him a clue, but they were in Chione's room. He didn't dare consider disturbing her now. He was stumped.

He mentally replayed the conversation. No, she was damned good at hiding what she didn't want the world to see. It made him wonder just how long she had been at it.

Irritatingly, he kept coming back to something seemingly inconsequential. *Even friendships are not immune, and professional relationships suffer too*…she had said. *Look at Mervyn and Batiste.*

For some reason the phrase echoed in his head. Repeatedly. *Look at Mervyn and Batiste.* And then an image of something Chione had showed him in one of Richard's journals popped into his mind's eye. *Drovetti in Thebes today, and in the company of C. G. B. Neither happy to see me. I am getting close.*

C. G. B. What was it that Eli had said? *But Gustavo Batiste? He's a bad character.*

Suddenly all the disparate facts connected. Captain Gustavo Batiste. C. G. B. Trey shot out of his chair, excitement and awe propelling him towards the stairs. He started to climb, had to refrain from shouting Chione's name in his exuberance. He came to an abrupt halt. What if he were wrong? She was in no state to deal with it. It would crush her.

He turned and descended, going to the back of the house and through the green baize door to the servants' quarters. He slipped through the back door, crossed the garden to the mews, and found the groom's quarters at the back of the stables. 'Eli,' he called. 'I hope to God you are not asleep.' He pounded on the door. 'Get your knife, your pistol and your best peg, man. We're going to the docks.'

Chione fled to her bedchamber. She'd hurt Trey; there was no mistaking the flash of devastation her harshly worded rejection had wrought. She was sorry for it, but he had spoken so tenderly and there had been something unquestionably significant in his expression. She had seen it and been at once elated and terrified, and suddenly terribly cognisant of her mistake.

She should never have let it get this far, should never have exposed herself so. She would have been smarter to go it alone, or to marry Orville Stockton, even. She would still be untouched, safe behind the unbroken mask of English reserve that was Miss Latimer. She wouldn't have had to face this fearful choice now, and she wouldn't be facing ceaseless remorse in the years ahead.

She stretched out on the bed, her tears drying. None of that seemed real yet. She felt strangely calm. It was done now. The choice had been made. How was it possible for a person to feel so horrible and yet so relieved all at once? For it was true, the terrible anxiety she had fought all day had drained away. An unnatural, empty lightness came in its wake—blessed numbness that eased the pain of loss and the sting of regret. Gradually, she relaxed and slept.

She awoke in Belzoni's Tomb. It looked much the same as it had this morning, except the flickering gas lights had been replaced with sputtering torches, and in the centre of the chamber sat a luminous, opalescent coffin. The alabaster sarcophagus that Belzoni had described in his book. Chione tried to sit up, but found that she could not move. She looked about and discovered she was surrounded by hundreds of the little *ushabti* figures that Belzoni had shown her.

A faint noise caused her to look to the centre of the room. It came again, from the coffin gleaming in the uncertain light. From its depths rose the gruesome figure of the mummy, its shining death mask still thankfully in place. Chione fought back a moan as the creature reached a sitting position, raised a ghastly arm and gestured to the multitude of tiny figures.

As one they came to life—called by their purpose. Created to be slaves, to do the dead pharaoh's bidding in the afterlife, they answered his summons. Horrified, Chione felt herself responding as well.

'No!' she cried, but her limbs were not her own to command.

'I'm not one of them!' She could not stop. Ever closer her legs carried her, until the withered, bandaged hand reached for her.

She awoke, gasping in terror. Sweat poured from her. She sat up in the bed, struggling for control. A vivid image of Eshe flashed in her mind; her mother forced to bend to a stranger's will. 'I'm not a slave,' Chione sobbed aloud. 'She was more than that. And so am I.'

She dropped her head in her hands and realised that she knew what her greatest fear was. And she knew where the coffer was hidden.

Chapter Eighteen

The morning was just a faint lightening in the eastern sky when Chione dressed and went in search of Trey. His room sat empty, his bed looked untouched. He had gone, then. She'd allowed her fear and feelings of inadequacy to control her, and she'd driven him off.

Still harbouring a faint glimmer of hope, she pushed through the door of the family breakfast room. Trey was not there, but his adopted urchin was going out the door on the other side of the room.

'Bartholomew, wait.'

The boy turned, snatched the cap from his head. 'Yes, miss.'

'Come here for a moment, please.'

She took a seat at the empty table. Bart silently advanced until he stood before her, his gaze fastened on the carpet at her feet.

'Have you seen Lord Treyford this morning?'

He looked up. 'No, miss. Stableman says how he took off in the night. Him and the old groom, the one with the peg?'

'Eli, yes.'

'They got in a hackney and left in the wee hours.'

'I see.' Hope flared briefly. If Trey had taken Eli, then

surely he would be back. She focused on the boy. 'How do you like being employed by Lord Treyford?'

Bart shrugged. 'I like it fine. The work's easy. The pay's good.'

'I'm glad. Lord Treyford likes you too. We all do. That is why I am going to ask you to put the silver back in the sideboard where you found it.'

The boy skipped back a step in alarm. 'How did you know?'

'I guessed,' Chione said, reaching gently for his hand. 'But I thought I might be right. I had a feeling, because you see, I used to be just like you.'

'You never!' he scoffed.

'Oh, but I did. It was in a city far from here—but I was most definitely a street rat.' She nodded at his look of shock. 'Yes, it's true. I know what it is to have no home, to sleep in the street, to forage for food, all the while trying day and night not to fall prey to worse dangers.'

'But how?' He waved a hand, speechless, to their comfortable surroundings.

'I was taken in by a kind man. He looked at me and saw more than just an urchin. He gave me a home and a family. For a time I still pocketed stray silver and hoarded food, but then I understood that he was truly offering me a better life. Just as Lord Treyford is willing to offer the same to you.'

He looked down. She doubted whether he believed her.

'It's tempting just to look at him as an easy mark, is it not?' she asked.

He glanced quickly up and then back down.

'You may look at him that way—and perhaps that will be what he becomes. No more, no less. But it will be up to you. I know we would be happy to take you with us when we leave London. Again, this decision will be up to you. You are free to refuse. Just understand that it would be your fear working against you, not lack of opportunity.'

She took his hand again. 'I know what I am talking about. I just let fear ruin the best thing that was ever offered to me. Now I have to try to make it right.' She looked at him, considering. 'Will you help me?'

Bart nodded.

She leaned in close. 'Can you pick a lock?' she whispered.

He looked surprised, but nodded again.

'Good. I have one last job for the two of us. Then, after this morning, I hope neither of us will ever have to steal again.'

It was still very early when the two of them stole out on to the street. Bartholomew led them on a roundabout path that avoided the main thoroughfares and kept to the residential districts. Not many people were out on these streets, just an occasional baker's boy or a maid here and there sweeping the steps to one of the grand houses. Twice they saw a fancy carriage pull up to discharge its late-night revellers. They stopped several times to ensure that they were not being followed.

It wasn't long before they reached Piccadilly and the Egyptian Hall. Carefully they circled around the back. Bartholomew had the back door open in the twinkling of an eye. They entered into a darkened workroom, filled with clutter and furniture left over from previous exhibitions. Chione was glad she had thought to bring along a satchel with a few basic supplies. The early morning light did not reach into the rooms. She pulled out two candles and a flint.

Quietly they eased into the exhibit. In the dim candlelight the Hall had the same eerie, sepulchral feeling as her dream. Chione wished, the thought fleeting and intense, that Trey was here with them. She pushed it away. She had left a note, but with any luck they would be back home with the coffer before Trey returned or anyone knew they had gone.

Silently they made their way through the exhibit, paying particular attention to the models and displays. At last, they found it. She hoped that it was it. A glass display case sat on a dark wooden base in the corner of the Entrance Hall. Inside sat an unassuming collection of objects: a plain bronze strongbox surrounded by the best of Belzoni's collection of *ushabti* figures.

'I believe the case is just a heavy glass box with no bottom,' she whispered to Bart. There was no one to hear, but she couldn't bring herself to speak out loud. 'Do you think you can help me lift it?'

'Can't we just break it?' he asked with a nod to her satchel.

'I would rather not. I think the two of us can handle it.' They set the candles down nearby and set to work. They did struggle with the weight of the case, and with the delicate task of lifting it without disturbing any of the objects it covered, but eventually they got the thing lifted off.

Reverently Chione ran her fingers over the pitted and stained surface of the ancient bronze chest. Could this plain and simple box truly hold the secret to a three-thousand-year-old mystery? There was no obvious lid to the box, seemingly no way to open it. Seamless and mysterious, it offered no answer to her question.

'I'll take one side,' she said low to Bartholomew, 'you take the other. We'll set it on the floor right here in front of the base.'

It was lighter than she expected. They set it down and she moved both of the candles closer.

Nothing. No marks, symbols or messages. Chione looked at Bart and lifted a shoulder. She thought a moment before a notion hit her.

'Help me tilt it up,' she said.

She'd been right. It was there—stamped in the thick metal base of the box. The outline of a scarab, a near replica of the bottom of Mervyn's piece. Her breath caught and her heart raced. After all this time, after everything that had happened to her family and her loved ones, this was it. She had found it.

Carefully they set it flat once more. 'Thank heavens it is not too heavy,' she said to Bartholomew. 'We've got to get this home as quickly as we can.'

They stood and had it lifted between them once more when the voice floated ominously out of the darkness.

'We shall save you the effort, Miss Latimer. Please, set it back down on the floor.'

Chione peered through the darkness towards the arched doorway. From the Room of Beauties a man emerged. His gorgeous white turban and his long, grey-shot beard marked him as a foreigner, but his wardrobe was that of an English gentleman: shining boots, black pantaloons and a form-fitting coat of the finest grey superfine. He even had a watch and fob stretched across his embroidered waistcoat. It was an oddly fascinating mix of cultures, but a cold hostility emanated from him as his dark gaze roamed over her.

'Who are you?' she asked. She and Bartholomew were still frozen in place, the bronze chest suspended between them.

He laughed. 'Ignorant child. I am Hassan.'

Behind him four men stepped out of the shadows. One of them was dressed in ragged Eastern robes; the others also wore English clothes, although of a totally different calibre. They were dressed more like stable hands than aristocrats. As they stepped closer, into the feeble light cast by the candles, Chione could see that while their leader looked sleek and fit, his men were a battered lot, adorned with old scars and fresh bruises. One of them was missing three of the fingers of his right hand.

'The coffer, and what is in it, belongs to us,' Hassan said in a flat voice. 'Put it down.'

She glanced about. She and Bartholomew were trapped in a corner. There was nowhere to go. Slowly she did as he ordered. Bartholomew followed her lead. As the weight of the thing reached a spot just a few inches above the floor she looked across into his frightened eyes and said, low and clear, 'Run. Find Lord Treyford.' With her foot she kicked out at the two sputtering candles.

The darkness fell, sudden and intense. The other end of the coffer clanged loudly as it hit the floor. Sharp words rang out and then the heavy sound of running feet. Chione tried to move quietly away, but she found her arm seized in a cruel grip.

'That was very foolish, Miss Latimer, and to absolutely no avail. My man will find the boy and he will cut his throat.' He spoke harshly again, ordering his men to light the gas lamps. A spark flared and the closest light flickered to life, revealing the icy expression in Hassan's face. Chione had expected to see anger, and its absence was unexpectedly frightening. This man radiated an indifference that rendered her as nothing, and forced her to believe that he was capable of anything.

'It's been you all along,' Chione said with an unnatural calm. 'You raided the house, and attacked us in Exeter. You have followed us, watched us. I don't understand. Who are you?'

He barked an order to his men and watched as they moved to cover the various entrances of the room before he answered. 'I have told you. We are the rightful owners of the Pharaoh's Lost Jewel. For millennia the story has been handed down in our village, kept alive by our tribe—the story of how the Jewel was stolen from one of our own. Many times have my ancestors tried to retrieve it, but I, Hassan, shall be the one to succeed.'

Chione still did not understand. 'Your tribe? Your ancestors?'

'Come, surely your grandfather has told you the tale?'

'The tale—you speak of the story of the architect's daughter?' The concept of so much time staggered her, but slowly the pieces of the puzzle began to connect in her mind.

'Of course,' he answered with a parody of a smile.

'Then, your tribe, you—you are all—the tomb robbers? The family the story speaks of?' She stared at him aghast. 'It cannot be!'

'It can be. It is. You have been too long in the West. Daughter of the Nile,' he scoffed. 'You have forgotten the timelessness of the East. Does not my family live among the same tombs built back when it all took place? We did not doubt. One day, we knew, we would retrieve what was stolen from us so long ago.'

He was right; it took an effort for her to bend her mind around the concept. 'But to hold a grudge so long?' Just to say it out loud left her unbearably sad. 'It is unbelievable.'

'It is not. The ancient dead have long provided us with a living. But now things are changing, now the Franks interfere.' He gestured at the exhibit around them. 'They steal our treasures. But they shall not have the Lost Jewel. This I have vowed.'

'I don't care what you have vowed,' Chione cried. 'The Jewel never belonged to your ancestor—he was not worthy. His wife was far more clever. If such a thing could belong to anyone, it would belong to the family of the architect.'

Hassan rolled his eyes and gripped her tighter. 'Who can predict a woman's trickery, eh? And you are not so clever as I. For three thousand years we have waited to avenge him.' He motioned for one of his men to retrieve the box. 'Now it is done.' He ran an assessing eye over the bronze vessel. 'A shrewd choice. I had expected something more ornate, more fitting. But the outside matters not, only the treasure inside.'

'I don't understand. You did not know what the coffer was either?'

He laughed. 'No. This is the brilliance of my plan. Over the years the details were lost. For a long time we knew only that the coffer and the Jewel existed. But stories of the Jewel began to circulate outside our village. I listened to the tales, sifted through them. Then I went to the elders. Someone did know where the coffer was, and that was information we could use.'

'Mervyn,' she said flatly.

'Yes. Rumour is a wonderful thing. It flies as fast as a bird. All it took was a whisper here and there into the right ear. We had found the hiding place, I said. It was only a matter of time until the coffer was ours.' He chuckled. 'In just a few weeks Mervyn Latimer was back in Egypt.'

'What have you done with him?' she whispered.

'I? Nothing. Your grandfather has enemies of his own and they got to him before us. I was furious at first, until I saw that the old man was as wily as ever. He'd hidden the coffer away again before he was caught. So I had hope. His enemies came to us, seeking an alliance. I agreed, but they are fools to think we would share the Jewel. I began to plan again.'

He released her and took a step away, running a brazen eye over her form. 'Your family is far more formidable than I first expected. I was shocked to find that you are no exception. When it finally came to you, I had not thought you would be such a creditable adversary.'

She sniffed in disdain.

'It is true. For months I have hunted you and yours. I did not expect you to ever turn the tables so neatly. Nor did I think to lose so many of my men. Have you killed them all?' he asked conversationally.

Chione raised her chin. 'You are the monster here. Not I.'

He sighed. 'I doubt they will fare well in your cold English gaol. But no matter. It is a small price to pay for the Jewel.' For the first time a true emotion showed in his face. An ugly hunger that grew as his gaze lingered on her. He reached for her again and involuntarily she took a step back.

'It is a great pity that you must die, but like your brother before you, you have too much knowledge.'

Tears welled and flowed over. 'You killed Richard,' she whispered.

'A clever lad. Nearly as clever as Hassan. He slipped into my country and found the coffer almost before I knew he was there. A merry dance he has led us all, no?' he asked with a glance about. 'But Hassan is the victor in the end.'

'But Mervyn,' she said desperately. 'Where is he now?'

'He is where he has been.' He shrugged. 'When it is discovered that I have won the prize, his fate will be more uncertain.'

He tilted his head, considering, then like lightning he reached out and grabbed her once more. Chione winced as he tore the pins from her hair. Her long locks tumbled down and he ran a caressing stroke along the length of one ebony strand. His eyes glittered. 'Would you like to see him one last time? A spirit like yours cries out to be broken.' He dragged her roughly against him. 'By all that is holy, I would like to make the both of you beg.'

Panic surged and she struggled, straining to free herself from his iron grip. He let go of her hair and used his free hand to slap her hard across the face. The smack of his hand against her flesh rang out loud in the dimly lit room.

Chione stilled, the stinging of her cheek awakening ugly memories and, unexpectedly, a hidden determination. Hassan's eyes flashed and his cruel mouth curved into a slow and wicked grin. Chione gathered herself and cast her glance about. Die she might, but she swore her death would not come cheap. Her eye fell on the table of *ushabti* figures.

Before either of them could make a move a peculiar grunt echoed from a dark corner of the room. Hassan gripped her tight and turned towards the door to the workroom. The henchman there, the one in the ragged robes, pitched forward and landed in a heap on the floor. He didn't move again.

Silence reigned, broken only by the rustle of the other men shifting where they stood, casting nervous eyes about the room. Hassan jerked his chin at one of them to investigate. Almost fearfully he approached his fallen comrade. He nudged him with his toe, and then turned him limply over. With a cry of alarm he reached down and picked up a small object, brandishing it aloft. 'It is as before,' he cried. 'The mark of the scarab!'

The other lackey started up. 'You see, Hassan! It is as I said. There is a curse on this treasure!'

'Stupid, superstitious fools!' Hassan dug his fingers tighter into Chione's arm and railed at his men. 'There is no curse!'

'Ah, but I'm afraid there is.' Everyone jumped when the new voice stole, calm and unruffled, into the room.

A thrill of hope surged through Chione. She looked up, searching. There, in the corner gallery. 'Mr Alden?' she breathed.

'What did I tell you?' raged Hassan. 'It is naught but an Englishman with a sling.' He peered into the darkened recesses of the gallery above. 'The woman is correct. It is the English scholar.' He gestured at his men. 'Are you women to be afraid of a bookworm such as him?'

'Hassan does not wish you to know,' Alden said evenly, 'but there is indeed a curse.' A flash in the scant light proved to be a gleaming pistol pointed unerringly in Hassan's direction. 'Any man who touches the coffer will pay for his transgression against the old gods. Your master thinks to let you suffer while he enjoys the spoils. I would do you all a favour to put a bullet through his black heart.'

'My men are superstitious, not stupid,' the rogue said with preternatural calm. 'They will kill the girl before they finish you. They will have the coffer and still I will have won.' He gestured to the henchman who still hovered over his fallen companion. 'Kill him.'

'You can try,' Alden challenged. 'Come on, then.' He kept his pistol trained on Hassan and beckoned the other man with a toss of his head.

'Do not waste your effort.' A woman appeared from the shadowed corner of the gallery. She stepped closer to Alden. Her silky tone and curling lips belied the fact that she too held a small gun and it was pointed directly at his head. 'I will deal with this English bookworm.'

Chione gasped. It was Madame Fornier, the woman Trey had suspected might be involved in this mess, the woman who had pressed herself against him in so blatant a manner.

Hassan's reaction was not so restrained. He swore mightily at the woman in Arabic before switching to French. 'What are you doing here? Are you stupid? Did I not tell you and your dolt of a husband to stand watch tonight?'

'Fornier is dead,' she replied in the same language. 'And there is no one left to watch. The prisoner has escaped.'

Hassan let loose with a string of foul invectives. His fingers dug cruelly into the flesh of Chione's arm. She cried out and strained to pull away, but her movements only served to bring the villain back to his senses. He cast a warning glare at the Frenchwoman and snarled at her, this time in English. 'Kill him, then. Quick.'

Alden did not move. His gun was still trained on Hassan. Madame Fornier lowered her gun an inch and protested, 'He is brother to a peer. Unlike the French, the English do not take kindly to those who kill their aristocrats.'

'What do you care for the English? Insolent woman! Do as I say.'

'He will be valuable if kept alive,' the woman argued. 'I dare say his family will pay us well to get him back.'

'And I dare say your precious Captain Batiste has already sailed with the morning tide! We will be lucky to escape ourselves, now that you have blundered so stupidly! Kill him.' He pointed to Alden. 'Or I will leave you to face the English authorities alone.'

Chione saw the woman hesitate, but then she raised her gun with resolution. Behind her something else moved in the shadows. A look of alarm passed over the Frenchwoman's face. In a flash of movement her arm swayed, the gun exploded and both she and Alden went down behind the railing.

'No!' cried Chione.

Like a rat, Hassan knew when an exit became prudent. 'Come,' he said, and his henchmen jumped to do his bidding. 'Bring the coffer and the girl. We go.' He turned her over to one of the two remaining men, whose grip was no gentler. Chione tried to shake him off. He only grinned and pulled her after his master, back towards the Room of Beauties and the front of the Hall.

They had only reached the pillars in the centre of the room when a loud crash sounded somewhere in the back of the building. Hassan quickened his step. 'Come,' he ordered again.

It was too late. 'Hassan!' someone called from behind them.

Chione stopped in her tracks. She stared disbelievingly over her shoulder. The figure stood awash in the flickering light of a gas lamp. He had a face that was lined and dirty, framed with straggling, unkempt hair. His clothes, literally in rags, hung on his thin frame. Chione's vision blurred with tears and it was not until the figure spoke that she knew for sure.

'Hassan, you old devil,' the man said. 'I should have known you'd figure somewhere in this.'

It was too much. 'Mervyn,' Chione choked, caught on a long, shuddering sob. 'Mervyn!'

He smiled at her briefly—one shining moment in which he conveyed love and pride and a subtle warning. Then he returned his focus to his enemy. Chione's eye was caught by movement behind him. 'Trey,' she breathed.

'A-yi,' Hassan sounded truly vexed. 'Like an evil omen you appear at every turn, Latimer. And you…' he gestured to where Trey stood behind the older man '…you are no better.'

'I will accept that as a compliment,' Trey returned.

'You have come too late this time, my old friend,' Hassan ignored Trey to address Mervyn. 'This time I will emerge victorious. I have the coffer and your granddaughter. You shall not block my way.'

'And yet here I am,' Mervyn said quietly.

'Not for very long, I am afraid. You are weak. I see that you did not enjoy the accommodations provided by your old rival.' A spark of amusement appeared in his flat, dark gaze. 'How glad I am to finally see you brought so low! The fact that this victory has been so long in coming only sweetens the taste.' He paused and glanced up into the empty gallery. 'How did you escape, if I may ask?'

Mervyn gestured behind him. 'The gods sent me help. They do not mean for you to have the Jewel. I am afraid it will once again be the bitter taste of defeat for you, my friend.'

The bland and impenetrable facade dropped over Hassan's

face once more. 'I tire of this nonsense.' He spoke aside to the henchman holding the coffer. 'Daoud, you will deal with the wretched English lord. Be sure that he pays dearly for his interference.' He reached into his coat and pulled free a short, curved scimitar, its blade catching the dim light. 'The old man I will kill myself.'

The pair of them advanced. Chione twisted hard and jerked her arm free, only to be caught up tight against her captor's chest. He pulled her hair mercilessly until she had no choice but to tilt her head back. Somewhere in front of her the fighting began, but she could see only the high, shadowed ceiling. The cold point of a blade pricked her throat.

'Latimer will win,' she ground out in Arabic. 'Allah has decreed it. He will destroy you.'

'If I kill you now, I can take the box and be gone before anyone wins,' he countered.

'I have a golden amulet,' she whispered desperately. 'I will give it to you if you let me go.'

He hesitated. 'Where is it?' His voice growled low.

'I have it. Under my skirts. Let me loose and I will give it to you.'

For several long seconds he wavered. At last greed won out. Chione had no doubt that he meant to take whatever she had and kill her still. He spun her around and pressed her up against one of the pillars. One hand pressed her shoulder back into the rough surface while his knee braced hard against her hip. The position gave her the opportunity to catch a quick glimpse of the rest of the room.

Trey fought Daoud with grim efficiency, judging by the flash of blades in their corner. Mervyn had a harder time of it. He rocked back and forth, avoiding the savage slash of Hassan's blade time and again. In his hand he held an object—

one of the candlesticks she had brought. Not much help against Hassan's deadly blade.

Her captor nudged her, pressing a leg between hers. Chione shook him off, extended her leg and very slowly began to lift her skirts. Glancing up, she saw his leering grin as he focused on the sight. She bent over and reached higher under her skirts, where her hands were hidden from his sight. Working fast, she pulled a knife from her garter—and watched dumbfounded as the man toppled at her feet. She stared down at him in stunned surprise. Blood ran from a gash behind his ear.

Chione looked up and found herself hauled into the arms of Trey. He tucked a blood-tipped *ushabti* figure under his arm, kissed her hard and whispered in her ear, 'I owed you that one.'

Together they turned and Chione saw why he had not used the blade that she had seen him with as he fought Daoud. It glinted now in Mervyn's hand, desperately trying to block the thrusts of Hassan's longer, far more lethal scimitar. She saw that he hadn't been quick enough more than once. A crimson slash showed clear across Mervyn's chest, another had severed the dirty sleeve of his left arm.

'Help him,' she urged Trey.

'I've already been told quite firmly to mind my own business.' Trey's tone conveyed his understanding. He nodded towards the two men, both of whom showed signs of tiring. 'I believe this has been a long time coming.'

Mervyn feinted, then dodged behind a display case. Hassan took just a moment too long in recovering. The older man came at him from the other side and drove his knife blade hard into Hassan's shoulder.

Red blossomed across his finely tailored coat, but his expression never shifted from its look of implacable determination. 'I shall not lose, old man. It is time the Jewel was returned to its rightful setting.'

'You are correct about that,' Mervyn panted. 'But such a course has nothing to do with you.' He struck hard once, twice, and again until Hassan was forced to retreat from the flurry of blows. But the Egyptian was too crafty to be forced into a corner where his manoeuvrability would be impaired. He struck back, seemingly without consideration for his damaged arm, definitely without any thought of mercy. Mervyn gradually fell back until he was once again braced against a pillar in the centre of the room.

Chione gripped Trey's arm. 'I don't care what he said, he needs help!'

'Wait.' Trey raised a hand. 'Look.'

She did. 'Eli!' she gasped. The groom stood braced in the doorway to the back workroom. A crash sounded and he looked over his shoulder, back into the darkness behind him. A low, silent form erupted past him, easily evading his reaching hand.

'It's the damned dog,' Trey said grimly. He picked his *ushabti* figure up again and took a step nearer the combatants.

Fiercely intent on each other, they had not noticed the new arrivals. Morty noticed them, however, and seemed to have no difficulty identifying the long-lost member of her family. She bristled, her raised hackles and her low, rumbling snarl signalling her deadly intent. She crouched and, moving faster than Chione could follow, launched herself into the battle.

Hassan's instincts were good, even if his blank indifference stood no chance against a four-stone missile armed with large teeth and the snarling promise of death. He turned away from Mervyn, towards this new and greater threat. One arm poised to protect his face and throat, the other raised to deliver Morty a sweeping blow.

But that moment's distraction was all that Mervyn needed. He blocked Hassan's strike with his own blade and at the same time struck a mighty clout to his temple with the candlestick.

The villain dropped like a stone, Morty following him down. The scimitar skittered across the room and Trey jumped forward to pull off the dog.

All of Chione's attention remained focused on Mervyn. He had fallen to his knees in the centre of the room. His head bowed, he braced a hand on a pillar. His breath came in great, rasping gulps.

Slowly, she approached. His shoulder, when she reached down to touch it, felt pitifully thin. He looked up and her heart thumped wildly to see the look he gave her. Love and acceptance, unconditional and beautiful, undeniably the thing she had missed the most all these months. This feeling inside of her now, it was the greatest gift he had given her, the one thing she had received from no one else in her life—she glanced back over her shoulder—save one.

She started to turn towards Trey, had a vague, silly notion of introducing Mervyn to the man who had rescued him, but a strangled cry sounded in the back of the room. As one they looked to see Eli still framed in the doorway, his hands restraining a desperate, fighting Will. At Mervyn's nod the groom let go. The boy stumbled, sobbing, to his father's arms. Chione's knees gave way and the three of them rocked in an endless, heartfelt and tearful embrace.

Chapter Nineteen

Trey refused to give in to emotion, despite the touching reunion that tugged at even his rusty heartstrings. That way lay danger and his most difficult task still waited. If he meant to get through it with any sort of dignity he must ignore the pain threatening to swamp him. He focused instead on clearing the havoc they had all so thoroughly wreaked.

Alden, thankfully, fared well. It was Aswan who had moved in the shadows and got to the Frenchwoman in time to misdirect her shot. The scholar cheerfully displayed the bullet-razed wound in his arm. 'I think this taste of adventure will hold me for a good long while,' he said with a grin. 'At least my brother never got me shot at.'

'She fights dirty,' was the entirety of the Egyptian servant's report, gesturing to the bound and gagged Madame Fornier.

Hassan sat next to her in the same state. He'd awakened from the blow to his head with his filthy tongue intact and Trey had tired of hearing everyone's ancestors maligned. Morty took the guarding of the prisoners on herself, her lip curled in a permanent snarl until Hassan lashed out at her with his boot. The dog took that as an invitation and helped herself to the shiny leather. Trey figured she'd take it off the villain's foot before too long.

The man Trey had bashed with the *ushabti* figure still lay unconscious. Daoud and the other henchman had disappeared in the confusion.

Trey sent one of the guards that Eli had brought back to Wapping, but Hassan's assessment of Captain Batiste had been correct. His ship had already sailed with the morning tide.

The rest of the men were given the duty of hauling the prisoners off to the magistrate's office. But as they filed past on their way out, Mervyn called for them to halt. He drew close and whispered long and fervently in Hassan's ear. The villain's back stiffened, his eyes went wide. He looked to Mervyn with a question apparent in his eyes. Mervyn nodded solemnly and then he gestured at the guards and they were gone.

Trey watched Will approach his father. The boy leaned against him, his eyes wide with curiosity. 'What did you say to him, Papa?'

Trey leaned in, wishing to hear the answer as well.

'I told him the truth. What he is looking for is not in that vessel.' The old man sighed. 'But an obsession such as Hassan's does not die an easy death, so I hope to point it in a new direction.' He smiled down at his son and ran a hand through his hair. 'The French did indeed abscond with some of the treasure Hassan seeks. Let them deal with him for a while.'

At last all of the details were seen to. Trey even had the display case put back together, minus the coffer, of course. He stood alone a moment, shoulders slumped in weariness and dread. Chione moved beside him and slipped her small, soft hand into his.

'Thank you,' she whispered. She looked at the newly restored display, not at him. He gave her fingers a squeeze.

'All this time,' she said low. 'He's been on Batiste's ship

all this time. It was no wonder he disappeared without a trace.' She glanced askance at him. 'How? How did you know?'

'It was something you said last night,' Trey answered. 'When you were telling me so eloquently how emotion destroys whatever it touches. "Professional relationships suffer too," you said. "Look at Mervyn and Batiste." For some reason that kept circling in my brain. And then I remembered Richard's words, in his journal. You showed them to me, do you remember? *C. G. B.* Captain Gustavo Batiste. I didn't know for sure, but it seemed worth a look.'

She ducked her head. 'You didn't tell me.'

'You were upset. I didn't know if I was right, and I wasn't sure you could handle it with equanimity if I was wrong.'

'No, you did the right thing. I was…distraught.' She sighed. 'Thank you,' she said again.

'He'll need looking after,' Trey said gruffly. 'Batiste had him locked in the slave hold.'

'And damned miserable it was, too,' Mervyn said, approaching from behind them, 'but I was allowed on deck when we were at sea. Batiste knew that I had too much to live for, I wasn't going to go over the side.' He looked at the small, roughly shaped figures in the case and then over at the coffer. 'He was after the Jewel, of course. He said he was going to hold me until I talked.'

'Then he didn't know you very well after all, did he?' Chione smiled.

'No, in the end, he didn't. I don't think he could bring himself to kill me, not because I might change my mind and tell him everything, but because I think he enjoyed having me at his mercy even more than he wanted the Jewel.' He sighed, a tired, heart-sore sound. 'He was particularly gleeful when he told me about Richard.' He took her other hand. 'I'm so sorry, Chione.'

She released Trey to embrace the old man fiercely. Trey

watched her grandfather hold her close and his own arms ached, because they would never again do the same. She no longer needed him. And she had made her thoughts on their betrothal clear enough.

'I want to go home, Chione,' Mervyn said into her hair. 'I want to sit down with Olivia in my lap and you and Will on either side. I promise, it will be a long, long while before I suffer the urge to get up again.'

'I understand and appreciate your sentiment, sir,' Trey answered before Chione could. 'Things are taken care of here. But I wondered if you wouldn't mind if Chione stayed behind with me, just for a bit.' He paused and glanced at her surprised expression. 'We have some business to finish, and a few things that need to be said in private.'

Mervyn looked from Trey's face, down to Chione's. 'I understand that you have betrothed yourself to this young man,' he said to her.

She flushed and hesitated. 'Yes, sir—but it was just a ruse. Mrs Stockton tried to take the children from me. Trey entered into the betrothal only to protect us.'

The old man regarded Trey soberly. 'It appears I am in your debt in more ways than one, sir. I suppose you are past the point of asking permission, but I thank you for doing so anyway.' He extended his hand and gripped Trey's tight. 'I trust you to bring her home safe.'

Trey nodded. 'Yes, sir.'

Everyone had gone. Trey took Chione's hand and led her to the first chamber. He looked around a moment, and then he moved the bench that Mrs Ferguson had sat knitting upon away from the mummy's case and angled it towards a colourful depiction of Isis embracing the Pharaoh.

'We are an odd pair,' he said, escorting Chione to the bench and waiting for her to settle in. 'We do our best talking when we've something else to look at, had you noticed?'

'No, I hadn't,' she said, intrigued. 'But it has been something of a pattern with us, hasn't it?'

Trey sat down beside her and for several minutes they sat without speaking. They were close enough on the bench to be lightly touching and he allowed the steady rise and fall of her breathing to calm him. A lock of her hair had fallen across his arm. He stared at it instead of the colourful relief before him and longed to touch it, to lift it to his face and breathe in the sweet scent of her, perhaps for the last time.

At last, she stirred. 'Trey, I—'

'No,' he said, ignoring the sudden press of her against him. 'Please, Chione. This is difficult for me. Let me say what I must before you speak.'

She nodded. 'All right.'

He reached inside of his coat and drew out a small box. 'While we were in Devonshire I sketched out what I wanted and sent it on to London. By the time we arrived, this was ready.' He opened it.

'Ohh…' she breathed, her fingertips travelling to her mouth to hide her exclamation of delight. 'It is beautiful.'

He hoped she thought so. He had been very specific and Rundell, Bridge and Co. had been happy to accommodate the Earl of Treyford. Tucked in its nest of velvet sat a ring of golden filigree. The front piece was in the shape of the Eye of Horus, with a blue lapis as the pupil.

Tentatively, she reached out, shooting him a questioning look. He nodded and she touched it gently. 'It is just exactly the colour of your eyes,' she said.

Trey shifted uncomfortably. 'I hadn't thought of that,' he said.

'But I am glad you like it.' He handed the box to her. 'There is a much more important gift I want to give to you, Chione.'

Still cradling the box, she looked up at him in question.

'Your freedom,' he said.

She drew a long, shuddering breath.

'I want you to know that I understand,' he continued before his courage gave out. 'The heavens know I am no prize for any woman, let alone, as you said, for one who carries heavy burdens of her own.'

Chione started to speak, but Trey raised a hand to stop her. 'Please. I understand that I have dived in and made myself part and parcel of this entire mess,' he said. 'But I am glad I have, because now we can finally put it to rest. The legend won't haunt you any more, Chione. The coffer is found, the Jewel— whatever it might prove to be—is safe and so is Mervyn. You are free—free to live your own life. You can go to America, just as you planned.' He faltered a bit, and paused to breathe deeply. 'Go—find your clean slate. Begin again. Go and be happy.'

He took the ring from the box and slipped it slowly on her finger. 'All I ask is that you wear this and think of me, from time to time.'

She smiled at him with tears in her eyes. 'May I speak now?' she asked with slight exasperation.

'Yes.' He braced himself for what he had no wish to hear.

'Thank you.' She stretched up, ran the fingers of both hands over his temples and curled them in his hair. 'You are the single bravest man I know, Niall Stafford, Earl of Treyford. Do you think that I am going to let you get away so easily?'

Incredibly, her words stung. He was attempting to be noble. For the first time in his adult life he was putting someone else's needs ahead of his own. Did she not take him seriously? Couldn't she see how deeply he felt, how he needed to fulfil her dreams?

She read his reaction. 'No, I am not talking of physical bravery.' She waved a negligent hand. 'Mervyn has us all beat in that category, at any rate. I am speaking of bravery that comes from the soul, emotional generosity—and that is far rarer and infinitely precious.'

One of her hands slid down, gently caressing his face, continuing on across his shoulder, down his arm, to take his hand in hers once more. 'I know, Trey. I know how far you have come. I realise how hard it was for you to share yourself with me, to open your past like a book and let me read the most painful passages of your life.'

She gripped his hand tight. 'Do you think I would reject you because you've entangled yourself in the chaotic mess of my life? Think back, Trey, to the day you first arrived at Oakwood Court. Would that man have taught Will the best canter transitions for his mount or sat in a coach all afternoon and let Olivia put ribbons in his hair? Would he have talked to me of my mother, and his own? Would he have seen my turmoil yesterday and thought to ease it by sharing his? Could he have ever shared his father's secret with me?' She shook her head. 'You've grown, Trey, you've taken a journey that few are ever brave enough to set out on.'

Trey felt peculiarly like crying. Her praise unmanned him. No one had ever said such things to him. 'Only because you showed me the way,' he said gruffly.

'Yes, but you shouldered me out of the way and far surpassed me,' she said, her tone rueful. 'And I could not bring myself to follow.'

'You were frightened.'

She sighed. Her eyes closed and she nodded. 'Richard knew, though, didn't he? My infuriating little brother knew that the hardest thing I could ever do was face the truth about myself.'

Gently he tucked the straying lock of hair behind her ear. 'Then your greatest fear…?'

She shuddered. 'Allowing the secrets of my past back into the light of day. I didn't want to face them again, or ever acknowledge that what happened then had anything to do with the person I am now.'

'It's done now. You don't ever have to worry about it again.'

She ducked her head. 'Yes, I do. I owe it to you.' She looked up and directly into his eyes. 'I want to tell you everything, for how can we begin our lives together if we are not on the same path?'

He kissed her then, couldn't have stopped himself if he wished. She exhaled, a long, satisfied sigh and then she melted against him. Her lips were warm and eager and tasted of exquisite promise—a pledge of days, months, years of such kisses. The promise of happiness.

She pulled back a little. 'Wait, Trey. I have to tell you.'

He made a sound of protest, but she gave him a pleading look.

'All right, then.' He pulled her comfortably against him and ran his fingers through her glorious hair.

She sighed. For several minutes she just leaned into him. Trey bent and kissed her neck, knowing she was steeling herself for a battle.

'You spoke of the lost little boy you once were,' she began, 'but I can tell you that he would have been no match for the angry little girl I used to be.'

Quietly she told her tale, telling him of Edward Latimer's death, of the harrowing journey cut short by her mother's captors. It was then her voice changed. 'They left us to die, Trey, like dogs in the street,' she said. It made Trey itch to get his hands on the bastards who caused that harsh, unforgiving tone. He listened in wonder and awe as she told of following after the men who had taken her mother, and of eventually finding her enslaved to a Frank.

'My brave, beautiful girl,' he whispered, kissing her temple.

'No. Not brave—furious. A new creature was born on that journey, a being of anger and plain stubborn refusal to be defeated. It is the side of me capable of hate and resentment. I thought she had gone when I found Eshe—but she was still there, lurking.'

Her voice grew quiet again. 'It was a good thing, I would guess, because I needed her again later, when the plague went through. The Frank caught it and my mother as well when she tried to nurse him. Richard and I found ourselves returned to the streets.'

She sat back then and looked at him, her expression hard. 'Do you understand? I was perhaps a little older than Bartholomew. A child alone with a toddler in the Egyptian slums.'

Trey met her gaze directly. To look away now, he suspected, would be the end of any hope for them. 'I don't know how you survived it,' he said simply.

'I did what street rats do, Trey. I stole, I cheated, I lied. I did worse.' She breathed deep. 'And then Mervyn came. He found us. I cried over Richard, kissed him goodbye and handed him over to his grandfather.'

'Why was it goodbye?' Trey asked. 'Didn't you know that Mervyn would take you too?'

'No, I didn't.'

'Why not?'

'Because Richard was Edward Latimer's son, but I was not his true daughter.'

He stared at her blankly. 'I do not understand.'

'I told you that Eshe had run away from her family—she wanted to see more of the world.'

'Yes.'

'She ran away with a Frenchman. A surveyor in Napoleon's grand army of engineers and artists. She lived with him, bore him a child. Me.' She ducked her head. 'But when the French were defeated he went home without us, without a second thought. It wasn't until a year later that Eshe met Edward Latimer. They fell in love, truly in love. She married him and he was the only father I have ever known.'

Trey sat, stunned. 'Then you are... Then Mervyn is not...'

'He is not my grandfather. Not by blood. You can see why I couldn't tell you,' she said, unable to keep all of the anguish from her words.

'I can see why you might think so at first,' he said, indignant, 'but surely later you might have got round to it!'

'I wanted to! I felt terrible, but I couldn't risk it. You railed at me for sacrificing myself for my family. What would you have thought had you known they were truly not my family?'

'You thought I'd be angry?'

She nodded and hid her face on his shoulder. 'I felt so guilty—I know I should never have agreed to the betrothal.' She gave a little sob. 'You deserve so much better in a wife!'

That statement, perhaps, shocked him even more than her revelation. 'What did you say?'

'It's true. You know it is. My mother was a slave, my father some unknown Frenchman. I lied to you. I lied to everyone—through my entire life. I let them all believe that I was someone I am not.'

'Stop it.' Trey's voice crashed through the empty room like thunder. 'You've sorely misjudged me if you think I give a damn about all of that.' He gripped her hard by the shoulders. 'Do you think I care who your father was? My father had noble blood—it didn't keep him from becoming a selfish, murdering bastard. Will you hold what he did against me?'

Anxiety still marred her pretty face, showed in every tense line of her body. 'No, you do not understand. It is not so much who my father was. It is who I am—what I have done. Must I spell it out?'

'I'm afraid you must,' he said gently, 'for I cannot imagine what you could mean.'

'I tried to change, to fit in here in England.' Her eyes rose to his. 'I never did, though.'

He started to speak, but she stopped him with a raised hand.

'No, it is more than my background. It is me—something fundamentally different in me. When I feel…I just cannot…' Her voice fell once more to a whisper. 'That angry, defiant girl—she still lives inside of me, Trey. I've never been able to rid myself of that part of me.'

'Thank God you haven't!' he said fervently.

'What?' She looked utterly shocked.

'You heard me.' He stood and began to pace between the bench and the wall. 'Did you think I didn't know about that bit of wildness inside of you? Good God, you beautiful, hare-brained idiot.' He turned and stared at her. 'Yes, I know that spitfire. I've seen her throw a knife at a bandit in a window, watched her lead her rag-tag family to safety with steely calm. She has saved my life—with a chamber pot, no less!' He came forward again and knelt before her where she still sat. 'She has rescued my barren heart, pressed her body against mine as she came apart. I love her, Chione, because she is a part of you.'

Her hands were shaking. He took them and held them safe in his own. 'You are not just the hissing, spitting Egyptian hellcat from the streets. Nor are you just the well-mannered little English girl. You, my dear, are an endlessly fascinating, sometimes infuriating mix of the two.'

A great, fat tear welled over and tracked down her cheek. She stared at him, her eyes narrowed, her gaze searching, as if looking for the lie in his face.

'I love you, Chione. All of you,' he said simply.

Tears spilled over. Her eyes closed. 'Thank you,' she whispered.

He gently wiped away the tears with his thumb. 'No more thanks, and no more tears. There is only one woman I want you to be right now.'

She made an effort to gather herself. 'Who would that be?' she asked archly.

'Why, the lover of the Niall, of course.'

She laughed helplessly, but it rapidly turned into a sob. Trey gathered her close and let her cry. Gradually it ended, although he still felt her tremble from time to time. Eventually she sat up and wiped her eyes on the ends of her dress. 'You are the only one,' she said. 'The only one who has ever seen all the pieces of me.'

'I'd like to see all the pieces of you. It's been a damned sight too long since I got the chance.'

She laughed. 'Yes, entirely too long.' She tugged at his hand. 'You wanted the lover of the Niall? Let's go, then.'

'Home?' He raised a brow. 'Because I don't think—'

'No,' she interrupted. 'There's a sofa in the back workroom.'

'Lead the way.'

She did, keeping her hand tucked in his like a child. It was no child that hiked her skirts and climbed aboard the sofa, however. She raised herself on her knees and pulled him to her with a finger hooked in his waistcoat.

She breathed in his ear and his skin heated all over. Then her lips slid around to take his own. She kissed him softly at first, then deeper, again and again until her lips were swollen and his cock surged to life, begging for its share of attention.

But something nagged at him. He broke their kiss and pulled back, looking down at the piece of furniture that she kneeled on. It was pink velvet and more than a little ratty. He could see it clearly, he realised, because the early morning light shone through the window. They would not have much time, but there was something that needed to be done.

'Wait here,' he said.

He left the workroom and went through the entire exhibit to the lobby. Ah. The place had been decorated as befitted the occasion. He pulled a large swath of fabric from the wall and returned to Chione.

He closed the door firmly behind him and propped a chair under the knob. He locked the door to the outside. Chione stared at him, puzzled, as he approached and held out a hand to her. 'Hop down from there a moment,' he said.

She complied and he shook out the length of fabric, completely covering the old sofa with cloth of gold trimmed in bright blue.

'There,' he grinned. 'I am going to make love to my Egyptian girl in a more fitting setting.'

She laughed. He swept her off of her feet and laid her gently down upon the shimmering fabric. He gazed down at her, his heart full. 'The most valuable thing I have ever discovered,' he murmured.

She rose to a kneeling position once more. Slowly she reached out to him, untucked the end of his neckcloth and pulled him closer inch by inch. Those brilliant eyes closed as she raised her face to his, even as her fingers worked at the knot. He leaned forward and answered her silent plea with a searing kiss, his own hands busy with his waistcoat buttons.

In mere moments, it seemed, he was bare from the waist up. Lightly Chione touched the long scar where he had once been razed by a knife across his ribs. She bent down and kissed the length of it with nipping, teasing, healing kisses. She did the same for the puckered wound on his left arm and every other mark she found, embracing and accepting each imperfection of his body, just as she had already done for his soul.

His breathing quickened and he fought back a moan. She was running her fingernails over his chest now, scratching lightly through the hair there, trailing teasingly around his nipples just as he knew she liked done to her. His blood surged and his self-control stretched to the thinnest thread.

He made a sound of protest as she drew back, a wicked gleam in her eye. 'You realise, Trey,' she said, her voice thick, 'that we still don't know what was in that coffer?'

'The coffer can go to Hades,' Trey said, turning his head to nuzzle the sweet dampness of her neck. He covered the swell of her breast with his hand and she sighed. He spun her around to get at the buttons of her gown and treat her to the same exquisite torture to which she had just subjected him.

Their coupling this time was like nothing Trey had ever experienced. Never had he given of himself with such openness and never had he been so rewarded. He worshipped Chione's body and savoured her every moan and twitch and whispered plea. When at last neither of them could wait a moment longer, he entered her fully on one slow, heavenly stroke.

She gasped and he felt her muscles tighten. In moments she went over, calling his name and rocking wildly beneath him. It was all the encouragement he needed. He pressed close, rode harder, drove deep and long and endless until he splintered apart and bright, shining joy flowed into him and out of him and he could not tell where Chione's pleasure began and his own ended. He threw his head back and cried out his thanks, for he finally knew that such distinctions didn't matter.

Some time later they still lay in a heap. Trey felt exhausted, sated, and infinitely happy. Until voices sounded in the exhibit outside. He raised his head and listened. After a moment the door knob rattled and they both jumped.

'Chione,' he said, reaching for his shirt. 'I've a sudden burning desire to know what is in that damned coffer. Let's go home.'

Chapter Twenty

As it turned out, it wasn't until the next day that their curiosity was satisfied.

Everyone was gathering in the comfortable family drawing room where Mrs Ferguson had planned a sumptuous celebratory tea. She was wheeling in a heavily laden cart as Chione arrived.

'Bannocks!' Olivia cried happily.

Everyone was there before her. Chione curled comfortably with Trey on a divan and sighed in satisfaction at the sea of faces around her. Mervyn had got his wish—Olivia sat in his lap, feeding him titbits while Will sat at his feet, competing with Bart in a bid to make all the muffins disappear. Jenny Ferguson and John Coachman mooned over each other in the corner and Eli slipped something in his tea when the housekeeper wasn't looking. Jack Alden sat a little apart, talking earnestly with Aswan, who was drinking cup after cup of strong tea.

'If only Lord Renhurst and Drake could be here, we would be complete,' Chione said to Trey over the hubbub of laughter and conversation. He squeezed her hand in response and she laid her head upon his shoulder. Such a small thing, but still it caused the spread of warmth and joy through her insides.

Finally Mervyn called for quiet and Aswan carried in the simple bronze box that had brought them all together. A hush fell over the room and Chione could see anticipation shining in every face.

'So many times,' Mervyn said solemnly, 'I feared this day would not come. Never have I been more aware of how truly blessed I am.' He smiled through the general murmur of agreement.

'But thank the heavens that we are all here, for now the time for secrets is past.' He glanced over to where Chione sat close to Trey and she flushed a little. 'Certainly, they have done us more harm than good. Yet still, I must ask of each of you—please do not talk of what will be revealed here today, at least until preparations have been made for the truth to come out on a larger scale.'

'Aye, we promise,' Eli called. 'Now can we open the coffer?'

'Not yet.' Mervyn laughed. 'First we must tell a story; one that only begins with the ancient Tale of the Tomb Robber and the Architect's Daughter.'

'Not everyone here knows that story, sir,' Trey said.

'Let Will tell it,' urged Chione. 'He knows it well.'

Mervyn smiled down at his son and Will told the tragic tale in his earnest boy's voice. Everyone shook their heads at the sad ending.

'It's so romantic,' Jenny said, wiping away a tear.

'Heathens,' Eli said in disgust.

'As Chione discovered yesterday, that tale has endured—literally lived on—for over three thousand years.'

'Hassan's family, his entire village in Luxor, they are the descendants of the notorious tomb robbers in the story,' Chione explained to the expectant group. 'They believe that the Pharaoh's Lost Jewel is in there.' She indicated the coffer. 'They have kept the tale, along with a thirst for vengeance, alive all this time.' She still could scarcely believe such a thing.

'They've continued the family occupation with some success as well,' Trey said wryly.

'What Hassan did not tell you, Chione, is that the architect's daughter had a family and it still thrives as well.'

Amidst all the exclamations and questions, Chione felt a little breathless. 'Tell us about them, Mervyn.'

'Of course. Chione, what was it that you used to tell Richard? That you worried that the daughter—her name was Nafré, by the way—would ruin her life?'

'I feared that she would let her anger blight her life, yes. I feared that she would never trust again.'

'It was a well-founded fear, for, according to legend, she nearly did let it spoil her life. She nursed her hatred for a long time, especially her resentment towards men. She could not find her way back to contentment. Eventually she left Thebes, abandoned her culture and civilisation in general. She crossed the desert and went to live in a remote spot on the Red Sea. Of course, she could not live entirely on her own, and with her new wealth she did not need to. A little village grew up on that wild and beautiful seashore, far from the caravan routes, visited only by an occasional sailing ship blown off course. She set up a matriarchal system and they flourished under Nafré's guidance, nearly cut off from the outside world.'

Chione's eyes widened. 'You found them,' she said, suddenly sure.

'I did, years ago,' Mervyn confirmed. He closed his eyes. 'I did, and, oh, what a remarkable thing it was. Their small little city is a marvel, a truly unique blend of ancient Egyptian, and later Greek and Roman influences. It is beautiful and pure. They are a simple society, in a lovely setting, always led by a woman—a descendant of Nafré.'

Chione's heart pounded. For the first time in her life she experienced true sympathy with the Latimer family obsession. A part of her longed to go to the spot that Mervyn described, to see for herself these people who had lived isolated for so long.

Next to her Trey sat at attention, staring hard at Mervyn. He started to speak, but the older man stopped him. 'Not yet, Treyford. It is time to open the coffer.'

That broke Chione out of her trance. 'But how?' she asked. 'There are no hinges, there is no seal to break.'

'Bring it closer, please,' Mervyn asked Trey.

Trey carried it over. The two boys made room for it, bouncing in their excitement. Mervyn made a gesture. 'Turn it over.'

Everyone gasped when the scarab imprint was revealed. From his coat Mervyn pulled his own scarab. He placed it gently into the depression in the coffer. It was not an exact match. The legs of Mervyn's scarab were too short, they did not extend as far as the legs stamped into the bronze.

A murmur of disappointment grew in the room, but Mervyn looked unperturbed.

'You have the emerald, I believe?' he asked Trey.

Trey nodded and pulled the jewel from his pocket. He placed it carefully into the indentation in the right wing.

'Push,' said Mervyn.

Trey did so, gently, and an extension sprang from the leg of Mervyn's scarab, filling the empty space and locking it into place.

'But we never found the other jewel,' Chione said, disappointed.

'Aswan,' Mervyn said.

The servant rose and approached. Very slowly he began to unwind his turban. At the end, theatrically, he produced a shining garnet stone—its shape a mirror of the emerald's.

'Aswan is a descendent of Nafré himself, and a very great friend to our family,' Mervyn said over the loud exclamations of wonder and delight. 'Please, Aswan, will you do the honours?'

Aswan settled the jewel into place and pushed. Again the leg extended and locked the scarab into place.

'Now,' said Mervyn, 'turn it back over, and then lift.'

Trey did and the bronze top and walls of the box lifted way, leaving the bottom and the contents revealed.

'Ohhh,' Chione breathed, gazing in wonder at the object on top: an elaborately decorated papyrus scroll. 'May I?'

Watching her closely, Mervyn inclined his head.

Gently she took it up, unrolling it with the utmost care. The detail was amazing. 'It's the legend,' she said in wonder. 'How old this must be!'

Aswan nodded. 'It is nearly as old as the legend itself.'

'It must be priceless,' she said.

'It is, Chione, as are the documents and journals with it,' Mervyn told her. 'It is *their* narrative: the story of each descendant of Nafré. That coffer contains their lives, their deaths, their history as a people. It is put into the keeping of each new matriarch—she who has always been called the Pharaoh's Lost Jewel.'

'Because, young miss,' said Aswan, 'despite the faithlessness of the father, Nafré always knew that her child was the most precious thing that she carried from that tomb.'

'We must return it!' Chione said. She stared up at Trey. 'You will help, won't you?'

There was tenderness in his gaze as he looked back at her. 'I think it has already found its true home, Chione.'

She stared at him, uncomprehending.

'Treyford is right,' Mervyn said gently. 'You are the Lost Jewel, Chione. You are the last descendant of Nafré.'

'Cor!' whispered Bartholomew.

'I should have told you long ago, but I was weak. Marie died, and I could not stand the thought of losing you, as well. I wanted to be sure you would be safe, and I wanted you to be ready to hear the truth, too.'

Chione had gone very still. Her heart thundered and her mind went dizzily awhirl. One thought emerged from the chaos and she clung to it. 'Eshe!' she said. 'She ran away because her family refused to live in the world. That is what she meant?'

'Yes. Eshe believed her people could not live in isolation any longer. The world is shrinking—she understood that. I had found them. A small party of French explorers found them too.'

'She left with them.'

'She did. She wanted to learn all she could so she could teach her people, Chione. She believed they must be prepared or else their way of life would be destroyed.' A bleak expression sobered his lined face. 'She was right. I have seen it happen in other places. They will fare so much better if they are gently taught, gradually shown how much the world outside has outstripped them.'

'It would seem to be a job for which you are eminently suited,' Trey said, settling back next to her and taking her hand.

She stared at him. What irony, when she had scorned the legend for so long. She thought of what Mervyn had said, and she knew that she hadn't been ready to hear such a thing. Until now. Until Trey had helped her reconcile her past with her present, and paved the way for her future.

'It is like a dream,' she said, staring into the cool blue of his eyes.

'It is not a dream, but your destiny,' Aswan said firmly.

'Think of the stories you could write!' exclaimed Will.

A million questions and concerns flooded Chione's head. She blurted out the one which felt the most urgent. 'You cannot leave again so soon,' she said low to Mervyn. 'Perhaps a map or perhaps we should wait…'

'You don't need me.' Her grandfather laughed and pulled Olivia close. 'And I am going nowhere for a good long while.' He tilted his chin towards the Egyptian man. 'Aswan will show you. It is his home.'

Chione leaned back into the comfort of Trey's embrace. 'It is all too much to take in.' She straightened suddenly and looked to Aswan. 'Wait—is the Jewel allowed to marry?'

'Of course.' He inclined his head.

'How do ye think she'd go about gettin' the next one then, aye?' Mrs Ferguson asked pragmatically.

Chione glanced back at Trey. It was not a decision she could make alone and she knew that the question danced in her face.

He smiled at her with approval and love and she had her answer.

'Mrs Ferguson raises a valid point, Chione. Perhaps you should consider an heir your first duty to your new family.' He paused mischievously. 'On second thought, we'll need two: a girl for you and a boy to take on the earldom. It might be best if we got to work on that right away.'

'I told ye,' grumbled the housekeeper, 'betrothed ain't married!'

REGENCY
Collection

*Let these sparklingly seductive delights whirl
you away to the ballrooms—and
bedrooms—of Polite Society!*

Volume 1 – 4th February 2011
Regency Pleasures by Louise Allen

Volume 2 – 4th March 2011
Regency Secrets by Julia Justiss

Volume 3 – 1st April 2011
Regency Rumours by Juliet Landon

Volume 4 – 6th May 2011
Regency Redemption by Christine Merrill

Volume 5 – 3rd June 2011
Regency Debutantes by Margaret McPhee

Volume 6 – 1st July 2011
Regency Improprieties by Diane Gaston

12 volumes in all to collect!

www.millsandboon.co.uk

REGENCY

Collection

*Let these sparklingly seductive delights whirl
you away to the ballrooms—and
bedrooms—of Polite Society!*

Volume 7 – 5th August 2011
Regency Mistresses by Mary Brendan

Volume 8 – 2nd September 2011
Regency Rebels by Deb Marlowe

Volume 9 – 7th October 2011
Regency Scandals by Sophia James

Volume 10 – 4th November 2011
Regency Marriages by Elizabeth Rolls

Volume 11 – 2nd December 2011
Regency Innocents by Annie Burrows

Volume 12 – 6th January 2012
Regency Sins by Bronwyn Scott

12 volumes in all to collect!

MILLS
BOON

www.millsandboon.co.uk

"To say that I met Nicholas Brisbane over my husband's dead body is not entirely accurate. Edward, it should be noted, was still twitching upon the floor..."

London, 1886

For Lady Julia Grey, her husband's sudden death at a dinner party is extremely inconvenient. However, things worsen when inscrutable private investigator Nicholas Brisbane reveals that the death was not due to natural causes.

Drawn away from her comfortable, conventional life, Julia is exposed to threatening notes, secret societies and gypsy curses, not to mention Nicholas's charismatic unpredictability.

www.mirabooks.co.uk

MIRA

England's Most Ruthless Queen

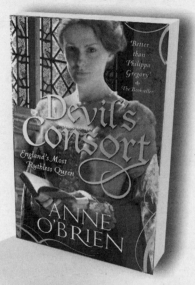

The story of Eleanor of Aquitaine is vividly brought to life by Anne O'Brien

Praise for Anne O'Brien

"Better than Philippa Gregory"
—*The Bookseller* on *Virgin Widow*

"With this winning book, Anne O'Brien has joined the exclusive club of excellent historical novelists"
—*The Sunday Express* on *Virgin Widow*

www.mirabooks.co.uk